The Thin Dead Line

By

Shane Gries

Chapter 1

Bagram Air Base
Parwan Province, Afghanistan
2010, Height of the Afghan War

The roar of jet engines temporarily drowned out the sound of tires crunching on gravel. Another C-17 cargo plane broke its bonds with earth, lifting off into the sky, its belly holding scores of lucky soldiers headed home on R&R, unlike Mark Foley and the rest of the poor bastards in his platoon. Instead of rotating back to "The World," he and the boys were preparing a convoy to roll outside the wire, headed for downtown Kabul.

He pushed the light button on his G-Shock and the time read 22:00 hours. The sun dipped below the horizon quite a bit earlier and twilight had already faded. There were few clouds and illumination was good, with the moon and stars shining brightly. Winter would be on them soon and the evening chill started to set in. Luckily, he had his body armor and SAPI plates to keep him warm.

The lieutenant had wrapped up their convoy brief and now some of the men worked as "ground guides," walking in front of their vehicles and guiding the MRAPs into position. They slowly lined up near the gate, each wearing a chem-light glow stick on the back of their helmets so the drivers could see them. Not that those were necessary, with the brightness of the night sky and the powerful headlights, the soldiers could be seen perfectly well.

Except for the drivers and the gunners up their cupolas, the men of the platoon milled about, waiting until the last minute to load up. The cramped interior of the vehicles was highly uncomfortable and since they'd be in them most of the night, each of the men put off the unpleasant experience as long as possible.

"Sarn't, why does the El-Tee have us rolling out this late? We'll be driving all night, then have to work all day tomorrow without sleep. This fuckin' sucks." Specialist Lee buckled the chinstrap on his helmet which hung awkwardly, sagging under the weight of a heavy set of night vision goggles attached to the front.

"Why? You got somewhere else you gotta be tonight, Lee?" Mark took a drag from his cigarette and slowly blew out the smoke. He usually smoked Marlboro Lights but those were expensive and the local Afghan brands available at the bazaar were much cheaper. He had one of the interpreters pick up several cartons and stashed them away in his hootch. The taste took a little getting used to but it saved him a bunch of money.

"It's not that, sarn't. It's just that the other platoons always get to pull their patrols during the day. We keep getting' fucked. The El-Tee is just kissing the CO's ass volunteering us for all the shit details." Private First Class Bates was Lee's best friend and the two of them were inseparable. When they weren't watching movies or talking about sports, they'd often be arguing with one another about some inconsequential issue, like an old married couple.

"The lieutenant doesn't get to pick the convoy times. The traffic on the roads is highly controlled and managed all the way up at Brigade. If it weren't, everybody'd be pushing their convoys out at the same time and we'd have traffic jams all up and down the MSR. So, we go when we're told to go and that's it." Mark took another pull on the cigarette, burning the cherry nearly down to the filter. He dropped it and ground the butt out with the heel of his boot.

"I think officers just like making shit harder than it needs to be." Lee made the last adjustments to his chinstrap while Bates held his carbine for him.

Mark hardly had any love for officers—especially lieutenants—but he wasn't going to give the two junior enlisted men the satisfaction of agreeing with them. "Look at the bright side, we'll roll into Camp Phoenix in time for breakfast, and morning chow there is the best in all of RC East."

"*Everybody load up! We SP in ten mikes!*" Lieutenant Simmons' voice cut through the chatter and background noise like a knife.

The men stopped standing around and made their way to the idling MRAPs, reluctantly climbing in through doors and hatches. The convoy was an eclectic mix of armored vehicles with a Buffalo mine-clearance model in the lead, followed up by Cougars and MATVs. The Cougar was an older design but could carry more passengers. Those were positioned in the middle of the column, while the newer MATVs were intermixed throughout. The entire lot made up a hodge-podge of up-armored wheeled transports, epitomizing the typical mounted patrol of the war in central Asia.

Mark strapped himself into the commander's position in the front passenger side next to the radio stack. He secured his four-point harness and tried to make himself as comfortable as possible, feeling the discomfort of the body armor on his shoulders and lower back. He sat in one of the Cougars and dreaded the idea of riding in the thing all night long. They'd been designed for the nicer roads of Iraq and their suspension systems were shit, totally inappropriate for operations in Afghanistan. They would feel every rock and pothole along the way during their journey, sending shockwaves up and down their spines.

It was shaping up to be a very long, unpleasant night.

Mark slipped the earphones from his headset into position and secured it to his helmet, adjusting the boom mike in front of his mouth. He toggled the key on the intercom. "Washington, you got me?"

"Roger, sarn't." The driver turned and gave him the "thumbs up."

"What about you, Cortez?"

"Got you Lima Charlie, sarn't," answered the gunner.

"*Guidons, this is Lancer Six. Sound off REDCON status,*

in sequence." The lieutenant's voice came in crystal clear over the platoon command net. Mark figured he must have finally got the commo guys to fix his radios. Probably right after that epic ass-chewing the CO gave him last time when his shit didn't work and the commander was demanding a report. The situation wasn't serious at the time, so the platoon sergeant let the company commander get good and pissed before jumping in and sending the information. Ass-reamings are good for lieutenants. Builds character after all.

Six vehicles and crews comprised the patrol and each of them checked on the net, starting with the lead. When it was Mark's turn, he reported in. "Lancer Six, this is Gun Three. REDCON 1. Over." The platoon leader acknowledged and the rest of the vehicle commanders reported in turn.

"All Lancer elements, this is Lancer One Six. SP, time now. LEEEEROY JEEENKINS!"

The first MRAP moved out and passed through the gate, running a serpentine through a series of concrete obstacles. Once clear, they picked up their speed along the airport road, giving each other tactical spacing. The gunners in their turrets faced out in opposite directions, with the trail gunner orienting his weapon to the rear, giving them all-round coverage.

The road itself was in terrible condition. Even though it was the main drag leading to Bagram—arguably the most important air field in all of Afghanistan—the thoroughfare was in an awful state. The asphalt was riddled with potholes, chunking away and in a progressive state of disintegration. And just as Mark had feared, he felt every bump pounding up his spine like a jackhammer.

It wouldn't be too long before they made it to the great Outer Ring Road where they'd hook left and head south toward Kabul. That road was in marginally better condition and would be a slightly smoother ride for the remainder of the trip. Irrigated fields flanked both sides of the road maintained by farmers of the area, punctuated by the occasional copse of trees. All the fields were empty now, with the locals snug in their beds. Or whatever the hell else the Afghans slept on.

Mark watched through the thick ballistic windshield as the column bounced along, trying to ignore the growing pain in his lower back, when a flash caught his eye off to the left about fifty meters from the road. It was almost instantly followed up by another, this one impacting on the side of "Gun 2" in front of them, showering the road in sparks. The detonation left stars in his eyes.

"RPG!"

Muzzle flashes from the nearby treeline sparkled and rounds smacked into their armored hulls. "Gun 2" rolled to a stop while everyone else slammed on their brakes. Gunners swung their turrets around and sent streams of tracers into the ambush line.

"Guidons, Lancer One Seven. Dismount and get off the trucks, now!"

Another flash, followed by a thunderous boom came from the treeline. The tail fire from a second RPG zipped past "Gun 1" like an angry lightning bug on crack. It barely missed the MRAP and the rocket flew off into the darkness, detonating in some poor farmer's field.

"Alright you guys, dismount and follow me!" Mark unplugged his headset, disengaged the combat lock on his door and jumped out. The rest of his men disgorged from the back hatch of the Cougar, tumbling out into the ditch. Men leaped from their vehicles all up and down the line while machine gunners hammered away at the insurgents.

Mark pulled his night vision goggles from the pouch attached to his rig. He fumbled with them for a moment trying to mount them to the bracket on his helmet, then flipped them down. He had the PVS-14 monocular, so the tube covered only one eye while the other was naked, taking in the natural light. It was designed this way to give the user better depth perception when walking or running, though it didn't help with the headaches after extended use.

Quickly surveying the situation, he saw the other squads

spilling out from their armored trucks, immediately going to ground. They took cover in a ditch on the left-hand side of the road. Some of the NCOs shouted orders to their men but the chatter of automatic weapons drowned out their voices.

Tracers zipped past in both directions, increasing in intensity as the platoon's gunners got into action. Toward the rear of the column a Mark 19 automatic grenade launcher began chugging in its slow rhythmic cadence, walking 40-millimeter shells through the grove of palms. Each tiny explosion sparked and flashed, filling the air with shrapnel.

Mark plugged into the squad radio attached to his kit and keyed up the platoon internal net. "Lancer One Six, this is Gun Three. We're set. What are your orders? Over"

"Gun Three, this is Lancer One Seven. One Six is off the net and nobody can raise him right now. Over." The platoon sergeant's voice strained. His gunner laid it on thick, forcing him to shout into the radio over the deafening noise.

Invisible rounds cracked overhead, intermixed with the occasional tracer. The enemy fire focused on the MRAPs and their armored hulls "panged" loudly when hit, the bullets splattering harmlessly off their thick skins.

The lieutenant's vehicle billowed white smoke from the RPG hit but the gunner up top was still in the fight, so the crew wasn't a total write-off. Standard procedure called for them to wait for the officer to dismount and join them before leading the assault. The problem was, the lieutenant hadn't got out of his stricken truck yet, and there was a good chance he was injured. Or worse. Meanwhile, with every passing second, the insurgent's fire grew increasingly accurate and it was only a matter of time before they started taking significant casualties.

"Come on you guys, let's move!" Without waiting for orders or taking the time to count noses, Mark took off at a full sprint. The rest of his men did not hesitate and fell in right behind him, headed straight for the ambush line.

After covering nearly fifty yards, he hit the dirt and opened fire while the men of his squad plopped down on either side of him and did the same. Bates took position off to his right, leaning into the bipod of his Squad Automatic Weapon, tearing off short bursts from the light machine gun. Lee lay in the prone off to the left, popping off rounds in a steady cadence.

Mark could barely make out muzzle flashes from up ahead but couldn't see where exactly the enemy was. He switched on his infrared illuminator, projecting a light invisible to the naked eye but perfectly visible through their night vision goggles. He shined the light on the insurgent position, quickly spotting several of them nestled among the trees, operating their crew-served weapons. He then switched on the infrared laser designator and marked them for the other members of his platoon. Immediately the friendly fire began to crescendo, focused on Mark's laser that danced on a Taliban gun crew. In an instant the converging fires from the entire platoon chopped up the three insurgents, rendering them into hamburger.

He swept the infrared flashlight further down the line looking for more targets but couldn't find any. *We need to get closer,* he thought to himself, switching off the light. "Get ready to move again. We're bounding forward!"

"Roger, sarn't." Lee fished a fresh magazine from his chest rig before tapping it on his helmet and slapping it home, chambering another round. Bates tossed aside an empty "nutsack" ammunition pouch before clipping a new one underneath the SAW. He deftly pulled a new belt of linked 5.56 ball and laid it across the feed-tray of his weapon before slamming the cover down into place. Satisfied that they were ready, Mark jumped to his feet and took off, headed into the fray.

Pumping his legs as fast as he could while wearing his full kit and body armor, he could already sense the fire from the Afghans slacking off. He saw some movement up ahead through the trees and could tell immediately they were running away.

When they approached the treeline, machine gunners on

the trucks stopped shooting for fear of hitting their own guys. "Come on!" Mark beckoned, firing his M-4 carbine on the run.

The Americans closed the distance in no time and were in the clump of bushes, on line with one another and clearing the insurgent position. Approaching the center of the ambush line, a muzzle flashed ten meters to their front and one of his boys yelped before falling to the ground. The enemy's Kalashnikov clicked on an empty chamber and Mark saw an Afghan toss the rifle away before digging into his combat harness. Closing the distance at a full sprint he watched the man pull out a hand grenade, fumbling with the safety pin.

Mark tackled the man in his midsection and they both hit the ground hard. The insurgent struggled, doing his best to get the pin out of the grenade but the American was bigger and stronger. As he squirmed underneath the weight of the squad leader, Specialist Lee came up and stepped on the Afghan's wrist before taking the grenade away. Properly disarmed, he stopped resisting and went limp.

While Mark stood back up his men already had their prisoner by both arms, zip-tying his hands together behind his back. Only then did he look back to see which one of his guys had been hit. "You guys alright? Who got shot?"

"It was me, sarn't. I caught a round in my SAPI plate but I'm alright." Bates' eyes were wide and he was out of breath but otherwise appeared okay.

Other members of the platoon raced past, intent on running down the rest of the ambushers. Mark knew they were long gone by now, and they were lucky to have the one prisoner. He looked the young man over before moving out. He was a teenage kid in typical Afghan dress, filthy and sporting a peachfuzz mustache and beard. The young insurgent reeked of body odor and spoiled milk, his eyes darting back and forth in fear. "Okay then, let's take little this fucker over and show him to the El-Tee."

Once they got back to the road, they found the lieutenant in the front seat of "Gun 2" talking on the radio, giving orders to the other squads while they cleared the treeline. Mark looked at the side of the truck where the rocket had impacted. It hit the rear passenger-side door and made a neat little hole where the shaped charge shot a hot plasma jet through the armor. He looked up at the gunner who was standing vigilant behind the spade grips of his .50 caliber machine gun. "Hey, Cherry, is everybody okay?"

The gunner in the cupola looked even younger than their prisoner, though he smelled better. "Roger, sarn't. The RPG hit us but the rocket passed just beneath the passenger seats. It missed McHale and Gomez by a couple of inches."

"Lucky."

"Yeah."

Mark heard the lieutenant giving orders to the rest of the platoon to break off the pursuit and load back up on the vehicles. He gave another glance at the enemy fighter. Since he had a Cougar and a large passenger compartment, the kid would be riding with him. *Great.* He thought to himself. *I'm going to have to spend the entire night riding in the truck with this stinky little shit. I really wish I had some air freshener right about now.* "Bates, Lee, take our guest and load him up on the truck."

Bates grabbed him by the arm and gave him a tug. "Let's go fucker. Hope you had fun taking pot shots at us tonight. Because by this time next week, you're going to be getting raped to death in Pole e Charkhi Prison."

***

One Month Later
Fort Campbell, Kentucky

The fresh air and bright sunshine swept away the cobwebs in Mark's brain. Rubbing his eyes, he purged the last vestiges of fatigue from the long journey. He sat in the backseat of the taxi resting an arm on his assault pack, containing all of the things necessary for his trip.

"You coming back on leave from Theater?" The cab driver glanced up and made eye contact through the rearview mirror.

"Yeah, I'm on R&R. I'll be home for nearly a month." Mark rubbed a hand across his chin, suddenly very aware of the stubble growing there. He had a shaving kit in his pack and thought about pulling over at a gas station or restaurant so he could run a razor over his face but pushed the thought to the back of his mind, anxious to get home.

"I figured as much, most of you guys don't wear your uniforms on planes unless you're coming back from the Sandbox. You coming in from Syria?"

"Naw, Afghanistan." Mark wasn't really in the mood for conversation but this guy was being polite and he clearly worked with soldiers before. "Did you serve?"

"Yeah, did a couple tours in Nam. Then retired as a First Sergeant. Did a civil service job after that and earned my second pension. After a while I got sick of fishing all the time and the Old Lady got tired of me sitting around the house so I got a job driving a cab. I kind of like it. Except for picking up drunk GIs on the weekend but I know how to handle 'em."

"I'll bet." Mark smirked, imagining just how the old First Sergeant would "handle 'em." The excitement grew as they passed through the enlisted housing area on post. He hadn't been away all that long, nearly six months total but it felt like it'd been years since he was last there.

"Anybody waitin' for you at home?"

"Yeah, my wife. I didn't tell her I was coming back for my mid-tour. I am going to surprise her." Mark stared at the window, watching some kids race by on their bikes down the sidewalk. They were wearing their bicycle helmets, and he thought about how when he was a kid nobody wore the things because they were for sissies. *Things change*, he thought to himself.

"Spend a dime, save a marriage," the cab driver mumbled to himself.

"Did you say something?"

"No. Nothing at all. Never mind."

The driver got quiet for the rest of the ride but Mark didn't care. He was too excited to talk and wanted nothing more than to reach his destination.Finally, they came up on his street. "It's that one there, third one on the left." They pulled next to the curb and checked the meter. He owed the old vet just over twenty bucks but handed him thirty instead. "Keep the change."

"Thanks." Mark stepped out onto the curb and shouldered his pack before looking back down at the driver. "And thanks for your service."

"No need to thank me, young man. You just enjoy your R&R, then get back safe. You hear?"

"You bet."

The taxi pulled away and Mark only lingered for a minute before heading to the porch. Cindy's car was next to the curb where she liked to park it, so she must be home. He was definitely going to surprise her. He couldn't wait. He pulled out the house key he had carried half-way around the world and back, inserting it into the doorknob. Slowly he turned it and gently opened the door, trying to be as quiet as possible. He silently entered and eased the door back shut again.

Sneaking around the living room he peeked around the corner into the kitchen but didn't find her there. He started to head toward the laundry room when he heard some talking upstairs. Creeping up the carpeted staircase, he moved like a cat, not wanting to make any noise at all. His heart pounded in excitement.

Making his way down the hallway toward the master bedroom the talking grew louder and he froze in place when he heard the voice of a man.

His heart continued to pound, only now the blood in his veins turned to ice. The voices of a man and a woman coming from his master bedroom were distinct. The woman's voice was definitely Cindy but he didn't recognize the other one. The two of them were carrying on and giggling.

Mark swallowed hard and continued to approach, the adrenaline surging now and his hands beginning to shake.

When he made it to the doorway he stood there in shock, staring down at his wife in the arms of another man. Their clothes were strewn all over the floor and the two of them were covered in a thin bedsheet, with the rest of the covers tossed off to the side.

He stood there for the longest time, looking at them, his chest heaving. Then, both at once, the two looked up and saw Mark standing there with a wild look in his eye. They sat upright together, as if jolted with electricity. Cindy screamed and the other man's jaw went slack.

"M.. Mark! *What are you doing here?*" She pulled the sheets up to her chin to cover herself.

A thousand thoughts raced through his mind and none of them were coherent. Images flashed and emotions boiled over. His face twisted in rage while hot tears ran down his cheeks, his fingers curling into fists.

The other man's eyes were locked with his own. They were held wide, with great furrows on his forehead. He was white, large and muscled, with a military-style haircut. He had a flattened nose from a fracture that never healed correctly and scar on his chin. The guy raised a hand in a sign of placation. "Hey now, let's talk for a bit. There's no need to do anything foolish here."

Something in Mark's mind clicked. He suddenly recognized the man. He was that new guy from Battalion staff, the sergeant who'd been selected to be their Rear Detachment NCO In Charge. He was the guy responsible for taking care of the needs of the families while the rest of the unit was deployed. It looked like he was taking particular care of Mark's wife.

His rage turned white hot.

Things suddenly came into focus. He dashed across the room to the closet and slid the mirrored door open.

"*Mark no!*" screamed Cindy, recoiling in fear.

He pulled out the Mossberg Model 590 and jacked a shell

into the chamber. Mark resisted the overwhelming urge to kill them both, raising the muzzle and touching off a round, sending buckshot slamming into the wall above the two lover's heads, intent on scaring them and teaching a lesson they would never forget.

He racked the slide, sending the empty hull flipping across the room, chambering another three-inch shell. The gun boomed once again in the close confines of the bedroom, blasting another tight pattern into the wall, showering the bed with chunks of drywall.

A third shot thundered in the enclosed space and buckshot hit the headboard, filling the air with shards of wooden splinters.

Mark worked the action again but the man in bed lunged toward him, going for the gun. They both struggled for control of the shotgun, the barrel of the weapon sweeping the room wildly. Mark's body pumped with adrenaline but that did not change the fact that the other man was significantly larger than he was. They grunted and gritted their teeth while fighting for control.

Mark pushed with all his might and the naked man moved back a bit. He kicked the intruder in the stomach, sending the man stumbling back. But his wife's lover still had a grasp of the gun, and fell backward, tearing it from his hands.

As if in slow motion the weapon fell to the floor buttstock first. When it hit, the gun went off sending another clutch of lead shot flying, hitting the other NCO in the chest near the right shoulder. He spun around, landing on the bed next to Cindy and she started shrieking.

Mark stood there, his eyes moving between his wife, her motionless lover, and the gun lying on the floor. Her screams turned into guttural sobs as she pulled the man closer to her, the white sheets quickly staining dark crimson.

At some point, the only thing he could hear was the sound of his pounding heart. The smell of gunpowder lingered in the air and he could feel nothing but the hot blood pulsing in his temples. His ears were ringing and he could see that Cindy was wailing but he could barely hear it.

The guy on the bed was not moving at all and as he stood there staring, a sense of doom descended upon him.

He needed to get out of there. Right now.

Mark bolted down the hallway and down the stairs, exploding from the front door out onto the porch. He started sprinting along the sidewalk putting as much distance as he could between him and the house.

The only thing he could think of was getting the hell out of there.

He kept running and running, barely noticing the sounds of sirens in the distance.

***

Six Months Later
Courtroom Annex of the Staff Judge Advocate
101st Airborne Division

Mark stared quietly at the legal pad sitting across the table from him. His Army lawyer had scribbled notes over several pages in barely legible handwriting. The room itself was spartan, with a few pieces of ancient government furniture scattered about, most of it in barely serviceable condition. There was an air conditioner blowing lukewarm air and mold grew on the wood paneling near the ceiling. The entire place probably appeared dated when it was first utilized sometime in the 1970's.

Without warning an armed MP came inside, holding the door open for the officer out in the hallway. A captain wearing a dress uniform came in, his hands full of soda pop and small bags of chips. He set them down on the table and without a word and the MP exited the room, closing the door behind him to stand silent sentinel in the hall.

"Sorry, they didn't have any Pepsi in the vending machine, just Coke." The captain slid the sweating can of soda across the table, then handed over a bag of chips. "You said Doritos, right?"

"Yes, sir. That's right. Thank you."

"No worries." The officer unbuttoned and removed his heavy jacket, adorned in ribbons and badges, draping it over the back of a nearby office chair. He cracked open his own can of cola and took a loud slurp. "They're still in deliberation. No telling how long they'll be in there."

Mark opened his own can and took a drink before pulling open the bag of chips. This was a rare treat that he didn't have access to this whole time he'd been held in pre-trial confinement. It wasn't much but it was something. "Sir, I just want you to know that no matter what the outcome is, I think you did a good job with the case."

"You say that now but hold off on your thanks until after the verdict is delivered." Captain Stemple wore a smile, betrayed by the sadness in his eyes. He loosened his tie and rolled up the cuffs of his shirt. "It's stuffy in here." He took another drink of cola before getting back to business. "So how are you doing? Are you holding up okay?"

"I guess I'm alright. I just feel numb. My wife cheated on me and stole my dignity. She cleaned out all of our accounts and took all my money. And now she and her boyfriend are trying to put me behind bars for something I didn't even do." Mark's expression grew dark. He put another chip in his mouth and the only sound in the room was him crunching it between his teeth. Then he looked back up at Stemple. "I can't believe she did this to me."

"Listen, you need to hold yourself together. Be happy that Sergeant Landreau survived his wounds. If he hadn't, the charges would have been more severe." Stemple picked up his notepad and flipped through a few pages, looking over some notes. Mark was surprised the guy could decipher his own handwriting, it was worse than a doctor's. All the other Army lawyers used laptops but Stemple preferred to use handwritten notes for some reason.

"Yeah, he survived so he could go on and testify that I

tried to intentionally murder him during my court martial." His face grew dark again. "Then my own wife gets on the stand and says the same thing. They both know the gun went off accidentally. They straight-up lied on the witness stand!"

"Mark, for what it's worth, I honestly believe you. So chin up, we presented our case and now there's nothing left for us to do but wait." Stemple opened up his own bag of chips and popped one in his mouth. He spoke while he chewed. "The court martial panels I've experienced in the past have all been very thoughtful and fair. I think you have a good chance."

"Yeah but if this were a civilian court I'd have a jury of my peers but in a court martial I have a 'panel' made up of colonels and sergeants major. I should have a group of junior NCOs sitting in that jury box."

"That's not how it works and you know it. Don't worry about that, it will be fine."

They were interrupted by a knock at the door.

"Yes?" Stemple said.

The door opened and an MP peered in to address the officer. "Sir, the deliberations are done. They are summoning everyone back into the courtroom."

"Already?" Stemple rolled his sleeves back down and began buttoning the cuffs. He looked over at Mark. "That went quicker than I had anticipated. Time to go."

***

Mark sat with his defense attorney, while the officer looked over some more notes. He knew the officer really wasn't studying them looking for anything new, he was burning nervous energy going over the pages. Even though the air conditioning was working fine, he felt the sweat begin to stick to his undershirt.

The prosecution sat at the other table, consisting of two other Army lawyers whispering to one another under their breath. Behind them were rows of cheap folding chairs, occupied by witnesses and other officers of the court. He stole a glance and saw Cindy seated next to that piece of shit Landreau. They were holding hands and staring straight ahead, doing their best not to make eye contact with him. He could feel the anger swelling within him as he looked at his wife's lover, with his broken nose and scarred chin, smirking.

Adultery is a crime in the military but somehow Landreau managed to get off with a slap on the wrist. Mark heard through the grapevine that he got nothing more than a letter of reprimand from the Commanding General and an ass-chewing. The thought of it made his blood boil.

Without fanfare a door opened near the front of the room and members of the court martial panel filed in and took their seats. It was a mix of senior officers and NCOs, all clad in their dress uniforms. He couldn't remember the last time he'd seen so many medals and badges assembled in one place at the same time. They said nothing and sat with their backs rigid, with stony looks on their faces.

"You good?" Stemple whispered in his ear.

"Yes, sir. I think so. Just nervous."

Stemple merely nodded in understanding. There really wasn't anything else he could say. It was only a moment longer before the judge entered from her offset chambers. She too was an Army officer but over top of her uniform she wore the traditional black robe.

Mark's gut began churning while the judge addressed the court. She went through a few procedural actions making standard statements and tapping of the gavel. He could barely focus on any of it and his mind raced. A trickle of perspiration ran down a temple and he wiped the sweat beading on his upper lip.

"Ladies and gentlemen of the panel, have you come to a verdict?" The judge pushed her glasses up the bridge of her nose with a finger. Her short brown hair was streaked with silver and the crow's feet were evident from the edges of her eyes. Her expression was neutral and well practiced.

"We have, Your Honor."

"Then please give your findings to the court."

The president of the panel was an infantry colonel who looked like he was about eighty years old. His closely-cropped hair was all gray and his face looked as if it were made of old shoe leather. When he stood however, he moved with a smoothness that hinted at tremendous physical fitness. He produced a pair of wire-rimmed reading glasses and perched them on the end of his nose before producing a few sheets of paper. Written upon those pieces of paper were Mark's fate. "Your Honor, members of the court, we the members of the panel have come to a unanimous conclusion on all charges."

"The accused will stand."

Mark nervously rose from his seat, feeling the shaking of his knees. He used the table to steady himself. He stared straight ahead at a spot on the wall, while the president read off each of the charges and the verdict for each. His head started to spin and his stomach did backflips and it took every ounce of his being not to void his bowels right then and there.

"Guilty on all counts."

More words were said by the judge as she read from prepared legal documents but Mark didn't listen to any of it. He didn't pay attention to his lawyer who quietly tried to console him. All he could do was look back at Cindy and her lover. The two of them finally made eye contact with him, sneering at him and nodding in approval of the verdict.

Mark gritted his teeth so hard he thought he would crack all of his molars, while they sat there smugly grinning.

He wanted to scream.

He wanted to lash out.

But he did nothing of the kind.

When the judge tapped the gavel, an MP came over and produced a set of handcuffs.

Mark meekly held up both wrists while the metal bracelets clicked into place.

He never looked back at any of them again, shoulders

slumped and gazing at his shoes while he was shuffled out of the courtroom.

Chapter 2

July, 2016
Dulles International Airport

Lieutenant General Art Kleinschmidt washed his hands at the sink of a crowded airport lavatory, with other passengers flanking him on either side. Dulles was a busy hub and people were busy relieving themselves and cleaning up before boarding. He pulled some paper towels from the dispenser to dry his hands when a series of aerosol air fresheners staggered at even intervals above the mirrors discharged, sending forth a delicate mist. They must have been installed incorrectly as most of the men lined up washing their hands grimaced when the chemical spray hit them all in the face. It was nothing more than a dusting but it was unpleasant.

Art used the towels to wipe it away, as it burned his eyes a little and the taste made him spit into the drain. "Seriously? What the hell?" He looked at the men to either side of him, noticing them suffering a similar reaction. One of them shrugged his shoulders and rolled his eyes while the other one cursed under his breath. It was just his luck to get hit with this stuff and now he was going to smell like a three-dollar whore for the flight back home.

He was about to try and wash his face when he stole a glance at his watch and saw it was well-past time for pre-boarding. *No time to dawdle, it's time to go. I'll clean up on the airplane*, he thought to himself. If he missed his flight, the next one wouldn't be until later in the afternoon and he'd miss an entire day of work. And there was too much to do to afford risking that, so he hustled out of there.

He crumpled up the used paper towels and tossed them in the trash, then excused himself as he maneuvered through a group of travelers just getting off their flight, trying to get out of the bathroom against the flow of traffic.

***

Art reviewed some of his notes while drafting up an agenda for the command and staff meeting he intended to convene later that day. He and his aide de camp were seated next to one another in coach after catching the red-eye out of Dulles earlier that morning. He'd been summoned out of the blue earlier that week for an unscheduled General Officers Steering Committee chaired by the Vice Chief of Staff of the Army. Not only was it unscheduled but it was also in-person and not the usual Video Tele-Conference everyone was accustomed to.

Art looked up from his notes, distracted by the aide's aggressive typing. He was tapping so hard, the general thought he might break his laptop. The major toiled away, drafting up some e-mails and the minute he found a WiFi hotspot, he was going to hit "send" and blow up about 200 inboxes scattered across the continental United States.

Art selected Major Dylan Garretson six months prior just after taking over as the Commander of the Combined Arms Center at Fort Leavenworth, Kansas. That was only one of his jobs however, since he also served as the Commandant, U.S. Army Command and General Staff College, and as the Deputy Commanding General for Combined Arms, Training and Doctrine Command. Since he was triple-hatted in such an important role, he had the pick of the litter when it came to an aide de camp, and Dylan was the best of the best. The young field-grade officer was a rising star and was a shoe-in for a "below-the-zone" selection to lieutenant colonel. He went everywhere the general did, and shadowed him day and night. It was a grueling job but aide de camp was a springboard to great career opportunities for junior officers.

"I hope you're typing an e-mail to your wife, telling her that the general is releasing you at a decent hour this evening so you can enjoy the long weekend with the family." Art peered over his reading glasses at Dylan, who masked his annoyance at being interrupted. Art knew the kid got agitated whenever he did it but the aide had enough tact and self-control to respond in a completely emotionless manner. If you looked up "Type A Personality" in the dictionary, it would have a picture of Major Dylan Garretson right next to it.

"No, sir, I'm drafting a message for the XO and the rest of the front office. We need to completely reshuffle your schedule for the weekend and the upcoming week before 'Close of Business' today." Dylan maintained perfect eye contact with his commanding general but kept on typing. Multi-tasking was like a religion to him.

"Okay but I still want to host the 4th of July function at my quarters this weekend. I'd hate to cancel that thing at the last minute."

"Yes, general, I'll let the XO know." Dylan turned his attention back to the computer, hitting the keys so hard Art was convinced everyone on the plane could hear him. He was getting some annoyed looks from a few of the passengers in the nearby rows who were trying to get some sleep before landing.

Art had been ordered to Washington D.C. to attend an extremely sensitive meeting. It was so sensitive in fact, that it was convened in a Top Secret SCIF in the basement of the Pentagon. The Vice had telephoned him personally to emphasize how important it was that he jump on the next plane and be there in person.

When he arrived, the small conference room was packed with senior general officers, all of whom Art had known personally for many years. Out of the twelve four-star generals in the Army, three of them were physically in the room for the briefing. The most unusual participant however, was the Army colonel from Fort Detrick, who was representing the U.S. biological defense program. Art introduced himself to the colonel and shook his hand, unable to ignore how pale and weak he looked. The man had bags under his eyes and his forehead was coated with a fine sheen of sweat, even though the air conditioner was working just fine in the room. When Art thought about the man's clammy dead-fish handshake, he unconsciously rubbed his palm on the leg of his trousers to get the cooties off.

The Vice, a four-star general and second-highest ranking officer in the Army, kicked off the briefing before handing it off to the Army G-2, Lieutenant General Amy Smith. Amy was the Army's senior intelligence officer and she had a lot to say. Well, she *always* had a lot to say but on this rare occasion her comments were actually relevant and to the point.

She said that Al-Shabaab and other Al Qaeda affiliates had successfully infiltrated the porous southern border with the help of local coyotes. Intel revealed that these terrorist cells brought with them a nasty biological weapon and that they successfully fanned out all over the country preparing to initiate an attack that would make the 9-11 Trade Center attack look like a Sunday school picnic.

When she finished, Amy turned the briefing over to the commander of Forces Command who discussed the ongoing deployments of active duty and reserve component forces all over the country to thwart the plan and deal with the emergency. The 101st Airborne was already in Washington D.C. and units were getting mobilized and deployed everywhere.

Lastly, the Public Affairs Officer got up and told them the White House wasn't yet prepared to make a statement. Recognizing that the American people might think it a bit odd that the country was suddenly going into martial law overnight, with manned checkpoints and curfews, they leaked a cover story to the press. Something about right-wing militias being a credible threat and preparing to use the Fourth of July as a symbol to strike a violent attack against the sitting government.

Throughout the briefing Art would glance over at the colonel from Fort Detrick and was struck by his odd body language and reactions to the presentation. The weird vibe made him uncomfortable as if the cover story about the militias wasn't the only smoke screen. He had the nagging feeling that the Islamic terrorist bio-weapon story was suspect as well. But he shrugged it off.

All that mattered to him was he needed to call an emergency meeting of his commanders and staff to get them taking action right away.

"Dylan, make sure the Chief of Staff gets the word out to cancel all non-emergency TDY. That includes travel for conferences, coordination meetings and even exercises. Also, the staff needs to give me some decision criteria for whether or not we should cancel classes next week at the Command and General Staff College. I'm sure if we do, the majors will be thrilled and the installation will be inundated with barbecue block parties in every cul-de-sac. Except for the nerds attending the School of Advanced Military Studies. They'll probably be clinically depressed if they don't have a stack of books for assigned reading each and every night." Art started coughing. He brought his arm up and started hacking into the crook of his elbow. It was a dry cough but a deep one and it kept going for nearly ten seconds straight.

"Sir, are you okay?"

"It's nothing, I just picked up a little tickle in the back of my throat. That's all." He felt warm and uncomfortable. "You might want to shoot a note to the doc while you're at it. Have someone drop a Z-Pack off on my desk before we arrive."

"General, if you're not feeling well, are you sure it's a good idea to go in this morning? Maybe you should go home."

"You know better than that. This information is too important and we have to get it out right away. I'll get a chance to rest up over the long weekend."

"I can cancel the party if you like."

"No, don't do that. I can power through this thing."

***

Kansas City International Airport
0814 Hours Local

Major Garretson's laptop rested on a baggage cart while he connected to the airport's WiFi. He was trying to get the e-mails launched out before their luggage arrived on the conveyer from the nearby carousel. Outside, the commander's driver parked his vehicle in the passenger loading lane, patiently waiting for the two officers.

Art checked his watch and shook his head. *That layover in Detroit turned what should have been a two-hour flight into a six-hour ordeal. This is going to be one long day.* He coughed again into his elbow, and rubbed a sleeve across his forehead to remove the beads of perspiration gathering there. He felt warm, even though the temperature inside the terminal was hovering around seventy degrees. *I sure hope the doc has that cold medicine waiting for me at the office.*

The best thing about the Kansas City International Airport was that it functioned more like a small municipal airport. Because of the overhead from running the three separate terminals after the TSA requirements came on board in the wake of 9-11, the place was no longer viable as a major national hub. Airports in Denver, Chicago, and Detroit picked up the slack, while Kansas City's turned into more of a local affair. It was bad for the local economy but great for air travelers since lines at check-in were short, as were the wait times to pick up luggage. For a big city airport, it had all the charm and feel of a small town commuter.

Art looked over and saw Dylan making calls on his cell phone while he sent more e-mails, he was like a machine. *I don't know what I'd do without that kid,* Art thought to himself.

When the bags came out he didn't say anything to his aide. He picked up both of their luggage and brought it over to his major. "Better close up that notebook, we gotta go. My first meeting is in forty-five minutes.

"Thank you, sir," Dylan said, accepting his baggage from the general. He turned his attention back to the phone while closing up his laptop. "Listen, I'll call you back. I have to go now."

The two of them walked out together and the driver opened up the hatch-back of the government SUV. As they exited the double doors, Art couldn't help noticing that a number of people from their flight gathered around the baggage carousel were coughing just like he was.

It's a little late in the season for the flu. I need to get some Vitamin C before this thing kicks my ass.

***

Garrison Headquarters
Mission Command Center of Excellence
Fort Leavenworth, Kansas
0845 Hours Local

The black SUV pulled up in front of the headquarters building with its classic 19th Century design sporting the unique clock tower. Fort Leavenworth was one of the oldest still-active U.S. Army installations, and many of its historical buildings were meticulously preserved and still in use. Even after the new military prison opened up, they turned the old one into office spaces and even a restaurant. Many of the old barracks were refurbished into offices for the various units stationed there, and most of them had dozens of ghost stories associated with them. Whether true or not, the stories were always entertaining.

The Commanding General and his aide de camp took their bags from the driver and headed inside. They were still dressed in civilian attire for the flight and were moved quickly so they could dig their uniforms out of their bags and get changed before their first meeting, scheduled in fifteen minutes.

"Sir, I'm headed to the locker room to change. I'll see

you shortly."

An NCO working the front desk looked up from her daily log and shot straight up from her chair, assuming the rigid position of attention. *"Headquarters, atten-shun!"*

"Carry on," Art said, headed for his office. He looked at the sergeant and though he didn't recognize her, he gave her a warm smile. "How are you doing, Sergeant?"

"Fine, sir." She stood with her back straight as if it were reinforced with iron rods.

"Excellent, you have a wonderful day."

"Thank you, sir."

Art entered the "Front Office" where most of his command group worked. As usual whenever he rolled in first thing after PT in the morning, the place was nearly full of people working on hundreds of routine tasks that kept things running. Phones rang, people chattered, and the incessant sound of fingers typing on computer keyboards blended into the background noise. The aides worked there alongside his eggheads in the Commander's Initiative Group, right next to everyone else.

He passed the offices of his Deputy Commanding General and the XO, who gave him a smile while talking on the phone. He ducked his head into the Chief of Staff's office as he always did, whether he had anything for the man or not. "Hey, Chief, we're back. Anything I need to know?"

The Chief of Staff was a senior colonel who'd served in the Armor corps for his entire career. His office was adorned with cavalry flags, pictures of tanks, Stetsons, a pair of ceremonial spurs in a shadow box, an unsheathed saber on his desk, and an obnoxious pair of bronzed tanker boots with their distinct leather straps and buckles instead of laces. "Good morning, sir. We got all your updates from Dylan and the XO rearranged your calendar accordingly. It's going to be a busy day, that's for sure. The first meeting is in fifteen minutes but I can delay it if you need some time."

"No, we can get started on schedule. I just need a few minutes to get dressed in my office."

"Roger that." The Chief of Staff cocked his head to the side. "Sir, are you feeling alright? You look a little flushed."

"I'm fine. I think I came down with something in D.C. but it's nothing serious. I'll see you in fifteen in the executive conference room." Art shouldered his bag and headed for his corner office, flanked by the sergeant major's office and his personal secretary. Tammy's official title was "Executive Assistant," but she always assured him that calling her a secretary was perfectly fine.

He poked his head into the office right next to his own. "Mornin', Sergeant Major."

The sergeant major looked up from his computer screen and smiled. "Good morning, sir. How was the trip?"

"Eventful. I'll tell you all about it later." Art went into his office and closed the door. The walls were covered in plaques and other framed memorabilia he had accumulated over a 35-year career. It represented merely a fraction of the "I Love Me Wall," with other items adorning his den at home. He needed to display it somewhere because his wife Maggie insisted that she did not want her home turned into a war museum and those things were restricted to his own personal spaces. A happy wife is a happy life, so Art complied.

He set his small suitcase on a modest conference table, opening it up and retrieving a camouflage uniform. The old general was accustomed to multi-tasking so he turned on his computer to check a few e-mails while he changed his clothes.

The cold medication he'd been promised sat there next to the keyboard, along with a bottle of water. He took the meds and washed them down quickly, nearly choking himself.

While tying his boots, a sudden wave of vertigo washed over him, forcing him to stop. Looking at the clock on his desk he saw there was still ten minutes until his first meeting. The dizziness was overwhelming and he decided to take a few minutes to rest.

He leaned back in the padded leather chair, lowered his

head, and closed his eyes.

Art didn't feel anything as he drifted off into oblivion, drawing his very last breath.

***

Dylan bounded up the stairs three at a time while checking his watch. He never liked cutting things this close and needed to make sure that everything was set for the boss.

Nobody even looked up from their computers when he entered the front office, not that he expected anyone to. He didn't bother stopping at his desk but did notice the inbox was filling up. It was days like this he wished aide de camps had assistants.

He made a beeline for the XO's office and went inside without bothering to knock. "Hey, sir, anything I need to tell the CG before we kickoff today?"

Lieutenant Colonel Harry Beckwith spit some tobacco juice into a plastic Coke bottle and screwed the cap back on. "Hi, Dylan. I got your messages and updated the CG's calendar. I printed out hardcopies and put them in his binder, along with read-ahead packets for his meetings today. Make sure he knows I programmed in some executive time from 10:30 to 11:30 this morning before his working lunch with the capstone course."

Dylan took the binder from the other officer, briefly flipping through the pages to make sure everything was in there and arranged the way General Kleinschmidt preferred it. The Old Man was usually easy to deal with but he was a quirky sort, and if his personal briefing binders weren't arranged in such a way, he had a tendency to get worked up and give his aide a tongue-lashing. "Roger, I'll let him know."

Without lingering he went straight to the general's office, finding the door still closed. Dylan and the sergeant major were the only people allowed to enter the general's office when the door was shut. Kleinschmidt had made it clear on his very first day that the aide had special privileges and could move freely in order to get his job done. And right now, his job was to get the binder full of read-ahead packets in Old Man's hands.

The secretary was on the phone but she put a hand over the transmitter, looking up at Dylan. "He's in there changing. Nobody else is with him."

"Thanks," he said, going up to the door and knocking. Hearing no response, he turned the knob and peeked inside.

The Commanding General sat behind his desk and faced toward the door. His chin rested on his chest with closed eyes, sitting there in his brown t-shirt and trousers, unmoving. He appeared to have fallen asleep in the middle of tying his boots. Dylan had seen him exhausted like this before after some of their longer trips when the jet-lag was beating him down, so it wasn't a big surprise. That was, until he noticed that the general's arms and face were covered in what looked like varicose veins.

Suddenly, Dylan got very concerned.

He darted across the office and put his hand on the Old Man's shoulder, shaking gently. "Sir, are you alright? General?"

Kleinschmidt raised his head slowly and Dylan was taken aback by the bluish color of his lips. His eyelids peeled open and the aide recoiled, finding the whites of his eyes the color of blood.

"Tammy! Call an ambulance!" Dylan leaned down over his commander. "Sir, you just sit there and relax. We're going to get you to a hospital."

Without warning, the general's arms flashed from the armrests of his chair and snapped around the aide's torso like a bear trap, pulling him in close. The young major had no time to react, taken completely by surprise. Only when his commander's teeth sank into his left cheek did he begin to pull away.

He writhed under the iron-like grip and started yelling as Kleinschmidt pulled away, tearing a sizable chunk of flesh from his face.

The secretary rushed in, hearing the commotion and froze in the doorway. The general saw the movement when she arrived and immediately released the aide, shoving him off to the side. Kleinschmidt bolted out of his chair and was on top of her in a flash, knocking the woman to the ground.

Opening his bloody maw, she held her arms up to protect her face. He sank his teeth into her forearms, biting over and over again. Her high-pitched screams sent a shockwave through the front office and everyone came running over, horrified by what they saw.

The sergeant major and the Chief of Staff grabbed their commander by each arm and did their best to get him off the poor woman, shocked by the general's strength. They could barely control him, fighting them like a wild animal.

After nearly two minutes of struggle and with great effort, they pinned the general to the floor. He continued thrashing about and when they subdued him, he let out a guttural howl. They were careful to keep their hands and arms away from his mouth as he continued to snap his jaw at them.

One of the other staff majors helped the secretary, getting the bleeding from her arms under control while the XO called for help on a landline.

In all the confusion the Chief of Staff realized that the commanding general's aide de camp was not there. "Anybody seen Dylan?"

The secretary winced while tears streamed down her cheeks. "He's in the commander's office. He got attacked too."

"You all hold him down and I'll check on his aide." The Chief of Staff let go of Kleinschmidt as the Deputy Commander took over. Turning to enter the office he was slammed backward against a nearby desk when the aide tackled him and took him to the floor.

He screamed in agony when the major bit into his neck and tore his carotid artery open, sending blood gushing onto the carpet in rhythm with his racing heartbeat.

***

Fort Leavenworth, Kansas
South Post
0935 Hours Local

"C'mon Foley, time to get after it." The MP stood next to him on the small bus while the door opened. After a short ten-minute drive, they'd arrived at their destination on the "civilized" side of the installation.

He popped his seatbelt and proceeded out the door and stepped onto the asphalt parking lot while the MP followed close behind. He stopped for a moment and surveyed his surroundings, just like he always did when he reported to his work-release program, five days a week.

Off to the right was the massive Lewis and Clark Building, a majestic affair of recent construction. It was where all the Command and General Staff College students went each day for their classes. But it was the summer break and except for the staff, there was no one working inside. The massive student parking lot across the way sat largely empty.

In the other direction was the post's golf course, which even at this time of day had retirees out on it, knocking balls around. They competed for space with the flocks of Canadian geese that enjoyed loitering there, year 'round. Some of the damned things were crossing the street with total lack of fear, while the morning commuters stopped their cars, allowing the silly things to cross unmolested.

It was a stark contrast to where he spent most of his time, locked up in the Disciplinary Barracks on the other end of the installation. Over there it was a proper prison with walls and concertina wire. On this side of the installation, it was like fucking Mayberry, with its quaint little manicured neighborhoods and moms running their kids to soccer practice. Which is why he liked working here so much, it almost felt like he wasn't an inmate. At least that's the illusion he allowed himself.

After the court martial they shipped him off to Fort Leavenworth to serve out his sentence. He was to spend the best years of his life behind bars, tamping down the simmering rage that ate at his soul.

His dad was embarrassed and ashamed of him, though he never said so out loud. He didn't have to, Mark knew by the way he spoke to him over the phone. He never wrote to him on the inside and he only received word through his mother, and most of that she probably made up to make him feel better. His mom on the other hand, kept in constant contact, writing to him constantly and even making great effort to visit him at least once a year. It was no easy task traveling all the way from Ohio, and it made him both happy and sad at the same time when she came to see him.

Mark's brother stood by him too and constantly pressed the Army to appeal the case. After a few years he asked his brother to stop, it was only bringing him more stress with the false hopes that all of this might get overturned and he could go back to a normal life. No, after a while he decided that it was better to accept his fate and move forward. It brought him a little more peace that way.

Life as a prisoner was tough on him at first until he got into the routine and figured out how to cope. Since all the other inmates were from the military, he figured things were different here at Fort Leavenworth than your typical federal pen. In any other prison he'd likely have had to join some sort of group for safety and social interaction. Here he didn't feel the need.

Most of the other prisoners were incarcerated for sex crimes. The enlisted were in for different types of sexual assault and the vast majority of the officers were in there for molesting children. They were a pretty vile group.

Since Mark was convicted for a violent crime, he walked in earning a great deal of respect from the other prisoners and they tended to leave him alone. He preferred it that way and liked being a loner inside. Even in his cell, barely a word was spoken between him and his cellmate.

It wasn't too long before he started looking into work programs. He needed to keep busy and to pass the time. Plus, he needed to learn a trade to prepare for that long distant day when he would be free and released back into society. He started off working in the metals shop, making all sorts of different things like pieces of decorative furniture. These items were for sale at a small shop on the installation and military families purchased them for a song. It was enjoyable work and it kept his mind busy but he was still trapped behind the walls of the prison.

One day he learned a position had opened up for a barber cutting hair at one of the annexes across post. After getting some training he'd be allowed to leave the prison grounds and work. The idea of being outside was more than he could have hoped for and he jumped at the chance. Now, Monday through Friday, every single week minus federal holidays, he would go to work near the Lewis and Clark Building. Regular people made appointments and paid a reduced rate to have their hair cut by an inmate wearing a brown jumpsuit. All supervised by a bored MP who spent the entire day sitting in a nearby chair, trying to appear like he was paying attention.

Mark took a deep breath of the fresh morning air and approached the door where another MP waited there to greet them.

"Hey Brody, have an uneventful shift?" The MP at the door didn't bother to look at Mark while he addressed the other guard.

"Roger, aren't. Pretty routine stuff." The young Specialist looked over at the red Ford F150 parked twenty feet away. "Is that the new truck you just bought?"

The NCO's face lit up. "Yeah, ain't she a beaut? I had 'em put the big knobby tires on it along with the tow package. She's still got that new car smell."

"Man, I need to get one like it someday." He walked over and gawked at the vehicle, glistening in the sun. Neither MP paid any attention to Mark, carrying on like he wasn't even there. He waited patiently, in no rush to be anywhere.

"You got plans for the 4th of July long weekend? Or are you working?"

"The wife and I were going to take the kids to Silver Dollar City down in Branson but I don't think that's going to happen now." Specialist Taggard used his hands to shade the sun while he peered through the windows, checking out the interior.

"Why? What happened?"

"What? You haven't heard?" Taggard turned around, looking at Matthews, crooked eyebrow held high.

"Heard what?"

"It's all over the radio and TV. The military deployments and mobilizations that started in Washington D.C. have expanded all over the country. There's National Guard troops occupying downtown KC right now, and movement all over has been restricted. They even declared curfews early this morning."

"That's crazy. What's going on?"

"Sarn't, you should probably listen to the radio when you start your shift. They say there is some sort of civil unrest in Washington and the surrounding areas in Maryland and Virginia."

"Yeah but why the fuck would they mobilize troops all over the country then?"

Taggard removed his camouflaged patrol cap and scratched his head before plopping it back in place. "The government isn't saying but the news anchors are reporting it's right-wing militias or something, trying to overthrow the government.

"That's nuts."

"Anyway, I don't really care. Except that it's fucked up my long weekend with Veronica and the kids. We think we're going to stay local now. Maybe check out the fireworks on post."

"Well, that sucks. Guess you'll get some barbecuing in over the holiday then." Matthews' phone chimed and he pulled it out of his pocket. He tapped in a response to the incoming text, then put it away. "Your wife coming over to pick you up this morning?"

"Naw. I live over in Ottawa Village and it's not too far to walk. The weather's nice this time of year." The young enlisted man walked slowly around the vehicle, taking his time to admire it. "Though I probably need to get home. Night shift always wears me out and I really want to get to bed."

"I hear that. I'll relieve you of your responsibility here and you can be on your way." The NCO had his back to Mark, pointing at him with his thumb.

"Thanks, sarn't. I guess I'll see you tomorrow then."

"Same bat time, same bat channel." While the junior enlisted MP strode off toward home, the NCO finally turned his attention to Mark, with his typical blasé expression. "Okay, Foley, you ready to get started?"

"Yes, Sergeant Matthews." Mark learned long ago to treat these MPs with deference. Most of them were okay but quite a few rode high on a power trip and loved to mete out petty tortures on the inmates, deserved or otherwise. Mathews wasn't one of those, but you never got too casual with the guards because if one of the others saw it, you'd get your comeuppance.

"Let's go then."

Mark walked into the barber shop nestled inside the nondescript single-story brick building. Under normal circumstances, there'd be four inmates working there but today it was just him. They were understaffed by two, and the other was recovering in the infirmary from appendicitis, so Sergeant Matthews had the distinct honor of watching over a single prisoner all day long.

Their first appointment wasn't for another half an hour, so Mark set to work prepping his station. He arranged his clippers and scissors along with all the other minutiae. While he did that Matthews settled into his chair against the wall next to the coat rack.

The MP had to adjust his gun belt while sitting down to make himself comfortable. The guards at the Disciplinary Barracks were like prison guards anywhere and didn't carry weapons inside the walls when intermingled with inmates. On the outside while supervising the work details, they wore the typical patrolman officer's kit, with nightstick, radio, handcuffs and sidearm. They also wore the new MP brassard on their left shoulder just above their unit patch.

Matthews paid Mark little attention, pulling out his smart phone and surfing the internet. He usually looked at social media or dating sites while the barbers took care of their customers. They weren't supposed to be distracted like that while on duty but it's what they all did.

After thirty minutes an elderly man came in, wearing a light jacket and sporting a nice head of white hair. It was old retired Colonel Davis, in for his weekly cut. He was there for a trim, whether he needed it or not. "Good morning boys, how are we doing today?"

"Livin' the dream, sir." Matthews never bothered to look up from his phone when responding to the old colonel. He slouched in the chair with his hat cocked back, exposing his forehead. It was a fairly disrespectful way to respond to the old man but he never seemed to take offense or mind.

"Would you like the usual, Colonel?" Mark was completely disenchanted with the Army and hated even looking at the uniform anymore. But the retiree knew he was an inmate and still treated him with dignity, so he felt obliged to reciprocate the courtesy. He was always particularly respectful to the old man, far more so than the MP sergeant slouching in his chair on the other side of the room.

"I think so, Mr. Foley. Just a trim if you don't mind."

"It will be no trouble at all." He gently held the old man's arm, helping him to settle into the barber's chair before draping the sheet over and securing it around his throat. Then he retrieved a comb and ran it through the white hair, starting their weekly ritual.

While Mark took his time with the trim, they'd talk about the weather and about the old man's grand kids. It was the same thing almost every week but it was refreshing in how normal it felt. It helped with the temporary illusion of freedom and a normal life. It was one of the few luxuries he allowed himself.

He never rushed cutting the colonel's hair, because he knew the old man enjoyed his time there too. Mark got the impression he was lonely and enjoyed the company. Since he didn't have anywhere else to be, it was no problem indulging the retiree.

This back and forth went on for quite some time, just like it always did, until the three of them heard a loud crash outside from across the parking lot. They all looked up and toward the window but couldn't see anything, and after a moment they got back into their routine. The barber and customer chatted, while the MP scrolled through pictures on his phone hoping to hook up with chicks.

The colonel suddenly became very serious. "You boys heard about the curfews and the check-points going up everywhere?"

"No, sir, I hadn't heard anything at all." Mark adjusted the clippers from a #1 setting to the #2 in order to get the proper setting for a skin fade. The old man still liked a military appearance and wanted a close taper around the ears and in the back of the neck.

"You wouldn't. The only time you get news is when you get access to the TV room after evening chow." Matthews smirked while he mocked the inmate's situation, never once looking up from his tiny screen. "Ain't that right, Foley?"

"Yes, Sergeant." His illusion of being a free man working on the outside was instantly shattered, dragging him back to the cold reality that was his life. Right then he felt like he was back behind the walls of the Disciplinary Barracks with nothing to look forward to other than daily exercise in the yard.

The colonel's cloudy eyes met his in the mirror, his face tighter than Mark had ever seen it before. "Mr. Foley, what are you in for? If you don't mind me asking."

Mark studied him for a moment, knowing the old guy was readying himself for disappointment. "I was convicted of a felony, Colonel."

"I see."

"Awe, come on, Foley. Don't be shy. Tell him what you did." Matthews finally put the phone down in his lap with both hands covering it. He was savoring the moment.

"There's not much to tell." He broke eye contact with the old man and turned his attention back to the clippers.

"You see, Colonel, Foley there got convicted of attempted murder."

"Is that so?"

"Yes, sir." Mark looked down at his shoes, his shoulders sagging a bit.

"That's right. He came home on R&R from Afghanistan and found some dude in bed with his wife, so he shot him. The only problem in my opinion, is that Foley only wounded the bastard and didn't kill him. He should have finished the job."

Mark's blood ran hot as the images ran through his mind all over again. The incident itself, the court case later on, and the lies that his wife and her lover told. It was against policy for the MPs to discuss the backgrounds of the inmates with civilians and this was highly inappropriate but as an inmate he had no real recourse. Filing an official complaint would have fallen on deaf ears, and he'd just turn Matthew's buddies against him, and some of those people were the sadistic sort. So, he said nothing.

"Is that true, Mr. Foley? Is that why you're here?"

Mark looked back up at the old man with a smile devoid of emotion. "That's what I was convicted of, yes, sir."

The old man's eyes softened and he extended a shriveled hand, gently patting the prisoner on the arm. "Life can be cruel sometimes, son. This too shall pass."

A moment passed without a word being said when a shrill scream from outside jolted them all. The three of them froze, startled by the sound.

"What the fuck was that?" Matthews sat up, nearly dropping his mobile device. Mark and the colonel looked at the MP and then back at each other.

Mark started toward the window but Matthews was up and pushed past him, looking outside. "Holy shit!" The NCO whipped around and stabbed an index finger at the inmate. "You stay here! Don't go anywhere, *you hear me*?"

"I'll be right here, Sergeant. You don't have anything to worry about."

Matthews nearly tore the hinges off the door, bolting outside and straight toward the parking lot.

"What the hell is going on?" asked the colonel, craning his neck to get a better look from his chair.

"I don't know, Colonel. Let me take a look." Mark went to the window and peered through it, trying to see what the commotion was all about.

Across the parking lot and out on the street two civilian vehicles had collided. Twisted metal and broken shards of plastic and glass were scattered everywhere. This was a residential area but it appeared as if one had hit the other at great speed based upon the severity of the damage.

On the far side of the wreck he could make out some movement. It looked like injured passengers but it was difficult to tell from this angle. A woman crouched over a man near the sidewalk, appearing to render aid. "It's a car crash. A bad one."

Matthews sprinted across the parking lot and he barked commands at the top of his lungs. It was hard to make out what he was saying.

The old man stood up, steadying himself with the armrest until he got his balance, then came over and stood next to Mark. They both looked out the window together trying to figure out what was going on.

Matthews never slowed his pace and tackled the woman crouching over the man lying on the ground. He was larger than the woman but somehow she wriggled out from his grip and managed to get on top of him. Mark could barely believe his eyes when he saw her face and hands coated in blood. She was snapping her jaws at the NCO like a velociraptor while he fought with every ounce of his strength to push her away. And it was clear that he wasn't going to last too much longer.

All sorts of confusing thoughts ran through Mark's mind. He didn't particularly care for Sergeant Matthews one way or the other but it was obvious the man was in trouble and he needed to do something. As a felon, he was not supposed to do anything more than stay put just as he had been told. But he couldn't. His instincts demanded that he do otherwise.

"Colonel, I think you best stay here where it's safe." Mark set the clippers on the bench and headed for the door.

"Mr. Foley, you heard what the sergeant said. You should stay here. I'd hate for you to get in trouble." The old man's eyes pleaded with him. In his younger years the old man would have been the first through that door, hell-bent for leather but those days were long behind him and he knew it.

"Don't worry. What'll they do to me? Send me to Fort Leavenworth?" He gave the retiree a wink and darted outside.

He crossed the parking lot and rounded the wreck in a matter of seconds, finally getting a clear look at the scene.

The man lying on the ground had human bite marks all over his neck and face, his eyes clawed out and dangling from their sockets. His shirt had been torn open and his chest was shredded, apparently by human fingernails. The sidewalk and grass nearby were slick with blood.

A few feet away the woman sat on Matthew's midsection and scratched at his face while trying to bite him. The NCO pushed back with his hands on her shoulders, trying to keep her bloody maw away. He squirmed and wriggled beneath her but she would not let go. The sounds she made were beastly and guttural, while his were of a frightened child.

"Hey, stop that!" Mark commanded, shouting as loudly as he could. Even so, he was completely ignored as if he weren't even there. He thought about tackling her but that's precisely what Matthews did and that maneuver didn't exactly work out for him. Then he saw the MP's nightstick on the sidewalk, dropped at some point during the brief struggle. Mark picked it up with both hands and gave it a swing, striking the woman across the back with a loud thud. She didn't even flinch at the blow, completely ignoring him while increasing the intensity of her attack on the desperate NCO.

He wound up the nightstick once again like a batter in the major leagues, before giving it the swing of his life. The baton landed at the base of her skull and she rolled off the soldier, into the grass.

Sparing a glance at Matthews it was evident he was injured. His face was covered in scratches and sprayed with flecks of blood and spittle from the woman's mouth when she attacked him. Leaning down to extend a hand to the MP he froze immediately when the woman rolled over and snarled at him. She was dressed in a tight exercise outfit with her blonde hair in a ponytail. She appeared to be in her late 20's or early 30's and would have been quite attractive except for the fact her eyes were a deep red, she was covered in blood, and her face contorted in an animal-like rage. The veins under her exposed skin were a dark spider web patchwork and her lips a dark blue.

What stopped Mark in his tracks more than anything were the eyes. It looked as if there was a hemorrhage in both of them as if she'd suffered a form of blunt-force trauma. They had an odd tinge to them, a sort of bioluminescence that sent chills down his spine.

Before he knew what was going on she was on her feet, limber as a jungle cat and coiled up tighter than a spring, ready to leap at him. Without thinking he swung the baton again, connecting with her temple eliciting a godawful howl from her.

The blow knocked her back on her heels and she bared her teeth at him, coated in oily-crimson saliva. The woman regained her balance and launched at him but Mark swung again, this time intentionally going for the head. The club landed with such force it made a sickening crunch, the skull giving way.

She stumbled from the hit and he sidestepped when she lunged, sending her sprawling on the grass. Thinking he had finally neutralized the threat he turned once again to the MP on the ground but he recoiled in horror when the woman leapt back to her feet once again, this time with one of the evil-looking eyes bulging out of its socket under the pressure of crushed bone and a horrible orbital fracture. Her "good" eye was locked on him like a laser and her jaw opened and closed in a rhythmic manner, saliva running down her chin and dripping onto her spandex crop top in stringy gobs.

Mark whacked her again. And again. And again. He knocked her to the ground, onto her back and she struggled to rise, hissing at him the entire time. He landed blow after blow, connecting with her head until he caved it completely in.

She finally stopped moving.

What was left of the young woman would be unrecognizable to any family member and Mark had to look away. He had killed people before but never like this and it turned his stomach. Moreover, he was pretty sure that as a convict, he had just done something that would put his parole off, indefinitely.

He looked down at the nightstick and his hands, both of which were coated in a sticky-red mess. There were bits of blood and brain everywhere and some of it coated the front of his brown prison jumpsuit.

I'm going to die behind bars now. That much is for certain. The dark thought filled him with dread. Still, he figured if he could save Matthews, maybe that would count for something.

Finally satisfied that the crazed woman was not getting up again he crouched down and leaned over Matthews. "Sergeant, are you okay?"

The MP's eyes were clenched shut and he moaned in pain. His arms and legs thrashed about before he began convulsing. He curled up on his side in the fetal position, every muscle in his body cramping up tight.

Mark didn't know what to do. Either for the soldier laying on the sidewalk or for himself. He looked up to see if there was anyone around who could help. It was then that he finally noticed what was going on around him.

Cars raced up and down the residential streets at top speed, their engines roaring at top RPM. Tires screeched in the distance and he was startled by the sound of gunshots. There were screams and people streamed out of the Lewis and Clark Building.

Across the street at the golf course a man clad in a white polo shirt drove his golf cart erratically across the green, not paying attention when his clubs fell off the back, spilling out on the ground. Someone similarly attired sprinted after him in pursuit.

A Blackhawk helicopter passed overhead, flying at treetop level. The chopper flew so low that the crew chiefs with their large aviator helmets were easily seen, pointing M240B machine guns from their firing ports, sweeping and scanning the ground below.

Something was definitely amiss.

Suddenly Matthews relaxed and laid sprawled out on his back. He lay still only for a moment before sitting straight up. When his eyes opened, he instantly looked up at Mark and his face took on the look of a predator. Spiderwebbed veins covered his face and his eyes had the same hemorrhaging.

A low growl rumbled in the MP's throat and he rose to his feet, eyes locked on Mark.

Instinctively, the prisoner brought the club to bear and caught the soldier in the jaw, knocking him back onto the sidewalk. Without bothering with the handheld weapon any longer, Mark stomped on Mathew's face, his leg working like a piston until he managed to cave the man's head in.

Finally, he stopped moving.

Still grasping the baton he looked over to the first victim the woman had been attacking. He did not move, his lifeless eyes staring to the heavens.

All around chaos reigned supreme. The once quiet little community on Fort Leavenworth spiraled out of control, the noise and confusion continuing to crescendo with each passing moment.

Think, damn you, think. Mark hyperventilated and his hands shook. *I'm up for parole in a few months and they'll never believe that I killed my guard and some other innocent woman in self-defense. I'll never get out and they'll bury me underneath the prison. I need to get the fuck out of here while I have the chance.*

He started stripping the clothes off Matthews and changed into his uniform right there on the sidewalk. Everything around was in utter pandemonium so nobody paid any attention to what he was doing.

Before putting on the dead MP's gun belt he dug his hand into the front pockets of the trousers and pulled out a set of keys. He looked over across the street at the red Ford F150 parked there and almost smiled. He clipped the belt into place over his hips and unholstered the handgun, pulling back the slide only a bit, checking to see if a round was chambered. It was and he slid the weapon back into its holster.

Dashing across the street he pointed the remote key at the vehicle, pressing the "unlock" button. The lights temporarily flashed and a loud chirp echoed off the brick building to its front. Before he got in the truck he looked up at the window and saw the old colonel standing there, his eyes wide and shaking his head. Ignoring the old man, he jumped in behind the wheel and settled in.

He looked around in frustration searching for a place to

insert the key but couldn't find it. Panic began to settle in as he thought he might not be able to make good his escape. Before he had a chance to give up, he saw there was an ignition button next to the steering column and he pressed it, the engine turning over and coming to life in an instant.

The controls for the transmission were strange and new but he figured those out in no time. He backed out of the parking space and looked both ways before heading out onto the street. People were driving like maniacs this morning and he didn't want to get side-swiped while in the middle of a prison break.

He headed south toward the main gate, the only plan was to put as much distance between himself and Leavenworth as he could. He'd figure the rest out as he went. There was no time for finesse in this particular operation.

Approaching the gate, he saw the guards there scrambling around. They were getting some barriers into position with the intention of stopping traffic both coming and going. Mark gunned the accelerator and picked up speed at a rapid pace.

One of the guards started waving his arms, trying to get him to stop but Mark mashed the gas pedal to the floor. He nearly hit the man, swerving off to the right and missing him by mere inches, then once outside the gate he slammed on the brakes before entering the intersection.

Now outside the installation, Mark saw an immediate difference. Things out here appeared to be relatively normal, with no panic and people driving their cars like normal. They waited patiently at the stop lights and everything.

It was a t-intersection so he had to make the first big decision of his escape. *Go left, or go right?*

Over to the right about a hundred meters away a couple of Humvees were parked on each side of the road. Soldiers pulled concertina wire and other temporary obstacles from the trucks, while others stood in the street with their weapons, halting individual cars as they attempted to pass.

That settles it, I'm going left, he thought to himself. He looked up into the rearview mirror to see if any of the gate guards were pursuing him. They weren't. After he blew past them, they went back to work locking down the base.

He waited as patiently as he could, waiting for the left-turn arrow to change from red to green. Each passing second felt like an eternity and his palms were slick with sweat on the steering wheel.

When it mercifully turned green, he pulled gently out and gradually picked his speed up to thirty five miles an hour. Up ahead, a blue steel bridge spanned a wide, brown river. He crossed it without fanfare and upon reaching the other side he was greeted with a sign next to the road that read, "MISSOURI WELCOMES YOU."

Chapter 3

2nd Platoon, Bravo Company
1st Battalion, 18th Infantry
Kansas City, Missouri
1005 Hours Local

Sergeant Dale Chamberlain was tired. Bone tired. They'd been at this for days now and there was no indication that the pace of things was going to slow down anytime soon. They received alert and deployment orders back at Fort Riley several days beforehand and since then it was a whirlwind of activity. He couldn't remember the last time he had slept, and didn't know for sure when he was going to get the opportunity. And the thought of crawling into his sleeping bag was the most delightful thing he could think of right now. It was a thought that seemed to dominate his mind, even though he had a thousand other more pressing things to do.

He rode in the commander's position of his Bradley Fighting Vehicle, standing on the seat so he could be out of the open hatch. It was much easier to see this way, and for safety purposes it was the way to go. They drove slowly along the shoulder of a busy roadway with civilian vehicles passing by, and any wrong move by the armored vehicle could result in a crash and lots of injuries. For the civilians anyway.

The Bradley was an Infantry Fighting Vehicle. It had tracks and a turret like a tank but also a modest compartment in the back designed to hold an entire infantry squad. It had decent armor to protect it and sported a 25 millimeter auto-canon, with a 7.62 millimeter coaxial machine gun mounted right next to it for additional firepower. The vehicle also had a dual missile launcher mounted to the side of the turret that could hold TOW anti-tank missiles but they were unlikely to be running into any enemy tanks in downtown Kansas City, so that wasn't likely going to get much use.

Chamberlain's track moved as part of a platoon column. There were four Bradleys in total and his was third in the order of movement. Under tactical conditions the gunner would scan for targets while they moved but since this was an administrative road march the barrel was pointed straight ahead and stationary. The gunner himself stood on his own seat, perched up through his hatch acting as a second set of eyes.

"You should get some sleep, Donahue. I got this right now." Chamberlain's voice croaked over the intercom while he spoke. He pulled his goggles up and rubbed his eyes before putting them back into place.

"I'm good, Sarn't. I'm not tired anyway." Private First Class Greg Donahue was a massive beast who barely fit inside the turret. He must have been terribly uncomfortable sitting in there for extended periods of time but the big corn-fed monster never complained about it. He was also the best gunner in the platoon, a point of irritation with the other crews whenever Chamberlain smugly compared gunnery scores with them. Which he did often.

A Suburban passed them on the road off to their left and the driver honked their horn at them. The passengers in the SUV had their windows rolled down and were waving at the soldiers as they drove by. Both Chamberlain and Donahue waved back and smiled.

"They must think we're here for the 4th of July parade or something. If they knew what we were really here for, they wouldn't be so happy to see us." Chamberlain's mind wandered back to the topic of his sleeping bag again, and then to the rest of the squad in the back of the track. He knew they were most likely strapped in back there, totally in the dark, and racked out. The thought of them sleeping back there while he was up in the turret made him more than a little envious.

"*Guidons, guidons, this is White One. We are going to turn off into the parking lot of that high school just up ahead.*

Follow me in. Over." Lieutenant Bethel sounded tired as well, which wasn't surprising since he'd been personally supervising and controlling the movement of the platoon since they left Fort Riley. The railhead had been somewhat of a clusterfuck when they loaded up but everything got sorted out when they got the Bradleys off the railcars in Kansas City. Not that any of it had been the lieutenant's fault but that hadn't stopped the CO from chewing his ass constantly. Of course, the captain was pretty smoked too.

The lead vehicle pulled into the parking lot while the other three followed behind. The sign out front read, "Park Hill South High School." During the school year the place would have been a beehive of activity with students getting ready to start classes at that time of day but it was summer break and the place looked like a ghost town. The platoon of four lonely IFVs had the place to themselves.

The lead track came to a halt and the lieutenant's pulled up right next to it. The others did the same and ended up in a neat row, just like they were parked back in their motor pool at Fort Riley. Under field conditions they would have set up in a circular perimeter but they were still treating this like an administrative movement.

"Go ahead and drop ramp. Then shut her down."

"Roger, sarn't." The driver complied, lowering the ramp from the back of the vehicle until it "thunked" down on the asphalt, before powering down the engine.

Soldiers unbuckled their restraints and emerged from the troop compartments into the early morning air. Walking down the ramps some of them shielded their eyes from the bright sun, while others stretched and yawned. None of them wore any of their kit but all carried their personal weapons and night vision gear. A soldier never went anywhere without their "sensitive items," a habit hammered into them since Basic Training. Some milled around, waiting for instructions while the smokers sparked up their cigarettes the minute they dismounted the vehicles.

Chamberlain removed his Combat Vehicle Crewman

helmet, better known as the "CVC," placing it inside the back of the turret next to the radio mounts. He fished his patrol cap out of the cargo pocket on the leg of his trousers and pulled it down on his head. He snatched up his M-4 carbine and exited the turret through the commander's hatch before climbing down the outside of the hull to join the others. It felt good to stretch his legs and move around a little.

***

Donahue squeezed through the gunner's hatch, pulling himself up and out of the turret. Climbing down he caught sight of their driver, Burbey, exiting the vehicle as well. He looked like he hadn't slept in a week.

"Man, fuck this shit." Burbey adjusted his cap while scratching the stubble growing on his chin. He slung his rifle across his back before following the gunner around to the backside of the Bradley where the rest of the platoon assembled.

"What are you bitching about now?"

"I can't believe we're not getting the four-day weekend off and we're here instead."

Donahue smirked, looking over his shoulder. He and the driver were close buddies, and he found it amusing whenever his friend was annoyed. "You had big plans or something?"

"Yeah, dude. I was planning on cruising down to Manhattan and picking up college chicks. There were all sorts of events planned, so the place was going to be overflowing with hot snatch."

"Who are you kidding? You'd just end up doing what you always do. Hang out in the barracks, playing video games, drinking beer, and jerking off to internet porn." Donahue's smirk turned to a wide grin while watching his buddy's reaction. The two of them rounded the back end of the vehicle as the last members of their squad wearily walked down the ramp. "Besides, you got nothing to complain about. I was supposed to be on my honeymoon this weekend."

"You mean you had something special planned with Candi?"

Donahue's expression shifted suddenly from mirthful to annoyed. "Dude, seriously. I told you to stop calling her that. Her name's Vanessa."

"Oh, I'm sorry. I keep thinking of her by her stage name." Burbey fished out a tin of Copenhagen and thumped it several times with his thumb before pulling out a pinch and sticking it between his lip and gums. "Those girls from Junction City are classy ladies. Is she still stripping at the same place you met her? What was the name of it again? *Den of Ecstasy* or something like that?"

"She's only still dancing because our housing allowance hasn't kicked in yet. Once that gets turned on she's going to quit her job." He motioned toward his buddy's can of snuff longingly. "Can I get a dip?"

Burbey handed the can to his pal before spitting on the ground. "Yeah, yeah. You know she just married you for the BAH. Oh, and the dental plan. That chick's got nice tits and a tight ass but got a fucked up grille. She's missing at least two or three teeth. Probably from smoking all that meth."

Donahue shoved in a fat dip and closed up the can before punching Burbey in the arm. "She's my wife you dick! Stop talking about her that way before I kick your ass!"

PFC Geoff Harris held his Squad Automatic Weapon by the carrying handle with one hand while lighting a cigarette with the other. Tobacco use was in sharp decline among the civilian population but it was popular as ever in the Army, much to the chagrin of the brass. "Did someone mention jerking off to internet porn and strippers? I could really use some stress relief. Hey, Gray, how about hooking a brother up? A little HJ in the back of the Brad?"

Private Lauren Gray emerged from the vehicle and squinted in the bright sunlight. She was the platoon's lone female and had only joined the unit a few months beforehand. "What? Are you serious, Harris? I wouldn't touch your dick with Johnson's diseased hand. Plus, if masturbation were an Olympic sport, you'd be a gold medal winner. You don't need my help getting off."

Johnson, who had been minding his own business up to that point, turned to them with a glare. "Hey, fuck all, y'all. How'd I get dragged into this?"

Private Dante Dubois started laughing at his friend's expense. "Man, that's what you get for hitting on Gray when she first got to the platoon. She didn't take kindly to it, and now she's got it in for you." Gray passed by, shoving her way past Johnson, giving him the stink-eye the whole time. "Hey, ain't this your hometown. I thought you said you were from here."

Johnson shook his head, pulling out a pack of cigarettes from his pocket. "Naw, man. I'm from St. Louis. That's on the other side of the state."

"Whatever, Missouri's all the same to me."

"That's 'cause you're a dang Cajun and don't know nothin' about nothin' outside of Louisiana." He tapped out a cigarette and put it to his lips before fishing around looking for a lighter.

"I'm Creole, not Cajun, you dumbass. There's a big difference."

"Not to me there ain't." Johnson lit his smoke and offered one to Dubois. He waited until Gray was out of earshot before lowering his voice. "Anyway, she wouldn't be so sensitive if that other chick that came here with her hadn't fucked the old First Sergeant."

"Yeah, I liked First Sergeant Gage. They relieved him quick after people found out about it. What happened to the female soldier… what was her name again?"

"Her name was Smith, I think. I heard she got reassigned to another battalion. I don't even think she got in trouble. Anyway, ever since that happened, Gray's been super sensitive about that kind of shit." Johnson took a deep drag and blew out the smoke. "I wish I would have known it at the time before I spoke to her at the club."

Harris leaned in, his eyes bright. "You mean, when you

asked her to go back to your barracks room with you and she threw a drink in your face? That shit was hilarious!"

"Man, nobody was talkin' to you. Why you buttin' into the conversation?" He flicked some ash on the ground and then took up a regal air. "Besides, I was inviting her up to participate in a campaign."

Dubois shook his head.

Harris gave Johnson a wry look. "You mean, you actually invited her up to your room to play Dungeons and Dragons?"

"Yeah, man. What's wrong with that?"

"Does that ever actually work?"

"Well. No, actually. But it might sometime."

"Dude, your game is weak." Harris chuckled as he walked off, clearly happy to have embarrassed his squad mate.

Dubois put a reassuring hand on his friend's shoulder. "Bro, don't pay any attention to him. He's a pole-smoker."

"Thanks, buddy." Johnson toyed with his "Thor's Hammer" pendant looking sanguine, then tilted his head to the slightly to the side, studying his friend. "Is there somethin' wrong? Why are you squirming?"

Dubois swallowed and wiped the sweat beaded up on his upper lip. "Man, I gotta drop a deuce. Bad."

Johnson's face lit up. "Ain't no porta-lets around here, and that school is all locked up. You best hold it, yo."

"I don't know if I can, I'm touching cotton already."

Johnson shook his head, taking a drag from his smoke while watching his pal hop uncomfortably from one leg to the other.

***

The platoon sergeant came stomping up from his track, looking even more pissed off than usual. His driver was over next to his Bradley doing push-ups and getting "smoked" by one of the other NCOs. It was probably for some minor infraction that was responsible for the "Platoon Daddy's" bad mood. Sergeant First Class Savage had been with the platoon for a couple of years, and was the logical choice for breaking in a new lieutenant, a job he was not particularly thrilled with. "Okay, everybody bring it in. The lieutenant has something he needs to put out."

The soldiers stopped milling about and gathered in closer, forming a semi-circle while the Platoon Leader came around and stood in front of them. He held a map in one hand and a plastic Coke bottle in the other, half-filled with tobacco juice. He had a large lump in his lower lip, from the big fat wad of chewing tobacco stuffed in there. It was likely the only thing keeping him awake from the looks of the dark rings under his eyes.

Bethel had come to platoon straight from the schoolhouse at Fort Benning only a few months beforehand. He was still plenty green and the soldiers often made jokes about him behind his back. Most of the NCOs put the kibosh on that sort of thing if they overheard any of it but privately they said the same sorts of things to each other when nobody else was around. Nonetheless, this was a normal occurrence for a rifle platoon, getting a new Platoon Leader then training him up.

"Gather 'round so you can see." Lieutenant Bethel laid the map out on the ground and kneeled down next to it. He pulled out an ink pen and used it as a pointer while he spoke. "While we were road-marching to this location the CO put out some instructions over the company net. Within the hour we are to set up traffic control points in these two locations." He pointed to a couple of nearby intersections on the map and his soldiers leaned in closer so they could see what he was referring to. "Once established we are going to shut down all traffic. Only authorized military and first-responders will be allowed to pass through. Any questions?" A few hands went up and Bethel pointed to Sergeant Cruz from 1st Squad. "Yes, go ahead."

"Sir, what's this about? All we know is we got alerted earlier this week and we've been working round the clock to get here. Now we're in downtown KC and running traffic control points? Why are we doing this? All we are hearing are rumors." Cruz had an edge in his voice that was unmistakable. Heads started nodding throughout the assembled group.

"I can only tell you what I know and that isn't much. Battalion says that there's a high probability of a terrorist attack planned to coincide with Independence Day. With lots of people out celebrating the holiday over the long weekend, the whole country is a target-rich environment. Units all over the United States are deploying as we speak to stop that from happening." The lieutenant scooped up the map and stood, facing his people. "Unfortunately, that's all the information we have right now. The CO is supposed to get a briefing from the colonel later this afternoon. After that, we'll likely know more. But in the meantime, we need to get these TCPs up and running. Any other questions?"

"Yes, sir. I have one." The platoon sergeant spoke up, cutting off a few of the others, indicating that this would be the last question and after that they were to get straight to work. "Since we're expecting a terrorist attack, when will we be getting issued ammo? The logistics package from Battalion isn't scheduled until later this evening and we'll need something sooner than that."

Bethel sucked at his teeth and took a deep breath before answering. "That's a great question. But unfortunately, there will be no ammo."

There were audible muffled reactions throughout the platoon, and a few mumbled curses.

"Sir, will all due respect, that's the dumbest thing I ever heard. How are we supposed to deal with a terrorist threat if we're unarmed?" the platoon sergeant said, shaking his head.

The lieutenant straightened up a bit, raising his voice loud enough so that everyone could clearly understand him. "It's like this. Under federal law we are not allowed to have any. It's called the *Posse Comitatus Act* and it precludes active duty personnel from carrying out law enforcement duties. We are only in a supporting role, and therefore will only be able to engage in administrative functions like setting up and running Traffic Control Points."

Harris raised his hand but didn't wait to be called upon before asking his question. "Sir, I saw Kansas National Guard troops earlier today with live ammo. They're in the Army too. Why do they get issued ball ammunition and we don't?"

Bethel sighed before going on. "I'm no lawyer but it's my understanding that those Guard troops are still under legal control of their governors and as such, are allowed to engage in law enforcement activities. Which means that they are allowed to carry live ammunition. And that's why the Kansas Guard won't come on this side of the city, because they have no jurisdiction here. We've been called in to assist on the Missouri-side of the border, because the Missouri Guard is spread thin covering down on St. Louis and their capital in Jefferson City."

"So, since we're active duty Army from Fort Riley, we can't carry live rounds. But the Nasty Girls from Kansas and Missouri can?" Sergeant First Class Savage was incandescent. It looked like he was going to blow like Krakatoa. "This is some fucking bullshit."

"I don't disagree. Any more questions?"

Nobody else bothered to raise their hand as a silent brooding settled in over the collective group.

"Okay then, if there are no further questions, let's get after it." Looking up from the map Bethel was distracted by Private Dubois. He kept bending his knees and shifting his weight from one side to the other with a pained expression on his face. "Is there something wrong with you, Private?"

Johnson grew a toothy smile from ear to ear. "Yes, sir. Dubois is about to do a Class I download in his pants!"

"Shut up fucker!" Dubois punched his buddy in the arm, nearly soiling himself in the process.

Bethel rolled his eyes. "Alright, dismissed!"

Without another word the platoon broke up and got to work, preparing their gear for the coming mission.

Near Platte City, Missouri
1015 Hours Local

Mark looked down at the dash and saw the pickup had three-quarters a tank of gas left. He wasn't exactly sure how big the tank was or how fuel efficient it was either. He could only guess how far the truck would get him.

In the back pocket of his newly acquired trousers, he could feel a wallet pressing into his buttock. Pulling it out, he opened it up to see how much cash was inside. *Almost a hundred bucks. Well, at least that's something.* There were credit cards in there as well, which he might be able to use. But if he did, they could track his movements and maybe catch him. *Not a good idea to use those unless I absolutely have to.*

He didn't know where he was heading, meandering through back country roads. He passed several farms along the way, with crops sprouting up through the rich soil. Every now and again he would pass the occasional farm house, usually with neatly manicured yards and brightly painted barns.

His mind raced and his heart felt as if it would leap from his chest any second. He needed a place to pull over and get ahold of himself before he got in an accident. He needed a minute to think. To process what had just happened back there, and figure out just what the hell he was going to do next.

Up ahead was a gas station out in the middle of nowhere. There was a customer filling up at the pump but no one else was around. Mark switched on his turn signal and slowly eased into the place, pulling into a parking space off to the side of the building. He put the truck in "park" and then shut the engine off before leaning forward, resting his forehead on the steering wheel.

The scenes of violence back at Leavenworth kept running through his head in a constant loop. The images would not go away, no matter what he did to push them to the back of his mind. *Come on damn you, focus! We need to figure out what to do next!*

He laid out the cash he had on the passenger seat next to the open wallet, doing a few calculations in his head trying to figure out how far he could stretch that money. He needed to get as far away from there as possible and that hundred bucks was all he had.

Next to the money was the gun belt, and in it was the unmistakable shape of an M9 pistol. He slid it out of its holster and dropped the magazine before pulling the slide back and inspecting the chamber. To his relief, it held fifteen rounds of nine-millimeter ball ammunition. He slid the magazine back in place with an audible "click" before checking the spare magazine pouches, finding them to be full too. *Well, at least I've got that going for me,* he thought to himself bitterly.

For a moment he contemplated taking the pistol into the gas station and robbing it in an attempt to gather up a little more cash but thought better of it. He wasn't a real criminal at heart, and besides, it would only bring more attention to himself and that's the last thing he needed right now. *No, the best thing I can do is try to slip away clean.*

The thought of the woman with her blood-red eyes, blue lips and snapping jaw flooded into his mind again, sending a chill down his spine. *What the fuck was wrong with her? And what happened to Matthews? This can't be real.*

Focus, goddammit. Focus! He pushed the terrible thoughts from his mind once again.

He opened the console of the pickup truck and found it nearly empty. Nearly but not totally. He reached in and pulled out a pristine 1911, .45 caliber, semi-automatic pistol. It was stainless steel and silver in color with nice wooden grips. Mark checked this one as well and found it loaded with an eight-round magazine and one up the pipe. Unlike the service pistol, this one was loaded with hollow-points for maximum damage. Mark whistled in admiration. He set the weapon back in the console and rummaged around, finding two additional magazines, fully loaded.

He leaned over and checked the back and found a long, hard, plastic case on the floor and a small pack on one of the passenger seats. He wrestled the pack over the headrest and set it next to the cash and gun belt, unzipping it and checking the contents. Inside he found a lock-blade knife, a poncho liner, a compass, some chemical lights, along with dry socks and other assorted items.

Matthews, I would have never pegged you for the survivalist type but I sure am grateful for the bug-out bag. Mark's stomach started to rumble and he was suddenly very aware of how hungry he was. *I just wish you had thought to put some energy bars in here or something.*

Zipping the bag back up, he turned his attention to the case laying on the floor in the back. He leaned over the seats and opened it up, his eyes growing wide. Inside was an AR-15 rifle, tricked out with modern optics, along with seven magazines full of ammunition. Upon inspection, each of the mags contained a full thirty rounds of soft-point hunting rounds, normally used for shooting coyotes in those parts.

He looked over his shoulder to see if anyone else was around that might have seen him messing with the weapons. To his relief there was no one, and he put everything away.

Mark sat quietly in the driver's seat and took a minute to evaluate his situation.

What do I do now? I've got a truck in good working order, a decent amount of fuel, a bit of cash, some credit cards, a bug-out bag and some weapons. I can get a ways down the road with the gas and the cash. If I run out, I can use the weapons to rob someone if I have to. His stomach turned at the thought. *I don't want to do it but I'm an escaped convict now and I just killed two people back there. If I bring any more heat on myself they'll come after me with everything they've got and I'll be lucky if they take me alive.*

No, I've got to stay under the radar… no robbing anybody.
He looked at the console and then at the gun belt. *I guess if I need to, I could try and sell the guns for money. That'd be better than robbing someone, and I could probably get a decent amount of cash.*

Leaning over, he popped open the glove compartment and rummaged around in it. He was relieved to find a couple of maps there.

Now, where am I going to go? Need to go somewhere safe, where I can disappear. He rubbed his temples while forcing himself to think. He could head off in any direction and try to disappear but he'd literally be a stranger in a strange land, trying to figure things out with no form of legal ID. He could try to find work like an illegal alien doing construction or something like that but he might get discovered. *Damnit, go with what you know.* His parents and his brother were in southern Ohio. *They'll hide me. At least for a while. Maybe even get me some money until I can find somewhere else to go.*

He couldn't think of a better option. Not with all the stress and the crazy images that kept flashing in his mind. All he knew for sure was that he couldn't just sit on his ass at this gas station taking all day to figure out a perfect plan. They'd be coming after him soon, and he needed to put as many miles between himself and Fort Leavenworth as he possibly could.

Looking down at the map he studied the routes available heading east. He had loads of options and thought about taking the secondary roads but the going would be slow. If he jumped on the freeway, he'd make the best time. *I gotta get moving, and I need to do it now.* The shortest route to southern Ohio was through Kansas City.

He studied the road networks in and around the city, then folded up the map and tossed it onto the seat next to him. He fired up the engine and pulled back onto the road, careful to observe the local speed limit.

This ain't exactly going to be the homecoming I've been

dreaming about all these years but at least it'll be something.

He checked his rearview mirror for the thousandth time to see if he was being followed as he pulled away.

***

Overland Park, Kansas
10:15 a.m.

Cassie rinsed out the dirty bowls the kids left on the counter from breakfast before putting them in the dishwasher. She plucked a couple of glasses out of the sink and put them in, filling it up as much as possible. After putting in some detergent she switched it on and looked down at her phone to check the time. She needed to get a move on because she had a lot to do and not very much time to do it.

She was still dressed in her sweaty exercise clothes after only just getting back from her spin class. The kids were downstairs playing video games and the dog was sprawled out on the couch watching her from across the room. When she made eye contact with him, the lazy beast thumped its tail up on and down on the cushions but otherwise didn't move a muscle.

Derek was upstairs getting cleaned up after his trip to Washington DC. He said he had a few things to do at the office but promised he would leave early so they could get a head-start on their weekend. The radio said something crazy about the Army declaring curfews later that night but Derek said if they got out of the city early enough, they could make it to Osage Beach in time. They always spent the 4th of July weekend at the lake and she didn't want to get stuck in the city.

Cassie knew if they got out of the house and on the road by three o'clock, they'd beat the rush hour traffic and make it there. The radio said that the lockdowns would be in place by six, so they didn't have any time to lose. She still needed to go to the store and pick up groceries for the weekend and pack them in the cooler. She could buy things over there but who knows if the stores would be open.

She thought about last year, with the kids playing in the lake with Dasher. The dog had even more fun than the kids did and would spend every day splashing around in the water, wearing himself out. Cassie was looking forward to Derek taking them out on their boat, and spending the evenings relaxing on the deck, with a glass of wine, watching the sun go down. But if she wanted to do any of that, she needed to get a move on.

She headed upstairs and ran through the mental checklist of things that still needed to get done. *Groceries, packing for herself and the kids, making sure they had the kennel loaded in the minivan for the dog... oh, don't forget the swim suits and the suntan lotion... are my sunglasses in the car? The list keeps growing!*

Getting to the top of the stairs she headed straight into the master bedroom, pulling the scrunchie from her hair and tossing it on the dresser, liberating her ponytail. She ran her fingers through her long blonde hair and curled up her nose when she saw the mess Derek had left. His suitcase was still open on the bed and the clothes he stripped off on the way to the shower were on the floor in a messy little trail. She hated it when he did that and she must have told him a thousand times to pick up after himself but he was like one of the kids and she was constantly cleaning up after him.

The water ran in the shower and the door to the bathroom was ajar. Cassie looked down at her phone again to check the time. Derek had been home for over an hour and he texted her that he was going to grab a quick shower before heading into the office. This wasn't like him.

She gently grabbed the doorknob and leaned in. "Honey, is everything all right? Are you still going in to work today?"

The only sound was the running showerhead and the water splashing on the tiles. She opened the door a bit more and peered inside. Derek stood there totally naked with his back to her, facing the shower. He stood there motionless with his head sagging at the shoulders.

"Honey? Is there something wrong?" Cassie went inside and he still did not move. She put her hand on his shoulder. She did so daintily, barely making any contact at all.

Feeling the hand on his shoulder, he turned to face her. His chin raised and his eyelids peeled back to reveal orbs of bright crimson. The jaw slowly opened and thick drool ran over blue lips.

She recoiled in horror. "Derek! Oh my god!" She took a step back, nearly tripping over her own feet. "I… I… I'm going to take you to the hospital!"

She snatched a robe from the hook on the back of the door and wrapped it around her husband. She did her best to cover him up, putting his arms through the sleeves and cinched the cotton belt around his waist, tying it for him. The whole while he did not move, only following her motions with his hemorrhaged eyes.

Then, without warning he grabbed her, his hands locked around her wrists like a vice.

Cassie yelped in pain and surprise, suddenly struggling with her husband, trying to break his grasp. He pulled her in close and his mouth opened wide, revealing cracked teeth.

She let out a high-pitched scream when those jagged teeth sank into her flesh, cutting through skin, flesh and grinding on bone.

Cassie cried out in agony when her husband fell on her, knocking them both to the floor. His jaws continued to bite, and his nails raked at her chest.

She continued to yell out until her voice grew hoarse, and the blood gurgled in her throat. Cassie continued on, with each subsequent cry growing ever weaker, until the only sound left was the patter of water from the running shower and the barking of the dog.

***

Tactical Command Post
1ˢᵗ Battalion, 18ᵗʰ Infantry
Kansas City, Kansas
1020 Hours Local

First Sergeant Kevin Landreau sat in the front passenger seat of his Humvee watching soldiers scurry around, trying to set up the battalion headquarters' control center. His driver quietly scrolled through social media sites on his phone, while message traffic crackled over the radio loudspeakers. He could have pitched in to lend a hand but preferred watching the Battalion Operations Sergeant Major struggle through the process, barking impatient orders at the enlisted members of the battalion staff.

They were in an industrial district of town, using some of the available parking lots to set up in. Military wheeled vehicles came and went, dropping off the odd piece of equipment here and there, before heading off to unknown destinations. All Landreau really cared about at that particular time was that the crew on his M-113 armored personnel carrier were getting his gear squared away at their company command post, located somewhere north of their current location, on the other side of the river.

He was none-too happy sitting there. He had talked Cindy into letting him go to a "high school reunion" that weekend, which was actually a secretive trip to Vegas with him and a couple of his friends. He was really looking forward to spending the whole time drinking, gambling, and maybe visiting one of the legal brothels he was always reading about. But instead, they got alert orders earlier in the week and all of his well-laid plans had gone to shit. So he had been busy the last few days taking his frustration out on everyone in the company, with the possible exception of his company commander, whom he barely tolerated.

Two Humvees pulled into the parking lot and parked over by the tent Sergeant Major Schell was setting up. It was the Battalion Commander and his Command Sergeant Major.

They dismounted their vehicles while the Battalion Operations Officer came up and spread out a map on the hood of the commander's vehicle.

The Company Commanders were clustered in a small group off to the side, and they motioned to each of their First Sergeants to rally up. Landreau watched his commander, Captain Bill Kieler, wave to him as well.

"About fucking time. We've been sitting here for nearly an hour already." Landreau plopped the "ACH" helmet on his head and buckled the chinstrap. "Alright, Perry. Monitor the radios while I'm in this meeting."

"Roger, First Sarn't." The driver never looked up from his phone while the senior NCO exited the truck, slamming the door back in place once he was out. It was getting hotter than hell already this morning but the Command Sergeant Major insisted that they all dress in full kit, so Landreau adjusted his combat harness over top of his heavy, and extremely uncomfortable, body armor.

"Hey, Lanny, how's it going?" First Sergeant Alexander from Charlie Company surprised Landreau, coming up from behind. He and his commander must have pulled up within the last few minutes unnoticed by himself or his driver.

"Oh, yeah hi. Didn't see you roll in."

"You don't have any extra power strips do you? My training NCO forgot to bring any, and now we can't hook up half our shit in the CP." Alexander adjusted the chin strap on his helmet while he walked, his ballistic eyewear fogging up in the thick morning humidity.

"He can check with my guys. If we got any extra, you're welcome to 'em." Landreau pointed to the assembling group of officers and NCOs up ahead. "You think they'll finally tell us what this shit is all about?"

"I hope so. I'm getting sick of my soldiers asking, and I don't have an answer for them." Alexander came up beside, he had to look up to make eye contact. "You know, Lanny, you get uglier with each passing day."

"That's not what your mom says."

"How'd you end up with that broken nose and scar on your chin?" Alexander smirked, his face wasn't going to win any modeling contracts either with all his shaving bumps and crooked teeth.

"It happened in a bar fight when I was stationed at Fort Carson. Some idiot was talking shit, so I taught him a lesson." The bar fight story was a carefully crafted lie that Landreau had been telling for years. The truth was that he had been driving home drunk from the bar and wrapped his car around a telephone pole. He fled the scene on foot and slept it off and got the alcohol out of his system before reporting it to the police. He told them he had fallen asleep at the wheel and he got off light. But the accident had left his face permanently scarred. The lie covered up for his crime and made him sound like a tough guy, which was the carefully crafted persona he created for himself and nobody was the wiser.

Coming up to the assembled group, the two First Sergeants saluted the officers who milled about. Each of them broke off and stood next to their Company Commanders, waiting for the Battalion Commander and his Command Sergeant Major to arrive. When they did, one of the NCOs called the group to "attention" and they saluted the colonel in unison.

Lieutenant Colonel Jerry Hamilton returned their salute in a leisurely manner. "At ease. Carry on." He was tall and lanky with a pronounced Adam's Apple, with cobalt-blue eyes and a large nose. He was a naturally talented runner, which he demonstrated often during battalion "morale" runs, much to the chagrin of most of his troops. "Okay, 'Three,' we got everybody?"

The Battalion Operations Officer nodded. "Yes, sir. Everyone's here."

"Good, everyone gather 'round." On the hood of Hamilton's Humvee, a map was laid out with its edges weighed down with military odds and ends to keep it from blowing away in a breeze. Not that that was an issue this particular morning since the air was stagnate and growing oppressively hot. Another typical summer day in Kansas. The Battalion Commander removed his helmet and set it down on the hood before pulling out an ink pen to use as a pointer. "I know you people have been in the dark and everyone has been asking a lot of questions and unfortunately I don't have a ton of information to share at this time. What we do know is that members of al Qaeda affiliates have infiltrated through the southern border and spread throughout the continental United States. We are told that synchronized terrorist attacks are imminent, set to occur on Independence Day. The G-2 says they will be attacking with biological weapons."

A few murmurs broke out from the back of the group. Command Sergeant Major Yates gave the talkers his patented stink-eye. "Everybody knock it off and listen up!"

"Thanks, Sergeant Major. Anyway, in Washington they are considering invoking the National Emergencies Act but haven't done so yet. So, for now the National Guard has not been federalized and are under authority of their respective governors. We active duty troops are in a supporting role to them. We'll be carrying out unarmed administrative support duties, while the Guard does the law enforcement piece. Our battalion will deploy in support of the Missouri Guard and local law enforcement just on the other side of the river. Our orders are to lock down all the major transportation arteries, keeping them free for authorized military and first-responder traffic. And there's lots of it. We also need to prepare the city for a curfew that begins at 1800 this evening." Hamilton looked up from his map and then at each of his assembled leaders. "Are there any questions?"

Silence.

"No? Well, then let's get after it."

***

Mark had both hands on the wheel, clenching it tightly. Traffic was backed up as far as the eye could see and was barely moving at all. Every lane was packed with cars and trucks, with the occasional dickhead cutting in front of someone else, trying to gain a few inches or car length, even though things were barely moving at all. Off to the left on the other side of the median the north-bound lane was jammed up just as bad. Everyone was stuck with nowhere to go. The only good thing about it was that they were actually moving, though at a glacially slow pace.

The windows of the pickup truck were down, even though the heat was smothering. He dared not use his air conditioner for fear of burning extra fuel, and he wanted to conserve every drop to get himself further down the road. At the moment however, he was half-tempted to ditch the truck and walk instead. He was pretty sure he could make better time that way.

He grabbed the map and spread it out on the steering wheel, studying it again. *There has to be a way out of this mess. If I don't get moving soon...*

Mark's mind raced and the terrible images came rushing back but he pushed them to the dark recesses of his mind. Those were replaced by cold, logical thoughts. And those were even worse. *What if this is all for me? What if they are shutting the roads down on a manhunt?* His stomach started to churn and his knee bobbed up and down uncontrollably.

Focus, damn you... focus! According to the road signs, I-70 was just up ahead less than a mile. If he got on that he could cut straight through the middle of the city and out the other side. It was the shortest way out but he had to get there first and that was no easy task with the way they were all crawling along.

To his horror he saw flashing lights up ahead, slowly

rolling up the shoulder in the north-bound lane across the way. It was local police and they pulled into the median before dismounting and heading over to the south-bound side. They were only a few car-lengths in front of him when the two officers split up and started halting drivers, leaning into their windows and talking to them.

Mark's eyes darted back and forth. He could see the exit and the on-ramp to I-70, it was only about half a mile away. He was in the extreme right lane and all he had to do was peel off onto the shoulder to bypass all this mess. *With the cops in the other lane, and the road completely packed, if I haul ass I could make it onto the exit and be on my way before they can catch me.*

He started to turn the wheels to the right but thought better of it. *No, just calm down. They're probably not after me. If I run then I'll draw attention to myself... gotta keep it together.*

Traffic continued to creep forward and the police checked each individual car, talking with all the drivers. Mark couldn't tell what they were saying and found it impossible to determine what this was all about. The radio kept going on and on about the governor declaring a state of emergency and for everyone to stay calm. *A state of emergency from the governor couldn't possibly be about me... could it?*

He saw one of the police officers heading his way now, and Mark quickly looked over at the pistol in the seat next to him, then looked back forward. *No, I am NOT going to shoot my way out of this.* He scooped up the gun belt and dropped it on the floor near the back seat, out of sight.

The officer approached the window and Mark did his best to look calm, though he was certain he looked anything but.

"Hello, sir. We're going to have you proceed another 300 yards, then ask you to pull over on the side of the road. We need to clear the highway for emergency services." The officer wore sunglasses and had a short-cropped haircut. Sweat beaded up on his forehead and ran down his temples from the midday heat.

"Sorry, officer. But I really need to get to my unit. Is there some detour I can take?" Mark felt his heart pounding but did everything he could to keep his facial expression neutral.

"Are you an MP?" The cop pointed at the brassard on Mark's left shoulder with the large letters "MP" printed in white.

In another life he would have considered a smart-assed response to the question but this situation was no joking matter. "That's right, officer. I am based out of Fort Leavenworth. I work at the prison there on post."

"Well, soldier, you are headed the wrong way if you want to get to Leavenworth."

"Yes, sir." Mark's mind was racing, trying to come up with a convincing story. He saw the cop look over and across to the passenger-side seat, inspecting the vehicle. The perspiration really started running down his back right about then. "I got caught in traffic while headed to my shift this morning. Thought I could find a short-cut around all this shit but all I did was get myself really stuck."

The police officer's expression softened. "Yeah, buddy, I understand. You're going to catch hell from your supervisor for being late for relief."

"Exactly. Can you help me out?"

"Sure thing. Pull out onto the shoulder, then roll up onto the exit ahead. Then you can take a U-turn and head back up to the base. I'll call ahead so nobody stops you." The cop started smiling. "Maybe you won't get your ass chewed too bad by your platoon sergeant."

"I appreciate it, officer."

"No worries. I was an MP too before I got out. Spent most of my time up at Fort Drum in a patrol car. Anyway, best of luck, and thank you for your service."

Mark was taken aback by the last part and didn't know how to respond. "Uh, yeah. You bet. Thanks again."

While he pulled off onto the shoulder the police officer grabbed the hand mike hanging from his epaulet and called ahead. His partner a short distance up the road merely responded with a "thumbs up" and waved Mark past, while holding the other cars in place.

Mark forced a smile and waved at the two cops while he pulled away, careful not to drive too fast.

When he entered the off-ramp and looped around entering I-70 East, he suddenly had the urge to urinate.

I'm surprised I didn't piss my pants back there. If I had, then I'd have really been screwed, he thought, proceeding along and driving deeper into the city.

Chapter 4

Independence, Missouri
1305 Hours Local

"Welcome to Burger King, may I take your order?" The tinny, disembodied voice crackled over the speaker, though barely intelligible.

Sheriff's Deputy Darin Jefferson leaned out the window of his patrol car, raising his voice to be heard. "Yes, I'd like three hamburgers, no pickle. Medium fries and a medium sweet tea."

"Anything else?"

"No, ma'am."

"You ordered three hamburgers minus pickle, medium fries and a sweet tea. That'll be $8.49. Please pull forward to the first window."

Darin pulled the cruiser up to the window and handed the girl his buddy's credit card, smiling politely at her, before retrieving it along with the receipt. He handed both over to his partner sitting in the passenger seat. "You know, you could at least change it up a little. Maybe get a cheeseburger, or heaven forbid, a salad."

Deputy Martin White accepted his credit card and slid it into his wallet. He grunted while leaning over to shove the over-sized thing into his back pocket. "That'll be enough with the fat jokes, dawg. You know I have a glandular condition."

Jefferson pulled the car forward to the second window where another teenage girl waited to hand off the paper bag full of food and the drink. He accepted it and handed it over before pulling off into the parking lot. "I didn't say anything about your weight. Just said you could at least change things up and maybe get something different."

White reached into the bag and retrieved a burger and the fries, spreading the wrapper out and squirting a couple of ketchup packets on it. "Yeah, sure. I've heard it all before.

Besides, if I got skinny like you, I'd have a harder time wrestling perps to the ground."

Jefferson's eyes twinkled and a smirk emerged on his face. "You gotta catch 'em first before you can wrestle with 'em. You can't run twenty yards to save your life. Plus, I don't know how you keep a woman so fine as you do, lookin' the way you do."

"That's because she recognizes a fine male specimen when she sees one. She likes a man with a little meat on his bones." White nearly consumed half the burger in a single bite, then grabbed a cluster of fries and dipped them in the ketchup.

Darin shook his head and reached for his lunch box, opening it up and producing a ham sandwich. "If you say so. I think she sticks around because you spend all your money on her."

"She sticks around because I give her sweet lovin'. I know you have trouble attracting the ladies, so if you ever want some advice, I'd be more than happy to assist." Martin talked while he chewed, sticking a straw in his mouth and sucking in some sweet tea to wash it all down. "You better hurry up and eat, skinny. The way we been takin' calls all morning, you might not get a chance to enjoy your lunch."

"Two-One, this is dispatch. We've got a 10-16 in your area. Sending the details now." The radio repeater came in clear as a bell over the car's internal loudspeaker, interrupting the both of them.

"Shit." Jefferson stuffed his untouched sandwich back into the box, pulling over the Mobile Data Terminal and punching in his pin. The screen lit up and the text box filled up with detailed instructions while the local map populated a location and route to their onboard GPS. "We've got a domestic disturbance three blocks from here. Injuries reported and EMS in enroute. Local PD is unavailable, committed elsewhere."

"Are you serious? Another one? This is our third one today. It's not even the weekend yet, what the hell is going on?" White shoved the rest of the burger into his mouth and stuffed the fries back into the greasy paper bag.

Jefferson flipped on the light bar, backed out of the parking spot and pulled out into traffic.

***

The cruiser came around the corner, rolling through a stop sign, barely slowing down. It was highly unusual to have this many calls so early in the day. Darin had only been with the Jackson County Sheriff's Department for three years and his experience was limited but this didn't seem right.

He and Deputy White worked traffic and normally spent their days handing out tickets but on rare occasions with the Kansas City Police Department stretched thin, they'd be called to help out. Usually local PD only got that busy late at night and on the weekends, not in the middle of the day. So he was scratching his head and trying to figure out what was going on.

The Fourth of July Weekend hadn't even started yet, and they were on their third domestic call of the day. What made it even more strange was that none of the calls seemed to involve alcohol or the normal arguments over booze, drugs, money or infidelity. These were physical attacks and the perpetrators were all out of their minds. Totally crazy, with blood-shot eyes and completely animalistic behavior. One of them even tried to bite him, though that had happened many times before when people were high on drugs. That wasn't particularly remarkable in and of itself, it was just the nature of the violence which was… different.

It was an older neighborhood in Independence, though it was well kept. The citizens trimmed their hedges and mowed their lawns, and the houses were in good repair. It was a fairly unassuming suburban affair, with nothing unusual about it, except for the two people rolling around on the grass in front of their house trying to kill one another.

A man and a woman were fighting, with the woman

sitting on top of the man. He had a large kitchen knife in his hand but couldn't slash at the woman, using his weapon hand to protect his face as she clawed at it. A crowd of neighbors assembled on the sidewalk, keeping a healthy distance, while some of them had their cell phones out, recording the altercation.

Darin tapped the siren, sending a loud chirp that drew the attention of the gathering crowd of neighbors clustered together on the sidewalk, watching the two adults roll around on the grass. The police car screeched to a halt and both deputies leaped out of the cruiser, making a beeline for the two struggling adults.

"Both of you freeze," Darin yelled, reaching for the taser mounted in the cross-draw holster strapped to his left hip. "Sir, drop the knife!"

Running past the crowd Jefferson noticed that there were two children on the sidewalk holding their arms and wailing. Covered in blood, a little boy and girl cradled bitten arms while a few of the adults attempted to dress the wounds. He felt the urge to help with the kids first but let it go, knowing full well he needed to stop the fight first. There'd be time later to deal with the little ones.

"Help me, she's gone crazy!" cried the man desperately holding on to the kitchen knife. He squirmed and twisted while the woman thrashed at him.

Darin couldn't help but notice that she looked like the others he'd seen on the domestic calls they answered earlier that day. The bloodshot eyes, the bluish hue to the lips, the varicose veins on the face—even cracked teeth and bloody saliva. And of course, the blind madness that consumed them, unresponsive to any verbal command.

"Same as the others," Darin said, drawing his taser and leveling it at the woman.

"Yeah," said his partner, taking up position near the struggling couple.

Darin pulled the trigger, launching two metal probes attached to thin wire leads. They struck the crazed woman in the chest, sending an electric charge through her body, making her muscles temporarily tense. The moment she stiffened, Deputy White—a man the size of an NFL linebacker—tackled her, slamming her to the grass.

While White subdued the woman, Jefferson dropped the taser and palmed the grip of his still-holstered Glock. "Sir, drop the weapon!"

The man on the ground was still laying on his back, his wide eyes locked with Darin's. He dropped the knife immediately and held his hands high. "Please, officer, don't shoot. She... she... tried to kill me."

White fought with the woman but he weighed almost three times as much as she did. She showed a surprising amount of strength, though it made little difference and White quickly handcuffed her. He kept a knee on her back while she lay belly-down on the ground, still craning her head back, jaws working like a snapping turtle.

Darin moved forward carefully to evaluate the man when two more vehicles came racing up. A K-9 unit pulled up to the sidewalk with an ambulance following close behind. More neighbors came spilling out of their homes, a number of them drawing in a semi-circle around the scene.

Paramedics dashed from their vehicle and descended upon the two crying children, shooing the civilians away. The other law enforcement officer darted from behind the steering wheel and opened up the back of her unit, securing a leash to a German Shepherd before it launched from its kennel, straining against its handler to get loose, barking up a storm.

The new deputy and her dog approached the gathering crowd and motioned to them, "Everyone get back, please. Give these people room to work."

More cell phones came out, recording the EMTs and the dog handler, while some focused on White who got the crazed woman on her feet. He had a hell of a time controlling her, careful to keep her snarling teeth away from him while he stuffed her in the back of their cruiser.

Darin leaned down over the man on the ground. "Sir, you may sit up." He flicked the kitchen knife a few feet away with the toe of his boot. "Do you want to tell me what happened?" The crying of the children a few feet away made it hard to focus, they were howling in pain and their blood was everywhere.

The man sat up and tears streamed down his cheeks. "My wife went down to the store this morning to pick up some groceries." He wiped his eyes with the cuff of his sleeve. "The TV said there's going to be a lockdown, so she went out to get some last-minute supplies." The man was hyperventilating and it made it difficult for him to speak.

Darin leaned in closer and put his hand on the man's shoulder. "It's all right, just calm down. Take a minute to catch your breath." He looked over at the paramedics who wrapped gauze around the bloody bite marks on the kid's arms. "Are they going to be okay?"

One of the EMTs, a guy named Gutierrez, looked up from his work. "Nothing looks life-threatening. I think they'll be okay but we gotta get them to the hospital right away." He shook his head. "We've been seeing this all morning, and they've already run out of bed space at Independence Regional. They're diverting us to Lee's Summit Medical Center."

"You guys good?" The K-9 handler approached, keeping her leashed dog close. It was Deputy Angela Carnegie, an officer they'd worked with on many previous occasions. She was a big-boned woman and strong, matching up quite well with her Alsatian named "Saxon."

"Hey Angie, good to see you. If you could keep this crowd back, that'd be great."

"Copy," she said simply, turning her attention back to the civilians who kept growing in number and getting in the way.

Darin turned his attention back to the victim. "You were saying?"

"My wife came back from the store crying, with a bite on her hand. I thought maybe a dog had done it but she said it was from a person." The man started shaking. "I wrapped it up in a towel and got ready to take her to the hospital when she went crazy and attacked me." The man's clothes had blood smeared on them but he didn't appear bitten, though he was covered in scratches all over his neck and face. He looked over to the deputy's car at his wife locked in the back seat, her face pressed against the window smearing blood and saliva across the glass as she scraped her teeth against it. He shuddered and averted his gaze, squeezing his eyes shut. People continued emerging from their homes, gathering around in morbid curiosity while Carnegie and her dog motioned them back.

"Hey! Come back here!"

Darin and the two other deputies broke their attention from the victim and crowd control duties to the shouts of the paramedic. One of the children, a small girl about seven years old with arms covered in her mother's bites, broke free from the EMT tending to her and darted off. Gutierrez tried to stop her but she dodged him, running around his legs, headed straight toward the growing group of bystanders.

The child ran snarling into the arms of a neighbor woman who was attempting to catch her, only to be rewarded by a savage attack. The child sank her teeth into the woman's bosom, eliciting a terrible scream. The woman recoiled, covering her fresh wound with both hands, releasing the girl. Now free, she instantly turned her attention to a man standing inches away and bit him in the calf on unprotected skin, well below the edge of his spandex shorts.

Some of the people stood there with mouths agape, while others pointed their cell phones at the action, as some descended on the child, trying to get her under control. All attention was focused on the seven-year-old sister while the nine-year-old brother turned, launching from the back of the ambulance and jumping on the back of Guiterrez, sinking his teeth into the man's spine at the base of his skull.

The paramedic howled in pain and dropped to the sidewalk while the young attacker let go and went straight for a woman pointing her cell phone camera at his little sister. He was on her before she knew it and started clawing and biting like a rabid badger.

Deputies Jefferson and White charged into the crowd, trying to subdue the two maniac children while Carnegie and Saxon did their best to keep people back.

Panic set in and the crowd dispersed, screaming and scattering in every direction. Darin almost got his gloved hands on the girl but she took off with amazing speed, intermixed with the crowd. Martin tried to grab the boy but the kid moved too swiftly and got away from the linebacker-sized peace officer.

A moment later the three sheriff's deputies and Saxon stood there in shock, their boots standing in fresh blood while Gutierrez whimpered as his partner attempted to render aid. All of them were facing the wrong direction and did not notice the original victim sitting on the grass suddenly turn and quietly jog off, disappearing between a couple of nearby houses.

Darin shook his head. "Can you believe this shit?"

Martin watched the crowd scatter with a blank expression on his face. "You want me to call this in?"

"Dispatch won't believe a word of it."

Angela knelt down next to her furry partner and stroked his head, trying to calm him as he barked at the fleeing civilians. "Are we going to pretend that we didn't just see what we saw?"

Martin shifted his weight uncomfortably, his huge mass casting a giant shadow on the lawn. "You mean that these people are turning into…"

"Don't even say it. It's too fucking crazy, and it can't possibly be happening!" Martin said, cutting his friend off before he could finish the sentence. "There has to be a logical explanation for all of this."

They all turned in unison to look at the snarling and spitting woman in the back of the police car. She was kicking and thrashing about, occasionally smashing her skull into the window, trying to escape. The wild, animal look in her red eyes sent chills down Darin's spine.

They all stood there silently for a long minute listening to the growing crescendo of screams around them that nearly drowned out the wails of sirens and gunshots in the distance.

***

I-635 North
1324 Hours Local

Mark didn't get onto the northbound lane headed back to Leavenworth like he told the police he intended to. Instead he kept right on going into the heart of the city. With all the cars stacking up in traffic jams he hoped that taking the shortest route would get him through all of this more quickly and once out of the city, it'd be smooth sailing across Missouri at least until he hit St. Louis but he could worry about that later.

Things here weren't much better than on I-435 South but he didn't bother obeying the traffic laws any longer, electing to drive deliberately along the shoulder. There were other people who had the same idea of course and he ran into the occasional log jam here and there but whenever he did so he dismounted and told the civilians to clear out for him as he had critical military business to attend to and he demanded they yield the right of way. His Army uniform, MP brassard, his sidearm, and most importantly his professionally delivered and hastily concocted lie fooled everyone, people clearing the way for him to proceed. And so he did.

He'd been on I-70 East headed through the middle of the city up until things got completely jammed up. In frustration he jumped onto I-635 North where at least the traffic wasn't at a total standstill. Even though it was moving, things were just crawling along.

The big, red Ford F150 made its way along the shoulders and grassy medians at a painfully slow pace, never advancing at more than ten miles per hour. But at least he was moving, unlike most of the others. Crawling along through the middle of the city with his windows down, he was suddenly hit with the smell of wood smoke. It was the unmistakable smell of Kansas-style barbecue and his empty stomach rumbled in protest. It was about then that he realized how hungry he was but he pushed the thought from his mind, staying focused on the task at hand.

He squeezed his truck past the traffic stalled out on the bridge spanning the Missouri River, ignoring the angry looks from civilians stuck in their cars. It was the second time that day he had crossed the meandering brown waterway but he hardly paid any attention to that. The occasional motorcyclist passed through the lanes of traffic, moving along much swifter than himself and he wondered if he should attempt to commandeer one. He discarded that thought too, knowing full well he didn't know how to operate a motorcycle and he'd just end up getting himself killed.

Before long he found himself in an industrial area and caught sight of another road sign reading, "Missouri Welcomes You." He realized that he had crossed over from Kansas, into Missouri, back into Kansas, and was now in Missouri once again. The novelty of that might have amused him at any other time but not now. At the moment he was fighting his way through the traffic, the frustration, and the building sense of panic welling up inside him.

The radio was on and he tried to glean whatever information he could from it by cycling through the various local stations. None of them were playing music and all were relaying news, some of it recorded from government authorities. Whenever he'd come across another broadcast he'd heard earlier, Mark would change the channel in hopes of finding something new.

"There is a curfew that will go into effect at 6:00 p.m. this evening on orders from the governor. All citizens are urged to…"

"Military units have deployed to Washington D.C. and northern Virginia. Residents of Alexandria, Fairfax, and

Arlington counties will observe..."

"The press secretary announced today that the President will make a statement to address the nation at 7:00 p.m. Eastern Time..."

Eventually he grew tired of the same messages and turned the radio off. It only made him more agitated and he was already so wound up that the knots in his stomach had knots.

He pulled out his map for the hundredth time, laying it across the steering wheel while he drove. He saw the river crossing and then the casino coming up on his right. Ahead there would be an interchange where he could get off and continue heading east. Mark roughly folded the map and set it aside and when he looked back up he couldn't help noticing the all-too familiar outline of Bradley Fighting Vehicle looming over the cars parked in the middle of the roadway up ahead.

The sweat that ran down his temples really started to flow now and the pace of his breathing picked up as the flow of traffic began to slow down. He considered jumping the median and going back the way he came but there was no way to get over with cars stacked up bumper-to-bumper. He pulled off onto the right-hand shoulder once again and made his way forward, his mind racing all the while.

***

2nd Squad, 2nd Platoon
Bravo Company, 1-18 Infantry
Checkpoint 7
1325 Hours Local

Specialist Geoff Harris adjusted the M-249 Squad Automatic Weapon, slinging it across his back. The useless thing hung around his neck like a millstone and he felt absolutely stupid carrying it. Of course it was stupid that they were on traffic-control duties wearing body armor, helmets, and even had their fucking gas masks strapped to their hips. To put the cherry on top, all of them wore brightly colored "road guard vests" covering the rest of their kit as a ridiculous accent to the rest of their silly attire.

They'd been posted here for the last couple of hours and patience was already wearing thin. The civilians got more and more hostile with each passing minute, each of them having a super-important reason why they were in a hurry to be somewhere. It was hot outside, the equipment was uncomfortable, and their four-day pass had been canceled. Frankly, Geoff was happy the fucking civilians were mad, they deserved to be as miserable as he was right about then.

Their orders were to keep the two center lanes cleared for first responders and military units with official business. Everyone else needed to have their identification checked before being allowed to pass. This had the effect of stacking up cars and trucks for miles but orders were orders and he was beyond giving a shit.

He walked past a Hyundai with the window rolled down. Private Lauren Gray was calmly talking to the driver who appeared to be a middle-aged woman. The two of them were smiling while they talked, and the lady happily handed over her license.

The women are always nice to Gray. They think it's cool that there's a "lady soldier" out here, so they give her an easy time. Us guys always have to deal with the assholes, Geoff thought to himself, walking up to the next vehicle in line.

The car was a white Prius and the dude behind the wheel looked pissed. Geoff walked up next to the door and the guy inside kept staring straight forward with his hands on the wheel, doing his level-best to ignore him. Geoff rolled his eyes and gently wrapped on the window with a gloved hand.

The window slid down with a hum, and the man looked up. "I need to be somewhere right now and you soldiers are making me late." The man almost spat the word "soldiers" when he said it.

"Yes, sir, I'm very sorry but we are required to check everyone's identification before allowing you to pass." Geoff tried to be as professional as possible while concealing his frustration. They'd been given orders to check IDs but none of them had any idea why, or what they were even looking for. The bad guys didn't exactly carry around ID cards with "terrorist" labeled on them. It was just another stupid and utterly pointless exercise the Army had them out there doing. This was total bullshit and he was definitely getting out when his enlistment was up.

"Is this really necessary? I have classes to teach. I'm a tenured university professor and I'm in a hurry. Tenured means that I'm 'full-time' you see, and I hold a very important position." The man's eyes squinted behind his wire-rimmed glasses and his lip curled from beneath his impeccably trimmed goatee. After an awkward moment of silence, the man's expression changed, as did his tone. Geoff had been in the Army long enough to recognize when someone was changing tactics on you. He retrieved his wallet and pulled out a driver's license along with faculty identification, with the name "Doctor Steven Rheinhardt PhD" prominently displayed on it. "Here you go young man. I know you're just doing your job."

"Thank you, sir." Geoff looked them over as if he were studying them, looking for something specific. Which of course he was not. He was putting on a show and since this guy was being such a dick, he was going to drag this out longer than it needed to be.

"So, where are you from?" Asked the man, obviously feigning interest in the young grunt. "Your English is excellent."

"I'm from Denver." Geoff didn't bother to look at him.

"No, I mean originally."

He'd been asked this question a thousand times before and on occasion would make the person asking feel like a real shithead. But the sun was blazing down on him, the smell of vehicle exhaust stung his nose, and he wanted to get this crappy day over with. "I was born in Korea but I'm adopted. I was raised by my parents in Denver." He didn't bother to add, *and they are both as white as you.*

"That's really great. We need more people here in this country like you. Can you speak Korean?"

He got this idiotic question a lot too. "Can you speak it?"

"Oh. No, I certainly can't. I was just curious."

"Yes, I'm quite fluent." Geoff couldn't speak a word of the language but he always enjoyed fucking with pretentious pricks like this guy. "Sir, your identification seems to be in order." He handed the cards back to the dickhead university professor. He didn't bother mentioning that he had a four-year degree from the University of Colorado and had joined the Army because he was bored with life. Geoff knew damned well what "tenured" meant, and also why this jerk felt compelled to announce his status. "You can be on your way."

He waved over to Burbey and Donahue who nodded, moving a single row of concertina wire and some orange road cones out of the middle of the road. The professor rolled up his window without saying a word and drove his Prius through the opening, and off to his very important job.

While the next car in line slowly pulled up to fill the now vacant spot, Geoff caught sight of a large red pickup truck approaching along the shoulder, nearly rubbing up against the concrete barriers on the side of the road. The driver was not doing anything reckless but he was clearly trying to get past the rest of the cars lined up. This guy too must have thought he was something special. Probably another doctor or something.

Geoff jogged over and stood on the shoulder, raising his left hand up while lowering his right and gently grasping the muzzle of his light machine gun. The big red Ford slowed to a halt a few feet in front of him and the driver gave him a friendly wave. The guy was dressed in an Army uniform.

He approached and was greeted with a smile.

"Sir, you can't bypass the traffic like this, you're going to have to get back in line with everyone else." Geoff used the obligatory "sir" since the guy's rank was covered by the seatbelt. He couldn't help but notice the MP brassard on his left shoulder though. Nobody liked the Military Police, so seeing this guy cutting traffic like an entitled ass only made him like the dude even less.

"Yeah, sorry about that. But I'm on official business and I have to get through. Please don't call me 'sir,' I'm sure as hell no officer." The soldier was covered in sweat and wore a smile about as sincere as the stripper's back in Junction City outside the gate of Fort Riley.

"Okay…"

"Sergeant. My name is Sergeant Matthews."

"Roger, aren't. You got your CAC card and a set of orders? I can't let anyone through who ain't got official business." Geoff could see that the guy was trying even harder to keep up the friendly façade.

"Unfortunately, no. Listen, this is real important. Can I speak with your squad leader?"

"Yeah, hold on." Geoff turned and waved over at the Bradley Fighting Vehicle parked in the median. His squad leader, Sergeant Chamberlain, stood on the back ramp talking to Sergeant Rash. He saw the waving and nodded with an annoyed look before coming over, weaving his way through the waiting cars and trucks.

When Chamberlain arrived, he looked none-too thrilled and the bags under his eyes were darker than they had been earlier this morning. "What's up?"

"I got an Army NCO here who says he needs to get through the checkpoint because he's on official business. But he ain't got no authorization."

Chamberlain walked up to the truck, greeted by the same fake smile. "My name's Chamberlain. Who are you?"

"I'm Matthews. I'm out of Fort Leavenworth and I need to be somewhere right now."

"We're getting a lot of that today." His expression was deadpan and his voice steady.

"Sergeant Chamberlain!" A voice called out from the Bradley. It was Sergeant Rash, the Bravo Team Leader and he was waving him over. "The El-Tee wants to speak with you on the radio. Says it's urgent!"

Chamberlain turned to the sweaty MP in the big red Ford and could see the uneasiness on his face. *Good*, he thought to himself, *I'll take any opportunity to inconvenience a fucking MP. They all need to suffer.* "Hold on a minute, Sergeant. My lieutenant's calling. I'll be with you shortly."

***

Mark watched Sergeant Chamberlain walk away toward the Bradley. His team leader was standing on the back ramp pointing inside to where the radios were located. Meanwhile, the rest of the soldiers were checking IDs and letting cars proceed while he was stuck on the shoulder.

Fuck, I shouldn't have drawn attention to myself. I just knew it!

He saw two of the soldiers look over to him, say something to one another and then laugh before getting back to their mind-numbing duties. They were obviously taking great delight in inconveniencing him. Mark understood them perfectly well, no soldiers liked MPs, particularly infantrymen. And since he had been spending years behind bars at the Fort Leavenworth Disciplinary Barracks, he wasn't very fond of them himself. But he had to keep up the act if he wanted to get out of there. Best to let them fuck with him a little bit so he could be on his way.

After a couple of minutes, Chamberlain emerged from the back of the track, looking even less enthused than he had before taking the call from his platoon leader. "Everybody stop what you're doing and pull it in!"

The soldiers standing next to open windows handed IDs back to the drivers, then serpentined their way through the parked cars over to their squad leader. The two manning the concertina wire and road cones simply left their post, looking bored as ever.

Mark watched them all huddle together, a few occasionally nodding while the NCO relayed the message from Platoon. It was a drill he himself had been through many times in the distant past, relaying critical information from the higher headquarters. Once complete, the group broke up with most of them headed to the front of the Infantry Fighting Vehicle where they began untying more bundles of razor wire secured to the engine access panel. Chamberlain came back over with that same neutral expression.

"Sorry, sarn't. Just got orders from my platoon leader and we have to lock this checkpoint down. No traffic moves without authorization. You got orders?" Chamberlain's face was red from the searing summer heat. His helmet cocked slightly back, exposing his forehead, and his chinstrap hung loosely under his jaw. The clearly evident five o'clock shadow and redness in eyes suggested that he hadn't seen the inside of his sleeping bag lately. He didn't even flinch when car horns began to honk, something that was particularly rude in the Midwest.

"Uh… well, I ain't got orders. You see… I fucked up this morning. I slept in and I missed movement. I was supposed to accompany a detail out to the airport to receive a Con Air flight. We were expecting some new inmates to ship back to Leavenworth for inprocessing. My platoon sergeant called me on my cell and ripped me a new asshole. Told me to get my ass out to the airport immediately or else he'd Article 15 me." Mark studied the other NCO's expression to see if he was believing this total bullshit lie. Chamberlain stood there like a statue and it was impossible to tell whether or not he was buying it.

"You're supposed to be out at the airport to pick up prisoners? Is that it?"

"That's right. I checked in, drew my weapon and then jumped in my POV trying to catch up with the rest of my unit." Mark shrugged his shoulders.

"Last time I checked, you weren't authorized to carry an issue weapon in a Personally Owned Vehicle, sarn't."

"Yeah, I'm not. But what was I supposed to do? Like I said, I missed my ride with the rest of the detail, and I'm trying to get out to them. My phone's been blowing up all morning and my platoon sergeant's fucking pissed at me. I really need to get moving."

Chamberlain stood there staring at him, and Mark shifted his weight in the leather seat uncomfortably. "You got your ID?"

Ice started to form in his stomach. He felt a lump growing in his throat and he fought the urge to swallow. He took a deep breath before answering, trying to keep the tremor out of his voice. "Ah, negative. I don't. You see, after I overslept and my leadership called, I raced out of the house so fast this morning I even forgot my wallet. So, I don't have my CAC card with me."

"Okay. Stand by." Chamberlain turned around and headed back to the Bradley. The other soldiers busied themselves reinforcing the wire obstacle running across the highway, while horns continued to honk and civilians began getting out of their cars in frustration.

Stay calm buddy, stay calm. He's just going to report the situation to his PL, and then they'll let you be on your way.

A few minutes later the squad leader returned. "I'm sorry, Sergeant. The El-Tee says he can't authorize any movement through the checkpoint right now. Orders from Battalion." Chamberlain pushed the helmet even further back and wiped the sweat from his brow with the sleeve of his battle dress. "He says he'll call it up to the CO and see if he can get permission though. But everybody's super busy right now and it might take a while. Sorry. For the time being you'll have to wait here like everyone else."

Mark simply nodded in understanding without saying a word, then watched the squad leader turn on his heel and head back over to the armored fighting vehicle.

***

Independence, Missouri
1335 Hours Local

"Dispatch, this is Two-One. Come in. Over." While deputy White transmitted, his voice crackled loudly in the hand-held radios affixed to the two other deputy's belts. It also came through loud and clear from Deputy Angela Carnegie's cruiser as well. "Dispatch, this is Two-One. How do you read? Over!"

"What do you think is wrong?" Jefferson cinched down the wrist restraints to Gutierrez on the gurney, while the other EMT dressed his wounds. The paramedic was already unconscious so they worked swiftly to get him in the back of the ambulance and more importantly, strapped him down securely in case he woke back up acting like the others.

Carnegie was out in the street with Saxon, keeping watch. She had his leash in her left hand while the palm of her right rested on her Glock. There were no people visible anywhere now after the crowd scattered. Most of the people retreated back into their homes, and except for the noise in the distance, things were quiet.

"Dispatch, this is Two-One. Is anybody out there? Over."

The woman in the back of the cruiser tried to reach through the grate from the back seat to get at White while he leaned into the car to use the radio. It was no use and she howled in frustration.

"Two-One, this is Two-Three, we can't raise dispatch either." The disembodied voice came from their buddy, Deputy Gary Stevens, a fifteen-year veteran of the Jackson County Sheriff's Department.

"Roger that, Two-Three. What's your situation?"

"You wouldn't believe me if I told you. The whole city is going crazy and people are literally tearing each other to pieces. We were attacked by a mob and forced to retreat. We're on the move now, headed back to the station to see

what's going on. Over."

"Copy. Good luck. Two-One. Out."

White put the mike back into the cradle, sparing a glance at the crazed woman. She lunged at him and he recoiled as she smashed into the steel mesh separating her and the front seat of the police car.

Jefferson finished securing Gutierrez and hopped out of the ambulance. "You better get out of here. Be careful when you get him back to the hospital in case he starts acting up like the others."

The paramedic nodded. "Don't worry, I'll be careful. Thanks for the help." He shook the cop's hand before jumping behind the wheel and taking off.

As the ambulance turned the corner Saxon started to growl. He lowered his head, bared his teeth and the hair on his shoulders stood straight up. He stared across the street at one of the houses whose front door was wide open. Carnegie looked down at him and across to the house. "What is it, boy?"

Two men burst from the doorway, sprinting straight at Carnegie and the dog. Their jaws snapped and their red eyes held wide as they closed the distance like a couple of Kenyan sprinters.

Saxon barked savagely while Carnegie adjusted her stance, her grip now firmly on the sidearm. "Halt! I order you to stop!"

The two crossed the yard and were on the sidewalk only a few feet from her in the span of a second. Carnegie unholstered her weapon and fired, the discharge of the weapon resounding in sharp pops. She aimed center mass just as her training demanded, sending jacketed hollow-points slamming into their chests. Angela was a good shot and her aim was true but neither of the attackers so much as flinched.

She let the dog go, and Saxon launched at the nearest one like a missile, knocking him to the ground. The Shepherd's powerful jaws latching onto the man's arm, not letting go.

Angela continued to stand her ground, firing rapidly at

the second one until he was nearly on top of her. She sidestepped out of the way at the very last second and tripped him, sending him tumbling to the ground. She turned to face him, re-aiming her pistol and gasped when he leapt back up to his feet, coming at her once again.

She got off another shot before the man hit her, sending her slamming into the street, the gun skittering off toward the curb. The man's teeth snapped at her face but she managed to gain some leverage. He was average in size and not athletic-looking but his strength surprised her. It wasn't enough though, since Deputy Angela Carnegie's favorite pastime was training for and competing in mixed martial arts bouts. She was a muscular woman, in top physical condition, and an expert grappler. Even so, she struggled with the maniac doing her best to keep him under control.

With tremendous effort, after what seemed like hours when in reality it was only seconds, Carnegie managed to ball up her attacker. She had him from behind, her arm like a vice around his throat in a choke-hold. It normally wouldn't take long cutting off the blood flow through the carotid arteries to the brain before the subject would slip into unconsciousness. But this one didn't seem to be bothered by it at all. He thrashed about, snapping his teeth and hissing, not slowing down one bit.

Angela grunted and strained, conjuring up every bit of strength she had. It wouldn't be long before she started to fatigue, and then the bastard might get loose.

Behind her she heard a loud pop, then saw a pair of legs standing next to her.

"You got him?" She craned her neck up to see Jefferson standing over them both.

"Yeah but this fucker is stronger than he looks," she gasped.

"Hold him steady." Jefferson leaned down and pressed the muzzle of his pistol against the crazed man's temple, careful to keep it pointed well away from Carnegie.

"No, wait!" She protested.

Another loud pop.

The man in her grasp went limp and her ears started to ring. She forced herself to look down to see a sizable chunk of her attacker's head scattered across the centerline of the street.

Jefferson leaned down and grasped the corpse's shirt, rolling it off Carnegie. She sat up and saw Saxon trot over, sniffing at the dead body next to her, the dog's body tense as a coiled spring. She looked up to see the other deputy disinterested in the person he'd just shot, instead his attention focused down the street. He clutched his service weapon with both hands, the pistol held at the low-ready.

"Why did you do that? He wasn't armed," she said, slowly getting back to her feet.

More gunshots rang out nearby and a guttural howl intermixed with high-pitched screams.

From around the corner of a well-trimmed hedge people came running. Seeing the law-enforcement officers and their cars they came straight toward them, some helping others, many concerned only for themselves. They first came on in ones and twos, then the number grew into at least a couple of dozen. Many of them carried small children who could not keep up on their own.

"Halt!" Jefferson yelled, still holding the pistol low.

Carnegie secured Saxon's leash and retrieved her Glock, struggling with the dog as it went nuts. White came up as well, the three officers spreading out and doing their best to form a line in the middle of the street.

The panicked people ignored the commands and continued on. Not only did they not stop on command, they kept on running past the deputies as if getting herded down the thoroughfare.

Then from around the corner, two adult males came sprinting from behind, chasing the others. One was a teenage boy and the other a middle-aged man. Both were covered in blood, covered in terrible wounds. They also had the red eyes, blue lips and spider-webbed veins on their skin.

The teenager zeroed in on a woman near the trail of the pack carrying a toddler. She was overweight and slow, barely able to keep up with the others. The diseased monster snatched the child from her arms while the middle-aged one grabbed the woman by the hair. They began shredding the child and its mother to pieces a mere yards in front of the sheriff's deputies.

Jefferson walked calmly toward the carnage raising his pistol, looking down the length of the slide focused on the front sight blade. He fired the weapon deliberately, taking his time to aim. The first round hit the teenager in the shoulder but the infected boy did not flinch, focused on disemboweling the shrieking toddler. He took a deep breath and continued moving closer, closing the distance, then took up the slack in the trigger before squeezing once again. The handgun bucked in his hands and a nine-millimeter hollow-point crashed into the attacker's skull.

The middle-aged creature paid no attention to the shots, singularly focused on sinking its teeth into the warm flesh of the flailing and gurgling woman. Jefferson shifted his aim to the left in a fluid motion before setting the sights on the man's head, firing once again. The second attacker fell on top of his victim, limp as a noodle.

Carnegie and White were suddenly there, covering the now-dead perpetrators. White, an African-American man the size of a bison, turned pale as a sheet and started to retch once he saw the small child's guts spread all over, some of it hanging from the dead teenager's mouth.

"What the fuck is going on here?" Carnegie said, rolling the infected corpse off the woman, its red eyes staring toward the sky. She didn't notice Jefferson calmly strolling up beside her, looking down at the woman who shook violently, gasping, choking and spitting up blood.

"I think you need to take a step back." Jefferson watched the victim begin thrashing around, clawing at the air.

"We need to get that other paramedic over here right now!" Carnegie holstered her weapon and leaned down toward the woman on the ground to render aid.

"I said, get back!" Jefferson commanded, his Glock pointed at the woman's forehead.

"What the fuck are you doing? Put that away!" Saxon suddenly put himself between Carnegie and the injured woman, growling with bared teeth while the hair on his back stood straight up.

The woman suddenly stopped thrashing about and leaped to her feet, shocking them all. Nobody as large as her should have been able to move that fast but she leapt to her feet with incredible agility. She turned to face Carnegie and snarled, the whites of her eyes beginning to flush red.

A shot rang out and her head snapped back. Her body collapsed with a wet slap on the asphalt. Jefferson stood there for a moment after delivering the killing blow, then slowly lowered his weapon. White turned and dropped to a knee, puking into a gutter.

Jefferson gently placed his hand on Carnegie's shoulder while she stood there dumbstruck. "I think we need to get in our cars and get back to the department and report what's going on."

Carnegie stood there in a daze, surveying the scene, unable to look away from all the bodies now littering the street. "Yeah... I think you're probably right." She turned her attention toward the dog. "*Saxon*, come. Let's get out of here."

***

Checkpoint 7
1720 Hours Local

Mark stopped cycling through radio stations and turned it off. The constant stream of news reports got steadily more confusing with stories of martial law and right-wing extremists being replaced by those of violence occurring all over the city. Over the course of a few hours the disc jockeys and reporters stopped talking about the curfews and the lockdowns, and quickly shifted to the anarchy breaking out all over. Eventually even these reports were replaced by the Emergency Broadcast System on every channel, telling everyone to stay in their homes.

That guidance didn't translate down to the soldiers manning the checkpoints, with them still enforcing no-movement orders on all major arteries, allowing only approved military and first responders to travel unfettered. The thousands of cars on the highways were stranded, with most engines still running so people could operate their air conditioners to avoid the stifling summer heat.

The honking of horns increased for a time and eventually petered out when people realized it was of little use. Now, more and more of them emerged from their vehicles to confront the soldiers, demanding to be let through. After hours of this, tempers were flaring.

Mark looked on while a mob of unruly civilians gathered around two of the infantrymen, some of them waving their fists and shouting at the top of their lungs. It didn't take long for the citizens to transition from "thank you for your service," to "I pay your fucking wages with my taxes so let me through!" If he weren't so frustrated himself, he might have laughed at the ridiculousness of it all but instead he sat there helpless like the others.

While half the squad dealt with the angry crowd doing their best to stay professional and polite, Sergeant Rash pulled a large cardboard box from the back of the Bradley, setting it down on the ramp and opening it up. He removed light-brown plastic pouches and began handing them out to the other half of the squad. Mark immediately recognized the Meals Ready to Eat—or MREs in Army lingo. His stomach growled loudly and he watched longingly as the young service members opened up the bags and started digging in.

After a few minutes of listening to his rumbling gut and feeling his mouth water, he tried to look away and focus on something else. The crowd was slowly growing and their protests got more animated with each passing minute. This was annoying but the sounds of sirens and gunfire in the distance started to really worry him. If things got much worse, he might never get out of there and it was only a matter of time before he was found out. If he couldn't run, he'd have to fight. He thought about the weapons he had in the truck but pushed that to the back of his mind. He wasn't interested in killing anyone else this day and he wasn't so sure he'd be willing to take another life to secure his own freedom. He was desperate but not *that* desperate. Not yet anyway.

"Hey, what're you doing right now?" The question startled Mark and he jerked a little as if he'd been hit with a jolt of electricity. It was Sergeant Chamberlain, standing there next to the open window of his truck, peering inside. He hadn't noticed him walk up and was taken by surprise.

"Uh, nothing I guess. Just waiting to hear back from CO and get permission to pass through." He wondered if Chamberlain noticed how uncomfortable he was.

"Well, if you ain't doing nothin', would you mind helping us out? These people are starting to get out of hand and I don't have enough people to deal with this situation."

Mark looked at Chamberlain and then over to his people. His eyes were drawn to the soldiers sitting on the ramp, bare-headed with their helmets sitting on the ground, wolfing down their cold MREs. His stomach made such a loud noise that Chamberlain couldn't help but notice. "I suppose I could help out. On one condition."

"Yeah, what's that?"

"If you give me one of those MREs over there, I'd be happy to lend a hand."

For the first time all day, Chamberlain showed a hint of emotion. The faintest bit of a smile almost emerged on his stony mask. "Yeah, sure. But you only get five minutes to eat. We got shit to do."

"Understood." Mark opened the door and stepped out onto the hot asphalt, securing the gun belt around his waist.

Maslow's hierarchy of needs kicked in and the thought of filling his empty belly overrode his desire to escape.

At least for the time being.

Chapter 5

Company Command Post
Bravo Company, 1-18 Infantry
1730 Hours Local

The command post, more commonly known as the "CP," was little more than a tent with some field tables and chairs arranged inside. In the center was a couple of speakers and remote handsets attached to thick, black cables running outside, plugged into the radio mounts of the First Sergeant's M-113 armored personnel carrier. Next to the remotes was a large map affixed to a piece of plywood, spray-painted olive drab. It hung from one of the support beams by pieces of parachute cord.

In the corner the company clerk, who doubled as the First Sergeant's track driver, typed on a laptop computer. One of the evening reports was due in less than an hour and the young specialist was working hard to get it out on time. They didn't have any WiFi so he had his cell phone hotspot switched on, ready to e-mail the report as soon as he was able. The Sergeant Major would be up the First Sergeant's ass if it got turned in late, and that meant he'd take it out on the rest of them. Shit rolls downhill after all.

On the other side of the tent's wall a generator hummed as it produced ample power to run the air conditioning unit the clerk had "procured," along with the tall, silver coffee maker sitting on the field table in the corner. Landreau poured himself some of the hot, black liquid into the plastic travel mug with the 1st Infantry Division logo printed on the side. The brew wasn't any good but it was hot and strong. Something he needed right about then as he contemplated yet another sleepless night ahead of them.

In the corner, curled up on the floor was Landreau's Humvee driver. He lay upon an issued air mattress, fast asleep. He'd been up most of the previous night, so he was trying to get a little shut-eye while he was able.

"You got that personnel status report done yet?" Landreau grimaced after taking a sip from the mug. The coffee had been on the burner all afternoon and it tasted badly burnt.

"Not yet, First Sarn't. I'll have it done in a minute." Sergeant Danny Medina didn't even look up while he typed, focusing on the screen while he spit tobacco juice into a paper cup.

"Once you're done with the perstat, send it up to Battalion, then make another batch of joe. This shit here is getting nasty."

"Roger, First Sarn't," Medina said, tapping away at the keys.

The tent flap opened up and in walked the company executive officer, First Lieutenant Scotty Truitt. He'd been with the company nearly three years now and XO for almost half that time. When he came inside the air-conditioned CP his ballistic glasses fogged up and he pulled them off right after removing his helmet, placing it on the field table next to the radio remote.

"Hey, Top. Any news on the crypto keys?" Truitt saw the coffee maker in the corner and headed to it as if drawn by an invisible magnetic force. He grabbed one of the paper cups stacked neatly next to it and poured himself a cup of the god-awful stuff. He took a sip and his face soured, so he picked up several packets of sugar and creamer and mixed them in, creating a hateful concoction.

"Not yet, sir. Battalion keeps saying the SIG-O is getting things unfucked but nobody has them yet. So we're still operating in the clear." Landreau kept his tone steady while addressing the officer but could barely stand him. He didn't like any officers but there were different shades of contempt that Landreau held for each individual one. The XO was down there near the bottom, mostly because he didn't feel the young man gave him the respect he deserved, ordering him around half the time like the commander often did.

"Awesome. The BC should fire the SIG-O, that fucking

guy can't ever seem to keep shit straight." Truitt sat down in a folding chair and kicked a leg up on the table, leaning back and stretching his neck before taking another sip from the cup. He still wore his body armor and kit, the sweat nearly soaking the sleeves of his battle dress jacket. "You get the word from the CO?"

"No, I haven't heard from him in a couple of hours." Landreau was disinterested in calling the commander on the radio, because the overzealous workaholic would likely saddle him with some meaningless task. He was perfectly happy to hang out in the nice air-conditioned CP and run the company from there.

"I ran into him after my meeting with the Battalion XO right before coming here. Big XO says that the resupply package will be ready back in the Field Trains within the hour, and that we need to escort the Log-Pac forward. The CO's out inspecting 1st Platoon and he told me to have you check in on 2nd Platoon while I head back to the Brigade Support Area and bring the resupply forward." Truitt took a deep breath and sighed, setting the cup down and rubbing his eyes.

"What about 3rd Platoon?" Landreau didn't bother to control the annoyance in his voice. He was not at all eager to put all of his gear back on and head out into the heat. Checking on the platoons was a waste of time in his opinion. The platoon sergeants were more than capable of taking care of their own business and if they needed anything, they'd call.

The XO looked up at him with a cocked eyebrow. "They're still sitting outside about a hundred meters from here in their laager site. Battalion's decided to keep them as the reserve until further notice."

"I can't believe we're in such a hurry to push forward the Log-Pac. There's plenty of supplies on the tracks and they can easily wait until morning."

"Normally we could. But 1st Platoon is a tank platoon cross-attached from Charlie Company. We haven't refueled any of the vehicles since we left the railhead, and those tankers will be out of fuel before midnight if we don't top them off. The tanks burn JP-8 like it's going out of style."

"The fucking tankers shouldn't be running their engines while they're out manning Traffic Control Points. They should still have plenty." Landreau frowned and crossed his arms, not moving from his spot near the blower that filled the tent with blissfully cool air.

"Be that as it may, we still have to do it." Truitt took another drink and poured the rest on the ground before crushing the cup in his hand and tossing it in the trash. He snatched up his Kevlar helmet and plopped it on his head, buckling the chin strap as he rose from the chair. "I'll be on the net if you need to raise me."

Landreau watched the lieutenant leave and shook his head in disgust. "Beltran, get up! We've got to go."

The exhausted driver stirred and groaned. "Roger, First Sarn't," he croaked, sitting up and letting out an audible fart before reaching for his gear.

***

Riverside, Missouri
1802 Hours Local

Juan Ochoa breathed heavily while fumbling with his keys. The screams on the other side of the door got his adrenaline pumping into overdrive and he struggled to keep it together. Finally, mercifully, he found the key and shoved it in the lock, turning the knob.

He burst into the small apartment to find it in complete disarray. Some of the cheap furniture lay knocked over, some of it damaged. There was broken glass and blood, with the place smelling of spicy food cooking in the tiny kitchen. To his horror he saw blood smeared on the walls and spattered on the floor. The screams were louder now, off in the master bedroom.

He charged in and saw a man kicking and smashing the door to the bathroom. On the other side Juan heard the muffled cries of his daughter and grandchildren. Inside of the bedroom was his daughter's boyfriend, a lazy alcoholic who went by the nickname Chico and sported a neck tattoo and gauged earlobes. At the moment he kicked and punched at the door, trying to break through.

"Mira, what the hell do you think you're doing?" shouted Juan. He may have been a fifty-five year-old man, well past his prime but he could still fight and he moved in to protect the only things in his life that held any value to him anymore—his girls.

The boyfriend spun around to face him and Juan gasped when he saw the young man's face. His eyes were red and his face covered in thick, blue veins, nearly as blue as his lips. It's the same thing Juan had been seeing all afternoon at different places in the city. It made his blood run cold. Chico rushed the older man, letting out a snarl while thick saliva dripped from his chin. Juan met him head-on and the two fell to the floor, all arms and legs.

The two of them made a terrible racket while they fought. Juan grunted and shouted, while Chico growled and snapped his jaws. As they struggled, they rolled around, knocking over a nightstand, sending a lamp crashing to the floor and shattering. While they fought the bathroom door cracked open and the daughter guardedly peeked to see what was going on.

Seeing her father on the floor with her psychotic lover she opened the door wide and shouted. "Chico, stop! What is the matter with you?" She stood there helpless with her children behind her in the bathroom sobbing.

"Maria, get the girls out of here!" Juan managed to grunt out, holding the boyfriend back while he tried to sink his teeth into raw flesh.

The woman bolted past into the other room and re-emerged seconds later with a kitchen knife in hand. She saw Chico on top of her father while the tears streamed down her face. "Chico, stop!" The lazy lay-about did not even acknowledge her, focused completely on attacking the older man. Seeing no other alternative, Maria plunged the knife in her lover's back. He did not so much as flinch, keeping up the attack on Juan.

She withdrew the blade and stabbed him again to no result. Suddenly she got swept up in a blind rage, sinking the blade into him over and over again like the needle on a sewing machine. Still, Chico did not stop.

Juan managed to keep from getting bit but some of the gooey saliva dripped into his eyes and mouth. The taste was sour and rancid. He had to blink to clear some of the goop from his eyes but things were quickly growing blurry.

Somehow, he managed to roll his attacker over and he got back on his feet. Maria still held the knife in her hand, ushering her three girls out of the bathroom and out into the living room. Chico too leapt to his feet, squaring his shoulders and preparing to lunge once again.

Glimpsing the girl's retreat from the corner of his eye and seeing the madness scrawled across the boyfriend's face, instead of having another go, Juan turned and ran instead. He heard the heavy footfalls behind him as they both raced for the door but Juan cleared the threshold and slammed the door behind him. He braced his shoulder against it, fully expecting Chico to come barging into the living room.

But he didn't.

The crazed young man instead beat on the door from the other side, howling in frustration at the top of his lungs, as if he didn't understand how to manipulate something as simple as a door knob. He pounded and kicked at it with frightening violence but the door held. If only just barely.

"Come on, Maria. Grab the girls and let's go!"

"Where are we going, Papa?"

"Anywhere but here," he said, scooping up the three-year-old toddler named Gina. Juan cringed when he saw the wounds on the girls, and it made his heart ache to hear them wail in pain. He so badly wanted to go back in that bedroom and kill Chico for hurting his girls but he saw what Maria did and it didn't even slow the maniac down. He decided to do the logical thing and get as far away from there as possible.

They ran from the apartment into the hallway to have their ears assaulted by the shrieks and cries coming from the other units in the building. What had played out in Maria's home seemed to be occurring to the neighbors as well. *Has the world gone crazy?* He thought to himself as he guided them downstairs and to the parking lot.

He stroked Gina's hair trying to calm her while Maria held the hands of the other two. He opened the doors of his car and they all piled in. The engine came to life and Juan pulled out into the street as fast as he dared, nearly getting t-boned by a mini-van racing down the road.

"Papa, we need to go somewhere safe," Maria managed to blurt out once they were moving. She had a dish rag wrapped around her forearm, soaked bright crimson. Her face contorted in pain but she kept it together, trying to stay calm and attend to the children.

Juan wore a Kansas City Chiefs jersey, splattered in blood. He tried to think but it was difficult to stay focused. The things he'd seen earlier in the day and what he'd just gone through made no sense. He would normally take them back to his house but the streets were a war zone filled with mobs of lunatics and people shooting at each other. All he knew was that he needed to find somewhere safe and he had to find it quick.

It finally came to him when he glanced down at his keys. He still had the keys to his place of employment and it would be the perfect place to go. He'd been working as a custodian at Park Hill South High School for the last ten years and with classes out for the summer, the place would be quiet and empty. There'd also be a nurse's station with bandages for the girl's wounds. That would be the perfect place to hide while everything around them fell apart.

His mind set, he turned toward the school. "It'll be alright girls. Papa will take care of everything."

***

Beltran drove the Humvee while carefully making their way through the packed freeways. Traffic stood motionless while a lane was kept open for official vehicles. They might have been able to drive faster if mobs of pissed-off civilians weren't loitering in the center lane, oblivious and completely in the way. The driver often had to use his horn to get people to move and by their reactions, it was clear they were all in a foul mood.

Even though they weren't able to move very quickly, it didn't matter because 2nd Platoon was fairly close to the Company CP. First Sergeant Landreau directed Beltran to head up to Checkpoint 7 first, because Lieutenant Bethel was over at CheckPoint 6 and he was in no mood to talk to an officer right now.

"Baker Seven, this is Baker Six. Over." The voice coming over the loudspeaker was from Captain Kieler, the Company Commander. He was relatively close, so the transmission came in strong and clear.

"Baker Six, this is Baker Seven. Over." Landreau watched through the windscreen as the rifle squad up ahead tried to clear the people from the road so his Humvee could approach. People weren't being very compliant and he was starting to get agitated. "Lean on the horn, Beltran." The driver did as he was told and a few of them reluctantly moved aside, while some woman in the group flipped them the bird as they rolled past.

"Baker Seven, be advised, I'm getting some disturbing reports from the Battalion S-3 on the command net. There's a fusion cell located at Brigade that is in direct communication with the National Guard units on both sides of the state line, and local law enforcement. We're getting word that things are getting out of hand in several parts of the city. How copy? Over."

Landreau scratched his chin and looked over to his driver.

"Sounds like the natives are getting restless eh, Beltran?"

The driver shrugged his shoulders with both gloved hands still firmly planted on the wheel. "I guess, First Sarn't."

"Baker Six, this is Seven. Do you have any details of the situation? Over." Somebody threw an empty Pepsi can at the Humvee, striking against the passenger-side window. Landreau flinched and a frown appeared on his face. He really wished he were back at the CP right now.

"Roger, we're getting word that riots are breaking out in Gladstone, Independence, Lee's Summit and Overland Park. The Kansas Guard has the situation under control in Overland Park but the other suburbs are having real problems. We should expect to have the checkpoints lock down local traffic on the major thoroughfares for the next several hours. We've been directed to divert traffic to side streets. What's your current location? Over."

"Baker Six, Seven. I am co-located with 2nd Platoon at Checkpoint 7. I will pass along the instructions. Over."

"Understood. Baker Six. Out."

Landreau set the handset on top of the radio set and unbuckled his seatbelt. "Well, things just keep getting better and better. I don't know why these people are so pissed off. They should just go back to their houses, pour themselves a drink and turn on the TV. Fucking civilians are soft."

"Roger, First Sarn't," Beltran drawled, his Alabama accent as pronounced as ever.

Up ahead they saw the Bradley Fighting Vehicle towering over most of the smaller cars, though it was dwarfed by the 18-wheelers that were sitting motionless along with everyone else. Getting closer he could see the soldiers dealing with angry civilians who shouted and shook their fists in the air.

"Okay, stop up there." Landreau gritted his teeth, watching more people begin gathering around his vehicle as they rolled to a stop. He wished he had a gunner up top in the cupola manning a machine gun right about now. Not that he had any desire to shoot anyone but someone up top behind the gun made them look more intimidating.

Two soldiers waved them forward and pointed to a spot next to the Infantry Fighting Vehicle. Beltran nodded in acknowledgement and pulled in next to it before putting the Humvee in "park" and shutting down the engine. Landreau got out of the truck, immediately accosted by a man in a polo shirt.

"Hey, are you in charge here? Can you tell us what's going on? Are we going to be stuck here much longer? This is fucking bullshit, you can't hold us here like this!" The man said, while Burbey and Donahue quickly stepped in between the angry citizen and their First Sergeant, protecting him with their bodies. Sensing that the Humvee carried a person of authority, the crowd gathered around tighter, getting uncomfortably close.

"Get those people back!" Thundered Sergeant Rash, emerging from around the front of the Bradley. He held his weapon across his chest with his firing hand on the pistol grip, finger off the trigger, pointing with his other free one. Landreau couldn't help but notice that there were magazines in all the carbines but knew no one had been issued ammunition. They must have put them in the empty magazine wells as a bluff.

The Squad Leader, Sergeant Chamberlain, emerged from the back of the track, shouting over the noise of the crowd. "First Sergeant, if you would join me over here, I can give you a SITREP."

Landreau felt incredibly uncomfortable and vulnerable at that moment. He'd never experienced anything like it during his time in uniform and it wasn't what he signed up for. He nodded to Chamberlain and brushed past the junior enlisted soldiers who were doing their best to keep the surly civilians at bay.

***

What the fuck am I doing here? I shouldn't have gotten myself talked into this. Mark thought to himself, staring down at an angry housewife sticking a finger in his face. By the way she was dressed he figured she was an upper-middle class type from an upscale suburb. Her makeup and hair were well done, and it appeared that she had spared no expense. This was juxtaposed against the shockingly crude words coming out of her mouth, most of them directed right at him.

"You cocksuckers need to let us through! You can't treat me like this! *My husband is a judge and he will bend you over the hood of my car and fuck you up the ass when he hears about this!*" Spittle flew from the woman's lips while she raged.

She couldn't have been more than thirty years-old, so she must have done well to bag a judge. *Fucking gold-digger,* he thought to himself, doing his best to keep his temper in check. "Ma'am, if you'll please calm down…"

"Calm down? Fuck you, soldier boy! Don't you tell *me* to fucking calm down!"

Private Lauren Gray seemed to materialize out of thin air, fully a head shorter than Mark. She carried the M249 Squad Automatic Weapon and the light machine gun looked awkward in her grasp. "Ma'am, we'll have you moving again soon. If you'll please return to your car."

The furious woman turned to the female soldier, looking like a pit viper ready to strike. "Listen you little bitch, I'm not in the Army and I don't take orders from the likes of you!"

Gray's expression remained neutral but her head canted to the side. "Okay, cunt, let me put it another way. You will close your cock-holster, get back in your car and sit quietly, or else I will butt-stroke you with this machine gun and you'll be spitting out those pretty veneers onto the sidewalk. Do you understand *me*, bitch?"

The other woman's eye's grew wide and her jaw went slack, utterly speechless.

Gray smirked with the look of a feral cat and leaned in

closer, almost nose to nose. "Now, *ma'am*, we would appreciate your cooperation."

Without another word the woman retreated, disappearing into the crowd putting as much distance as possible between herself and the two soldiers. The cluster of people nearest them witnessed the exchange and they calmed down a little, not yet ready to push things too far.

Mark was relieved to have Gray intervene, knowing there was very little he could do to a civilian woman if she got out of hand. If he laid so much as a finger on her the rest of the men in the crowd would have come to her rescue, whether she was being a fucking bitch or not. They would not however get in the middle of a female soldier giving the woman a beat-down, though they might protest some. A few of them would simply look on, completely and totally aroused.

"Well done…"

"Gray, saren't. My name is Private Gray." She looked up at him through a pair of darkened ballistic glasses so he couldn't see her eyes. It was a good practice when doing crowd control since it made it harder for people to read your emotions. If things got sketchy you'd still look as if you were in complete control and cool as a cucumber, even if you were about to piss your pants in fear.

"Nice to meet you. My name is Sergeant Matthews. I'm a prison guard out of Fort Leavenworth." It got easier for Mark to tell the lie now the more times he said it and it was easier to remember all the little details he had sprinkled in there for color. It didn't really matter all that much though, since he was doing his damned best to figure out a way to get back on the road and put some miles between himself and this place.

"A guard at Leavenworth? How'd you end up here with us?"

"It's a long story. I basically ended up in the wrong place at the wrong time." *That part was the truth*, he thought to himself, his attention suddenly drawn to the Humvee pulling up to the Bradley. The civilians started gathering around the light military truck, with a few "Karens" in the group, looking like they wanted to speak to the manager. "Who's that pulling up over there?"

Gray craned her neck so she could get a good look. "Oh, that's the First Sergeant." Her voice took on an acid tone and she spit on the ground.

Mark's curiosity got the best of him. "Should I even ask?"

Gray didn't say anything at first, her gaze fixated on the figure inside the Humvee. "Me and this other female were the first two women to get assigned to the company several months ago right after we graduated infantry training at Fort Benning. The *First Sergeant* had us report to him after hours, in his office, alone."

"He didn't… well… you know." Mark couldn't bring himself to say it out loud.

"Rape us? No. But he did ask us both to have sex with him. I turned him down. The other female didn't. She liked the attention and men in positions of power." Gray shifted the uncomfortable weight of the machine gun, the sling digging into her neck. "Anyway, when she got caught fucking one of the other NCOs the First Sergeant was quick to punish them both and get them kicked out of the company for fraternization. The fucking hypocrite."

"Shit. Sorry to hear that." Mark took off his patrol cap and wiped the sweat from his brow with a sleeve. He put the cap back in place and dug a water bottle out of his cargo pocket, taking a drink. Unlike the infantry squad he was with, he didn't have a helmet and body armor on. So whenever the thought of how hot and uncomfortable it was outside crossed his mind, he'd take one look at them and feel better knowing he wasn't nearly as miserable as they were.

"It's tough being the only female in the company you know. The guys are constantly trying to get in my pants but I ain't like that. Some are more overt, some are sly and try to be friends with me. But their motivation's always the same. I hate it here. I joined the infantry as a woman so people would respect me but I have to put up with this bullshit constantly."

"I don't know what to say."

"You don't need to say nothin', sarn't."

"Why are you telling me this?"

"Because you ain't in my company and I ain't got nobody to talk to. Nobody I trust anyways."

He nodded in understanding but didn't say anything else, watching the First Sergeant get out of the Humvee. People closed in on him, raising their voices and it was hard to see him at first and when he did, he froze and dropped the water to the ground, spilling the remaining contents.

There was no mistaking the broken nose and the scar on the man's chin. It was that bastard Landreau, the one he caught sleeping with his wife and the same one that lied and got him sent to prison.

Now the son of a bitch was standing there a few yards away and if he recognized Mark… well… that could not happen. Mark's heart started racing and he instinctively reached for his pistol but stopped himself short.

No goddammit, not this way. He thought to himself. *I've got to get out of here.*

"You okay, sarn't? You look like you seen a ghost." Gray stared at him through her dark sunglasses.

"Ugh, yeah. I just need to use the latrine."

"Good luck with that, they ain't dropped off the porta-potties yet and there ain't exactly any bushes around here. I know, 'cause I gotta pee real bad and I can't exactly squat by the side of the road."

"I'll be back in a minute." Mark went straight for the nearest guard rail and kicked his legs over the side before heading down the grassy embankment, headed straight for the underpass.

He could almost feel Gray's eyes on his back while beating a hasty retreat.

***

Mark looked at his watch again, pacing back and forth beneath the underpass going over things in his head. Cars passed by, some of them speeding recklessly but he couldn't care less. He was trying to figure a way out of this thing. He felt like a cornered cat.

Immediately above his head was the overpass with the infantry squad and the one man in the world that would immediately identify him and send him right back to prison. *What are the fucking odds?* He thought to himself, kicking an empty soda can, sending it flying.

After jumping the guard rail he was going to make a break for it but he didn't get twenty yards before he felt the car keys jangling in his pocket. Without the pickup truck he wouldn't get very far and he needed the wheels. He entertained the thought of hijacking some poor civilian's car but he wasn't prepared to do that. At least not yet. He might have been a felon on the run but he still felt a bit of humanity. Besides, he wasn't guilty of the thing he'd been convicted of.

He thought about the two people he killed back at Leavenworth and shook himself. *No, that was self-defense. I didn't mean to kill those people. Besides… they were sick or something. Not right in the head.*

Mark knew the only way out of there was to get back in the pickup truck and back onto the road. He stopped pacing, cocked the patrol cap on the back of his head, exposing his forehead and put his hands on his hips while staring down at the ground.

Then, someone from behind him put a hand on his shoulder. It startled him so badly he jumped nearly a foot in the air. He snatched the pistol from its holster and spun around, almost tripping over his own feet.

It was Gray.

"Whoa! Sorry, I didn't mean to scare you!" She held both hands out in front of her defensively, with the muzzle of the Beretta pointed at her nose.

"Jesus Christ, I could have shot you." Mark took a deep

breath and lowered the gun, his shoulders drooping as he did so. "What the hell are you doing down here?"

"Sergeant Chamberlain told me to come get you. You were gone almost half an hour, I thought maybe you run off or something." Gray's posture relaxed as well as Mark put his gun away. "I guess you just needed to take a dump real bad."

"Yeah... that was it," he lied, shifting his weight and adjusting his gun belt.

"Anyways, the El-Tee called on the radio. We gotta break down the checkpoint and head out. We're supposed to link up at the rally point and get a mission brief. He said some National Guard guys are in trouble and they need help and the CO's sendin' us." She too was shifting her weight uncomfortably but it wasn't nervousness.

"What about the First Sergeant? Is he still up there?"

She cocked her head at an angle. "No, he took off right after the El-Tee called. Said he needed to get back to the CP. Why do you ask?"

"No reason, just curious." He took a deep breath and sighed. "You still need to pee?"

"Yeah."

"There's some bushes on the other side of the underpass. I'll stand guard while you go so nobody walks up on you." He pointed over his shoulder with a thumb extended.

"Thanks, sarn't!" She wasted no time and took off like a shot, shrugging off the sling of her machine gun as she did so.

***

Gray followed him back up the slope, her shorter legs having to work twice as hard to keep up. The traffic was moving again now with people leaving in an orderly fashion. By the looks on their faces the anger and frustration was beginning to melt away. The red pickup sat there on the shoulder while the other cars and trucks passed by, one by one.

Now that the checkpoint was breaking down and vehicles were allowed to go, he'd be on his way. With luck, he'd be back at Mom and Dad's house by midday tomorrow. Then he could lie low for a while.

Getting back up top, Chamberlain and the rest of the squad gathered around the Bradley, some secured rolls of concertina wire to the vehicle while the rest stowed other gear. As the junior enlisted worked, Rash gathered them over. A couple of drivers beeped their horns in annoyance while they jay-walked across the highway.

"Gray, you help Burbey and Donahue secure the jerry cans," Chamberlain ordered, pointing to the equipment still sitting on the shoulder next to the tracked vehicle. She acknowledged and got to work, ignoring the rest of them. He then turned his attention to Mark. "Sergeant Matthews, I hate to do this but you need to come with us. We've got a situation developing and we need your help."

"Now wait a minute, Sergeant. I was more than willing to help while traffic was shut down at the checkpoint. But I need to get going. My platoon sergeant is going to fucking murder me as it is." Mark swallowed hard and his hands trembled.

Chamberlain's jaw muscles clenched. "Come with me please." He stepped off the ramp and went around the other side of the Bradley where the others couldn't see. Reluctantly, Mark followed him, dreading what was about to come next.

"Sergeant, before you start, I am not assigned to your unit and I have a job to do…"

Chamberlain held up a hand and cut him off. "Listen to me, this isn't business as usual. Just take a look." He held out his arm and pointed off to the east where thick smoke curled toward the sky. Fires burned all over the city and the pops and cracks of gunfire were everywhere. "Shit is getting real out there and we need your help. Now, whatever mission you were on getting convicts is either over, or has taken a back seat to other priorities. If you want, I can have the El-Tee call your platoon sergeant if that makes you feel better."

"Uh… no… your lieutenant doesn't need to call my platoon sergeant." Mark's mind started racing again, trying to figure a way out of this but couldn't think of anything. He needed to buy some time. "No, I'll call my platoon sergeant and let him know where I am then."

"Good. I figured you'd see it our way." Chamberlain's thumbs were in the arm-holes of his ballistic vest, holding it open as much as possible, trying to get some airflow inside. His shirt was soaked all the way through and his skin had a red tinge to it.

"When do we leave?"

"We roll in five mikes. Gotta link up with the rest of the platoon at the rally point near the high school. El-Tee will give us the CONOP after we get there."

"Okay, I need to grab some stuff out of my truck real quick."

"Hurry up, man. We don't got all day."

Mark nodded and took off, once again threading his way through the slow-moving traffic on the highway overpass. He unlocked the pickup and went inside, grabbing the "bug-out bag" and weapons the real Sergeant Matthews had stashed inside. He opened up the console and stuffed the 1911 into the pack, then pulled out the hard case with the rifle before locking the truck back up again.

If he wasn't able to make it back to the truck, at least he'd have this stuff with him when he got the opportunity to make a break for it. He wasn't planning on hanging around with this platoon any longer than he had to and was singularly focused on getting the hell out of there.

***

Four Bradley Fighting Vehicles parked neatly next to each other in the empty parking lot in the same places they had occupied earlier in the day. The lieutenant chose this place as his rally point since it was familiar to all of them and easy to get to with the roads all jammed up. Unlike earlier in the day, things were getting sporty out there in the city and the reports coming over the radio were getting more outrageous with each passing hour.

"All right, everybody gather 'round," barked their platoon sergeant. Sergeant First Class Savage looked like he'd been chewing on barbed wire all day, right after wrestling grizzly bears. He did not appear to be in any mood to mess around and the soldiers acted accordingly.

Lieutenant Bethel made his way to the center of them all, taking a knee and spreading the map out on the ground for all to see. He took his helmet off and ran fingers through dark blonde hair, soaked in perspiration. "Anybody got a cigarette?"

Harris pulled out a pack of Marlboro Lights and offered it to his Platoon Leader. "I thought officers didn't smoke, El-Tee."

"I had to file a waiver for the exception to policy." Bethel accepted the pack, pulled one out and handed it back to Harris. He produced a lighter from an otherwise empty grenade pouch attached to the front of his body armor. "Thanks." He looked up and couldn't help notice the one soldier standing there with no helmet or body armor, wearing the distinctive "MP" brassard on his left shoulder. "Wait, who are you?"

"That's the MP that's been working with 2nd Squad today. The one I told you about earlier." Savage stood there scanning the other members of the platoon, making sure they were paying attention and not playing grab-ass like they had a tendency to do.

"Oh, yeah. I remember. What's your name?" Bethel lit his cigarette and took a deep drag before putting the lighter away. He paid no attention to his driver and gunner who were busy placing an acetate overlay on top of the map displaying their operational graphics.

"Matthews, sir. I'm Sergeant Matthews. I'm a prison guard out at Fort Leavenworth." All eyes of the platoon were on Mark while he nervously lied to the officer. He felt like they could all see through his masquerade, and it'd only be a matter of time before they had him zip-tied inside a Humvee headed back to the Disciplinary Barracks.

"Sorry about shanghai'ing you but we need every swinging dick right now."

Savage loudly cleared his throat, drawing the lieutenant's attention. He jerked his chin over, pointing it at Private Gray, the lone female in the bunch.

"Yeah, I mean… we need every soldier we can get right now. We've got our hands full. Do you need the CO to call your chain of command to let them know where you are, or are you good?" The lieutenant took another drag before tapping some ash onto the ground.

"No, sir. That's not necessary. They know where I'm at and I'm accounted for." The sweat started to trickle down Mark's back once again and he swallowed the lump in his throat. "I'm here to help out any way I can. Whatever you need."

"Sounds good, welcome to the team. Alright, everyone bring it in." The platoon crowded in even tighter, some straining to see what was on the map. "Okay, Battalion called down and said that there's a Missouri National Guard unit east of here in trouble. It sounds like they were dealing with some looters and things got out of hand. Apparently, they're outgunned and pinned down. We're going in for a show of force and if necessary, get them out." Bethel pointed to the location on the map with an alcohol marker and some of the grunts began whispering to each other. "Any questions?"

Hands went up throughout the group.

"Yes. Weber, what is your question?"

Private First Class Weber looked unsure of himself. He looked over at his Squad Leader to check if it was okay before going on. The NCO gave him a nod first before going on. "Sir, if those Nasty Girls... I mean National Guardsmen are outgunned, then what good are we gonna do? We don't have no ammo to fight with. We'll be outgunned too."

"Great question. We're going to roll in there with four Bradleys and we're going to point our Bushmaster auto-cannons at the bad guys and bluff." He took another puff from the cigarette and rose to his feet. "And if that doesn't work, then we park the tracks between the Guard guys and the looters so the Guardsmen can fall back. Deer rifles and zip guns can't penetrate our armor, so we'll be fine. Once the Weekend Warriors are safe, we drive out of there at our leisure. Pretty simple. Any more questions?"

The soldiers stood there silently, some looking at each other with skeptical expressions on their faces.

"Okay, we roll in five mikes. We're running out of daylight and we need to get them out of there before it gets dark. Order of movement is 22, 21, 24 and then 23 bringing up the rear." He took one last pull from the cigarette then dropped it to the pavement and ground it out with the heel of his boot. "Let's move!"

***

US 69
Gladstone, Missouri
2010 Hours Local

The Four Bradley Fighting Vehicles traveled in a column down the road in a tight formation. Under tactical conditions they'd space themselves out at least a hundred meters but since there was no danger of anti-tank weapons or artillery, they kept their spacing much tighter. They also moved "administratively" with gun barrels pointed over their front decks so they didn't hit any obstructions along the way.

A few cars and trucks raced past going in either direction, all of them moving in violation of the curfew. The smell of burning wood, rubber and plastic stung their noses as they moved deeper into the city and the evening air cooled a little becoming somewhat more comfortable than in the middle of the day.

The Bradley Commanders all stood in their cupolas for better visibility to direct the drivers, who were buttoned up underneath heavy hatches. The constant sound of gunfire all around made them cautious, in case someone felt like taking a pot-shot at them.

Two police cars came screaming down the middle of the street with lights flashing and sirens wailing. Their engines roared as they came at the Infantry Fighting Vehicles barreling down the street at nearly 100 miles per hour. They practically crashed into the armored vehicles, swerving out of the way and missing by mere inches, gunning their engines and racing down the street and quickly out of sight.

"Maverick One-Two, this is White One. Over" Lieutenant Bethel commanded the column from the second vehicle, looking down occasionally at the map board laying on top of the turret in front of him. In violation of Army regulations and probably half a dozen other government safety policies, he smoked a cigarette while in a military vehicle. He had to cock the boom mike on his helmet off to the side while the Marlboro dangled from his lips. "Maverick One-Two, this is White One, your push. How to read me? Over."

"White One, this is Maverick One-Two. I read you loud and clear. How far away are you? Over." The disembodied voice came in staticky but clear enough. Though it was difficult to tell over the noise of the track, and the chatter on the platoon internal net, the person's voice had a tremor in it.

"Roger, we're almost there. You should be around the next corner. What's the situation? Over."

"White One, Maverick. I've got four gun trucks and

twelve personnel. We're pinned down in the parking lot of a strip mall, just outside the liquor store. You can't miss it when you roll up. We were ordered to stop the looting and got in over our heads here. I've got two wounded and we need immediate extraction. Over!"

No sooner did the transmission end when the infantry platoon rounded the corner coming into full view of the strip mall. The parking lots in the area were mostly abandoned, with the occasional car parked here and there. Many of the shop's doors and windows were smashed with the ground covered in shards of glass. The gas station immediately across the street was an inferno with flames climbing over twenty feet into the air, churning oily, black smoke skyward.

Over in the center of the strip mall was their objective, with a large neon sign that read, "Joe's Liquor Emporium." The door and windows were blasted to bits with the outer walls full of bullet holes. Outside, over fifty yards away four Humvees were parked with a dozen National Guard soldiers huddled behind them for cover. The trucks all had crew-served machine guns but none were manned and all stood silent.

"Guidons, this is White One. Advance on line. 22 and 21 break left, while 24 and 23 break right, come up on the flanks of those gun trucks. All BCs button up, we don't need any snipers taking anyone out. Over." Bethel disengaged the safety locks and lowered himself inside the turret, pulling the hatch down as he did so, seating it in place with an audible "thunk."

The Bradleys split up by section, coming up alongside the beleaguered Guardsmen on both sides and slowing to a halt. All four turrets pointed into the liquor store with their menacing but completely unloaded, 25mm auto-cannons. A couple of shots rang out from inside and the bullets smacked harmlessly against the armored hulls.

Chapter 6

Gladstone, Missouri
2012 Hours Local

The inky-blackness of the Bradley's troop compartment wrapped around all of them like a shroud. Between the darkness and whine of the engine, Mark felt like he was in a sensory-deprivation tank. Under any other set of circumstances he might have drifted off to sleep but the images of what happened back at Leavenworth kept assaulting his mind. He fought to push those ideas away only to have them replaced with the realization that he needed to get away from these people as fast as he could.

Then, the movement of the vehicle stopped and the engine began to idle. He sat there in the dark with the other members of the squad, strapped in with no idea what was happening outside until the turret access door slid open, bathing them in a faint blue glow. Sergeant Chamberlain slithered through, still wearing his crewman's helmet and looking like he hadn't slept in a month.

"Everybody listen up. We're here. Just off to our immediate right is the El-Tee's track and beyond that is four gun trucks with the National Guardsmen taking cover behind them. To our front is the strip mall where the looters are holed up. On the lieutenant's signal, we're going to drop ramps and you guys are going to dismount, grab their wounded and put them in the back of 21. Everybody understand?"

Several of them acknowledged and everyone began unbuckling seat belts and getting their kit sorted. Sergeant Rash switched on the light and did a quick visual check on everyone to make sure they were set. Chamberlain scurried back into the turret, slamming the turret shield door shut behind him.

Without warning the ramp yawned open and the compartment flooded with light, forcing the squad in back to squint. Rash sat closest to the opening and burst from his seat, getting out and looking around, trying to orient himself. The others kept their seats and Mark did the same, mimicking the others. He didn't know what their standard procedures were, so he played along, monkey see, monkey do.

Rash peeked around the side of the track to get a look at the store fronts to get a sense of the threat, then leaned in to address the squad. "Okay, we're about thirty or so meters from the liquor store where the shooters are located. I can't see any of them so they must be hunkered down inside. I can see the Guardsmen, so when I say so, you guys follow me." He peered around the corner one last time to check if the coast was clear. "Okay let's go!"

Rash bolted off and the others rushed out the back of the track, hot on his heels. Mark took up the rear, bent over while he ran to keep his head low. Unlike the others, he had live ammo on his person and the Beretta firmly in hand.

They ran past the lieutenant's track toward the National Guard soldiers who waved frantically at them. The six covered the ground in seconds and tumbled down next to the others who clustered around the wheels, using the axles and engine blocks of the unarmored Humvees as cover. The bodies of the vehicles were peppered with holes all over.

"Who's in charge here?" Sergeant Rash crouched down next to the command truck, identifiable by the extra radio antennas.

"I am. My name's Lieutenant Boehm, I'm the Platoon Leader."

Rash jumped with a start when another soldier sprinted over and nearly crashed into him. When he looked to see who the asshole was that almost knocked him over, he found himself practically nose to nose with his lieutenant who sported a shit-eating grin.

"Hi, I'm Tony Bethel, the 2nd Platoon Leader. What's the situation here?" Bethel was bare-headed and didn't have any of his kit on. He'd just wormed his way through the turret access door and ran over. He looked naked without a weapon and body armor.

"Local law enforcement called for help hours ago. Things are falling apart all over the city and nobody knows why. We rolled in here to stop some looters who were robbing all the stores and managed to disperse most of them without any trouble. Right up until we ran into this group who proceeded to shoot the shit out of us." Boehm pointed to the three soldiers laying on the asphalt near the adjacent Humvee. "They got hit early on, and ever since we've been in a Mexican stand-off."

Bethel nodded and scratched his chin. He had a baby face and while many of the other soldiers in his platoon were sporting dark five o'clock shadows, he had nothing more than peach fuzz. He might have been twenty-three years old but he could have passed for an eighth-grader. "You don't have a cigarette I could bum off you? Do you?"

Boehm looked confused, looking at the boyish-looking officer and his NCO. "Uh… no, I don't."

Harris, who was crouched down behind the lieutenant, shook his head. He pulled out a cancer stick and handed it to his Platoon Leader. "Sir, I thought officers were rich. Can't you afford to buy your own smokes?"

"I don't buy cigarettes, I'm trying to quit." Bethel accepted the Marlboro and lit it before stuffing the lighter back into his pocket. "Sergeant Rash, police up their wounded and put them in the back of my track. I don't have any dismounts so there should be plenty of room." He turned to the National Guard officer. "Lieutenant, once we get your wounded loaded up you should get in your trucks and come with us, we'll escort you out."

Mark helped one of the wounded up, while the other members of the squad grabbed the others. They kept low, taking care not to expose themselves to the store front. One of them was hit in the arm and could walk, while the other two required more assistance. They groaned loudly in pain, and one of them was terribly pale from blood loss. While they moved the injured, someone from inside took a shot at them, hitting the ground near Mark's feet.

Boehm shook his head and pointed toward the store front. "No way. You active duty guys back me up. We're going to get some payback for what those fuckers did to my men!"

Bethel took a deep drag from his cigarette and cocked an eyebrow. "Listen, dude. I don't have authorization to do any law enforcement activities. My mission is to get you and your people out of here. If you don't want to go, fine. But we're rolling out of here and getting your wounded evac'd to the aid station."

"Bullshit, you guys are gonna help us, I've got a mission too!" Boehm's face turned red and he clenched his fists. His people were looking at the two officers, some of them with a pleading look in their eyes. Whoever was in that liquor store was cornered and in no mood to go down without a fight.

"Dear god, help us!" A shout pierced the air, suddenly drawing all of their attention. A group of men and women ran toward them across the parking lot coming from around the far side of a restaurant located behind them, completely oblivious to the danger of getting caught in the middle of a firefight. They either didn't notice, or didn't care.

"Wait, you people stay back!" Over a dozen of them came rushing on, ignoring Bethel's commands. He turned to his own people, not paying any attention to the Guardsmen crouched around him. "Sergeant Rash, keep those people out of here!"

"Yes, sir." Rash secured his empty carbine, holding it at the low-ready. "Come on, you heard the El-Tee. Let's go!"

Mark watched the rest of the squad leave the relative safety of the Bradleys and rush off toward the panicked civilians. He hesitated for only a moment, getting to his feet and taking off after them. Without the weight of the body armor and helmet, he caught up with the in no time.

The people sprinted toward the soldiers flat out, the slower ones trailing behind with no one waiting or helping the others. It was as if they were in a race and all of them were competing for the gold.

As they got closer to the people, dozens more came from around the corner of the same restaurant, hot on the heels of the others. These new people however did not call out for help but instead let out a howl that turned Mark's blood cold. They all had blue lips, spider lacing on their exposed skin and the red eyes that were unmistakable at over a hundred yards away.

Mark stopped immediately in his tracks, mouth agape, watching as a deluge of humanity came pouring around the side of the diner. Within a matter of seconds, the dozens turned to hundreds, and more kept coming as if a giant spigot had turned on.

"Rash, stop! We have to get your people out of here!" Mark yelled at the top of his lungs and all heads looked back at him. He pulled the pistol from its holster and held it in both hands at the low-ready. "Come back! Do it now!"

"Matthews, what are you talking about? Come on, man!" Rash and the others kept running forward, trying to meet the civilians and hold them back, trying to keep them out of the line of fire. They looked confused and frustrated at the MP, who stopped and refused to take one step further.

"I said stop, damn you!" Mark raised the M9 with one hand and fired two shots into the air.

The soldiers stopped and looked at him incredulously, while a freight train of human bodies kept surging toward them. They only turned to look in the other direction when they heard the high-pitched screams. The runners with the red eyes were catching the slower people and tackling them to the ground, jumping on them in piles and literally ripping and tearing the flesh from their bones.

Rash and the others stood dumbfounded as men and women were rendered into strips of bloody meat, consumed by ravenous packs of the undead. There were hundreds of them and more kept on coming, a steady stream that seemed to have no end. Their howls and the shrieks of the victims sent chills down their spines.

The squad stood, frozen in horror at the unbelievable sight watching them fall one by one, some trying to fight, others begging and crying for their lives. All of them torn to pieces.

Some of the civilians ran past the stationary soldiers, seeking safety in the Bradleys and Humvees. A couple of the women embraced Johnson and Dubois, sobbing uncontrollably. Every one of them were out of their minds with fear.

Rash stood there quietly as civilians ran past, completely entranced, watching a wave of flesh-eaters coming on straight at him. The carbine hung limply on its sling across his belly, while his hands stood useless at their sides.

"Fuck me," Mark said to himself. He bolted forward once again until he was up with the others, Rash to his left and Gray to his right. He brought the handgun up and started popping off rounds into the approaching mass. They were still fifty yards distant, which was too far away for a pistol but he was less interested in landing a kill shot, and more concerned with snapping them out of their fugue. "*Get moving, all of you!*"

"Dude, what are you *doing*? Have you completely lost your mind?" Rash looked back and forth between Mark and the carnage unfolding a short distance away.

"They aren't what you think they are, now run!" The slide locked back on an empty magazine. Mark thumbed the release catch and dropped the empty, catching it in his hand and stuffing it in a cargo pocket. He snatched a fresh one from his gun belt and slammed it home in the magazine well before hitting the release catch, chambering another round. "*Go!*"

Johnson turned to Dubois with wild eyes. "Let's get the fuck out of here yo!" He turned tail and dashed off to the rear toward the Bradleys with Dubois right behind.

The sprinting monsters at the front of the pack continued to latch on to the people in back as their endurance failed. It was mostly women since they couldn't run as fast as the men, making terrible sounds as they died. The howls intermixed with high-pitched cries, many of them begging for mercy only to be savagely consumed. With each passing second more and more of them emerged from the surrounding buildings, spilling out into streets, sidewalks and parking lots, all of them drawn to the noise and commotion. Mark stood his ground, taking methodical, aimed shots, most of which landed harmlessly in and among the growing mass of mindless, salivating, flesh-eaters. Gray came over and grabbed Rash by the arm. "Sarn't, we gotta get back to the rest of the platoon!" She tugged at his jacket before taking off herself, doing her best to catch Johnson and Dubois who were already half way back to the tracks.

Once Gray took off Mark looked Rash, his eyes hard as diamonds. "It's your funeral, buddy." He took off like Usain Bolt, leaving the Team Leader standing there by himself.

Rash saw the wave coming on, then noticed others in the distance coming at them from every direction. "Fuck this," he said to himself, before heading off to catch the others.

Lieutenant Bethel and the rest looked on while the squad fell back, intermixed with a small group of fleeing civilians, all of them chased by a growing mass of inexplicable horror. He slowly stood up, staring at the chaos, not bothering to crouch under the safety of cover. His mouth hung open and he dropped the still-lit cigarette from his fingers, falling silently to the ground.

"Get in the tracks! Get in the fucking tracks!" Mark shouted as he ran, suddenly at the front of the pack and waving the others on.

Bethel shook himself out of it and looked down at Lieutenant Boehm, still hunkered down behind the engine block of his Humvee. "You should get your people loaded up on your trucks and follow us out of here."

Boehm looked up at Bethel then back at the hundreds of runners headed their way. He said nothing and did nothing, only shifting his weight from one knee to the other while his soldiers looked at him pleadingly.

"Fire 'em up, we're rolling!" Bethel bellowed, scrambling up the side of his Bradley Fighting Vehicle and climbing up on top of the turret before lowering himself into the commander's hatch. He pulled the crewman's helmet down over his ears, ordering his driver Hartman and the rest of the platoon to start up their motors over his boom mike.

The engines coughed to life, blowing puffs of dark exhaust from the manifolds as Mark and the rest of 2nd Squad scampered up the ramp of 23, plopping themselves down into their seats. Some of the soldiers from the other squads helped a few of the civilians get aboard, stuffing themselves inside the armored hulls in and among them while the drivers raised the ramps. The last one "clunked" into place while the National Guardsmen scrambled into their Humvees, pulling the doors shut as the wave of undead slammed into their vehicles.

The horde flowed around them, surrounding the Bradleys and Humvees on all sides with hands outstretched, reaching up at the commanders perched atop their turrets and at the Humvee gunners in their cupolas, standing behind pintle-mounted machine guns. Some mashed their bloody faces against the ballistic glass of the trucks, gnashing their teeth at the horrified passengers looking back at them from inside.

Shots rang out from inside the liquor store and the noise drew scores of runners inside. The rate of fire reached a frenzy, intermixed with desperate screams before being replaced by the sickening sounds of flesh ripped from bone.

Inside the troop compartment of Bravo-23, Mark switched on the light, illuminating the inner armored cocoon in light-blue glow. The soldiers sat with chests heaving, gasping for air, trying to catch their breath.

"Man, what the fuck is happening out there?" Dubois tore off his eye-protection and wiped the sweat from his face. His hands shook and his dark skin was visibly pale even under the poor lighting. Johnson rocked back and forth in his seat grasping his "Thor's Hammer" pendant, while Gray cupped her face in her hands. Rash stared straight ahead into the nothingness, his face devoid of any emotion while Harris looked like he was watching a game of tennis, his head going back and forth, looking at Mark and Sergeant Rash.

Mark heard the engine idling and felt the gentle vibrations through his seat and wondered why they weren't moving. They all could hear wailing, moaning and howling just outside their armored womb. They also heard the distinct sound of blood-soaked hands slapping on the side of the hull.

Mark got up and made his way toward the front of the track, stooped over while trying not to bang his unprotected head against any of the heavy conduit or communication boxes attached to the inner hull. He had to step over the legs of the others who tried to make space for him as he clumsily stumbled forward in the cramped space.

He banged on the turret shield door trying to get the Squad Leader's attention. Nothing happened so he banged some more only to have Rash slap him on the shoulder.

"Chamberlain's a little busy right now." Rash wore a Combat Vehicle Crewman's helmet, jacked into one of the nearby communication control boxes. He was talking to the Squad Leader over the vehicle intercom but no one else in the back could hear the conversation.

"What's going on outside? Why aren't we moving?" Mark struggled to make sense of what was happening outside but between what he had experienced back at Leavenworth, and what they had just seen, he was pretty sure they needed to get the fuck out of there right now.

"Like I said, he's busy. The lieutenant's trying to get things organized up top and when I get a chance I'll ask."

"Let me talk to him," Mark pointed toward the crewman's helmet sitting snugly on Rash's head.

"You ain't in charge of shit around here, Matthews. Now sit the fuck down and be quiet." Rash scowled at the other NCO and his hands curled into fists. The other junior enlisted crammed in back with them watched the exchange in silence, none daring to intervene.

"Fuck this." Mark turned around and took measure of the

situation in the dim-blue light. Right in front of his nose was the release mechanism for the cargo hatch, situated above all their heads. The hatch was placed there so personnel in the back of the Bradley could open up a large opening to feed TOW missiles into the launch unit located on the side of the turret without exposing themselves to small arms fire. The hatch also doubled as a secondary egress in case the ramp or troop doors were blocked or damaged. Mark grabbed it and yanked hard, the spring located on the heavy, armored hatches hinge assisted in popping it open a few inches. He got underneath it and used his whole body to push the thing open the rest of the way until the clam-like door slammed down on the back deck of the fighting vehicle, engaging the combat locks that held it open, flooding the inner compartment with daylight.

"What are you doing? Close that goddamned thing!" roared Rash, who reached up and tried to grab Mark.

Mark kicked him in the center of his chest, the boot landing firmly in the center of the ballistic plate inside his body armor, knocking him back down inside the track. He climbed outside and stood up top on the back deck of the vehicle, immediately behind the bustle rack mounted to the backside of the turret. He was shocked to see hundreds of blood-soaked people surrounding them, clawing at the sides of their vehicles with hundreds more streaming in from every direction.

Off to the right was the Platoon Leader's track and past that were the National Guard gun trucks. The undead rocked the Humvees back and forth, tossing the gunners around to such an extent, they had to grip the guns and cupola rings as tightly as possible for fear of being launched over the side and into a sea of snapping jaws. The moans, howls and screams from the dead drowned out nearly everything else, bringing everything into laser-sharp focus.

"What are you doing up here? Get back inside with the others and button that hatch up!" yelled Sergeant Chamberlain from his commander's hatch located in the turret, only a few feet away. His eyes darted around them, held wide.

As much as they tried, the flesh-eating mass could not climb the backs or sides of the Bradleys because they were far too tall and steep. The front slopes of the vehicles were at an angle however, and a few clawed their way up, some grasping onto the rolls of concertina wire secured there for a handhold. Their dead flesh ripped and tore on the razor wire but they did not notice, singularly focused on the living meat-sacks perched atop the vehicles.

"Look behind you!" Mark pointed to what used to be a teenage boy wearing a torn and bloodied Metallica t-shirt who came lunging at Chamberlain from the other side of the turret. He snatched up his M9, pointed and shot the creature through the forehead, sending the lifeless husk tumbling over the side of the track onto dozens of others down below reaching up at them and howling. A young woman who must have been attractive before half her face got chewed off came up right after the teenage boy and Mark shot her too, the body falling backward and knocking back a few of the others trying to get on the vehicle from the front.

A machine gun chattered off to their right when a National Guardsman cut loose with his M240B. Jacketed slugs flew into the crowd in a steady stream, most hitting the creatures in torsos and limbs to no effect. Only an unlucky few took a round to the head, finally putting an end to their suffering.

The dead climbed up on the hoods of the Humvees with much less effort and two of the gunners got dragged from their perches, literally kicking and screaming. The infected crawled inside the trucks through the open cupolas and even over the din, the muffled cries from the people inside could be heard as teeth sank into flesh and bone.

Another gunner opened up just like the first, sweeping the weapon wildly in panic. The arc of bullets flew wide, stitching up the side of Lieutenant Bethel's Bradley, bouncing and ricocheting in every direction. Bethel, from his position, was on the radio giving instructions to the Platoon when one of the bullets caught him in the neck. He collapsed inside the turret, hosing the interior with arterial spray. Mark crouched down trying to make himself as small as possible as a few of the errant rounds cracked past his ear.

In seconds the Humvees were completely swarmed, covered in writhing bodies, their gunners finally silenced. Mark was back up, taking careful shots and keeping the climbers at bay while Chamberlain looked on with mouth agape.

The slide locked to the rear on an empty magazine and Mark slapped in his last remaining, handing the weapon to the Squad Leader. "Here, take this. Aim for the head. It's the only thing that stops them!" He leaned back down into the open cargo hatch, shouting down at the squad hunkered below. "Hand me up that Pelican case and my assault pack!" He pointed to the gear he took from the pickup truck.

With a confused look, Harris grabbed the case and pack, handing them up. Mark opened it up and removed the civilian AR-15, loading it with a single magazine. He unzipped the assault pack and took out the stainless steel 1911 pistol along with the spare ammunition and stuffed it into his holster. He tossed the remaining six rifle magazines back down to Harris. "Take these and make sure everybody gets one."

Chamberlain carefully popped off shot after shot, keeping the front deck of his track clear, while dozens of the snarling beasts clambered up on the other Bradleys in the platoon with nothing to stop them. Two of the other track commanders ducked down inside, pulling their hatches shut and buttoning them up tight, safe from the threat. The lieutenant couldn't do that, and some of the creatures were already worming their way inside, the muffled screams of the gunner clearly audible over all the other noise.

Mark pulled the charging handle back on the military-style rifle and loaded a round into the chamber, then peered down the holographic sight perched on top of the receiver. It was a red-dot style and something he was familiar with. He looked over to Chamberlain who wore a pained look on his face as he serviced another flesh-eater with his nine-millimeter. "We need to get the fuck out of here right now!"

Chamberlain said nothing, continuing to shoot as another zombie mounted the front deck. It was getting easier for them now, with new ones using the freshly killed as a stepping stool, and there were only a few cartridges left in his magazine. He stayed focused on the threat and completely tuned out the rest of the world, and that included Mark.

"Goddamnit," Mark said to himself through clenched teeth, shaking his head in frustration. He reached up and pulled the combat crewman's helmet from Chamberlain's head with the NCO barely noticing, before placing it on his own. He adjusted the mike in front of his mouth and toggled the transmit key. "Guidons, guidons, this is 2-3. We are rolling out, back to the rally point at the high school. Follow our lead. Over."

"2-3, this is 2-4, negative. The lieutenant hasn't given the order to move, and last time I checked, you're not in charge around here. Over!" The platoon sergeant's voice boomed over the radio.

"2-4, this is 2-3, I saw the lieutenant go down. He's had it. Now, we're pulling out of here and heading back to the high school. You can follow us or stay here if you like. Up to you. But either way, we're going. Over." Mark saw the slide locked to the rear on the pistol once again, Chamberlain patted his pockets looking for a spare magazine that wasn't there. He handed the rifle to the man and took the M9. "Here, trade ya. There's a round in the chamber and she's got a full mag." The Squad Leader nodded and took the weapon, immediately putting it into action. Mark toggled the transmit key in the opposite direction, opening the circuit for the internal crew intercom. "Driver, move out. Head back the way we came."

"Roger that!" came the excited response from Burbey, who slammed the vehicle into gear and mashed the accelerator to the floor while the exhaust manifold belched a big, black cloud of smoke.

The track lurched forward and peeled off to the left, barely avoiding smashing into the store fronts. The undead standing in front of the vehicle were knocked to the ground and many got crushed into the asphalt under the weight of the steel tracks, leaving behind a gruesome trail of gore. The other drivers of the platoon watched through their periscopes and fell in behind 2-3, not paying any attention to tactical spacing and none of them keen to be left behind.

Mark stood on the back deck of the track, the spaghetti cord from the crewman's helmet stretched to its limit, connected to the radio stack inside the turret. He spoke with the Burbey giving him directions, since the drivers could not see very well while buttoned up inside. While safely protected, the periscopes simply did not give adequate visibility for the drivers and they relied upon the Bradley commanders to tell them where to steer and when. As they did so, Chamberlain stood in the hatch bare-headed with the AR-15, keeping watch.

Driving away, hundreds of the dead chased after them from the parking lot, flooding the street with reanimated bodies, some emerging from buildings and storefronts along the way. Mark ordered them to increase their speed until they were nearly at their maximum speed. The creatures pursuing them displayed shocking strength and speed but they were still creatures trapped in human bodies and were accordingly limited in their capabilities. It didn't take the column long to get away, though many of the runners managed to keep up for an alarming amount of time.

Mark held on to the bustle rack to steady himself and squinted in the wind, the smell of burning plastic and rubber stinging his nose and making him cough. The images scrolling through his mind kept flashing and he transcended from panic to numbness. *Maybe I should have stayed at Leavenworth. I'm beginning to think my prison cell might be safer.*

***

Captain Bill Kieler lit the propane burner of a camp stove sitting on the hood of his Humvee. He poured tepid water into a canteen cup before digging into a pocket for a packet of instant coffee. Through the windscreen of the vehicle he saw his driver fast asleep, his helmeted head leaning against the doorframe of the truck. A sense of envy washed over him as he tried without success to remember the last time he'd gotten any sleep. He wasn't going to get any tonight, that much was sure.

He'd been checking on the platoon earlier in the day but stuck around to help out because they were so short-handed. Unlike the rest of his command, 1ˢᵗ Platoon was on loan, cross-attached from Charlie Company. It was also a tank platoon and not infantry, which under combat conditions would give his unit a tremendous boost in firepower but was more of a millstone around his neck given the current mission they had. Infantry platoons boasted over thirty personnel but the tank platoons had half that many—all of them crewing their vehicles. This made them a poor fit for traffic control points but they had to work with what they had.

They set up a tank section here at Checkpoint 2 and dismounted the tankers. All eight of them worked the traffic control point, dressed in their Nomex jumpsuits and wearing body armor and the rest of their kit over top. They looked like fish out of water but they executed their mission without complaint. At least not in front of the captain anyway.

Off to the west the sun sank down near the horizon, giving everything an orange glow. The color was particularly pronounced due to all the smoke in the air from fires burning throughout the city. It would have been beautiful if it weren't for the caustic stink and the racket of gunshots and sirens coming from every direction. The radio too was full of constant chatter and the reports coming over it were getting tougher to believe. Even if only half of the shit being reported was true, there was no denying that things were coming apart at the seams and nobody was keeping a lid on it.

He adjusted the burner until it hissed with an even blue flame. He carefully perched the metal canteen cup up top and waited patiently for it to boil, rubbing his exhausted eyes and yawning loudly.

A couple of sirens grew steadily louder, accompanied by the sound of roaring engines. Down the street two police cars raced toward them with lights angrily flashing. A couple of the men manning the checkpoint stood in the middle of the road with empty rifles strapped across their chests and light-wands in hand, waving desperately at the cops to slow down. If they continued barreling down the street they'd run right into the concertina-wire obstacle and make a hell of a mess.

The police saw the M-1 tanks parked on the road and the soldiers waving at them and slowed down, rolling to a halt. They were Kansas City PD, and two of them dismounted their cruisers, headed straight for the tankers holding the light-sticks. The cops were animated and loud, making it clear they wanted the wire moved so they could be on their way. Their behavior seemed almost manic.

Kieler sighed and set his helmet on an immaculately groomed head before snapping the chinstrap in place. He tried to stretch a little but it did nothing for the pain in his shoulders and lower back, brought on by heavy body armor he'd been wearing for days on end without a break. He calmly walked over and the volume of the voices grew louder in direct correlation with the officer's frustration.

"Can I be of assistance officers?" Kieler's voice croaked from fatigue.

One of the cops glanced down at the rank on the army officer's chest. "Yeah, Captain, you need to open this road up and let us pass, and you need to do it right now. There's no time to explain!"

Two more police officers emerged from the cruisers, one carrying a pump-shotgun and the other with an M-16 rifle. Both of them nervously fingered their weapons, facing down the road they had just come from.

Kieler held a hand up to placate them, doing his best to de-escalate the situation. "Okay, okay. I need to call my headquarters for clearance, then I can let you pass. It'll only take a minute."

"We don't have no fucking minute, Captain! Those things are right on our ass!" The cop didn't bother to wait for a response, immediately going over and grasping the roll of wire with his gloved hands, pulling it out of the way. The two junior enlisted soldiers looked to Kieler with pained expressions on their faces, standing there frozen in place.

"Now hold on a second," Kieler said, feeling as if he were losing control of the situation, and that simply couldn't happen while the soldiers were watching. He moved forward to physically stop the police officer when a series of howls pierced the air. All heads turned down the road where scores of people began emerging from side streets and alleys. They were running flat out, right toward the checkpoint. "What the..."

"Come on, Bevins! Give me a hand with this shit!" shouted the cop to his buddy, both of them wrestling with the razor wire, pulling it off to the side and leaving an opening more than large enough for both of their cars to pass through. The patrolman with the M-16 popped off several shots from the standing position, aiming into the growing mass of runners.

"What in god's name are you doing? Are you crazy?" Kieler yelled. He couldn't believe that law enforcement officers were cutting loose with live ammo like that. They might kill somebody that way.

The cops ran back to their cars, all of them jumping back in. The lead vehicle squealed rubber on pavement and nearly ran over one of the soldiers as it raced away. The second one stopped for a second with the window rolled down. "Captain, you need to get your people out of here as fast as you can. Get in your vehicles and go if you know what's good for you!" He then punched the accelerator and took off, barreling down the road, with light-bars flashing.

Kieler watched the cruiser race off, quickly disappearing out of sight. *What in the world is going on? Has the world gone completely crazy?* He tried to work out in his mind what he had just witnessed but none of it made sense. All he knew was that he had to keep this checkpoint locked down, and get a report up to Battalion.

"Uh, Captain? I think you need to take a look at this." The platoon sergeant, a lanky guy named Schwartz, placed a gloved hand on the Company Commander's shoulder, trying to get his attention. He pointed down toward the wretched mass of undead swarming down the thoroughfare, coming straight toward them at a full sprint. They boiled out of the shops and side streets, spilling out into the road with the nearest ones four hundred yards away and closing in fast. The way some were running, they'd have little more than a minute before the fastest ones would be on top of them.

"Sergeant, get your boys in the tanks. Then park them bumper to bumper in the middle of the MSR and block it. Orient your gun tubes in their direction, that oughta discourage them. Got it?"

"Roger that." Schwartz nodded and gathered up his men. They clambered up onto the big, armored beasts and got inside, firing up their turbines in a matter of seconds. They pulled into the center of the road and pointed their main guns toward the mass of runners headed their way, which did exactly nothing to slow down their advance.

Kieler climbed up top to get a better look, astonished to see how fast they came on. Hundreds of them howled and shrieked as they ran and as they drew closer, the terrible faces and the wounds that covered their bodies became evident. "Dear god," he said to himself, shocked at the sight.

He stood transfixed, reaching for the hand mike when the mass of flesh-eaters washed over them like thousands of army ants.

Chapter 7

Missouri River Bridge
2015 Hours Local

Lieutenant Scotty Truitt sat in the passenger seat of his Humvee sweating and growing more pissed off with each passing minute. There were civilian vehicles everywhere, weaving past trying to get wherever the hell they were going. That made it nearly impossible for them to make any progress and they were moving at a snail's pace. It was well past curfew and the fucking civvies shouldn't have been out there in the first place, and all the checkpoints were supposed to be keeping the roads clear.

He was leading the company's logistical package, or "log-pac," forward to the platoons. He had fuel trucks full of JP-8 to top off the tracks and tanks, along with heavy trucks loaded with spare parts, barrier materials and most importantly, hot chow. Their convoy tried to snake through the mess but the civilians kept pulling in the way, darting to and fro in their cars, forcing them to halt every few feet or so. It was maddening to say the least. Now they found themselves in the middle of a bridge spanning the Missouri River, hopelessly stuck and it was starting to get dark.

The speaker-box mounted next to the radios was alive with chatter, both at the company-level and battalion. Reports rolled in describing murder and mayhem all over the place, with law enforcement and even the National Guard asking for backup. The ever-increasingly desperate calls started to make him feel uneasy, which only added to his frustration.

"*Battle Axe Six, this is Vanguard Three. Over.*" The disembodied voice was that of the Battalion Operations Officer, also known as the "S-3." He directed the various units within the battalion while the commander was on the move, which he often was. The "3" was usually a man of light-hearted humor and a quick wit but over the last several hours, his tone had grown noticeably sharper. *"Battle Axe Six, I say again, this is Vanguard Three. How copy? Over."* *Captain Kieler must still be out on foot helping with the Traffic Control Point and that idiot driver of his is probably sleeping again, not monitoring the radios,* Truitt thought to himself, frowning. "Vanguard Three, this is Battle Axe Five. My Six element is dismounted. I will relay. Over."

"Roger, Five. We cannot raise the Battalion Reserve. Nobody is monitoring the net and you need to get that fixed ASAP. Need you to posture them at RedCon 1, time now. Acknowledge."

The Battalion Reserve was their 3rd Platoon co-located with the Company CP and the First Sergeant. *And another thing. Why the fuck isn't the First Sergeant out here leading this log-pac? It's his damned job after all. He's the most useless NCO I've ever met. For the life of me, I'll never figure out how the bastard got his stripes.* "Vanguard Three, this is Battle Axe Five. Wilco. I'll make it happen. Over." Truitt grabbed the other transmitter, the one dedicated to the company internal radio net. "Battle Axe Seven, this is Battle Axe Five. Over."

"Battle Axe Five, this is Battle Axe CP. Battle Axe Seven is unavailable right now."

"Battle Axe CP, this is Five. Somebody go find the First Sergeant and get him on the radio right now, before I reach through this handmike, wrap the cord around your neck, and give it a yank. *Over!*" Truitt took a deep breath to calm himself, knowing full-well that losing his temper was counter-productive but found it increasingly difficult to keep his emotions in check. It wasn't helping that things were at a dead stop right in the middle of the bridge and they were stuck there like a cork in a bottle.

"Guo, I'm going to go take a look and see what the hell is holding us up," Truitt said to his driver, unbuckling his seatbelt while opening the door.

"Roger, sir."

Truitt carefully opened the door so he didn't hit the car

idling right next to his vehicle. The female driver inside looked up at him with a pleading look on her face. In the backseat her two kids sat in car seats, asleep and blissfully carefree. He nodded to her and forced a smile.

He pulled his M-4 carbine from the Humvee and readied himself to trudge up to the front of the column when someone came running along the shoulder, near the edge of the bridge off to his right. Then, another came from the other side, sprinting as fast as their feet could carry him while running between the vehicles, careful to dodge the rearview mirrors as he went.

Moving up the line, more and more people dashed past, none of them stopping or saying a word. Curious, the people sitting quietly in their air-conditioned cars started emerging to get a better look up ahead to see what the commotion was all about. The number of people rushing to the rear quickly increased at an exponential rate, with many people yelling and cursing as they shoved their way through the opened car doors and stationary gawkers.

Then, in an instant, the mood among the people changed and something spooked the herd. Seemingly at once those that stood trying to get a better look took flight, creating a stampede to the rear. The rush of people pushing and shoving their way past nearly knocked Truitt over while the volume of screams began to steadily crescendo.

People no longer ran serpentine between the open car doors any longer with many simply running over tops of the stranded cars. Panicked feet smashed windshields while denting hoods and trunks with all semblance of order dissolving in a matter of seconds. Children and the elderly fell to the ground, trampled to death in seconds while others leapt from the bridge into the swirling brown waters of the Missouri. Truitt watched a father fling his small children off the side then fight off three maniacs while his wife jumped in after her children. The deranged trio bit the man while he flailed and struggled on the hot pavement, blood gushing from multiple wounds.

Small packs of attackers chased down the slower and weaker, taking them down and doing unspeakable things to them. Truitt stood there in shock as scores of hunters dispatched their prey while they begged and pleaded for their lives.

Soldiers from the resupply column poured from the cabs of their trucks, tossing aside weapons and body armor to lighten their load so they could run away faster. In many cases they elbowed and shouldered the civilians out of their way, faces etched with panic.

"Get back in your vehicles, all of you!" Truitt shouted at his people in an attempt to rally them, though he could scarcely be heard over the growing chaos all around. In a matter of seconds, the cries of individuals grew until it sounded like thousands of people cheering at a sports stadium. He tried to push his way upstream to at least get control of the soldiers when he was knocked flat on his back.

Dozens of feet kicked or stepped on top of him. He brought his arms up to protect his face and curled into the fetal position, unable to get back to his feet. He tightened his body up as tightly as he could, letting out a yelp when a particularly heavy person stepped on one of his ankles. The punishment continued on for what seemed like an eternity but in reality was over in less than a minute, and then it was suddenly over.

He cautiously peeked out from his arms, both wrapped around his face, to see that the mad rush was over. There was noise still all around but at least he was no longer being stomped into the pavement. He struggled to get back to his feet while balancing himself against a silver Hyundai whose passengers had abandoned it with the engine still running.

The madness swept through them all and continued on, leaving him and other survivors in its wake. He looked on in disgust to see that most of the military vehicles he brought with him were also empty, their occupants high-tailing it out of there with the others. High-value and sensitive military equipment lay strewn about, tossed away like garbage in direct contravention to all of their training. That more than anything upset him, as soldiers should have been far more disciplined than that.

"I've got to call this in," he said to himself, bracing himself against the car before taking his first step. He let out a yelp when he put pressure on his injured ankle, limping badly. His Humvee was only a short distance away and he needed to get to the radio located inside.

He gimped along as best he could, mostly hopping on his good leg until reaching the front of his Humvee, grabbing onto the front-mounted brush guard to hold himself upright. Both the passenger and driver's side doors hung open, with no one inside. *Motherfucker. First thing I do when I get back is fire my driver and get a new one*, he thought to himself, gritting his teeth.

He hopped toward the passenger-side door, focused on the radio transmitter hanging from a piece of parachute cord only a few feet away. If he could get a report off, he might be able to get some assistance.

Moving forward with great difficulty he heard a scraping and shuffling off to his left. Turning to see what the noise was, he found himself staring almost nose-to-nose with something that once resembled a human being. His skin turned to gooseflesh as the thing shifted its head ever-so slightly, studying him before hissing the word, "Ssssoool-jjjerrr."

Before Scotty Truitt could react, the thing was on him. He struggled impotently when it knocked him back to the ground, snapping its teeth at his face. It took every bit of strength he possessed to keep it from biting him, calling out for help. He realized it was no use when he saw other red-eyed monsters coming in from every direction, drawn by his cries.

And then in a matter of seconds, things went black.

***

"First Sarn't, the XO says he needs to speak with you on the radio." Specialist Beltran stood hunched over his senior NCO, trying to wake him without actually touching the man. He'd shaken him awake once before and almost got punched in the mouth for his trouble. The First Sergeant had a reputation for being a bit cranky when roused from sleep.

"What is it?" Landreau croaked, barely even stirring.

"There was a message from Battalion that he wanted to pass on. Said he wanted to talk to you right away." Beltran stooped over while inside the close confines of the M-113 armored personnel carrier. First Sergeant Landreau had sealed it up tight and was lying on one of the bench seats, using it as a bunk. He used his gas mask for a pillow, covering himself in a lightly-insulated poncho liner for comfort. He'd turned off the radios in the track to get a little peace and quiet, and had been fast asleep for quite some time now.

"I told you not to wake me up unless it was an emergency." Landreau's head was covered by the field blanket and he did not move. He hoped it wasn't important and that Beltran would go away. The junior enlisted soldier often disturbed him when it wasn't necessary tending to err on the side of caution, always seemingly at the most inopportune moments. Like when he was trying to get some shut-eye.

"The XO sounded like it was, First Sarn't. He sounded upset."

Landreau growled, then ripped off the poncho liner, tossing it aside. He threw his legs over the side of the bench seat and sat up, blinking away the sleep. He exited the APC through the troop door, emerging from its armored cocoon. The first thing that hit him was the smell of burning plastic and rubber hanging in the air, suddenly aware of the sound of small-arms fire all around them in the distance. These were no longer the single shots from civilian-owned arms, these were the staccato sounds of automatic weapons. The kind that the military possessed. It became suddenly obvious that things were very, very wrong.

Just to their north stood one of the many bridges spanning the Missouri River. Military personnel were posted there on both ends and traffic was still moving, though it was official vehicles only. It was well-past curfew so there weren't any civilians moving about. At least not here anyway.

On the other side of the park, 3rd Platoon milled about between their vehicles, waiting for instructions. They talked quietly with each other, clearly spooked by events beyond their understanding.

He stomped over and tore open the tent flap to the CP and ducked inside. There he found the company clerk, Sergeant Medina, talking to someone on the radio. "What's going on? What does the XO want?"

Medina set the handmike down and stood up, pointing over at the map. "First Sarn't, you're not going to believe this shit. Half the city has gone up in some sort of insurrection. There's fighting all over the place. Battalion says that the Missouri and Kansas Guard are in running gunfights all over the city. It's fucking bad."

"What do you mean?" Medina had a tendency to be overly dramatic sometimes, so getting the details was important.

"Police and military checkpoints are being overrun. Looters are setting fires all over the place and there are reports of unarmed mobs attacking in just about every sector. The Kansas boys seem to be keeping things under control but the Missouri side of the river is a fucking shitshow." Medina pointed to different symbols drawn on their tactical maps to help describe what was going on. The picture he began to paint, along with sights, smells and sounds of things going down all around them took hold. "In addition to that, First Sarn't, Battalion ordered the XO to bring 3rd Platoon to 'Redcon 1' and have them stand by. It looks like they might order them into the city to reinforce a couple of strongpoints."

"What's Captain Kieler's status? Why isn't he up on the net?"

"We can't raise him. In fact, nobody at Checkpoint 2 is answering the radio. It's like nobody over there is monitoring the net." Medina indicated the bridge off to their south on the map. "The XO is leading the logpac and last reported being stuck in traffic here. He wanted to talk with you but we can't seem to raise him anymore either."

Landreau studied the map and considered what he'd just been told. Military and police units everywhere were under attack. Checkpoints were being overrun and shit quickly spiraling out of control. It also didn't escape his attention that their CP was on the wrong side of the river since those Missouri boys were failing to keep law and order. It was crystal clear what he needed to do. "Medina, call 3rd Platoon and have them switch over to our unofficial 'emergency frequency.' Then, break down the CP and get everyone on the road. We're heading back to the Kansas-side of the river, where we'll re-establish the Command Post. Got it?"

"But what about the other platoons and the CO? Shouldn't we tell them first?"

"No time for that right now. We need to fall back and re-establish ourselves in a more secure area. We cannot support the company if we get compromised. Now stop arguing with me and *move!*"

***

Park Hill South High School
2056 Hours Local

The platoon pulled into the same parking they occupied earlier in the day before things fell completely to shit. They managed to shake hundreds of runners that chased them down the streets by pushing their engines as fast as they dared. Running a tracked armored vehicle at its top speeds is nothing like driving a car or a truck fast, if you took a corner the wrong way you could throw or snap the steel track which would send the vehicle flying ass-over-teakettle, likely killing or severely injuring everyone inside.

Even though the platoon shook most of its pursuers, more came out of the woodwork as they drove down the cluttered city streets. People with shredded clothing, horrific wounds and blood-red eyes launched from doorways and windows, chasing the sound of their vehicles.

Arriving at the high school they slowed to a halt and several dozen runners caught up with them, quickly surrounding the tracks. There weren't nearly as many as before at the strip mall, so the number was somewhat manageable.

Chamberlain began taking aimed shots with his rifle, blowing the heads off a few when Mark put a hand on his shoulder. "Hold up. We don't have a lot of ammo to spare."

Chamberlain nodded and safed his weapon, looking at the MP, waiting for instructions.

The Bradleys halted in a column with no tactical spacing between them. Mark got the platoon sergeant's attention before keying the transmit button. "Two-Four Actual, this is Matthews. Over."

Sergeant First Class Savage grimaced back at him from the turret of his track before responding. "*Send it, Matthews.*"

"Roger, there's only a couple dozen of these crazed-fuckers here. Recommend we neutralize them without wasting any precious ammunition." Mark stood on the back deck of the IFV, while the heads of the squad members in the back poked out of the cargo hatch like a family of meercats, trying to get a better look at their surroundings.

Savage looked down at the raving monsters clawing at them all from down below and frowned. "*Do it. Grease your tracks.*"

"Roger. Moving." Mark gave him the thumbs-up before toggling the internal intercom. "Driver, get ready to move.

When I give the word I want you to start driving deliberate circuits around the rest of the platoon, and crush these fucking monsters flat under your tracks. Understood?"

"You got it. That's why we call 'em 'crunchies,' right?" Burbey sounded all-too excited from down in his driver's hatch.

"Okay then, driver move out."

Mark gave precise directions to Burbey while they ran laps around the rest of the stationary Bradleys. At times they came in so close they scraped the side-armor panels, squishing the undead between the heavy plates, and mashing them into the pavement under their steel tracks. They all tried to ignore the sound of bones cracking and skulls popping under the weight of their IFVs. Most of them had to look away, not comfortable witnessing the grisly scene as they crushed them one by one. They kept it up for only five minutes or so before crushing the last of them.

All of the Bradley commanders and gunners stood in their open hatches wearing grim expressions on their faces. All of them except for Lieutenant Bethel's track.

"Two-One, this is Matthews. Can you read me? Over." Mark knew that at the very least the driver was still alive, or else the track wouldn't have followed the rest of them here.

"*Matthews, this is Two-One Delta.* I'm okay but I don't know what happened to the El-Tee or our gunner Fernandez." His voice shook and sounded husky, like he'd been crying.

"Roger that, Two-One Delta. You just put your track in 'park.' But stay buttoned up until I say otherwise. Matthews, out." Mark handed the CVC back to Sergeant Chamberlain and pulled out the stainless steel 1911. He pulled back the slide and let it slam forward, chambering a fat .45 auto hollow-point. "I'll be back in a minute."

He gingerly circled around the turret, then leapt from the front slope of the track onto the ground. He nearly slipped in a slick matte of gore. Once he regained his footing, he climbed up onto Lieutenant Bethel's vehicle, keeping the handgun trained on the open hatch. The sun dipped beneath the horizon and it got difficult to see so he pulled the flashlight from his duty belt, turning it on. He carefully pointed the light and the weapon into the hatch while peering inside.

Down below, three undead creatures squirmed on top of Bethel's dead body, pawing and biting at the turret access shield, smearing it with blood and saliva. It was as if they could smell the living people in the back of the vehicle through the perforations in the metal, and were attempting to get at them but their simple minds could not figure out how to work the latch to disengage the sliding door. Which was the only thing that was keeping the passengers in back from being rendered into zombie chow.

When the flashlight shined down on them, they looked up at once at Mark with those terrible eyes. The sensation of an electric shock passed through him and he opened fire. The first round caught one harmlessly in the shoulder. It clambered up at him, closing the distance in a heartbeat. The second round caught it in the face and sent it tumbling back down on the other two. Momentarily immobilized, he popped off another two rounds and finished them before yelling, "Clear!" He looked down to see his hands trembling.

Mark stood there on the Platoon Leader's track unable to move and didn't notice that after a few minutes, cautiously, deliberately, hatches creaked open and ramps began to drop. Soldiers warily emerged, looking in every direction for danger while NCOs organized them and got them busy establishing a security perimeter.

Intermixed were a few civilians who managed to get on board before they took off, now found themselves milling about nervously, unsure of what to do. Two of them were armed but were careful not to accidentally point their weapons at the soldiers.

Sergeant Savage pulled the CVC from his head and dismounted his vehicle, slinging an empty carbine across his back. "Squad Leaders on me!"

Mark snapped out of his daze, realizing that while the senior leaders of the platoon met, the junior NCOs had work to do. He instinctively climbed down off the vehicle and met up with Rash, helping to get the others organized.

***

Landreau's agitation continued to rise and he found himself barking orders at everyone to move faster. It had taken far too long to break down the CP so he made them abandon most of the equipment. Tents, generators and even their precious air conditioner got left behind when they mounted their vehicles and left the site, headed for the nearest bridge and the relative safety of Kansas.

His M-113 armored personnel carrier drove in the middle of their scratch convoy with a section of 3rd Platoon in the lead and the remaining section pulling up the rear. He didn't want to ride in his Humvee, preferring to ride in the APC. It just felt safer.

"Medina, why have we stopped? Are we across the bridge yet?" Landreau sat on the bench seat in the dark all by himself, with only the faint blue light to illuminate the space. He could have opened up the cargo hatch to look outside but there were reports of snipers with deer rifles all over the place and he didn't want to take the chance of sticking his head up where it could get shot off.

"No, First Sarn't, we ain't across the bridge yet. The Guard guys have us halted and Sergeant Siegel's on the ground talking to one of them manning the checkpoint."

"Fuck," he said to himself, completely exasperated. He yanked the handle on the troop door and opened it up with a loud creaking groan. It was dark outside now and some of the street lights were flickering on. The small column was halted in a neat row, facing a couple of Humvees behind a hastily assembled barricade. Out front was 3rd Platoon's lead section led by its platoon sergeant, who stood next to his track talking to a couple of guys from the Kansas Army Guard.

Landreau dismounted and headed off for the cluster of men, very much aware of the flurry of activity going on all around them. He couldn't help but notice that these Guardsmen were combat engineers, working at a frantic pace. Some of them handed down boxes and crates from the backs of 5-ton trucks, while others cut lengths of time fuse, crimping it into blasting caps. Others taped together blocks of C-4 plastic explosive and some were even removing World War II-vintage TNT, preparing that as well. It appeared that they had emptied out a local Ammunition Holding Area and grabbed the first items they saw. And it looked like they brought out enough explosives to turn the entire Midwest into a giant, smoking crater.

When he got closer he heard Sergeant First Class Siegel, and the man was even more animated than usual. "Listen, we need to get through to the other side and I don't have a written authorization. My First Sergeant is obeying orders from Battalion."

Landreau adjusted the pouches on his plate carrier so his rank was clearly visible before approaching. "What seems to be the problem here?"

A Staff Sergeant from the Kansas Guard with a big gut and a bushy mustache tore his attention from Siegel and eyed-up Landreau with a look of contempt. "Listen, bud, we've got orders to allow no traffic to pass unless they have a written authorization from the governor."

"Sergeant, we're federal troops and don't work for any governor, so you need to let us pass."

"No-can-do. The boys over in Missouri have lost control of the situation over there, and the governor of Kansas gave us orders to seal off the border. There's some sort of outbreak going on and we ain't lettin' it cross the state line. We're going to drop this bridge in the river in a few minutes." Engineers set stacks of charges at strategic points all along the structure. Friction igniters were getting attached to lengths of time fuse, while others wrapped clusters of charges with det-cord.

"Well, then there's no time to lose. You need to let us cross right now. My Battalion Commander says I need to get this platoon across so we can attach them to one of your Guard infantry units and reinforce it." It was a total lie but Landreau needed to come up with something that these Kansas boys might find to be in their own self-interest.

The Staff Sergeant with the bushy mustache looked over his shoulder and did a quick estimate. "Alright, Top. I reckon you got ten minutes before we light this thing off. If you ain't on the west side by then, you're going to get blown to smithereens. It's your funeral."

"Don't worry, we'll be clear and we won't get in your way." He could feel the other man's mood soften.

"All right then, you can go."

Landreau turned and shouted to his men while running back to his track. "Move 'em out, get over this bridge and make it quick!"

In less than a minute, Landreau had his people on the move, toward the safety on the west side of the river.

***

Dave Savage spent his entire adult life in uniform just like his dad, and his grandfather before that. Grandpa fought the Germans in Italy and southern France during Operation Dragoon. Dad served with the 173rd in 'Nam and re-upped for a second tour before going back to Bragg. Neither one of them talked about the wars they fought in until after Dave himself had seen action in the early days of Iraq. Of all of the things he'd seen and heard from all their time in uniform, none of it compared to what Dave had witnessed within the last hour. It was truly shocking and he struggled to reconcile it. In the meantime, his training kicked in and he operated in auto-pilot, doing the things he was hard-wired to do through muscle-memory.

"What's the status of those wounded Missouri Guard soldiers?" Savage cradled his helmet in the crook of his arm while wiping his brow. The Team Leaders scurried about getting the fire teams organized, while gunners guided the Bradleys into a tight perimeter known as a "coil" formation, with turrets facing outward.

Specialist Aggie "Bags" Bagdasarian administered aid to the three wounded while eavesdropping on the conversation. She, like all the others, liked to listen in when the senior NCOs spoke. It was the best way to figure out what was going on. She stood up and joined the tight knot to interject. "All three are stable, sarn't but in serious condition. We need to get them medevac'd out of here quick. One's gut-shot, right below the ballistic plate. Another took one to the leg and the third is shot in the arm."

"Thanks, Bags. Try to keep them comfortable until we get some help."

"Roger that, sarn't." She excused herself from the group and went back, tending to the injured.

"Okay, give me a LACE report."

Chamberlain looked up from his boots and even in the failing light, the dark circles under his eyes were evident. "We've got a couple of jerry cans of water, so we're okay for now. Our guest showed up with a rifle and seven mags which he distributed to my squad. Everyone except for the driver and gunner have one rifle magazine. It ain't much but it's something. No casualties and we're 100% on the rest of our equipment."

"What about you two?" Savage directed his question at the other two Squad Leaders, Frakes and Bates.

"We're the same except 'Black' on ammo," Frakes said.

"Same with us," said Bates.

"How's the fuel situation for the Brads?" Savage pointed a thumb at the big armored beasts sitting there with engines idling.

Frakes was first to answer. "Not great, we're down to a quarter tank. If we don't get refueled soon, we're going to be walking home. And I sure as shit don't want to be walking anywhere right now. Especially not in the dark." Everyone looked down at the mashed body parts and viscera smeared all over the parking lot around them.

"Everyone got their nods?" Savage realized that his night vision goggles were stashed in his rucksack and he was going to need to dig them out. He was certain he had fresh batteries for them, since he had insisted on detailed pre-combat checks and inspections before they left Riley.

"Affirmative. The Team Leaders are getting them mounted as we speak," said Bates in his deep West Virginia drawl. He was tall and lanky, the product of Scots-Irish coal-miner stock.

"Good, because we're going to need them. Alright, those wounded Guardsmen have ammo on them. Distribute that to your squads. That should get the rest of the platoon up to one mag per man. I will call to get the status on our log-pac. We should have a hot-refuel inbound soon." Savage looked at each of them to ensure they understood his instructions.

Frakes looked around nervously before clearing his throat. "Guys, can anybody explain what is going on? This is something straight out of a horror movie."

The NCOs looked at each other, no one wanting to be the first to say anything for fear of sounding crazy. Savage didn't want to say anything either but he was in charge now and had to say something. "Word from Battalion was there was a terrorist group about to release a bio weapon. That must be what this is." The mood was cool and he didn't feel like he'd convinced them. Probably because he hadn't completely convinced himself. "Look, it doesn't matter. Right now our responsibility is force protection. Keep your people alive. Defend any uninfected civilians if you can but take care of your people. Once we make link-up with the rest of the company, we'll get clear orders and take things from there.

"Frakes and Bates, collect magazines from the wounded and distribute them to your people. Chamberlain, hold up for a sec." When the other two left Savage gazed over at Matthews who was getting his adopted fire team organized and assigning them sectors of fire. He lowered his voice before going on. "So, what's the deal with the new guy?"

"Matthews, you mean?"

"Yeah."

"He seems to know his shit. He's impressing the hell out of me. Frankly, I never would have dreamed an MP would be this squared away. I hate to admit it but he saved my ass back there." Chamberlain wore a sheepish look and shifted his weight.

Savage nodded in agreement. "I think he might have saved all of our asses back there."

"What do we do now? I don't feel like spending the night out here."

"Get yourselves organized and I'll call the CO. He ain't going to fucking believe any of this but we need to tell him." Savage wasn't looking forward to explaining how Lieutenant Bethel got killed. He kind of liked the kid and the young lieutenant was learning fast. If he'd have made it, he'd have probably made a really good officer. Lord knows, Savage had seen a whole lot worse in his time. This whole situation was completely insane.

***

Jefferson dodged a cluster of the freaks, hunched over a victim sprawled out in the middle of the street. They fed on the poor bastard, tearing chunks of flesh from his body. The sheriff's department cruiser weaved quickly around them, barely missing a car abandoned on the road, its doors hanging wide open. The noise of the engine and the squealing of tires drew the attention of the undead and they took off in a sprint after the deputies. They did not see or care about the second vehicle, boldly stenciled with "K-9" on the side following close behind. It rammed them with a steel brush guard and one of them fell down, crushed under the tires, while another rolled up onto the hood and over the windscreen, cartwheeling in mid-air, then slamming into the ground with a loud "smack."

White turned and watched her slam into the two creatures, not slowing down at all. He picked up the transmitter from its cradle and keyed the mike. "You okay back there, Angie?"

"*Yeah. But that last one cracked my windshield all to hell. It's getting difficult to see.*" They switched off their sirens and lights earlier in the evening after realizing that it was drawing more of the things toward them. It was like ringing the fucking dinner bell and once they realized what was going on they turned the things off. Once the sun went down, they used their headlights for a little while until they realized that that too was attracting the things. So now they drove down the streets as fast as they dared, completely blacked out. It may have drawn fewer of the creatures in but it made navigating through the city quite a bit more challenging. "*We need to find a safe place to hole up. You got any ideas?*"

White turned to look at Jefferson who stared straight ahead, hands firmly affixed to the wheel at the two and ten o'clock positions. He hadn't said a word in a while. "Not sure right yet. So far, every place we've tried has had those things hanging around." They turned a corner and saw a large building up ahead that looked like a school. The parking lot was largely empty except for several Army vehicles and some dark shadows moving around. "Wait, hold on. I think I see something." He pointed ahead, turning his attention back to his buddy. "Darin, you think those are soldiers up there, or more of those things?"

"Don't know, man. But it's worth checking out. If those soldiers are infected maybe we can get inside that empty school and spend the night. Then we can figure out our next move."

He nodded and keyed the transmitter once again. "Angie, there's some soldiers next to a school just up ahead. We're going to check it out."

"*Copy. I'm right on your tail.*"

***

Mark saw the two cars approaching and whispered to the others around him. "You stay here and hold your fire. Remember, if I give the order to shoot, go for the head. None of this center-mass stuff." The others nodded in understanding, peering down the length of their weapons at the two cars.

He stood up and clicked his flashlight three times as a signal to the oncoming cars. It was difficult to see and the electrical grid was down in this part of the city, so none of the street lights were on. As they grew nearer he saw that they were police cars, which made him uneasy. He knew that they would have no idea he was a fugitive but he still couldn't shake the feeling that they were coming for him.

Upon seeing the light, the two cars turned and headed straight at them and Mark motioned to them to slow down. To his relief, they complied, coming to a controlled halt a few feet in front of him.

Two officers got out of the lead vehicle, while a single cop dismounted from the second, going around to the rear of her car. When she emerged, the woman had a German shepherd on a short leash.

"Hold up there," Mark said. He had his AR-15 rifle across his chest with the barrel pointed at the ground but it was obvious that he was ready to bring it into action in a split-second if need be. "Who are you? Identify yourselves."

"Jackson County Sheriff's Department. I'm Deputy Darin Jefferson, this large fellow is my partner Deputy Martin White. And over there is Deputy Angie Carnegie. The hairy one is Saxon. Who are you guys? National Guard?"

Sergeant Chamberlain approached, having heard the exchange and interjected. "No, we're from Bravo Company, 1-18 Infantry out of Fort Riley. Well, most of us anyway. What's your situation officer?"

Jefferson looked over at White and then to Carnegie. She

shrugged her shoulders. "You might as well tell them."

Jefferson turned to Chamberlain and Mark. "I don't think you're going to believe what we have to tell you."

"Try me," Chamberlain said, trying to keep his voice down.

"We usually work traffic and only get involved in other types of calls when local PD asks for backup. Imagine our surprise when we spent all morning responding to domestic disputes all over the place. Only these weren't the normal kind where some drunk meathead is slapping his old lady around. People were biting each other. A lot." Jefferson paused to see if the soldier was taking this seriously, or if he was going to scoff. He didn't.

Angie couldn't hold back. "At first we'd get the victims loaded into ambulances and take the perps downtown but it didn't take long before the ambulances stopped showing up and dispatch quit answering the radio. For a while we coordinated with the other units patrolling in different parts of the county but the things people said were crazy. Then one by one, people checked out. Most said they were going home to protect their families, and when ordered to return they just switched their radios off and stopped responding."

"Yeah but that's not the worst part," White said apprehensively. "I think people are coming back from the dead." He swallowed hard. "I think people are turning into zombies."

There was an uncomfortable silence. Chamberlain wanted to choose his words carefully, not wanting to sound like a lunatic himself. He spat on the ground and adjusted the weight of his rifle. "We saw some of that too. I'm not sure if I'm ready to call them 'zombies' or anything but people are definitely infected with something. It's probably related to that bio weapon we've been hearing about. At any rate, it is what it is. We've got people going insane, biting each other and spreading the infection. And for whatever reason, only head shots seem to slow them down."

"It slows them down permanently," Matthews said, not

wanting to volunteer his experience back at Fort Leavenworth.

The platoon sergeant came over, his fire-plug build and grumpy demeanor as menacing as ever. "Chamberlain, get your people ready to move." He looked at the sheriff's deputies and their dog but did not address them directly. "We can't stay out here in this parking lot all night, we're too exposed."

"Where are we going then?"

"We'll hunker down in there." Savage pointed to the darkened high school with his chin. "We'll set up a strong-point until we get this sorted out."

The sharp crack of an explosion pierced the air and the ground rumbled. All heads jerked to the west, straining to identify the cause.

"Holy shit, it sounds like somebody just set off a nuke!" Jefferson blurted.

"That was no nuke, those were demo charges." Savage stared off into the darkness. "Things are getting serious. Time to quit jaw-jackin'. Get the tracks locked up and let's get our people inside. Let's move with a purpose!"

Chapter 8

Park Hill South High School
2242 Hours Local

Mark swept the weapon around the corner, using the light mounted on the front handgrip to see. There were rows of grey lockers, punctuated by bulletin boards, water fountains, and doors leading to classrooms. Nothing stirred and the only sound was their own gentle footfalls.

He wore a helmet and body armor, with night vision goggles mounted but flipped up and not in use. He preferred to use "white light" when clearing buildings but kept the nods ready in case they needed to go dark. The gear belonged to the lieutenant's gunner, Fernandez but he wouldn't be needing use of it any more.

He waved the others forward and they took a knee next to him. He whispered, speaking only as loudly as he needed to in order to be understood. They hadn't secured the entire building yet and there was no telling whether or not one or more of those things was inside with them. If there was, he didn't want any nasty surprises. "This area appears to be clear. Set up security and I'll report in. Dubois, you're in charge. I'll be back in half an hour. If any of those things come this way, hold this position. If you can't, fall back to the rally point in the gym. Understood?"

"Roger, sarn't." When the MP was well out of sight he turned to his buddy, Johnson. "What does this place remind you of?"

Johnson wiped a bead of sweat from the tip of his nose. His ballistic glasses fogged up again and it was getting difficult to see, so he took them off and shoved them into a cargo pocket. "This is reminding me of that campaign we did while at NTC. When our party was hunting for the maiden's treasure in Draken Castle."

"That's the one. Remember when the party was moving through the dark subterranean caverns with nothing more than torches to light the way. The sounds of dripping water and the occasional screech of a rat, with the smell of death in the air."

"Then we got ambushed by those orcs… that was a close one."

"Are you two seriously talking about Dungeons and Dragons right now?" Gray lay on her belly in the prone, her light machine gun shouldered while she scanned the darkness with a night vision monocular lowered over one eye.

"Yeah, so? What's the problem?" Dubois answered indignantly. "You don't think we should participate in role-playing campaigns?"

"Is that what you call it? 'Engaging in role-playing campaigns?' It's playing Dungeons and Dragons. And you're insufferable nerds. You should be pulling security, not talking about elves and shit."

Johnson smirked. "Keep it up, Gray, and you'll never get invited again to one of our sessions."

"Is that a promise?"

"Whatever."

***

Mark entered the teacher's lounge and found the other NCOs gathered there, bathed in the glow of a battery-powered lantern one of them had brought from the tracks. Most of them sat around the table, all of them bare-headed, some with arms crossed and heads lowered, grabbing a little sleep before the platoon sergeant arrived. There was a coffee pot in the corner on a table which he looked at longingly but with no electricity, there'd be no java. He'd just have to fantasize about it.

Savage walked in right behind him and some of the guys nudged their sleeping buddies awake.

"How's the security situation?" Savage looked to his Squad Leaders, all seated around a long conference table.

As senior Squad Leader, Frakes spoke up first. "We've

set up a tight perimeter in the main building since we don't have enough bodies to secure the entire facility. We barricaded the entrances and exits, so we don't think anything's getting in. The Bradleys are all locked up and secured, sitting outside close by if we need to get to 'em."

"Good. As you know I took a detail up to the roof with some dismount radios." The assembled NCOs leaned in closer while Savage spoke. He had their full, undivided attention. "We haven't been able to raise anybody from the Company command element. The CO, XO and even the First Sergeant are off the net. I can't even get the Company CP to acknowledge us. I was able to get the tank platoon on the horn and they said they can't get anyone else on the net either. They got through to Battalion though and relayed some information to us."

"What'd they say?" Bates had his body armor and kit lying on the floor behind him. It was much cooler inside the school and he tried to dry the sweat from his uniform. It was the most comfortable any of them had been in a couple of days, which only made them sleepier.

Savage sat down at the head of the table, set his rifle on the wooden conference table and sighed. "Is there any coffee?"

"We can't brew any up without power," Chamberlain said, pointing to the pot sitting on the table in the corner.

"Didn't one of you geniuses think about bringing in a propane stove from the tracks? I know most of you guys packed camp stoves in your shit." Savage was so tired he looked like he had aged at least ten years in the previous two days.

There was an uncomfortable silence for a short while before Frakes broke it. "We didn't think about it. We locked up the vehicles and got in here so fast, we left our rucks and duffle bags behind. We can go back out and get them if you want."

Savage rubbed his eyes. "No. It took us long enough to barricade the doors and clear this portion of the school. I don't want to have to do it all over again. Plus, from up on the roof we could see all sorts of runners moving around outside. It's best that we just stay put until morning." He set his helmet next to the weapon and tossed his ballistic eyewear inside. "So here's the situation."

The other NCOs leaned in closer as the platoon sergeant spoke.

"The CO was with one of the tank sections when they went off the air. The lieutenant over there thinks the section got overrun, or else they would have heard from them by now. So now there are two tanks left with crews but they are critically low on fuel. They are only running their gas generators to keep the batteries charged up so they can use the radios. Those things are running around everywhere, so they are buttoned up inside of their tanks and pissing in empty water bottles until help arrives. They are basically stuck in place."

"What about the fuel trucks in the logpac?" Mark felt exhausted but wasn't nearly as sleep-deprived as the rest. He looked fresh compared to the others, though he sure didn't feel that way.

"The logpac never arrived and nobody knows what happened to them. Battalion says that the XO left the Field Trains with them hours ago, and that at last report they were stuck in traffic. Nobody's heard from them since."

"Without any JP-8 we will be walking home," Bates interjected.

"Yeah, well, it gets worse." Savage propped his feet up on the conference table and leaned back in his chair. He grimaced while trying to stretch out and relieve the kink in his back. "Battalion says that the governor of Kansas ordered the Guard to blow the bridges over the Missouri River to keep the outbreak isolated on the east side. So they fucking did."

"Motherfucker!" Chamberlain slammed his fist on the table, startling the others. "Are you saying we're trapped over here?"

"Calm down, Dale. Take it easy." Savage spoke soothingly, resisting the urge to snap at his subordinate. "Things are confused all over the place and all order in the city has broken down. But we're here together, we've got our equipment, so we're going to be fine. I just need everyone to keep their shit together. Understood?"

A few of them responded with half-hearted "Hooahs," acknowledging their leader.

"This is what's going to happen. We're going to spend the night here. Put your people on one-third security so they can take turns getting some sleep. Then, in the morning we load up on the tracks, link up with the tankers, and get back to Battalion."

"How are we going to link up with the tanks and get back to Battalion with the bridges blown and no fuel?" Frakes wasn't challenging his platoon sergeant, he merely sought clarification on two of the most obvious problems confronting them.

"We can substitute diesel for JP-8. Then we can head north and dog-leg west toward Kansas. It's a longer route but we can make it." Savage peeled off his gloves and tossed them in the helmet before running fingers through greasy hair.

"That's great, Boss. But how are we going to get the diesel? With the electrical grid down all over the city, we can't just use our government credit card at the local service station to top off. The pumps won't work." Bates had an edge to his voice which he didn't bother to keep in check, and some of the more junior NCOs in the room looked at him with astonishment. Surely Savage would pounce out of his chair and pound the Squad Leader to dust with his fists. Except that he didn't. The platoon sergeant maintained his composure, though it was clear that it was becoming difficult to do so.

"You let me worry about that. In the meantime, I want you to get your people bedded down. Yourselves included. I need everyone rested up before we head out tomorrow. Now, let's get after it."

***

"First Sarn't, I think you need to come outside." Medina found himself in the unenviable position of waking the First Sergeant once again. Like always, he kept a healthy distance from the senior NCO, in case he decided to lash out.

Landreau came out of his haze, feeling even angrier this time. They'd found a good quiet place to settle in and he made it clear that he didn't want to be disturbed. As much as he wanted to roll over and go back to sleep, he couldn't ignore the shouting going on outside of the track. "What the hell is going on out there?"

"It's the Battalion XO and he's really pissed. He told me to get you right away."

"Sonofabitch." Landreau grumbled while slipping on his boots. He didn't bother to tighten the laces or put on his kit before going outside. On the other side of their perimeter a Humvee with a trailer was parked next to one of 3rd Platoon's Bradleys. Even in the low light he recognized Major Denney, who was flailing his arms around and yelling at Sergeant First Class Siegel. He wasn't sure how the XO managed to find them out here but it was clear the man was not happy. He strode over and mentally prepared himself for the verbal assault that was inevitably coming. "Sir, can I help you with something?"

Denney hadn't noticed the First Sergeant approach while he was chewing the other NCO out. When he turned, his eyes were fire and his voice was nearly hoarse. "Yes, First Sergeant, you can help me by explaining why in the fuck you are here and not forward with the rest of your company!"

Landreau had spent a bit of time dreaming up a cover

story but he still felt nervous. He needed to be convincing. "Captain Kieler ordered us to displace to the west side of the river. He said things were getting untenable on the Missouri side and wanted us to move to a more secure location."

"Captain Kieler said that?"

"Yes, sir."

"Do you even know where Captain Kieler is right now?"

"He's with our attached tank platoon. He's been there all day." Landreau swallowed the lump growing in his throat and concentrated on not fidgeting.

"Are you in contact with anyone up there? Or anyone else for that matter?"

"No, sir. We were having trouble reaching the TOC and with our command net. We figured everyone switched over frequencies, so we did too. I thought we'd be up on commo sooner or later."

"You switched frequencies and didn't tell anyone? Then when you still couldn't communicate, why didn't you send a runner to the TOC? You know where it is after all." Denney glared at the senior NCO, his jaw muscles flexing.

"I guess I didn't think about it."

"Where's your Company XO then?"

"He was leading the logpac earlier. He should be back with the Field Trains by now."

"Well, he's not. Your Company Commander was overrun hours ago while manning a checkpoint. Your Company XO was last seen in the middle of a bridge when the logpac was also overrun. There weren't many survivors but the few that made it back had a pretty grim tale to tell," Denney growled. He bared his teeth, speaking through them while trying to keep himself under control. The man was furious and he shook with rage. "First Sergeant, I am having a very difficult time believing you right now. You abandoned your post and took the Battalion Reserve with you after we explicitly ordered it forward on a rescue mission. We've got half the battalion stranded inside the city, with wounded personnel we can't evacuate at the moment. The situation is a total shitshow at the moment and you are back here sleeping. What do you have to say for yourself?"

Landreau didn't have a good response but when in a tight spot, it always helped to deny everything and make counter-accusations. "Sir, that's not true. We did not abandon our post, the CO ordered us to displace. Besides, the Sig-O never got us the proper encryption keys or frequencies, so it's his fault we've had commo issues. We've been doing everything we can to stay up on the net!"

"Listen to me very clearly. In one hour's time, refuelers and supply trucks from the Brigade Support Area will arrive here. You will personally lead them, along with the Battalion Reserve forward and link up with the rest of your company. The US-69 Bridge is still intact, since we managed to stop the Kansas boys from dropping that one into the Missouri River before they had a chance to light the fuse."

"But, sir, it's a war zone over there. We don't have any ammo."

"We managed to get some and it will be included with the supply convoy. It's small arms ammo but it will be enough. We don't have any 25-millimeter for the Bushmaster auto-cannons yet, or 120-millimeter rounds for the tanks but we have ball ammo for rifles and machine gun rounds for the coax's.

"Once you consolidate the company, prepare to secure the rail yards at daybreak. We got reports that it's a bloodbath down there, and we need to get it back up and running right away. Since Lieutenant Baker is the last surviving officer he will be in command. What are your questions?" Denney had a hard look on his face but had calmed down enough that he was no longer shouting.

"None, sir."

"Good. Let me be perfectly clear, if you happen to fall back without permission from Battalion and fail to come up on the radio again, I will personally see to it that you face a court martial." Denney did not linger. He jumped into his Humvee and the driver sped off.

Landreau watched the Humvee leave their small Assembly Area and whispered under his breath, "Fuck that guy." He turned to face the platoon sergeant for 3rd Platoon who was pretending not to eavesdrop on the conversation, standing twenty yards away. "Siegel, get your people ready to move, we head out in an hour!"

***

US-69 Missouri River Bridge
0320 Hours Local

Sergeant First Class Don "Bugsy" Siegel stood in the turret of his Bradley, directing the clearance operation the best he could. He'd been out on the ground at first but the demands for SITREPS from Battalion kept coming in and the First Sergeant wasn't being very helpful handling them.

The column consisted of his mechanized infantry platoon, the Bravo Company Command Element, a refueler, a supply truck, a few Humvees, and an M-88 armored recovery vehicle. The M-88 was a massive beast and they had it in the lead, using its built-in plow to push abandoned cars out of the way. The infantry squads were dismounted and clearing things forward while they moved. The grunts did their best to go up ahead, putting larger trucks and vans in neutral and steering them while the M-88 nudged them off into the shoulder. It was slow, methodical work but they made progress.

Reports of lunatics and murderers flooded over the radios all day long and there was shooting in the distance all around them. They hadn't run into anything like that however, finding the streets empty of all people. Living ones at least. The soldiers ran across dozens of dead bodies along the way, many left in a ghastly state. The sight of the mutilated victims put them all on edge and they moved cautiously.

Up front the lead squad, led by Staff Sergeant Villalobos worked in buddy teams, snaking their way through the empty cars and trucks, weapons shouldered and at the ready. Behind them the roar of the M-88's engine and the squeaking and popping of its steel tracks was punctuated by the crunching of plastic and metal as it pushed vehicles from the road. As bad as the congestion was before, it was even worse on the bridge, with the traffic channelized here. Up ahead, even in the dark they could see the outline of the Army trucks from the earlier logpac sitting in the center of it all, quiet and unmoving.

He directed his people forward, boot soles crunching on bits of broken glass, not saying a word, leapfrogging the understrength fire teams forward. Then he caught sight of movement up ahead, darting back and forth between vehicles, some of which still had their engines running with doors hanging ajar. He held his gloved hand high, palm open and forward, giving the signal to "halt." The other members of the squad mimicked the hand-and-arm signal, passing it back until everyone stopped moving forward. "Blue Four, this is Blue One. Over."

"Blue One, Blue Four. Send it. Over." Bugsy Siegel normally had a very upbeat and positive attitude, usually cracking a joke or bringing levity to the situation no matter how stressful it was. On this night however, his voice sounded like it was crawling out from the pit of darkness.

"Roger, Four. We've got contact, front. Looks like civilians. Over." Villalobos squinted at the green screen inside of this night vision monocular. The picture was grainy, the movement still pretty far off, a hundred meters at least. What he did see was silhouettes dashing back and forth, a few here and there, all of them making their way toward the squad and the rest of the column.

"Can you make out how many there are? Are they hostile? Over."

"Four, this is One. I can't tell for sure. What are your orders? Over."

Siegel flicked on a red-lens flashlight and shined it on his map, wishing for the hundredth time that the GPS was working. Their orders were clear, get to the other side, link up with the rest of the company, and prepare for their follow-on mission at daybreak. And if they didn't get moving faster, they were going to fall way behind schedule. "One, this is Four. We need to continue pressing forward. The Rules of Engagement dictate that you are authorized to defend yourselves. Get those people cleared and deal with them appropriately. Over."

Villalobos saw the civilians getting much closer now, running and not walking. He signaled to the others to get down behind cover and they readily complied, pointing their weapons at the darkened figures drawing closer. *Deal with them appropriately. What the fuck does that even mean?* he thought to himself. "Roger, Four. Standby." When the first couple of people got within twenty meters or so, the Squad Leader stood and raised his voice to get their attention. "You people, halt! You are in violation of the curfew. Turn around and head back to your homes, that is an order!"

The ones in the lead snapped their heads in his direction, noticing him for the first time. They had been running before but now they picked up their pace even faster, dashing straight at him. Others took notice as well, and they seemed to appear from nowhere by the dozens.

"I said halt!" Villalobos raised his muzzle into the air and fired three shots from his M-4 in quick succession. He wasn't a big fan of warning shots but he wasn't in the Middle East, he was in America, and he was in no mood to start smoking civilians.

A grenadier further forward stood behind the door of a Kia, "Stop right there!" He raised his hand with his weapon slung across his chest. Two of the runners leapt from the hood of Taurus and slammed into him, taking him to the ground. He began shrieking the moment they sank their teeth into his flesh. Then the rifleman off to the left fell, crying out for help, while the monsters on top of him growled like wolves on a fresh kill, ripping chunks from him.

"Holy fuck. *Open fire!*" The Squad Leader leveled his

weapon and snapped off rounds quickly. The infrared laser emitter mounted to the side of his carbine shined brilliantly in his night vision device. The laser dot danced on the chests of the oncoming runners while he shot them repeatedly. Seeing their Squad Leader go hot, the others opened up too, sending forth a hail of jacketed slugs, smashing into metal, glass, meat and bone. To their horror it did not slow them down and the noise only seemed to draw out more of them, working them into a frenzy.

Perched atop his Bradley, Siegel tried to get a report from anyone as the crackling of small arms fire picked up in an instant. He watched in horror through the green screen of his night vision goggles when scores of infected swept over his men, not slowed down one bit by the punishing wall of fire. In an instant their weapons fell silent while knots of the creatures piled on top of his people, ignored by dozens who charged past them, coming on toward the rest of the fresh meat.

***

Park Hill South High School
0340 Hours Local

Savage ran up the darkened staircase using a headlamp to light his way. The mental cobwebs were thick and he did his best to clear his mind by getting the blood pumping through exercise, bounding up the stairs three at a time. He'd left his gear down in the teacher's lounge, which they'd turned into a makeshift bunkhouse, electing only to carry his M-4 carbine. It felt good to be free of the body armor and kit, wearing only his boots, trousers and brown t-shirt.

Coming to the door at the top of the stairs he switched off the light and proceeded outside into the cool evening air. The door was propped open with a cinder block, and it stayed ajar while he stepped out onto the roof. The moon was a waxing crescent giving off little illumination but without cloud cover there was ample light. Near the ledge his driver had the duty of radio watch this shift, and he had the long-whip antenna up as high as it would go for best reception. He sat next to the radio set, stuffed inside a rucksack, with the handmike held to his ear. Savage quickly strode over holding the carbine by the pistol-grip with the muzzle hanging down, physically shaking his head, trying to clear it.

"What's up, Rojas?" He stood looking over the ledge, out toward the city. The building only stood three stories high but it did give them a little elevation. A few glows from raging fires contrasted against the darkened skyline. The sounds of violence echoed faintly in the distance while the beating rotors of a helicopter thrummed overhead.

"It's First Sarn't. Says he needs to talk to you." The gravel covering the rooftop made it uncomfortable to sit, so Rojas put his plate carrier on the ground and sat on that. It wasn't much of a cushion but it was better than nothing. His eyes drooped and his shoulders sagged, underscoring the soul-sucking exhaustion they all suffered from.

"Wow, it's a miracle. He's finally up on the net." Savage's anger welled up in his chest and he resisted the urge to spit. The First Sergeant always managed to ghost on them whenever things got sticky and he had been true to form since the moment they arrived in Kansas City. He took the mike from Rojas and put it up to his ear while scanning down below. "Battle Axe Seven, this is White Four. Over."

"*White Four, this is Blue Four. Battle Axe Seven is on the horn with Battalion right now. I will relay for him. Break.*" Siegel sounded tired like the rest of them but there was something else there. He sounded rattled. "*We attempted to cross the US 69 bridge a short while ago and were unsuccessful. We had to fall back. Over.*"

"I thought they blew all the bridges. You mean there's one still standing? Over."

"*Roger, there's one still left but we couldn't get across. Over.*"

That's just typical, Savage thought to himself, resisting

the urge to smash the handmike on the concrete guardrail. "Can I ask why? Over."

There was a long pause that dragged on noticeably for several seconds before the response came.

"*We were clearing a route over the bridge when we got attacked by mobs of civilians.*" Siegel's voice tremored and he broke the transmission again, taking a moment to regain his composure. "*Dave, you wouldn't believe the things we saw. These people… there were hundreds of them… they just…*"

"Let me guess, they started biting and eating people. Is that it? Over." The images of the infected pulling the gunners out of their Humvees kicking and screaming while ripping them apart ran through his mind. He suddenly didn't feel very sleepy any longer.

"*Yeah, that's right. All the crazy reports we've been hearing all day. They're true.*" Siegel paused before going on. "*I lost half my dismounts trying to clear the bridge. We opened up on them but it didn't even slow them down.*"

Savage lowered his head and shook it. He looked down to see Rojas looking up at him. He forced a smile at the young soldier to try and reassure him. "Blue Four, White Four. You have to shoot them in the head, it's the quickest way to put them down. Over." *Of course we could have told you this earlier if you had bothered to monitor the radios*, he thought bitterly.

"*Roger, that's good to know. I'll pass the word. In the meantime, we are trying to consolidate and reorganize ourselves. We fell back a few hundred meters but those things followed us. I think they're drawn by the noise of the vehicles and gunfire. We're all buttoned up in our tracks and they're swarming all over us. First Sergeant is talking to Battalion, trying to figure out what to do. Until then, you guys are on your own. How are you set? Over.*"

"We're hunkered down and okay. I've got two dead including the El-Tee. We picked up three wounded Guardsmen that need attention, and a few stragglers. We're good on food and water and we managed to scrounge a little ball ammo but we need fuel for the tracks and the tanks. Over."

"*Roger. I don't think we'll be able to make link-up with you before daybreak. Over.*"

"Understood. We'll stand by."

"*Good luck, Dave. I hope you guys make it out of this okay.*"

"Thanks, Bugsy. We'll be alright. See you later. White Four, out." Savage sighed and handed the mike back to his driver. "Well, Rojas, it looks like it's going to be another long day ahead of us."

***

1ˢᵗ Battalion, 18ᵗʰ Infantry
Tactical Operations Center
0358 Hours Local

Lieutenant Colonel Jerry Hamilton got out of his Humvee and looked up at the sky, inhaling the cool air. He leaned back with hands and his hips, trying to stretch out and get a little circulation flowing. He barely noticed when the other vehicle pulled up beside his own and the passenger hopped out, going through a similar ritual of his own.

"How are you feeling, Darin?" Hamilton knew his Sergeant Major was hurting but would never say so. He'd spent years in the airborne community and the injuries were beginning to catch up with him.

"I'm okay, sir. Just getting' old." Command Sergeant Major Yates wore his night vision goggles perched on the top of his helmet attached to a "rhino mount" and tied off with parachute cord to the rest of his kit.

"Is your back doing alright?"

"It's felt better. I popped a couple of Motrin a short while ago, so I ought to feel better before long." A faint glow off on the horizon signaled the coming of another day. Yates unclipped the NVGs and stuffed them into a pouch affixed to his harness. "Looks like BOB is finally coming up. It's a good thing, it'll help me wake up. I haven't felt this tired since Ranger School."

"I think I was better rested in Ranger School. Well, shall we?"

"After you, sir."

Hamilton briefly composed himself before approaching the small tent, attached to a M-577 armored command post vehicle. He opened the tent flap, pulling the hook and loop fastener apart, making a loud tearing sound. He went in without fanfare and the Sergeant Major followed close behind.

"The Battalion Commander!" shouted one of the staffers seated next to a set of radio remotes. Everyone inside shot straight up, coming to the rigid position of "Attention." One of the captains stood up so fast he knocked his metal folding chair over with an audible clang.

"Carry on," Hamilton said nonchalantly, taking a moment for his eyes to adjust to the bright lights inside the command post. He unbuckled the chinstrap of his helmet and removed it before taking his ballistic glasses off as well.

Radio reports poured in over the speakers and staffers settled back down in their seats, answering the calls that rolled in. The officers and NCOs clustered around workstations, segregated by their military specialties. The intelligence analysts dominated one side of the Command Post while the operations personnel were on the other. In the middle the Staff Sergeant Major and the Executive Officer choreographed everything, processing the information that kept coming in, while sending reports and updates to the Brigade Headquarters.

In the center stood a white screen and a projector attached to a laptop computer displayed a computer-generated operational picture. Lines and symbols covered a detailed map of the city, indicating the locations of friendly forces and operational control measures. Over on the right side in a corner, the Ops Sergeant Major worked with a young Specialist, updating an old analog map covered with acetate overlays. It was a common practice to update the low-tech tracking systems in case the computerized systems failed, which they sometimes did. Usually when someone forgot to refuel one of the generators.

Hamilton sank down into a seat designated just for him while the Sergeant Major made a beeline for the "silver bullet" coffee maker off in the corner. He plopped the helmet onto the field table in front of him, peeled off his gloves and tossed them inside. "What's the update, XO?"

Major Denney took a sheaf of papers from the Intelligence Officer and handed it to Hamilton before spitting tobacco juice into an old plastic Coke bottle. "Here's the latest report on what we're up against. Division sent it down and it's labeled 'Secret,' though I'm not so sure how much of a secret it is anymore."

Hamilton flipped through the papers, skimming through most of it and when he got to the last page he casually handed it over to the Sergeant Major who sat down next to him. The senior NCO had two steaming cups, handing one to his commander before mechanically looking at the report. "We got briefed on most of this at Brigade before we got here. Bottom line, there's some sort of infection loose that's burning through the population, spread mainly through bodily fluids. The victims lose all higher mental functions, and they go completely feral, attacking and spreading the disease. Is there anything else?"

"That's the gist of it, sir." The XO set down his spit bottle and turned to the Intelligence Officer. "Anything else to add, Jenny?"

She tapped away at a computer, pulling up some new information and projected it on one of the main screens. "Yes, sir. Reports are coming in indicating that the infection manifests itself differently in each individual. Some people get taken over by it, while others die; similar to being bitten by a snake bite. The information is very incomplete." She shifted uncomfortably in her chair before making eye contact with the senior officers. "The other, more pressing concern, is that the infected seem to not feel pain and are not easily affected by gunfire."

Hamilton sighed and scratched his chin. He took a sip of coffee from the disposable paper cup and grimaced after swallowing the bitter stuff. He wondered why they had the paper kind and not the Styrofoam but then realized his focus was wandering. It was getting harder and harder to concentrate. "We've been hearing that a lot but it doesn't make much sense. What do you make of it?"

All eyes in the tent were not on her, curious of the answer. Captain Jennifer Kwon cleared her throat and sat up straight. "The Brigade S-2 discussed this with the Brigade Surgeon and he believes that the infected should die like anyone else but since they don't react to pain, they need to be neutralized in a more direct manner."

"Meaning what, exactly?"

"Head shots will kill them instantly. Presumably a shot to the heart will do the same. Taking out their legs will immobilize them but only if the bones are broken it seems."

Hamilton nodded gravely and his knee bobbed up and down unconsciously. "This makes me sick to the pit of my stomach that we're talking about how to kill American citizens. Is there any other way to neutralize them without killing or maiming? There must be something. I mean, this is merely an infection and the scientists will figure out a cure sooner or later. We just can't go around massacring innocent people. This isn't what we do."

Kwon sat in her seat quietly.

"Okay, thank you, Jenny." Hamilton retrieved a small notebook from a cargo pocket and pulled it out of the plastic bag he kept it in. He opened it up and jotted some notes before going on. "XO, give me a SITREP on the rest of the battalion."

"Roger, sir." Denney spit in the bottle again before screwing on the cap and setting it down. He used a laser pointer on the main screen and circled various positions with it. "The situation remains unchanged. All the companies are trapped in the city on the east side of the river. Without ammunition, most of our personnel are locked down for the night, unable to get out except mounted. There is extremely limited fuel—especially for the tanks—and any attempt to drive out through the mangled mess of abandoned cars and trucks right now is very risky. Especially in the dark." He pointed to another cluster of vehicles on the Kansas side of the border. "We managed to scrounge some ammunition and sent the battalion reserve forward to make a crossing of the Missouri River but they suffered heavy casualties and turned back. They got attacked by a mob of the infected, and well… it went sideways."

"Can we get help going back in from the Kansas Guard?"

"No, sir. They aren't playing nice. The governor gave them strict orders to defend the state line and they aren't doing anything to help us out right now. Until federal mobilization orders come from Washington, we don't have any authority to make them do anything. The good news is that we got a vocal order from the President suspending Posse Comitatus and Division is pushing ammo and additional equipment from Fort Riley but that will take quite a while to get here. Plus, there's another problem."

"I already know. They briefed us at Brigade a few minutes ago. In order to get those shipments of ammunition and additional equipment they need to send them in via rail and the railyards are a complete shitshow." Hamilton looked over at his Sergeant Major who sat there stone-faced. The worry lines on his forehead were as pronounced as ever. "We've got to secure the railyards first thing this morning or else. Did you send the Warning Order to Bravo Company?"

"Yes, sir. Once we get the battalion reserve to them with the resupply, they should have enough combat power to carry out the mission."

"Is there anyone else available?" Hamilton studied the virtual map taking mental note of all the various positions of his subordinate units. They were scattered all over the place, distributed at the checkpoints they had been ordered to man the previous day.

"No, sir. Not really. Bravo Company is relatively intact and their 2nd Platoon is consolidated at a high school, ready to roll. Everyone else in the battalion is scattered to the four winds. It'll take us most of the day just to get them consolidated into something resembling their original formations."

"Fine. Get the word out. Once ammunition is distributed, I want people to fire in self-defense only. Civilian casualties are to be kept to an absolute minimum. These people might be infected with something horrible but there will be a cure someday soon and I can't have our people committing acts of mass atrocity. Also, I need Brigade to get us the Rules of Engagement as soon as possible. Is that understood?" The Colonel's tired eyes were hard and this issue was not up for debate.

"Sir, with all due respect, I'm not sure how we are going to clear and secure the railyards if our people run into these packs of the infected if they are only allowed to fire in self-defense."

"You heard me, XO. This is not up for debate!" He stabbed a finger at Denney.

"Yes, sir." The XO's posture stiffened.

Hamilton took a deep breath and his tone softened. "Now, when will the reserve be moving again?" Hamilton gave his Sergeant Major a knowing look. "Is First Sergeant Landreau still in charge over there?"

"He is, sir. But the Battalion S-3 is enroute to their location as we speak. He plans on personally taking charge and leading the reserve." Denney's face did not betray any emotion, though it was common knowledge he was highly frustrated with Landreau. "Major Fuentes should be there within minutes and I expect they'll be moving again within the hour."

"Good. I'm headed there as well to oversee their

preparations." Hamilton stood and put his helmet back on. "Give me a call if there are any further developments."

"Yes, sir."

***

Landreau sat on the bench seat inside of his M-113 armored personnel carrier with forearms resting on his knees, staring down at the diamond-plate flooring, illuminated by the hull-mounted light in the corner. Medina sat on the seat across from him, monitoring the radio while Beltran sat up front in the driver's position, head resting on the brow-pad, fast asleep. The engine idled quietly as they recharged the batteries and all would have seemed peaceful except for the bloodied palms slapping the side of the vehicle, accompanied by the moans and the screams of the infected who tried to find a way inside.

The Battalion XO had basically threatened to court-martial him if he ran away again but they hadn't had any choice. They got mobbed while trying to clear that bridge and they lost nearly half the platoon's dismounted infantry before the remaining survivors clambered up the sides of the tracks with those creatures hot on their heels. If they hadn't turned around, they might have lost all of them. *If I hadn't ordered everyone to fall back we would have lost a hell of a lot more people, that's for sure*, he thought to himself, doing his best to rationalize his decision.

"First Sarn't, it's Vanguard Three on the radio for you." Medina's voice croaked hoarsely, he'd been up all night without any rest. His disheveled hair looked as if it had never seen a comb. He fully extended his arm, trying to hand off the hand mike as if it were radioactive, its cord dangling across the mid-section of the APC's troop compartment.

"Vanguard Three, this is Battle Axe Seven. Over." Landreau cringed, waiting for the response.

"Battle Axe Seven, this is Three. I am co-located approximately fifty meters from your location. You are to get

your people moving, time now. Get them across the river. We have to get our units resupplied and we need it to happen ASAP. Acknowledge." The Battalion Operations Officer's voice came across with an icy tinge.

"Vanguard Three, Axe Seven. We lost nearly half the dismounts attempting that a short while ago. I don't think it's possible to get our personnel across that bridge."

"Seven, this is Three. You will make that crossing and you will do it now. The sun is coming up and you will have excellent visibility in no time. We are continuing to lose personnel in the city because they have no ammunition to defend themselves. Every minute you delay, costs more of our people their lives. Over."

Landreau shook his head in frustration. "Roger, understood. We will move out shortly."

"And another thing. Vanguard Six wants civilian casualties kept to a minimum. Your people are to shoot only in self-defense. Acknowledge."

"Is he fucking crazy?" Landreau said to himself, staring at Medina in disbelief. "Uh… roger, Three. Understood."

***

Siegel monitored the conversation between Major Fuentes and the First Sergeant. He wasn't quite sure what to make of the instructions about keeping casualties to a minimum when these monsters were literally ripping people to shreds. It was yet another reminder of why he fucking hated officers. "Battle Axe Seven, this is Blue Four. I monitored your traffic with Vanguard Three. I'll initiate movement. Over."

"Roger, Bugsy. Make it happen. Seven, out."

"I'll make it happen alright. It'll probably be the last thing I do," he said, looking over at his gunner Specialist Hackworth, sitting inches away from him inside of their Bradley. He rotated the turret, scanning through the optic mounted up top, trying to see whatever he could outside. It didn't look good.

"How's it look out there Hack?" Siegel had his own commander's optic to look through but he didn't want to. He'd seen far too much already this day.

"It don't look good, sarn't. There's even more of those things running around than before. You got a plan?"

Siegel screwed up the courage to look through his commander's sight and frowned. "Yeah but it ain't a good one."

"Better than nuthin' I suppose."

"Famous last words, dude."

***

Siegel put out his plan over the platoon net and received tepid responses in return. The boys were none-too excited about any of this, particularly after what they'd been through a few hours before. As reluctant as they were, they executed precisely on their platoon sergeant's order.

All the vehicles shut their engines down and went totally quiet, allowing an eerie silence to settle on them all. The infected clustered around the armored hulks still focused on getting inside. A few managed to climb up on top only to walk off the sides, falling onto the others below. Things stayed quiet like this for precisely five minutes.

On Siegel's signal, the M-88 recovery vehicle at the head of the column roared to life, belching thick black smoke from its exhaust manifold. The driver gunned the engine rhythmically, the sound echoing down the streets. Then he put the transmission into drive and started to move, albeit at a crawl. The heavy steel track squeaked and popped, adding even more noise to that of the massive engine. Most of the infected to their front were nudged aside but a few fell under the tracks, crushed flat.

The noise acted as the siren's song and drew the creatures from every direction. Those that clustered around the other vehicles in the column suddenly lost their interest, instantly drawn to the new stimulus. They mobbed the recovery vehicle, losing interest in the Bradleys and leaving them behind.

"That's it. *Now!*" Siegel ordered over the platoon radio frequency.

At once the cargo hatches on top of the Bradleys back decks popped, their clamshells yawning open and locking to the rear while the dismounted infantry inside poked their heads out into dawn's early light. With only two or three of them left per vehicle there was plenty of room to move and they instantly picked up sectors of fire on opposite sides of their tracks.

The drivers of the Infantry Fighting Vehicles fired up their engines as well, falling into formation behind the M-88. The moment they did so, some of the infected once again found them interesting and came running. Some bounced harmlessly off the outer hulls but others climbed up the equipment lashed to the side. Those that clambered up found themselves staring down the barrels of M-4 carbines whose reports cracked and popped excitedly.

The column picked up speed and hit its stride and in short order, they were back on the bridge, clearing it. The M-88 focused on pushing cars out of the way, avoiding the larger vans and trucks when possible. They came to a point where they had to push an 18-wheeler but it jackknifed, utterly blocking the route. The mechanics inside the recovery climbed out and hooked a heavy winch to the back of the huge truck while their buddies on top of the armored recovery vehicle provided covering fire. They managed to clear it out of the way at great risk to themselves.

Lieuteant Colonel Hamilton rolled up in his Humvee, pulling up next to his Operations Officer. Nobody got out of their vehicles and the gunners up top scanned nervously behind their pintle-mounted machine guns. When he saw the column crawling along with the infantry on the tracks shooting wildly at incoming runners, he grew incensed. He jumped out of his vehicle and stomped over to Major

Fuentes' truck. Seeing his commander, Fuentes cracked the window about an inch, not eager to get out from behind protection.

"Damn it, Delmar, I thought I made it clear to minimize civilian casualties. It's a massacre up there!" Hamilton pointed off toward the reinforced platoon, his face growing bright red.

"Sir, it was my understanding that our people were to shoot in self-defense. You can see that they are being attacked by groups of the infected." Fuentes looked out past the colonel, worried about him standing there out in the open with all the crazies running around. "Would you like to get into my vehicle while we speak? It's not safe standing outside, sir."

"No, I will not! I am not going to cower inside the safety of a vehicle!"

The roar of the engines and the report of the rifles stirred up even more of the dead. They came on in groups of twos and threes, drawn to the action and the noise like moths to the flame. The platoon held them off, if barely. Getting a headshot on a running human being is difficult for extremely well-trained troops in the Special Operations community. Line grunts did not train for that sort of thing, practicing routinely to shoot "center mass" from stationary shooting positions. Now, these people fired from moving platforms at small targets moving along at a full sprint. It took the line grunts many shots to score a hit, and usually it occurred when they were within a few yards of their targets when it was difficult to miss. Bullets flew everywhere.

Hamilton went back to his vehicle and slammed the door when he got inside. He grabbed the transmitter from a hook fabricated from a piece of parachute cord. "Battle Axe Seven, this is Vanguard Six. You are causing far too many civilian casualties up there. I am ordering you to stand down. Bring your people back immediately. We will figure out another way to get across. Six, out."

Chapter 9

Park Hill High School
0445 Hours Local
Second Day of the Outbreak

Savage stood up and yawned while he stretched. The early morning sun felt good on his face and started to clear the cobwebs from his head. At his feet his gunner and driver dozed blissfully on either side of the dismounted radios sitting snugly in their field packs, with long-whip antennas reaching toward the sky. It was nice out now but later in the day it would get brutally hot on the rooftop and they would have to leave a man up there, since that's where they got the best reception.

"*Red One and White Four, this is Vanguard Three, your push. Over.*"

"*Vanguard Three, this is Red One. Over,*" said Lieutenant Baker, the tank Platoon Leader, sounding as if he'd just woken up.

Savage wondered why the Battalion S-3 was calling them on their company command net. Whenever that happened it was never a good sign. "Vanguard Three, this is White Four. Over."

"*Red and White, listen up. The Blue element is having a tough time getting to you. We had to pull them back to the Tactical Assembly Area to consolidate and reorganize. We will find a different route and get the resupply to you, it's just going to be somewhat later in the day. I know both of your element's vehicles are running on fumes but your people are secure, so hold your positions until we make link-up later today. Acknowledge.*"

"*Vanguard Three, this is Red One. We're buttoned up in the tanks and safe but it's going to get uncomfortable in here when the sun starts blazing down on us. And most of our water is strapped on the outside of our vehicles and we can't get at any of it with the infected people running around.*"

Over."

"Roger, Red One. You'll have to deal with it for the time being. We can't get help to you any quicker but it will be coming soon." Major Fuentes did not sound convincing, not even a little bit.

"Vanguard Three, this is White Four. We're in good shape here at the school. No issue with us. Over." Savage did some mental inventory in his head. With the power still out, water pumps at the school weren't working but they still had water in the jerry cans. The freezers in the cafeteria didn't have anything inside but they did have some MREs and if they rationed them, they'd be fine for a couple of days. Ammo was far from plentiful but at least they had a little, which was something.

"Red and White, I will be sure to give you an update as soon as I am able. Sit tight, and we'll get to you soon. Vanguard Three, out."

Savage sighed while looking out from the rooftop. With the sun finally up he could make out more details of their surroundings. Off to their west was a large wooded lot with some houses on the far side of it. To the south were a baseball diamond and football field with more houses beyond that. To the east some small businesses sat dark and silent and to their north a four-lane road with a suburb just beyond it. Off in the distance however, plumes of smoke reached for the sky accompanied by the sound of beating helicopter rotors.

The look of it was peaceful, though eerily so. Under normal circumstances the area would have been quiet but never *this* quiet. It was unsettling. Then, off to the east, in the cluster of small businesses, the crackle of small arms fire erupted.

Savage snatched up his pair of binoculars and focused on the buildings off in the distance, trying to get a better look. From his perch he could not make out much but did make out the shattering of glass from the impact of bullets. From the sound of it, those were civilian weapons and not military.

He lowered the binoculars and reached for the radio to send up a report when he caught sight of some motion in the corner of his eye. From the cluster of homes off to the northwest came individuals, then small groups, sprinting to the sound of the guns. They crossed the four-lane road cut through the northern parking lot of the high school headed off to the east, drawn by the sounds of the shots.

Not wanting to be seen and draw any attention to himself, Savage crouched low and continued to watch as things unfolded. He tried to count them at first but quickly found himself unable. There were simply too many.

Rojas and Becker started to stir. "What's going on, sarn't?"

"You two stay down," Savage whispered harshly, motioning with his hand for them to stay low. The driver and gunner looked at each other in confusion. "And keep your voices down."

Savage picked up the handmike to send his report as scores of runners passed by the school, nearly all of whom possessing ghastly wounds all over their bodies. "I have a feeling we're going to be here awhile," he said to himself.

***

Specialist Vince Rossi sat in a swivel chair he'd found in one of the classrooms, staring down a gloomy hallway. When they first arrived the evening prior, everyone pulled security from the prone while laying on their bellies, just like they would in the field. But the tile floors were cold and uncomfortable so it didn't take long before they started "improving their position" by acquiring items to make sentry duty a little less miserable. The chair was for one of the teachers and while not super comfortable, it was better than sprawling out on the floor.

The sun came up and rays of light streamed through the windows at the end of the hall, finally providing some illumination. Still, after days of grabbing meager amounts of sleep here and there, he felt exhausted. He ran his hand across a stubbled chin and remembered that his shaving kit was still on the Bradley, secured outside in the parking lot.

The platoon was short on NCOs so Rossi served as the Alpha Team Leader in 1st Squad. As a card-holding member of the "E-4 Mafia," he was non-too pleased to be saddled with the leadership assignment. It meant he had to keep some separation from his other junior enlisted buddies, and it didn't even come with a pay raise. They had talked about making him a Corporal to lend some authority to the position but somehow the paperwork never seemed to get processed and he remained a Specialist with all of the responsibility of an NCO, with none of the perks. It fucking sucked.

He checked his watch and looked at the time. *Got a huddle at 0600 and I gotta make sure everyone is up in about fifteen minutes.*

Rossi looked over at Specialist Jesse Beekhof, curled up on a field air mattress underneath a poncho liner. He slept soundly, gently snoring and not moving a muscle. Next to him lie most of his kit and the M-249 light machine gun propped up on its bipod.

He sighed deeply, feeling envious of the other soldier, wishing he too could be catching forty winks. Rossi rocked back and forth in the swivel chair, barely noticing the squeaking sound it made. He also didn't notice when his eyelids began to droop, eventually closing completely as his rocking slowed down and then came to a stop.

Somewhere in his sleepy haze he heard a dripping noise. It wasn't a steady rhythm, which is why it seemed so out of place. Something thick splashed in inconsistent drops on the tiled floor behind him. He forced his eyelids back open again and swiveled the chair around, not bothering to get up.

Standing there in the gloom was a thin man with greying hair with stooped shoulders staring down at him. He wore a Kansas City Chiefs jersey and even in the low morning light he could see it was covered in blood. Looking up he could just make out the man's face and when he saw the red eyes and blue lips with thick saliva dripping off the man's chin, the realization hit him all of a sudden like an electric shock passing through his body.

The creature moved in a flash and Rossi had no time to react. Its jaws sank yellowed teeth into his face, forcing him to let out a high-pitched screech.

Specialist Beekhof sat up immediately and turned to see the thing clawing and biting his Team Leader. He froze at the sight and before he knew it a woman and three small children came out of nowhere and jumped on top of him.

Their desperate cries echoed down the empty hallways.

***

"What the fuck was that?" Staff Sergeant DeShawn Frakes had spent three combat tours overseas and had seen his fair share of fighting and killing, yet he had never heard anything like the sounds coming from around the corner. The visceral, animal sounds made his blood run cold.

"It's Rossi and Beekhof!" Private Ho snatched up his weapon and stood up, dressed only in his t-shirt and trousers with his boots untied.

"Come on, let's go!" Frakes grabbed Private Piel by the arm and the three of them took off.

They ran past several classrooms and rounded the corner, nearly running into five creatures coming their way. Sticky red blood covered the man, woman and three young girls and upon seeing the soldiers they snarled and charged straight toward them.

Piel froze in his tracks, getting hit full on by the girls. The woman went for Ho and the man in the Chiefs jersey came at Frakes. The NCO snap-fired his carbine and stitched the creature across the chest with a burst, not slowing it one bit. He managed to get off another burst, catching it in the face and dropping the runner in its tracks.

Piel howled in pain and Ho grunted and struggled, pinned up against some lockers. Frakes had to side step in order to get a shot on the woman, careful not to hit his man in the process. She caught sight of him and jerked her head in his direction as he fired, making him miss. The rounds flew wide and traveled down the length of the hallway, smashing into some large windows, sending shards of glass flying out into the parking lot.

His second burst took half her head off and she collapsed to the floor. The two soldiers then turned their attention to the tiny attackers covering Piel and dispatched them in seconds, their tiny bodies sprawled out on the cold tiles.

Frakes bent down to check on his subordinate and found him with several small bite wounds all over. "Medic!"

At the end of the hallway more figures gathered outside, peering in through the broken panes. Then, all at once, dozens of them stormed inside headed toward the source of the noise and the smell of fresh blood.

***

Angela Carnegie assisted Specialist "Bags" Bagdasarian cleaning and re-dressing a wound on one of the National Guardsmen, an older guy named Huntzinger. They used the cafeteria as a makeshift aid station and assembly point where the wounded and the civilian refugees hung out. Other than the restless moaning from the wounded, it was quiet in there.

They'd ended up with five civilians rescued from the strip mall. Two of them were a middle-aged couple with their seventeen-year-old daughter. The man was named Roberts and said he was a banker. He and his wife looked as if they'd been running marathons recreationally for years and they were both armed. He kept his Ruger Mini 14 no more than arm's-length away at all times, while his wife Cynthia clutched her Glock.

The other two civilians were a couple of Hispanic teenagers and neither of them spoke English. Specialist Rodriguez from 3rd Squad did some translating and learned that they were boyfriend and girlfriend. They worked as housekeeping staff at one of the local hotels when the outbreak occurred and they'd barely managed to survive. They huddled together closely with the girl resting her head on the boy's shoulder.

It was peaceful in the cafeteria and everyone felt safe. Right up until gunfire thundered in the hallways outside.

Saxon started barking and the soldiers and deputies went for their weapons while the civilians looked on in alarm.

"What's going on?" Jefferson blurted out, scooping up his Remington 11-87.

White shouldered his M-16, keeping it at the low-ready. "How the hell should I know? You think I've clairvoyance or something?"

"Clair-what?"

"Never mind, you stay here and I'll go look." Jefferson went to the nearest door and carefully opened it, peering down the barrel of his shotgun. He flipped on the barrel-mounted light. The noise from the gunfire got much louder the moment he went outside.

At the end of the hallway at an intersection he saw several people flash past, running at a full sprint. He couldn't get a good look at them but he was fairly certain they weren't soldiers. The shots from the other part of the building gradually rose in intensity and he carefully made his way forward, taking particular caution when rounding corners. He didn't feel like running into any nasty surprises.

He found himself near the front office when he swept his tactical light on two figures crouched over a third. The two bit and clawed at the third who struggled helplessly underneath.

Jefferson did not hesitate and blasted both of them with 00 Buck. The semi-automatic shotgun roared in the enclosed area and blew their heads apart. The limp bodies fell atop the victim, who twitched uncontrollably. He kept the weapon trained on the third and saw it was one of the soldiers from the platoon. He looked like he wasn't even old enough to shave and he gurgled blood while looking pleadingly at the sheriff's deputy.

Jefferson shook his head in regret. "I hate to do this kid but I don't have a choice. Sorry." He pointed the gun at the young grunt's head and pulled the trigger.

The shots and sounds of men shouting orders to one another rapidly grew closer. He did a quick look around, found the soldier's M-4 carbine and slung it across his back before retreating back to the cafeteria. He was even more cautious than he had been before but arrived without further incident.

Walking through the door he found himself staring down the muzzle of an M-16.

"It's me, get that thing out of my face." Jefferson pushed the barrel off to the side into a less lethal direction.

"Sorry, bro. We're getting a little jumpy." White meekly lowered the weapon. "Did you see anything out there?"

"Boy, did I..." Before he could finish his sentence the door behind him flew open and three soldiers came bursting inside. Two of them assisted the third who looked like he'd just lost a fight with a rottweiler. They set the injured man down next to the wounded Guardsmen while their chests heaved.

"Bags, take care of Piel. He got bit by some... kids." Private Ho's wild eyes darted from right to left and his chest heaved, nearly out of breath.

The three sheriff's deputies looked at each other with a knowing look.

"You gotta get him the hell out of here." Jefferson pointed at Piel with his shotgun, finger resting gently on the trigger.

Ho stood up, getting between the barrel of the weapon and his buddy. "What the fuck are you talking about? He's my buddy and he's hurt."

Bags moved toward Piel but Carnegie grabbed her by the arm and held her back. "Don't get near him. Trust me." This elicited a confused look from the medic whose hard-wired instinct was to rush in to help.

"He's going to turn into one of those things. He's infected like the rest. He might turn slow or he might turn quick but sure as shit, *he will turn.*" Jefferson didn't point the shotgun at Ho, keeping it trained on Piel, just on the other side of Ho's legs. If Piel so much as flinched, he'd blow Ho's knees out from underneath him and nail the bitten soldier.

"How can you possibly know that?" Ho grasped his own weapon in a menacing manner, though he hadn't pointed it at the deputy yet. The other soldier, a guy with the name "Adams" written on his nametape crouched next to his injured friend, looking back and forth at the two facing off.

"He knows it because we watched it happen at least a dozen times yesterday during our calls. We seen a lot of shit yesterday, I'm here to tell you," White interjected, his M-16 at the ready as well.

"We don't leave anyone behind and that's that…" Ho jumped when a shot rang out. He spun around to see Piel with a clean bullet hole in his forehead. The female deputy stood over him with pistol in hand. After dispatching the wounded soldier, she brought her Glock up and pointed it at Ho.

"I recommend you stand down. I didn't want to do that but Jefferson's right." Angela Carnegie held the weapon with both hands expertly. There was little doubt she knew how to use it.

"*What the fuck have you done?*" Ho bellowed, he still held the carbine in his hands, raising it in Carnegie's direction. Saxon began to growl, baring his teeth.

"I wouldn't do that, bud," White said.

The door burst open and Staff Sergeant Frakes spilled inside with Cruz and Maravich hot on his tail. The two junior enlisted slammed the door shut behind them and leaned their shoulders into it. Within seconds a loud thumping began on the other side as the dead tried to force their way in.

Frakes pointed to the wounded Guardsmen and the civilians sitting up against the wall. "Police these people up because we gotta go. *Now!*"

***

Once the shooting started Mark and Dubois sprinted down the hallway and got down in the prone next to Gray and Johnson who covered the area in front of the library.

"They're inside. First Squad's in contact. Scan your lanes.

The sounds of pitched battle resonated throughout, gunshots punctuated by shouts and screams. Intermixed in it came the animal howls that they'd become all too familiar with. Nervously they watched and waited, sweat dripping down temples and off the tips of noses.

A man came running up from their rear in the gloom. "It's me, Chamberlain, hold your fire," he whispered loudly.

Mark got up on a knee and Chamberlain got down next to him. "Matthews, I need you to hold this position for five minutes, then get your people and fall back to the Bradleys out front in the parking lot."

"Why? What's happening?" Mark looked down at his watch and set the timer.

"The perimeter's been breached. We've got infected civilians, dozens of 'em, running around inside. The platoon sergeant gave the order to un-ass the AO, so we're bugging out in the tracks."

"Roger, understood."

"Five minutes, then you get back to the rest of us. If you're late, you're walking home." Chamberlain did not look like he was kidding.

"That bad huh?"

"Yeah, it's that bad."

Mark nodded. "Then we'll see you soon."

"Good man." Chamberlain clapped him on the shoulder, then took off back down the darkened hallway.

***

"Pull the piano out of your ass and pick up the pace!"

Burbey shouted to Donahue who lagged behind the others.

"Eat a bag of dicks!" Donahue puffed while carrying a rucksack with a dismounted radio, spare batteries and other gear stuffed inside. "Besides, weren't you supposed to be taking this shit?"

"Not my turn, I had the duty yesterday, so suck it up sweetheart." He gulped down two breaths of air. "Besides, carrying the weight is just an excuse. You run like pregnant yak."

Donahue struggled for wind and panted heavily. "We can't all be skinny little shits like you, dude."

"Knock it off, the both of you. Pick up the pace or else!" Sergeant Rash scolded.

Harris took point, running down the corridors, quickly checking each intersection with his rifle before moving onward. In the rear, Sergeant Rash pushed them forward, occasionally turning around to see if they were being pursued. They'd made it halfway already but the noise around them did not inspire confidence. Things were falling apart, quickly.

When he spun around again he caught sight of two figures behind them rounding a corner. They stopped for a split second, sniffed at the air and then sprinted toward the fleeing infantrymen. Unencumbered, the infected moved with incredible speed.

"Contact rear!" Rash picked up the pace and caught up with Donahue within a few paces. He pushed him in the back of the heavy rucksack to help move him along a little faster.

The adrenaline kicked in and the four of them bolted but the dead closed the distance in no time. Rash, conscious of the limited number of rounds in his single loaded magazine, resisted the urge to shoot as long as he could but he didn't have a choice any longer. "Keep going!" He shouted to his men before stopping and spinning around. He dropped to a knee, taking up a steady firing position and tried to get his breathing under control.

The two runners came on fast and Rash flipped the safety

catch from "safe" to "semi" while trying to get his red dot on the first one's head. Once he did, he squeezed the trigger and the little carbine boomed in the enclosed space, making his ears ring.

The head snapped back and the creature tumbled to the floor with a wet slap. Rash shifted his aim to the second one and snapped off another shot. The thing got so close that its limp body fell on top of the NCO, knocking him to the ground, splayed out on top of him. He struggled awkwardly and got the thing off him in time to see dozens more coming around the corner, emerging from where the first two came.

"Oh shit," Rash said to himself as the mob came rushing at him.

***

"Ditch all your shit. Ammo, weapons, night vision and water only. Oh, and keep the ballistic eyewear. Do it!" Mark tossed his helmet and shrugged off his body armor while the others did the same. The Kevlar and E-SAPI plates in their plate carriers weren't going to protect them much against bites but the weight sure would slow them down. Everyone in the fire team dropped the armor and put their Fighting Load Carrier vests back on, which carried the bare minimum for survival. When he saw everyone had done like him, he gave them a thumbs-up. "You all good? Alright, let's go. Johnson, you got point. Haul ass and don't stop for shit. Everyone else, keep up!"

The four of them took off at a sprint, pounding down the hallways. The sounds of gunfire and panic tapered off and Mark knew there was one of two reasons for that. Either the rest of the platoon was wiped out, or they had already left the building, leaving him and his fire team alone inside with a horde of ravenous flesh-eaters. Either way, it was time to get the hell out of there.

They moved as fast as they could, barely bothering to check the corners, knowing full well that lingering a few seconds too long might spell disaster. It didn't take long before Gray started to lag behind the others, her short legs unable to keep up. Dubois passed her and caught up with Johnson leaving her behind. Mark grabbed the light machine gun she carried and dragged her by the tactical vest as she struggled to keep pace.

Approaching the sound of random shots up ahead, Mark suddenly realized they needed a new plan. The infected were drawn to the noise and if they got closer to the entrance where the shooting came from, then they'd probably run right smack into a group of the dead and then things would get a little sporty.

"Johnson, take a left up there," Mark huffed, pulling Gray along.

"What? That will take us further from the rest of the platoon." Johnson didn't even sound winded, he probably could have run even faster, leaving the rest of them behind.

"Just do it!"

They peeled off to the left and barreled down a long corridor flanked by empty classrooms until they reached a double door marked "Fire Exit." Johnson stopped and looked back quizzically. Mark shouldered his way past him with Gray in tow, slamming into the push-bar and spilling outside. They all squinted in the bright early sunlight.

Mark took the lead and headed toward the sound of fighting and the unmistakable rumble of Bradley engines turning over around the corner of the building. In the distance they saw figures darting between houses and buildings but none of them seemed particularly interested in their group. At least not yet.

Coming around the side of the building they stopped for a second to assess the situation. The Bradleys were still parked side by side just as they had been all night but the crews were aboard now getting them ready to move. The ramps were sealed up tight and the dismounted infantry climbed up top, facing out and orienting their weapons toward the runners steadily streaming in. Even the small group of civilians and sheriff's deputies were there, either helping or doing their best to stay out of the way.

Clusters of the infected gathered around the tracks trying to claw their way up toward the fresh meat but the grunts beat them back with rifle butts and boots, saving their precious ammunition. There weren't that many gathered around the vehicles yet but their numbers grew with each passing second. Mark tried to work out the best course of action in his head, running through all the options in his mind. There were half a dozen runners between them and the Bradleys, and he considered signaling to the others to create a distraction to draw them away so they had an opening.

He got ready to walk out into the open and wave his arms at the others when the Bradley on the far end pulled away, heading toward the road. The second one in line wasted no time and fell in behind the first, while the remaining two fired up their engines.

Mark turned to Gray, handing her his stainless 1911 pistol. "You know how to use this?"

"Yeah, my dad had one and taught me how to shoot it." She took the handgun from him, popped the safety catch and pulled the slide back a bit to check to see if a round was in the chamber. There was, so she eased it back forward.

"Good. I'll carry the SAW so you can move faster. Try to keep up." Mark turned to the others. "That's it, time's up. It's now or never. Follow me!" He darted off, leading the way. He slung the M-249 across his back and shouldered the AR-15 while running straight toward the nearest track. The grunts up top caught sight of the fire team and waved them forward, shouting encouragement.

A third Bradley pulled away but the commander atop the fourth and final one ordered the driver to remain stationary. The dead focused their attention at the noisy soldiers perched up high on the armored beast making all the noise and did not notice Mark and his team closing the distance toward salvation.

About twenty yards out, one of the creatures caught sight

of the movement and howled. This drew the attention of some of the others and a group of the things broke away from the Bradley, charging straight at Mark and the rest.

He stopped, planted his feet shoulder-width apart, raised the rifle, taking in a deep breath and letting it out slowly. He settled the red dot in his optic on the lead one coming on, pointing it at the bridge of the nose. Squeezing the trigger there came a loud crack along with the familiar springy sound resonating through the stock into his cheek. Things seemed to slow down and his field of view focused to a soda straw. He shifted aim to the next one and fired, then moved on to the next.

The moment Mark opened fire, Dubois and Johnson took notice. Trailing ten feet behind on either side of Mark, the two of them halted and opened up as well. The Bradley found itself in the line of fire and the dismounts standing on top scrambled to find cover, huddling behind the turret to protect themselves from an errant shot. Moreover, they dared not shoot at the dead for fear of hitting their comrades on the ground. All they could do was watch and pray.

The infected sprinted toward the fire team, not in any way deterred by the gunshots as more and more of them fell. The deafening noise only spurred them on, working them into a frenzy. Their numbers dwindled until only two remained and they sprang at the closest person, who happened to be Mark.

They slammed into him with incredible force, knocking him down on his back. Mark nearly had the wind knocked out of him and struggled to regain control. The two things, one man and one woman raked at him with their nails and tried to bite him. He held his AR-15 across his chest and did his best to hold them back while angry jaws snapped. He pushed and he squirmed but the things were on him and they would not let go, clawing and biting.

The female wriggled her way up and her mouth opened, exposing teeth covered in a sheen of oily foulness connected by threads of thick saliva. He could not stop her as she came at his face. Mark squeezed his eyes shut waiting for the inevitable when a loud "pop, pop, pop" rang in his ears. Then, all of a sudden, the bodies on top of him stopped moving and went limp. When he opened his eyes, Gray stood over him with the 1911 pistol cradled in both hands.

Before he could get his wits back, Dubois and Johnson were pulling the bodies off him, then helping him to his feet. Gray was already off and running toward the Bradley while the soldiers up top came from behind cover to reach down offering their hands to pull them up.

On his feet again Mark started off with the others in the fire team well ahead of him. He didn't notice that a dozen of the infected came rounding the corner of the school, hot on their tails. He did notice when some of the men on top of the Bradley started shooting at something behind him which only motivated him to run faster.

Up ahead Gray, Dubois and Johnson got pulled up while some of the others shot at his pursuers. When he was inches away from the track, runners came streaming around from both side of the vehicle, their wild eyes focused on him like a laser. He reached up and grabbed the lip of the armored apron, only to feel hands latch on to the fabric of his uniform near his shoulders, lifting him off the ground. His dangling feet came within inches of varicosed hands clawing the air at him.

"They're clear! Let's go!" Someone shouted and the IFV lurched forward, crushing a number of the dead under her steel tracks.

Mark sat upon the back deck, his chest heaving, gently rocking as the Bradley crossed over a ditch and up onto the road, falling in behind the rest of the platoon. He looked back in a daze, watching a growing mass of runners chase after them, unable to keep up.

"You okay, Matthews?" Mark turned to see Sergeant Chamberlain hunched down beside him, holding onto the bustle rack to steady himself.

He took off the ballistic glasses, spattered with a thick,

red goo. He wiped his face with a sleeve, careful to keep any of the toxic goo from getting in his mouth. "Yeah, I think so. Though I might have to change my shorts."

Chamberlain cracked a smile and slapped him on the shoulder. "I'll have the supply sergeant bring up a fresh pair the next chance he gets."

***

Intersection of I-29 and Route 45
0549 Hours Local

"Red One, this is White Four. Over." Sergeant First Class Savage keyed the handset while looking down at his map encased in plexiglass. On one side it held the standard 1:50,000 scale military contour map and on the other he mounted a standard road map of the Kansas City area. He flipped between the two from time to time to orient himself.

The platoon picked its way through neighborhoods and side streets to link up with the two stranded tanks attached to their company. With no help coming from the west side of the river, Savage meant to link up and consolidate their people. Plus, Lieutenant Baker was the last remaining officer in the company and while not permanently assigned to their unit, he was the highest-ranking person left and technically in charge. They couldn't just abandon him and the others. Though he had been tempted to after all they'd been through in the last twenty-four hours.

"*White Four, this is Red One. Nice to hear your voice. Over.*" Baker sounded tired but in good spirits.

"Likewise, Red One. We're about half a klick out from your position and inbound. Still picking our way through a mess of smashed and burned-out cars. I think we shook off the last of our 'friends' about a klick back but those things keep coming out of the woodwork. Over."

The Bradleys maintained a tight formation snaking their way through the congested mess dodging the largest of obstacles while rolling over the rest. Commanders tried to ignore the occasional body sprawled out on the ground in front of them while mashing them into the pavement. The stench of burning rubber and plastics hung in their noses while the muffled sounds of rifle and pistol shots echoed in the distance. Up ahead the unmistakable silhouettes of M-1 tanks came into sharp relief against the backdrop of stalled-out civilian traffic.

"Driver, stop." Savage toggled the switch on his Combat Crewman's helmet from intercom to transmit as the IFV slowed to a halt. "Red One, White Four. We are approximately fifty meters to your twelve o'clock position. Over."

"*Roger, White Four. We've got eyes on you. Over.*"

"Understood. So, I hope you have a plan, sir, because my tracks are running on fumes right now and it's a long walk back to Kansas." Savage checked around his vehicle to see if they had any "unwanted guests" in the area. To his relief there were none, and he was happy to see the other NCOs perched in their turrets doing the same. Everyone had their head on a swivel.

"*Well, you ain't going to like it but it's our best option. Over.*"

"Go ahead and lay it on me, sir. I don't think this day can get much worse."

"*I wouldn't say that. It's still awfully early.*"

***

"Who's the fucking genius that came up with this plan?" Harris sucked on the end of a red rubber hose until a rush of diesel fuel gushed into his mouth, nearly choking him. He pulled it out and jammed it into the plastic jerry can at his feet. He spat out the wretched stuff in disgust, making an awful sound.

"Will you keep your voice down?" Mark scolded. "You know noise attracts those things. Now quit your bitching and let's get this done." On either side of them Dubois pulled guard while Johnson and Gray manhandled fuel cans up the line bucket-brigade style up to the nomex-clad tank crews standing atop their massive battle wagons. Once up top, they'd affix the flexible spigots and dump the precious liquid into their empty fuel cells.

Down the line Staff Sergeant Bates had 3rd Squad siphoning diesel from another eighteen-wheeler abandoned fifty yards down the line. Instead of lugging the cans by the handles, he ordered his people to put them in empty rucksacks in order to move them more easily. Mark felt dumb for not thinking of that as well while Sergeant Medicine Bear and PFC Weber brushed past them.

"Sorry, Sarn't," Harris whispered hoarsely, spitting some more onto the ground, his face contorted in a pained expression. He looked over just beyond the M-1s to the Bradleys parked one behind the other. Donahue stood up in the gunner's hatch next to Sergeant Chamberlain and waved at him sarcastically. Harris stuck up his middle finger in response which elicited a Cheshire grin from the other. "How come we don't just fill these cans up at one of the gas stations we passed along the way to get here? All the juice we need is sitting in any one of them."

Mark rolled his eyes and shook his head. "Because with the power grid down, the pumps won't work. And until we can get our hands on a generator, this is our best option."

"I guess." He looked over at the Bradleys parked a short distance away. "Why am I stuck down here on this shit detail while Donahue and Burbey get to sit their fat asses on the track? They never do anything and get away with bloody murder."

It was Dubois' turn to shake his head. "You know the track crews never dismount unless they absolutely have to. They's allergic to work. Plus, the two of them are known homosexuals." He shifted his weight from one knee to the other while watching carefully for any movement. He then patted the pocket on his left shoulder, checking to see if he had any cigarettes left.

"Is that true?" Harris broke his concentration from the fuel can with a surprised expression on his face. He nearly pulled the hose out unintentionally. "It might explain some things. Wait, no they're not. Didn't Donahue just marry that stripper from Junction City?"

"Yeah, man. But that don't mean he don't like to go both ways." He lit a menthol and took a deep drag before stuffing the pack back into his pocket.

"Will you two cool it? We've got work to do and you can bullshit later." Mark checked his watch and noted that they'd been at this for nearly an hour. It was a slow-go affair and his nerves got a little more frayed with each passing minute. Filling up tanks and Brads one jerry can at a time was glacially slow and the platoon was spread thin, working while maintaining a secured perimeter. *At this rate, it'll be nightfall before we get the vics topped off*, he thought to himself, watching the tankers haul up another hard plastic container.

The early morning sun warmed their faces and woke them up from their drowsiness but Mark knew in a couple of hours it was going to get miserably hot again. He did a mental inventory of their water supplies because it wasn't going to be too much longer before they needed to begin worrying about that as well. Then, in mid-thought, a familiar steady drumming sound grew louder from the east. Heads turned skyward, some shielding their eyes to see a Blackhawk helicopter making its approach toward them.

The chopper came straight toward the soldiers and they all stood, gawking at the aviators flying overhead. It went a short distance off to the west and then circled around them before coming to a hover. The markings on the tail clearly identified it as belonging to the Missouri Army National Guard.

Without any warning, the co-pilot tossed a water bottle from the window and it fell to the earth only a few feet away from Mark and his team. Looking up at the helo, the co-pilot gestured down toward the plastic bottle he'd just discarded.

Mark jogged over and quickly saw that there was a note inside. He looked up at the Blackhawk and gave the "thumbs up." The co-pilot reciprocated and the Blackhawk nosed forward, flying away back in the direction it came from.

He unscrewed the cap and tapped the note out to see a message scrawled on a piece of notebook paper. It read: *You people need to get moving. There are thousands of infected headed your way. They'll be on top of you in minutes. Go now. Good luck.*

"Good lord." He stood up and turned to the junior enlisted soldiers who were now looking up at him in confusion. "You two police up the others and get back to the track. Move it!"

Mark took off toward the nearest tank where Lieutenant Baker and Sergeant Savage stood, going over the situation. He had to work his way through the bucket-brigade work detail to them, nearly shoving one of the other NCOs aside as he did so. He was greeted by surprised looks from the two leaders when he waved the piece of paper in front of them. "This is a note from that chopper pilot. We're going to have company real soon and we need to un-ass this place!" He handed the note to the lieutenant watching his eyes grow wide as saucers.

"Yokey, how much diesel did we get?" Baker called out to his gunner who supervised the refueling of the tank. He sat upon a small folding chair perched on the back deck of the vehicle, leaning back with his ankles crossed, his fingers steepled and a bored look on his face.

"We only got about a third of a tank so far. The other crew's about the same. Why, what's up Loo-tenant?"

He turned to the infantry NCO. "Sergeant Savage, how much do you have for the Brads?"

"Almost nuthin', El-Tee. We're running on fumes."

"According to the pilot we've got thousands of those things headed our way right now. We gotta go. Load your people up and follow us. We'll take the lead."

"Where are we going, sir?" Savage unslung his rifle and straightened his chin strap.

"I don't know yet but anywhere is better than here."

A sickly howl echoed from down the road, quickly joined in by others. From the top of the trail Bradley a couple of rifles barked, then several more punctuated by the sound of men barking orders. In a matter of seconds, the howls grew into thousands of cries.

Baker looked to the two other NCOs. "Time's up, let's roll!"

Chapter 10

0813 Hours Local
Day Two of the Outbreak

The soldiers scrambled back into their vehicles, tossing their fuel cans aside. Rifles cracked and popped, burning through their precious, dwindling supply of ammunition, firing into a charging mass of infected humanity. Some of the dead fell from the carefully aimed fire, trampled under the feet of hundreds of others streaming in from behind.

The turbines of the tanks came to life while the Bradley's engines turned over in quick succession. Lieutenant Baker stood in his hatch, waving to the others to follow while adjusting his crewman's helmet. The tanks launched forward dodging abandoned cars where they could, rolling over and crushing those they couldn't. As much fun as it would have been to simply smash all the cars and trucks, doing so would have run the risk of throwing track and that would have been a fatal mistake with those things swarming them.

The ramps of the Infantry Fighting Vehicles slammed shut with audible "clumps" and they fell in behind the M-1s. The cargo hatches on the back decks were again open with the infantry facing out. They husbanded their rifle rounds, only firing if one of the infected climbed up onto one of the vehicles to protect the vehicle commanders who stood in open hatches in order to effectively see and issue orders.

The mass of undead came at them like a wave breaking at the beach but the tanks plowed through them without slowing down. The creatures fell beneath the steel caterpillar tracks, mashed into pulp instantly, crushed under sixty tons of combat vehicle.

Baker glanced over to see Sergeant Yokey standing up and gazing out from the gunner's hatch, located next to his own. Yokey bore a huge, shit-eating grin.

Yokey toggled the intercom key. "I guess this is why they call 'em 'crunchies,' right, sir?"

"You need to seek professional help. You know that?" Baker shook his head, pulling a pair of Nomex gloves on his hands before adjusting his map board in front of him.

"Hey, sir, you ever heard of the old punk band *Method of Destruction*?"

"No. Why do you ask?"

"Because they had this song called *Hate Tank*."

"You're going to sing it for me now, aren't you." It was a statement rather than a question. Yokey was always bringing up dumb shit at the most inappropriate times.

When you see it coming, the shit runs down your leg
A rumble of disaster, it's much too late to beg
You didn't heed its warning, as it's parked up on your house
Your baby's crushed to pulp, you're cornered you cry out
The Hate Tank... The Haaate Tank
The Hate Tank, THE HATE—TANK!

Baker rubbed his eyes, listening to Yokey's terrible singing voice assault his tortured ears. He held up a gloved hand to stop him from doing any more. It was like listening to a baboon fucking a house cat on a hot metal roof. "Seriously? You're making this shit up."

"No, sir. Honest, it's a real song. They got another real good one about A.I.D.S. You should hear it sometime."

"Okay, dude, I get the picture. Remind me never to go to a karaoke bar with you. Like, ever."

***

First Sergeant Landreau rocked back and forth inside the M-113 Armored Personnel Carrier. The lights were on and he studied a map while listening to the radio chatter coming across the net. They'd made significant progress after hours of frustration and managed to make link-up with several platoons from the battalion, re-supplying them before moving on.

He chafed at the insult to his ego after the colonel chewed him out and threatened to relieve him. It didn't help that Major Fuentes was riding along, embedded in their column, micro-managing the operation. He didn't need any of these overbearing officers looking over his shoulder and telling him what to do. All officers did anyway was make more work for them, and frankly he was getting sick of it.

The two other platoons managed to consolidate and even scrounge a little fuel. They reported massive numbers of infected in their area with most in pursuit. Major Fuentes was basically commanding the battalion reserve now, with Landreau and his headquarters element just along for the ride until they linked up with the rest of Bravo Company. Then he'd get dropped off with them consolidating all of the surviving company elements back together again, minus their 3rd Platoon who would remain the battalion reserve for the time being.

"Battle Axe Seven, this is Red One. Can you read me? Over."

"Red One, this is Axe Seven. Got you Lima Charlie. What's your situation? Over?"

"We've been forced to retrograde from our position due to a large number of—not sure what to call 'em—infected? Over."

The colonel made it clear that Lieutenant Baker was now in command of the company since he was the last surviving officer. It was bullshit of course, since Baker was a tanker and his platoon was only temporarily attached to the company. The kid shouldn't have been put in charge, *he* should have been in command as the senior Non-Commissioned Officer. "Roger, we are five minutes out from the Logistics Release Point. Do you anticipate any issues getting to the LRP? Over."

"We're barely limping along and almost out of gas but we'll make it. Over."

"Roger, see you soon. Battle Axe Seven. Out."

***

Major Fuentes leaned up against his Humvee and set his helmet on the hood. He let out a loud yawn before digging in a pouch hanging off his kit and retrieving a pack of chewing gum. He'd been a smoker in his younger years but managed to quit after several attempts. Being in full kit under field conditions always brought back the old urge to smoke but he fought it back with gum. Grape flavor was his favorite.

He was happy they'd managed to get two of the companies resupplied and linked back up. It had been a hell of a challenge, particularly with the colonel's orders to minimize the number of infected casualties but they'd figured it out. They still had to cap a few here and there but it wasn't as bad as he'd feared. Now all he had to do was get Bravo and Alpha companies squared away and then they could move on to the next event. And Brigade was already loading them up with missions.

The massive fuel trucks lined up in a row and their crews busied themselves pounding in grounding stakes and prepping for a "hot refuel." They'd done it countless times at home station and at the National Training Center at Fort Irwin, California. This would be more of the same, only in an urban environment.

Off to the side the Distribution Platoon stacked crates of small-arms ammunition and began the process of breaking them down. They'd keep this operation moving as fast as possible, handing over ammo cans while the tracks and tanks topped off. The occasional rifle shot along their hastily established perimeter told him that they had no time to waste, and if the experiences earlier in the day were any indication, there'd be a mob of infected on them if they lingered at the LRP for too long.

Glancing over to the other end of the site, First Sergeant Landreau and his company headquarters laagered. He couldn't wait to get that sonofabitch out of his hair. The guy really chapped his ass.

"Sir, it's Battle Axe Six, he says they are one minute out," said Fuentes' driver, leaning out the window of his Humvee.

"Okay, tell him to bring his people into the LRP. We're all set up and waiting for him. Tell him this is a hot refuel and they need to make it quick." Fuentes put his helmet back on and adjusted his body armor, looking up at the sky. There wasn't a cloud in it and temperatures were already hot. He could feel the sweat trickling down the small of his back.

"Roger, I'll let them know."

"First Sergeant, your people are one minute out. Get ready to make link-up," Fuentes shouted over to Landreau, who simply nodded in acknowledgement.

***

North Flora Avenue
North of Northgate Park
0930 Hours Local

The Bradleys ran out of fuel shortly after pulling out of the checkpoint. They managed to get enough distance between themselves and their flesh-eating pursuers to buy them a little time. Crews and dismounts hit the ground running and set to work hooking up heavy steel tow bars, attaching the Infantry Fighting Vehicles to the tanks. Each of the tanks now towed two Brads in tandem, driving carefully so as not to bend or snap the fragile linkages, for if they did, they'd have to leave the valuable piece of equipment behind. They had to drive slow—too slow for anyone's comfort--but they were also too close to the LRP to leave anything behind now.

Mark stood on the bench seat in the troop compartment, staring out over the side of the track, watching and scanning through the optic of his weapon. It wasn't much different from his first combat deployment in Iraq when he was a brand-new private. The looks, smells and sounds brought all sorts of unpleasant memories flooding back. Of course, none of them were nearly as unpleasant as the new memories he'd been making in the last couple of days.

They wanted to take the highways and major thoroughfares but they were all a total mess. It was much quicker and easier to negotiate the side streets and lesser avenues but the going was slow. And the problem was, it didn't matter how fast or slow you drove the tanks, those turbines burned through fuel at the same rate—roughly three gallons per mile. So faster definitely would have been better.

Rolling through business districts and residential areas certain common themes played out. Mark and the others tried their best to ignore the corpses littering the sidewalks, yards and parking lots along the way. Clouds of flies gathered around and turkey vultures circled overhead in some places. As unpleasant as that was, at least it was reassuring when the corpses didn't awaken from death's slumber and come after them, giving chase.

They also saw hastily hand-crafted signs everywhere indicating that there were survivors. Spray-painted bed sheets and walls were marked with, "SOS," or "Alive Inside," or even "Help Us!" Scores of people leaned out of second and third-story windows calling out to them as they drove by, begging them to stop and take them but there was nothing they could do for them. The men and women in uniform turned their eyes away from the desperate survivors, scanning their lanes and looking for threats.

Often, one or more of the infected would catch sight of them and give chase. They usually didn't present an immediate threat so the soldiers ignored them and drove on.

Their column rolled through a suburb headed southbound toward the Logistics Release Point established in one of the local parks. Off on a side street running parallel to their own Mark and Gray caught sight of a pickup truck moving along at high speed. In the bed were two men keeping one hand on the roll-bar to steady themselves, while holding rifles in the other. Seeing the military vehicles, they quickly peeled away, putting as much distance as possible between themselves and the military convoy.

"We've been seeing pickup trucks and SUVs all morning cruising around but whenever they see us, they haul ass. Why do you suppose that is?" Gray peered down through the optic mounted to the feed tray cover on her M249 Squad Automatic Weapon. The bipod legs were folded underneath and the weapon rested on the top deck of the Bradley, facing out. She had a rifle magazine inserted into the backup mag well, and with fewer than ten rounds of ammo left, she'd be lucky if she got off more than two bursts before she was out.

"That's because they are out scrounging for supplies. With the grid down, the stuff in their refrigerators and freezers will be used up or spoiled within a couple of days. Maybe sooner in this heat. They're all out grabbing as much water and non-perishable food they can find." Mark wiped a bead of sweat from the tip of his nose and felt the familiar trickle down the crack of his ass.

"Why are they running from us then?" Gray stood on top of a case of MREs sitting on the bench seat below so she could stand high enough to see over the side of the track.

"They think we'll arrest or shoot them for looting. That's why." The bill of his patrol cap rubbed up on his ballistic glasses uncomfortably, so he pushed it back a bit, exposing his forehead. The breeze at least kept the glasses from fogging up too badly. "Frankly, if I were in their shoes, I'd be doing the same thing. Policing up as much food and water as possible, then hunkering down for the long haul."

"What about the civilians we keep passing in the buildings waving and shouting at us?"

"Those people are waiting to be rescued. There are basically two types of people running around out there now. The people waiting for help to arrive, and those that are organizing, helping themselves and their neighbors. Care to place a bet on which type survives the longest?" Mark smirked, though the smile did not reach his eyes.

"Do you think we'll get things back under control soon?"

"I hope so, Gray. I sincerely do."

***

To his right they passed a sign that read "North Highland Ave" and the small column threaded the needle between two apartment complexes. All of the dismounts carefully scanned as they passed through, having seen many creatures dart out from dozens of places like this all morning. They'd also dealt with a few random civilian snipers along the way which was also nice. As Team Leader he was painfully aware that each of them had fewer than five rounds of ammunition apiece, having expended nearly everything else and cross-leveling what remained. They were in no shape to get caught up in another running gunfight.

Up ahead things opened up and there were woods on either side of the road. Leaning over the side he could just make out the first of a series of large Army trucks, parked neatly in a row. All of them accompanied by soldiers milling around.

They'd finally reached the LRP.

Sergeant Chamberlain leaned over the bustle rack and hollered down at Mark. "Matthews, we're nearly there. When we stop, I need you to get everyone moving with a purpose. Load up the ball ammunition first, then the link, then water and food, in that order. We ain't got a lot of time. Got it?"

"Roger!" With Rash dead, Mark assumed the position of second-most senior NCO in the squad, making him the de facto assistant Squad Leader. Since Chamberlain would be busy with refueling the track, Mark needed to police up the dismounts and get everything else. He knew with all the racket they were making and the number of infected that had been chasing them, along with their slow speed, they didn't have the luxury of lingering around any longer than they had to. They had to get out of there, wham, bam, thank you ma'am.

Moments later their vehicle eased to a halt next to one of the large green, Army refuelers. The fuel handlers, clad in their camouflage Nomex uniforms immediately ran out the hoses handing the nozzles to the crews. Troop doors loudly creaked open and the dismounts spilled out, shuffling off toward the Support Platoon who were already grabbing green metal cans loaded full of 5.56 and 7.62 NATO.

"All right you guys, let's go," Mark said, practically pushing the dismounts out of the track. They jogged across the road to the Humvees and trailers along with other light trucks with their bounty stacked neatly behind them. Off to the side the sheriff's deputies and civilian stragglers dismounted as well. The law enforcement officers pitched in to lend a hand while the civvies stood around, doing their best not to get in the way but not wandering off too far. They had no intention of being left behind.

Track and tank crews set to work unhooking and re-securing the tow bars while the dismounts went after ammo, water and food. In that order. Each of them grabbed an ammo can in each hand and ran back to the tracks, then raced back over. Some of the Support Platoon soldiers did the same—all of them working like hell to get the job done fast.

Bags worked with 3rd Squad to carefully move the wounded Missouri Guardsmen, transferring them to a couple of Medevac trucks with bright red crosses painted on the sides. They assisted the one that could walk and carried those that couldn't in litters.

Carnegie had turned off her cell phone in order to save some battery life but now pulled it out to check and see if she had any messages. There were still no bars and no messages waiting for her.

"Still no signal?" Jefferson asked, adjusting his utility belt adorned with handcuffs, pepper spray, radio, taser and sidearm. He slid the nightstick into its ring before pulling on a pair of black leather gloves.

"No. Nothing. I think the cell towers are still down." She turned the phone off again and stuffed it back into a pocket.

Saxon looked up at her lovingly and she petted him gently on the head.

People began emerging from the nearby apartment buildings, some of them armed. They started moving toward the military perimeter in small groups, mostly by family. Sergeant Savage saw them coming and hopped down from his track, walking briskly over to the law enforcement officers.

"Deputies, would you mind helping out with crowd control? We need to keep those people back." It was an order and not a request. Sergeant Savage was busy getting his people synchronized and didn't need a bunch of refugees slowing up the operation. Besides, there wasn't much they could do for them right now.

"Will do, Sarge." Jefferson patted his buddy on the shoulder. "Come on, Martin. Let's go do a little community engagement with the local citizenry."

"I'll stay here with them." Angela Carnegie pointed to the five civilians the soldiers picked up at the strip mall. They never wandered far and had no intention of being left behind. She knelt with one knee on the ground, petting Saxon while he sat there calmly, gently panting.

Mark worked feverishly, snatching up a couple of cans of 7.62 link when he heard a conversation behind him.

"Who's in charge here?"

"Sarn't Savage is but he's over on the tracks with the Squad Leaders, First Sarn't," Harris said. "I guess Sarn't Matthews is senior over here right now."

Mark heard "First Sergeant" and instantly recognized the voice. He stopped in his tracks and the pit of his stomach turned to ice.

"Matthews? Who's that?"

"He's that MP over there, First Sarn't. We picked him up yesterday and he's been helping out ever since."

"Is that so? Introduce me to him."

"Roger, First Sarn't," said Harris.

Mark could hear them approach and the ammo cans

sagged in his hands. His mind raced, trying to figure a way out of this but nothing came to mind. The only thing he could think of was to run. But with only a handful of rounds left for his weapons he wouldn't last long in the city. Plus, his feet suddenly felt like they were full of lead and he could barely move them. He was like a trapped wild animal.

He bent his knees slowly and lowered the cans to the ground, then unsecured the restraint on his holster, freeing up the sidearm.

"Sarn't Matthews, the First Sarn't would like to speak to you," Harris said.

Mark turned around to see the both of them standing there. Landreau's face could not be mistaken for anyone else's with his broken nose and scarred chin. Now his mind was awash with even more unpleasant memories. Ones that he'd never forget.

"Sergeant Matthews, is it? My name is First Sergeant Landreau." He stuck his hand out to shake. He had a smile on his face, making instant eye contact. At first, it didn't immediately register whom he was looking at, it was just another NCO. It took a couple of seconds before the light bulb flickered on and the faint smile melted away. His eyes grew wide, the look of shock washing over his face. "*You!*" He hissed. "*It can't be!*"

Mark's eyes squeezed into slits. "It's been a long time. I see you've been promoted, *First Sergeant*," He heard himself say the words, almost as if disembodied from himself. He stood there with his left hand planted on his hip, while the right rested on the pistol grip of the automatic, still snug in its holster. "You don't look as if you've changed a bit."

Harris looked about as confused as a person could be. "Wait, *you two know each other?*"

Landreau said nothing, his face turning pale. The others didn't notice when his hands began to tremble. His mouth turned to cotton and his Adam's apple danced as he swallowed.

"Oh yes, we know each other. We go back a long time.

Don't we? *First Sergeant?*" Rage swelled in his chest and the veins on his temples throbbed. He had to tamp it down in order to maintain control but it became infinitely more difficult with each passing second. He was a ticking time bomb and was about to blow.

"W…where did you find this man?" Landreau stammered. He quickly wiped away the sweat beading on his upper lip with the back of his hand.

"He showed up at our checkpoint yesterday. We were short-handed so Sarn't Savage asked him to help out." Harris looked back and forth between the other two, offput by the vibe he was picking up. The tension was palpable.

"That's not possible."

"Sure it is, *First Sergeant*. It's just like Harris said." Mark's fingers wrapped around the pistol grip and the M9 slowly began to slide out. He fought the urge to burn the man down right then and there but stopped himself short. It took every fiber of his being. "I've been pitching in and lending a hand."

"This man is a fugitive. He must have escaped somehow. I want you to disarm him immediately and place him under arrest!" Landreau took a step back from Mark, pointing a shaky finger at him.

"First Sarn't, I don't understand." Harris swallowed hard. Around them the men and women continued to work in a frenzy but as the volume in their voices grew, people couldn't help but take notice.

"I gave you an order, Specialist. Now, *do it!*" Landreau reached for his own pistol, clumsily fumbling with the holster. He used both hands trying to free the weapon.

"*Sergeant Savage, Sergeant Chamberlain, you need to come over here right now, I think we've got a problem over here that needs your attention!*" Harris yelled across the way to the two NCOs who were busy herding cats. They looked annoyed, then suddenly concerned when they saw Mark and their First Sergeant squaring off on one another, tensely fingering their sidearms looking like they were about to go full-on "High Noon."

"What the fuck?" Savage said to himself, before turning to his 2nd Squad Leader, standing a few yards away who was helping his crew lash a heavy tow bar to the hull of their Bradley. "Chamberlain, come with me!"

The two NCOs dashed over, coming around both flanks of the two belligerents. Their look of confusion mixed with a sense of growing alarm.

"First Sarn't, is there a problem here?" Savage interjected.

"Yes, you need to place this man under arrest. *Immediately!*" Landreau faced the platoon sergeant with a look of fear that took him by surprise.

"First Sarn't, can you tell me what this is all about?" Savage spoke calmly but he did not take his attention away from the way the two other men gripped their still-holstered pistols. Neither one of them was screwing around and the situation was deadly serious.

"He's a fugitive. Escaped from prison. Disarm him before it's too late!"

"Come on, First Sarn't. Matthews is a prison guard stationed at Leavenworth. He's been working with us for the past day and he's been a huge help. I think there's a misunderstanding here," Chamberlain said soothingly.

"The First Sergeant and I have history together," Mark said, fighting to keep his voice steady. "You see, several years ago, over in Korea, my partner and I busted him hanging out at an off-limits establishment after curfew. We apprehended him after a bit of a scuffle—we may have knocked him around a bit since he didn't want to come quietly—and then turned him over to his chain of command. I heard they took some rank from him over the incident. He's been stalking me on social media ever since, constantly harassing me. I can't believe we've run into each other like this." The words flowed smoothly. He ad-libbed the story as best he could, improvising and embellishing along the way, hoping the yarn he weaved seemed convincing enough.

"That's his problem with me, plain and simple. He wants payback."

"That's a lie! *I'll fucking kill you!*" Landreau snapped, yanking the handgun from its holster.

Savage pounced on the First Sergeant, wrapping his arms around him and spinning him away, careful to keep the weapon pointed in a safe direction. The fireplug-shaped platoon sergeant held onto him like steel bands around the staves of a wooden barrel. Strong as an ox, Landreau could not break free no matter how hard he tried.

"*Let go of me you sonofabitch!*" Landreau thrashed about helplessly, squirming and flailing while Savage leaned back, picking him off the ground.

Chamberlain flashed a hand onto Mark's shoulder, holding it firmly but not hard. He used just enough force to get the man's attention, to let him know that this was as far as he was willing to let things escalate, and not one bit further. "Steady, Matthews. We don't need this right now. We got bigger fish to fry."

Mark watched Savage wrestle Landreau, dragging him off while trying to talk sense into him. He felt the firm hand on his shoulder and looked at Chamberlain and after a moment as if a trance were broken, his muscles relaxed and he let out a deep breath. "Roger, sarn't. I'm okay."

"You sure? Because a second ago you looked like you were going to shoot the First Sergeant." Chamberlain cocked his head at an angle, giving a quizzical look.

Mark eased the pistol back into the holster and removed his hand, letting it dangle by his side, suddenly conscious of the fact that the entire platoon was staring at them. "I'm good. Thanks for intervening."

"Yeah, no sweat." Chamberlain's hand started kneading Mark's shoulder in an impromptu massage. "Anyway, you need to calm down. Top's a fucking asshole, we all know that but he's still the First Sergeant. Try not to kill him, okay?" His face softened and he cracked a smile. "You wouldn't want to end up locked up back at Leavenworth. I heard the other inmates don't treat former MPs very nicely inside the prison."

Mark returned the smile. "Yeah. I heard that too."

Looking over Chamberlain's shoulder Mark saw Deputy Carnegie standing in the street trying to restrain Saxon. The woman was solidly built and very muscular but she struggled to barely keep him under control. The dog barked like crazy and strained at its leash, coming completely unglued.

***

Sergeant First Class "Bugsy" Siegel carried his weapon at the ready, resting it on top of his magazine pouches affixed to his plate carrier. It was already so hot and humid his ballistic glasses fogged up with each step to the point where he could barely see. Still, he needed to get off the track and stretch his legs in order to wake up. He really felt like he was reaching the end of his endurance and if he didn't catch some shut-eye soon, he might collapse.

He'd set up the platoon in a perimeter next to Northgate Park, straddling the road, surrounding the Support Platoon. His men secured the LRP so the rest of Bravo Company could roll in and top up unmolested. After the disaster at the bridge earlier in the morning, things had gone much smoother. Though with the Colonel's restrictive Rules of Engagement in place, it made things particularly difficult. And it didn't help having the Battalion S-3 and the First Sergeant riding along micromanaging things either.

His Bradleys were spread out with one positioned in each of the cardinal directions. He trudged wearily over to where Bravo 32's position was on the western edge of the perimeter just short of the treeline. The dismounts—few in number now after the morning's fiasco—were spread thin between the vehicles, filling the gaps. Meanwhile, turrets on the IFVs scanned from left to right, looking for potential threats. They hadn't been issued any 25mm auto-cannon rounds for the Bushmasters yet but they did have plenty of ball link for the coaxial machine guns. So at least they had something.

Up ahead Corporal Sparks stood with M-4 carbine in hand, shifting his weight from side to side. He too watched the woodline and was probably at least as tired as the rest of them.

"How's it going, Sparks?" Siegel approached from behind and his voice gave the Corporal a start.

"Oh hey, Sarn't. I'm doing okay." He looked relieved when he saw his platoon sergeant standing there with a sympathetic look on his face. Sparks visibly relaxed after nearly jumping out of his boots. "Is everything going smoothly back there?"

"Best as I can tell. I talked with Sergeant Savage and he said they had some close scrapes over the last twenty-four hours."

"Yeah, well join the club I guess. It's been touch and go for us all day."

"That's for sure." Siegel admired how nice some of the apartments looked adjacent to the park. He couldn't help but notice the crowd of people emerging from them, headed toward their perimeter, many of them clutching weapons of all variety. Two cops emerged from their perimeter and met them half-way, doing their best to keep the people back.

A shouting match erupted in the center of the perimeter and the two of them saw the First Sergeant going off on another soldier they did not recognize. Even from here they clearly saw the "MP" brassard on his arm but had no idea who he was. Whoever the guy was, he had the First Sergeant so worked up that he started reaching for his sidearm.

"What the fuck is going on over there?" Siegel said, under his breath.

The two of them watched while Savage and Chamberlain went over to defuse the situation. Sparks snorted in delight when Savage tackled the First Sergeant and dragged him away.

"What do you suppose that was all about?" Sparks said, bemusedly.

"Fuck if I know, buddy."

"Top looked pissed."

"He sure as hell did. I'm going to have to ask Savage what happened later."

A dog started barking and Siegel turned to see a female sheriff's deputy holding a German Shepherd's leash. The animal pulled as hard as it could and the officer leaned back with her full weight to keep the dog from getting away from her. It was slightly unsettling that the canine strained with every fiber in its being to break free and come straight at Siegel and Sparks.

***

Vanguard Tactical Operations Center (TOC)
0945 Hours Local

Lieutenant Colonel Jerry Hamilton found himself in a foul mood and the Command Sergeant Major tried his best not to agitate the Old Man any more than necessary. The two of them walked briskly toward the TOC, ignoring the soldiers on work details around them snapping to attention and rendering parade-ground salutes.

Hamilton tore open the tent flap and ducked inside with Sergeant Major Yates following right behind him. Inside he found the battalion staffers working hard, processing reports both from their higher headquarters and their subordinate units. The Battle Captain saw them walk in and quickly announced their presence. "*The Battalion Commander!*"

Everyone immediately stood erect, coming to the position of "Attention."

"Carry on," Hamilton said, quickly removing his helmet and setting it down on a field table, nearly knocking over a plastic Coke bottle filled with brown tobacco juice. "XO, give me a quick status update."

The other officers and NCOs in the tent settled back into their chairs, picking up handmikes and tapping away at computer terminals. The Battalion Executive Officer came over, holding a double-hulled metal mug in his hand. He had a five o'clock shadow and dark rings under his eyes.

"XO, you look like shit. When was the last time you got any sleep?" Hamilton plopped down on a folding chair and tugged his Nomex gloves off, tossing them on top of his helmet. He removed his ballistic glasses and vigorously rubbed his eyes.

"I dunno, I don't remember. Maybe last month? I forget. Besides, I probably ought to be asking you the same question." Major Denney took a sip from his mug and winced.

"Noted. Anyway, what's going on?" Sergeant Major Yates brought over two cups of joe and handed one to Hamilton before sitting down next to him.

"Roger, well we've managed to get Charlie and Delta Companies topped off and consolidated at the Charles B. Wheeler Downtown Airport. Bravo Company is now all linked up at the LRP much further to the north at Northgate Park, located here." The XO pointed at the projected image on the left-hand screen dominating the center of the TOC. "Alpha Company has linked up all their platoons near Riverside but they're out of gas. They are standing fast until the S-3 can bring up Distro Platoon. We've got the Scout Platoon and Mortar Platoons back here on the Kansas-side of the river pulling route security and guarding the command nodes. We're about to issue the Warning Order for securing the rail yards, and anticipate transmitting the WARNO at the top of the hour."

"Casualties?" Hamilton blew on the inky-black liquid before daring to take a sip. It was bitter but not burnt, so at least that was something.

"Bad. We've got twenty-three confirmed KIA and another forty-four Missing. On top of that, we've got a dozen wounded. Four shot dealing with criminal elements and one broken arm from falling off a Bradley."

"What about the other seven?"

Denney cleared his throat. "Infected, sir. They've got whatever is burning through the city. I went down to check on them down at the aid station while you were out and…"

"And what?"

"They had them lashed down, and well…" he cleared his throat again. "Well, sir, it ain't pretty."

"I can imagine. Anyway, I…"

"Gentlemen, I have flash traffic from Brigade!" The Battle Captain rushed over to the table and interrupted the briefing, startling the XO and annoying Hamilton. "The Missouri Guard reported thousands—maybe tens of thousands—of the infected are moving in massive groups. They're calling them 'herds.' The general direction of movement is from east heading west."

Hamilton raised his hand to calm the flustered young officer down. "Okay, Randy, take a deep breath. This is somewhat concerning but what's the issue? Our people have their tracks and tanks, so they've got plenty of protection. Why is this such an emergency?"

"Sir, the issue is that orders just came down from Topeka to the Kansas boys. The State Adjutant General ordered that they seal the border and not let anyone across. They are going to drop the remaining bridges over the Missouri River within the hour!"

"What? You're joking!" The XO suddenly seemed very awake.

"No, sir. Division has been trying to get the Kansas TAG on the phone but he refuses to answer. The last thing he said was that until he and his people get mobilized, they take their orders from the Governor and that's what he intends to do. He went on to say that any active-duty units caught on the Missouri-side of the border after that needed to remain there until further notice."

"He can't do that!" The XO blurted out.

"What does Brigade want us to do?" Hamilton got to his feet, spilling his cup of coffee while picking up his gloves and helmet.

"The Brigade Commander hasn't issued any guidance yet. They said to stand by and await further instructions."

Hamilton studied the map. Without bridges nearly his whole battalion would be stuck in the city. They might be able to evacuate them by helicopter but would end up leaving nearly all their equipment behind. Except if they struck north and then west. "Okay, everybody take a deep breath and calm down. If we need to, we can push the companies toward Leavenworth and cross there. They'll have to cover more ground and it'll take a lot longer but it's doable."

The Battle Captain collected himself and lowered his voice but he was still keyed up pretty bad. "Sir, they said that anyone still on the Missouri side after 1130 hours this morning stays over there. No exceptions. They don't want anybody bringing the contagion over here."

"Does the Adjutant General in Kansas know we have tanks? We aren't that easy to stop." Hamilton picked up some paper towels and began cleaning up the spilled coffee.

"The Brigade Commander mentioned that."

"And?"

"And the Kansas TAG said that his people had TOWs and Javelins, with orders to use them."

"He's bluffing," said the XO. "Right?"

There was a long silence while Hamilton pondered what to do. If he pulled them out, then he'd give up the city and it would consume itself in a matter of days. He was still convinced that they'd still find a cure for whatever the infection was, eventually. Letting the infection burn through the entire population however, would make it exponentially harder to help those who were sick—they had to limit the outbreak as best they could. But if he left his people in place, they'd be stuck with dwindling supplies, caught in the middle of the hot zone and he'd probably lose a lot more of them. And while he was pretty sure that the Kansas TAG was bluffing about shooting at his people if they forced a border crossing, he wasn't particularly keen on finding out. Blue on blue was not an option.

The Sergeant Major looked up at his commander, speaking up for the first time since entering the TOC. "Sir, we need to get our people out of there, ricky-tick. Unless Brigade deliberately orders us to hold them in place, then I recommend we go 'Sua Sponte' and redeploy our companies back here. We ain't got a lot of time to think about this. If our people get stuck over there, there's no tellin' how many KIA and MIA we'll have by this time tomorrow. Hell, we might lose the whole battalion."

Hamilton looked down at his Sergeant Major, locking his gaze and saying nothing. The TOC suddenly got very quiet and all eyes were on them. The two stared at one another for a long moment and then he nodded.

"Okay, XO, get on the command net. Order all of our people back, and tell 'em to do it now. There's no time to waste!"

Chapter 11

"Did you see that?" Sparks said, breaking his attention away from a First Sergeant being dragged across a street, while a German Shepherd lost its ever-loving mind.

"See what?" Siegel turned around and caught a glimpse of a silhouette darting between some trees in the park. He squinted to get a better look, then saw a few more. Within the span of a few seconds, it turned into more than he could count. "Oh shit."

In the growing crowd of civilians gathering outside the north side of the perimeter a woman's scream pierced the air, quickly followed up by the popping of gunshots. Panic struck them almost at once and a large group of civilians broke into a stampede, devoid of any order.

Sparks realized what was moving in the treeline, raised his M-4 and opened fire. He dropped to a knee, firing in three-round bursts. Siegel snatched the transmitter of his squad radio and keyed the mic, "Guidons, guidons, this is Blue Four. Contact! Out!"

The coaxial machine gun mounted in the turret of the Bradley off to their left opened up, sending a stream of hot lead into the once-serene park. The jacketed slugs tore into the trees, sheering off limbs and bark, sending splinters of wood flying. All along the line, the dismounted infantry joined in with the fusillade, first as a crackle then as the buzzing of a chainsaw.

It did not deter the dead.

The infected came on in a monstrous mass, locking in on the noise and the smell of living flesh. Scores of them fell under the murderous fire, collapsing onto the manicured grass, falling next to picnic tables and public barbecue grills. On the north side they slammed into the civilians looking for rescue, falling on the men, women and children with ravenous intent. The shrieks and cries from the victims made the soldiers cringe.

Siegel raised his carbine and fired as well, working the

232

trigger like mad. He peered through his Aimpoint optic and did his best to put the shaky red dot on the heads of the snarling beasts. With them moving at a sprint it made getting a bead nearly impossible and he missed nine out of ten times.

He fired until his bolt locked to the rear on an empty magazine. He fingered the release catch and dropped the mag to the ground while snatching another from his load-carrier, in a fluid motion he'd practiced a thousand times. Slamming the magazine home, he loaded another round into the chamber and fired some more, and as their attackers closed in, it became much easier to score killing hits.

Siegel tuned out all of the noise around him, focusing on the task at hand. He fired round after round, dropping one after the other until something hit him from the side.

A woman was on top of him dressed in a business suit, her neck and face a shredded unrecognizable mess. One eye was gone but the other shone red. Her right cheek and lips were largely torn from her face, flapping loosely as chunks of meat, hanging on scraps. But the jaw and the teeth were intact and she opened her mouth to reveal a nearly black tongue, dripping in an oily goo.

He pushed her back, his forearm under her chin, pushing back against her throat. "Sparks, help me!"

He turned his head to see six of the things fall upon Sparks. He punched and he kicked, then yelled in anger before his tone turned high-pitched and guttural.

Then, he felt a sharp vice-like pressure on his neck cutting through his skin.

And in an instant, many more were on him.

***

The people broke into a panic and bolted past Jefferson and White, nearly knocking them over. Some tried to make a break for it, back to their apartments, while others tried to find safety with the soldiers of Bravo Company. They both unslung their long guns and tried to take aim but it was impossible to get a clear shot on anything with the civilians intermixed, running in every direction.

"Come on, man. I think it's time for us to go." Jefferson raised his pistol and aimed it at one of the creatures chasing a young boy. He snapped off several shots and missed, barely able to aim properly at a moving target with the open sights. He winced when the thing grabbed the child and had to turn away, unable to watch.

White fired the Remington 11-87 12 gauge, sending nine lead pellets crashing into the brain-pan of an infected UPS delivery man. The head exploded when all nine pellets hit the skull almost simultaneously, sending shards of bone and brain flying in every direction. He put the bead on another, disintegrating the head of an infected housewife, sending the rest of the carcass rolling into the street.

Jefferson grabbed White by the collar of his shirt. The skinny deputy could barely move his giant partner but it got his attention and broke him from his spell. He nodded to his partner and the two of them proceeded to haul ass.

They didn't make it ten feet before a stray bullet hit Jefferson's leg just above the knee, making a terrible mess of it and sending him crashing to the pavement.

"Oowwwww! Fuck me, I'm hit!" Jefferson's face contorted in pain. He tried to sit up and when he caught sight of the awful wound he nearly passed out.

"I got you, partner, just hang on!" White lifted him with a grunt, pulling him over both shoulders in a fireman's carry.

"Aaaaahhhh, it hurts so fucking bad!"

"Try not to think about it, I'll get you out of here." He shuffled forward, one hand holding his buddy, the other holding the 12 gauge by the receiver. He focused on the soldiers. If he could make it over there just a few yards away, they'd be okay. It was only a little further.

Things were a chaotic mess and now bullets flew in every direction. But if he could just get them both on board one of those Bradleys they'd be okay.

Something hit him in the back. Hard.

Jefferson wailed and White lost his footing, taking a painful face plant into the asphalt. White got back up on hands and knees while Jefferson lay in front of him. Trying to pick his friend back up, he saw the man pointing to something behind him. He turned to find four drooling beasts standing there studying him with those evil eyes. They barely moved after knocking him down, rather, they stood stationary, curious about him.

The shotgun had gone flying and it was too far away so he went for his service pistol. The moment he reached for it the four infected leaped upon him, wildly attacking.

Jefferson went for his pistol and brought it to bear. The weapon shook terribly, barely able to aim with the pain in his leg. He squeezed off the first shot and one of things went limp. The others didn't even notice, too focused on biting and raking White with their nails.

He shot another, then another, and finally finished the last one but it was too late. White bled from multiple wounds, mostly protective in nature.

White sat up, outstretching his arms to inspect the wounds. They were ghastly and he bled like a stuck pig. Then, he struggled back to his feet and clumsily picked Jefferson back up again.

"What are you doing? Aaaahhh… owwwww…." Jefferson still held the Glock 19 in his hand while his friend carried him, shuffling toward the perimeter. There were bites on his legs too and he walked with a terrible limp. It seemed as if his entire uniform was soaked in his own blood.

"Don't worry, partner," he grunted. "I'll get you out of here."

***

The entire outer perimeter from the nine o'clock to twelve o'clock positions erupted in a staccato of gunfire. The cracking of rifles, punctuated by the tearing sound from the coax machine guns on the Bradley Fighting Vehicles.

Major Fuentes supervised the overall operation at the LRP when all hell broke loose. He saw more infected than he could count pouring through their sieve-like outer cordon. They simply didn't have enough people or vehicles to even slow them down. It reminded him of the scene in the movie *Platoon* when the battalion was being overrun. Only right now, he didn't have any air support to "Drop everything on my poz."

Dismounted infantry were going down all along the line and the infected flowed around the Bradleys like water. Over on the hot refuel line, the drivers and fuel handlers scattered, running in every direction. The tank and track crews tossed nozzles to the ground, spilling JP-8 everywhere before wiggling back into their vehicles through open hatches.

"Get to your vehicles and form up! We'll uncoil and head out through the twelve o'clock position," he shouted to nobody in particular. It wasn't like anyone was paying attention to him, the whole site was degenerating into utter pandemonium.

Tank and Bradley commanders stood in their turrets with carbines, shooting the infected off their vehicles while drivers fired up the engines. A driver of a refueling truck climbed into the cab and nearly got the door shut but got yanked out and he fell into the clutches of a group of the crazed beasts, who tore him to pieces. More of the dead clambered into the backs of the field ambulances and began feeding on the wounded National Guardsmen while the medics ran for their lives.

A female sheriff's deputy worked with her K-9 to protect a small group of civilians. The dog launched itself toward the nearest infected that endangered them, latching on with its maw, then the officer would calmly approach and dispatch the creature with a single pistol shot to the head. They did this methodically and as quickly as they could manage, making their way over toward 2nd Platoon who started to move their Bradleys away from the refuelers.

It was complete chaos and Fuentes had to get to a radio,

and quick.

He headed off toward his Humvee parked a short distance away. An unarmed soldier raced past, oblivious of his presence, only to be nearly knocked over by the two of the undead giving him chase. He got maybe ten yards before one of the snarling creatures took notice of him and came on fast. The thing actually spoke to him hissing, "Sssssooooljerrrr!" It sent chills down his spine and he nearly wet himself. Without thinking he shouldered his rifle and put a double-tap into the thing's forehead and it dropped at his feet. He had to shake himself out of it before moving on.

He tuned everything out and focused on his up-armored Humvee just up ahead. The front passenger-side door was open and after what seemed like an eternity, he made it, ducking inside and slamming the door shut. Through the bullet-proof windshield he saw armed civilians and soldiers firing at the infected without regard to each other. It was a Polish firing squad and friendlies shot each other to pieces while the maelstrom swirled around them.

Over to his left, his driver rested his helmeted head against the glass of the driver's-side window. It was a hell of a time to be taking a nap.

"Brewster! Brewster, wake up!"

The driver did not stir.

Fuentes reached over and shook him. "Wake up damnit! We need to start rolling, right now!"

Brewster slowly turned to face the officer, revealing a bite mark on his left cheek. Fuentes gasped when he saw the spiderwebbed veins on his skin, the blueness of his lips and the blood-red eyes.

"Rrrrrooojjjeerrrr, ssssssirrrr," it said, before lunging at him. Brewster moved in a flash, faster than Fuentes had ever seen him move before. The young infected soldier came straight at him, trying to get over the radio stack that separated the two of them. Luckily, the driver's seatbelt held him in place, and he clawed at the major in vain.

The Operations Officer jerked backward with a start. He

pushed himself back as the hands reached out trying to grab him and pull him toward those wicked teeth. He fumbled with the release catch on the door and finally got it. The door flung open with his weight pressed up against it, and he fell to the ground, onto his back. He crab-walked backwards, doing his best to put distance between himself and the thing that used to be his driver. He made it a few yards and then stopped, barely conscious of the madness playing out around him.

His chest heaved and his mouth was dry. A thousand mental images flashed in his mind and he did everything he could to get a grip on himself. Then, just as he began regaining his wits, he heard a high-pitched growling, much akin to a puppy's.

He looked up to see a little girl, not more than five-years-old staring down at him. Her blonde hair was matted in blood, with dark, oily saliva running down her chin. The redness of her eyes made her look like the spawn from hell.

Fuentes reached for his rifle only to realize that it was still sitting in the Humvee.

The child pounced on him, sinking her tiny incisors into his arm, slicing through the fabric of his uniform and puncturing the skin.

His howls of pain were drowned out in the cacophony that enveloped them.

***

Yokey and Baker dropped down into the massive turret and pulled their CVCs over their ears. They dropped in so quickly, Yokey nearly landed on top of his loader. The driver pulled down his hatch with an audible "clunk" and fired up the turbine with a high-pitched whine.

"Aronson, tell me you got the coax up," Baker said, plugging his crewman's helmet into the spaghetti cable hanging next to him. He adjusted the seat so he could stand on it at "nametape-level" outside the hatch. He adjusted the leather chest-holster that held his empty 9mm pistol.

"Negative, sir. We were too busy topping off and unhitching the tow bars from the baby tanks. We didn't get a chance to grab any ammo." Aronson looked sheepish, bracing himself for the inevitable ass-chewing.

"Good job, dipshit. You're a loader with nothing to load. What good are you?" Yokey was quick to hand out the tongue-lashings. It may have been the lieutenant's platoon but it sure as shit was Yokey's tank, and he didn't have a whole lot of patience when the crew failed to do the right thing. "I should make you get out and fucking walk."

Baker toggled the intercom. "You up, Cooper?"

"Roger, sir. Everything's good to go. Where shall I take our chariot?"

"Good question. Stand by." Lieutenant Baker swept the area with his gaze, trying to take it all in. It was a fucking mess and people were all over the place, and it didn't look like anyone was in control. Largely because there wasn't. He keyed the transmit button on his radio. "Guidons, guidons. This is Red One. Everybody mount up, we're pulling out in one mike. Over."

Yokey popped his head up from the loader's hatch located right next to the tank commander's. He rested a hand on the M-240 machine gun secured in its pintle mount. It was nothing more than a useless boat anchor without any ammunition. He whistled and shook his head. "Well, this is nice. Any idea what we're going to do, El-Tee?"

"We're going to do what we always do." Baker looked over at his gunner and lowered a pair of goggles over his eyes. He always wore an olive drab cravat around his neck, fashioned into a bandana, cowboy-style. He pulled it up to cover his nose and mouth.

"You mean we're just going to make it up as we go along?"

"Yeah, something like that." He pointed to the western woodline where the infected continued to emerge from. "We need to do something about that and take some pressure off the grunts so they have time to get on their tracks. But we don't have any working weapons."

"Oh, I wouldn't say that." A shit-eating grin grew from ear to ear.

Baker sighed. "You thinking what I'm thinking?"

"Yup. It's crunchie-time."

"Cooper, did you monitor?"

"As if I were sitting next to you, m'lord."

"Okay then, driver, move out." Baker waved over to the other tank crew, signaling them to follow. The Tank Commander nodded in understanding.

The two armored behemoths lurched forward and drove straight into the park, right at the mass of infected humanity. They moved out at a deliberate speed, turning into the larger clusters, smashing them into the neatly manicured grass. The giant steel caterpillar tracks mangled flesh and infected bone, while tearing up the soft terrain, leaving bloody, gory indentations in their wake.

They worked in a pattern, moving back and forth, passing in front of the breached perimeter, doing their best to take the pressure off the beleaguered grunts. Then, all of a sudden without any warning, Baker's ears were assailed by Yokey's awful singing voice.

Its treads are stained with blood
Of victims who had pride
Some thought they'd defy it
All of them have died
Destruction in its wake
The mangled corpses rot
If you think you'll survive… NOT!
The Hate Tank
The Hate Tank
The Hate Tank
The Hate Tank!

***

"Come on you guys, get the lead out!" Mark double-fisted cans of 7.62 link, his rifle slung across his back, egging on the other members of the squad. Sergeant Chamberlain released the First Sergeant. Landreau took one look at the oncoming wave of the dead and bolted like a scalded cat.

The things came on running flat out. Some had no shoes and ran on bloody feet, leaving crimson footprints in their wake. They made all sorts of noises but the animalistic howl drove a spike of fear into the living's very souls.

Johnson took a knee, rubbed his "Thor's Hammer" pendant for luck, then steadied himself and paused between breaths before taking his first shot. He took aim at one chasing a truck driver from the Distribution Platoon. He slowly squeezed the trigger, surprised by the crack of the report. The creature's head snapped back and tumbled to the pavement. The driver didn't even bother to look back and kept on running.

"Nice, you must have rolled a Nat 20. You suppose these zombies are controlled by a necromancer? Or do you think this a product of the fade, or maybe a death curse?" Dubois crouched down next to his friend and snapped off a couple of rounds, stopping a couple more who were feeding on one of the medics who'd finally stopped thrashing about.

"I'd say necromancer is a possibility but do you think it's an epic level, or do you think he has some friends? Because this is more than one casting's worth and he's controlling it. Huh, you think the chaplain can turn undead?"

Gray came down with a thud next to them and set her SAW up on its bipod. "Are you two idiots actually talking about Dungeons and Dragons at a time like this?" She put her optic on a cluster rounding the platoon sergeant's Bradley. Her weapon spat jacketed slugs in short bursts, cutting them down, dropping them in their tracks.

Chamberlain fired his weapon on the run, engaging at point-blank range so he wouldn't miss. He was clearing a path while Mark followed close behind, headed straight for the track with the name "BOHICA" stenciled on the TOW launcher. Up in the gunner's hatch, Donahue fired his carbine rapidly, sending a steady stream of spent brass flying, pirouetting to the earth.

The tanks were running amok, grinding the dead into mush, running parallels along the western side of the perimeter. The dismounted infantry was scattered all over the place and unsynchronized. Some were mounting the tracks, others tried to hold their ground. Nobody appeared to be overall in charge.

Chamberlain slapped a fresh mag into his weapon and popped two infected in the head who ran at him with hands outstretched. He never slowed down and hopped over the two motionless corpses while pressing on. When he reached the front slope of his IFV, he dropped his carbine, letting it hang limply by the sling. With both hands he grabbed the armor side plating and stuck his foot in the steel stirrup located there, expressly for that purpose. As he lifted himself to the front slope of the vehicle three of the dead came around from the far side of the vehicle and lunged at him. They got hold of his legs and yanked them out from beneath him, making him land face-first on the track. He clawed at the armored engine compartment, feverishly grasping for a handhold that wasn't there. In the span of a second, he was on the ground and they were on top of him. He made an awful gurgling sound after one of the things tore out a chunk of his throat.

Mark was only a few feet away when he watched Chamberlain go down. He stopped and immediately tossed the ammo cans up onto the back deck and clambered up the side after them. He spared a quick look down at the Squad Leader and then looked away. It was not a pretty sight. Then he reached for his AR-15 and carefully aimed. He squeezed the trigger three times, barely noticing the loud "pop, pop, pop." The infected lay sprawled out on top of the NCO who looked up at Mark with a pleading look in his eyes, blood gushing from his nose, mouth and the wicked wounds covering his body.

Mark swallowed hard, took a deep breath and then settled the red dot on Chamberlain's forehead. He pulled the trigger and then turned away, squeezing his eyes shut.

When he opened them again he saw Harris running up, while the others covered him.

"Give me your hand!" Mark reached down and Harris grabbed it. He pulled with all of his strength, and managed to help him up. "Lay down some covering fire for the others and help them up too!"

"Roger, Sarn't!" Harris brought his Squad Automatic Weapon up and hammered away. Links and brass showered the top deck while he pushed back the oncoming onslaught with hot lead. When the others saw Mark waving them on, they began leapfrogging forward, two laying down supporting fire while the others moved up, just like they'd been taught at Fort Benning.

Mark climbed up onto the turret paying no attention to Donahue standing there in the hatch, plugging away, running through mag after mag. He dropped the ammo cans inside the Bradley Commander's station, then lowered himself down after them.

Ripping open the sealed metal cans, he pulled out the linked ammunition and settled them into the hopper on the right side of the turret, linked all of the rounds together into a single belt, then ran it into the feed chute. Struggling with some of the battle-tracking gear, he finally got the coax doors open to reveal the weapon. He wormed his arms into the tight space and opened the feedtray cover, then slid the linked ammunition in place. Once done, he slapped the cover closed and pulled the charging cable, locking the bolt to the rear, ready to fire. Then he closed the doors up and secured everything in place.

The engine was idling so he knew the driver was probably okay. He pulled on the Combat Vehicle Crewman's helmet and toggled the intercom. "Driver, are you up?"

"Roger, I'm good. Who's this?" Came Burbey's puzzled response.

"It's Sergeant Matthews. Are you ready to roll?" Mark flipped the switch turning the turret power on before disengaging the locks. He punched the button marked "coax" and armed it, then peered through the commander's sight, grabbing the override joystick located to his right.

"Where's Sergeant Chamberlain?"

"He's dead. I'm in charge." Mark grasped the controller while looking through the sight. He scanned the turret to the west, seeing hundreds of the undead headed their way. The tanks drove past, turning many of them into mush but there were far too many for them to deal with, and they were spread all over hell's half-acre.

He zeroed in on the infected closest to the vehicle that made it through the tanker's grisly gauntlet. He squeezed the trigger and felt a slight sense of elation when the coaxial machine gun roared to life. He was careful to take headshots and was grateful that the weapon had been properly bore-sighted. He swept the turret left and right, slicing through the waves of undead, stacking their motionless carcasses in steadily-growing windrows.

Unable to ignore the moving turret and the suddenly active coax machine gun, Donahue lowered himself into the turret to see what the hell was going on. He looked on in shock while Mark aimed and fired the weapon, wreaking utter havoc. He clicked on the intercom. "Sarn't, you want me to take over?"

Mark looked over to see Donahue sitting in the gunner's seat, staring over at him with an incredulous look on his face. "Yeah, take over." He gave the hopper a quick glance. "I burned through about half the ammo. You have another 400 rounds left. Keep those fucking things back so we can get the dismounts loaded. Got it?"

"Got it." Donahue settled in and peered through his gunner's sight and took over, letting fly with streams of hot death. "You mind telling me how you know your way around a Bradley turret? This is obviously not your first time in one." He loosed another burst, tearing three of the infected nearly in half.

"Long story. I'll tell you later." Without another word he took off his helmet, climbed back out of the hatch, and stood on top of the rotating turret, taking a moment to survey the situation.

The track on the western part of the cordon belonging to 3rd Platoon sat stationary, spraying the park wildly with coax. It was swarmed with infected, like ants covering a juicy grub. Fortunately, the entire crew was buttoned up inside and completely safe. He couldn't see anything wrong with the running gear, so it appeared they were capable of moving out under their own power any time they wanted to.

On the north side, the dead intermixed with panicked civilians and a gruesome fight was playing out, and even though many of the civilians were armed, they were losing. Badly.

Inside the perimeter all order had broken down. The members of the Distribution Platoon cut and ran, leaving idling trucks, weapons and other equipment scattered all about. An M-88 recovery vehicle's massive engine roared, belching thick, black smoke from its exhaust manifold. It cruised casually through the area with a squad of infantry sitting on top, shooting down the dead and racking up an impressive body count.

The company command element sat motionless around the First Sergeant's track. All of them huddled inside their vehicles, locked up tight, contributing absolutely nothing to the fight. Mark couldn't see him but he knew Landreau must have been buttoned up snug as a bug inside his M-113, completely safe and sound. *I swear to god, if I had any armor-piercing rounds for the 25mm Bushmaster, I'd fucking blow that track in place and send that sonofabitch straight to hell where he belongs*, Mark thought to himself, looking down at the silent auto-cannon conspicuously sticking from the turret of their Bradley.

A bullet smacked the armored turret right next to his foot and ricocheted off harmlessly. Mark crouched low, suddenly very aware that there was no fire discipline anywhere and people were shooting all over the place, and sometimes at each other. *We need to get this clusterfuck under control, and right now.*

Something hairy caught his eye down below, near the back deck. Emerging into view came the muzzle of a German Shepherd. The look in its eyes betrayed its fear as the animal wasn't accustomed to being lifted up off the ground but somebody down below was definitely hoisting him up.

Mark slid down to lend a hand but was interrupted by a shout.

"Don't touch him! He bites!" Underneath the dog, Deputy Carnegie pushed the dog up onto the top of the IFV. She pushed him up from behind, with his tail tucked firmly between his legs. The animal was as formidable and fierce as any of them had ever seen but right now being lifted up off the ground he looked like a frightened puppy.

Standing behind Carnegie were the five civilian refugees they had rescued at the strip mall the previous day. The man named Roberts with the Mini 14 guarded their rear while the others climbed up on the track.

Harris pulled up the girl named Consuela and eased her down into the troop compartment through the open cargo hatch, then reached down for the other teenage girl while her parents watched in the other direction, their weapons drawn. The Hispanic boy helped lift Bailey Roberts up to Harris, and once the second girl was secure, the soldier put out a hand to the teenage boy who couldn't speak a word of English.

Coming up fast came Gray and Johnson, while Dubois pulled up the rear. They helped the last of the civilians and then each other, drilling a couple of the dead that got a little too close for comfort.

On the next track over, Sergeant Savage motioned off to the north with a knife-hand, indicating his desired direction. Mark nodded and gave the thumbs-up, then lowered himself back into the turret, putting the CVC back on his head.

"Nearly black on ammo, Sarn't." Donahue didn't look

up, his head resting on the brow-pad, gazing through the sight. He worked the gun controls with both hands, completely focused on the task at hand.

"Shit, alright. We'll see if we can get back over to the pallets of ammo stacked behind the trucks." Mark looked over and saw numerous infected between them and their cache. But it didn't seem like something they couldn't fight their way through. As bad as it was, it did look manageable. "Okay, on my order we'll drive over, then we'll clear everything around it and grab some ball and link, smash and grab style. Got it?"

"Roger," said Burbey, who started revving the engine.

"Driver, move out."

The Bradley took a hard left, pivot-steering away from the refueling truck. Burbey changed gears and the track lurched forward covering the distance in seconds, grinding one of the undead into the pavement along the way.

Mark leaned over the bustle rack, and shouted down at the passengers in the troop compartment through the open cargo hatch. "Okay, we are going to stop next to Distro Platoon's vics. When we stop, you're going to get out and toss in as many cans of ammo as possible while me and Donahue cover you. Understood?"

There were eight nods of understanding, two sets of confused looks, and one hairy individual who panted with his tongue hanging out.

In the time it took to issue his instructions, the vehicle crossed the road and pulled up next to the cache of green metal cans, neatly stacked on top of wooden pine pallets. "You ready, Donahue?"

"Roger that, sarn't."

"Let's do this."

Mark and Donahue wiggled their way up through their hatches with their rifles and immediately started engaging the dead. There weren't too many in the immediate vicinity so they managed to clear them in short order.

"Driver, drop ramp!" Mark changed magazines and

scored a lucky shot on a runner who seemed a little too interested in them. Luckily for them, most of the undead focused on the civilians and Distro Platoon soldiers running around. They were much easier prey.

The ramp whined as it lowered, then came to a rest with a deep thunk. The passengers in back poured out and grabbed olive drab cans, tossing them inside the Bradley. There was no time for neatness or finesse, and they handled the things roughly.

Saxon stood sentinel with the hair on his shoulders standing straight up, growling but not venturing far from Carnegie. Though they didn't understand the instructions, the two teenagers named Angel and Consuela quickly figured out what was going on and pitched in, tossing cans of ball and link like the others. Meanwhile, Mark and Donahue fired their rifles like mad as more and more of the infected became interested in their little operation. They kept it up for a short while but they began to draw a crowd. The kind of crowd you didn't want to draw.

"Last mag!" Shouted Donahue. He dropped all of his empties inside the turret. He didn't want to lose any because it was hard to say when they might get a fresh supply of magazines if they tossed them away.

"Me too!" Mark said. He leaned back over the back of the turret again. "Everybody back inside. *Now!*" The motley group charged back up the heavy armored ramp and when the last one was clear, he gave the order. "Driver, raise the ramp."

Without a word it came back up. Burbey gunned the engine to make the motor work faster and it closed with a loud thud, followed up by the clicks of the locking mechanism falling into place.

One of the dead pulled itself up onto the front deck of their track, locked onto Mark with its awful eyes. He lowered his AR-15 and fired but the round impacted in the thing's shoulder, affecting it not at all. The bolt locked back to the rear on an empty magazine, his last one. The creature scurried up toward him at lightning speed and he almost didn't have time to unholster his sidearm. It took him three rounds of panic fire before he landed one in the thing's face. It slumped back down, falling wetly on a few rolls of concertina wire lashed to the engine compartment.

The company command frequency crackled to life with the voice of Sergeant First Class Savage. *"Guidons, guidons. Police up everyone you can and mount 'em up. We roll in one mike. All stations acknowledge."*

"White Four, this is Bravo Two-Three. Over." Mark surveyed the area and the dead were thinning out. The surviving civilians scattered, drawing away most of the infected with them. The few that remained were getting steadily swatted down by increasingly accurate fire from grunts perched atop their tracked vehicles.

"Send it." Savage sounded exasperated and in little mood for argument.

"We've nearly got things back under control here. There are cargo trucks, fuelers, and equipment lying all over the place. There's probably personnel from the Distro Platoon hiding out around here. I think we should secure the area, search for survivors and police up any equipment and rolling stock we can before moving out."

"No time for that. The last bridge in our sector is getting rigged to blow by our Jayhawk friends. We've been told by Battalion to get back right now, or else we risk getting trapped over here without any support." Savage broke the transmission, presumably to collect himself and calm down before going on. *"Now, like I said, we roll in one mike. Anybody that don't mount up gets to walk home. Acknowledge."*

Mark tossed the handset down in disgust as the first of the Bradleys pulled out of the LRP, headed off to the north.

"Sarn't Matthews!"

Mark looked down to find Harris trying to get his attention. He pulled off his CVC and leaned down. "What is it?"

"Over there!" Harris pointed off to their right, roughly fifty yards away. The large sheriff's deputy carried the other, skinnier one. Both of them looked a fright. The big guy swayed and stumbled as he walked, fighting to stay upright. It was impossible not to notice that he was covered in nasty bites.

"Cover 'em!" Mark brought his weapon up and carefully fired, clearing a path for the deputy. Some of the others joined in, doing their best to keep the ravenous beasts at bay while White trudged forward.

When he finally made it to the track, he heaved his friend up, while the rifle squad reached down and grabbed him. Jefferson let out a god awful sound when they did it, dragging his bloody leg up the side of the vehicle. When they got him inside, he passed out from the pain.

They all looked down at White and he smiled at them. His eyes were red and his lips blue. He held his shotgun in his right hand and waved at them with his left. "Y'all get goin'. Ain't nothin' left for you here now."

The other armored vehicles fell in after each other, snaking along up the road, not waiting for Mark or his people to fall in. With each passing second the distance kept growing wider.

He nodded down at the sheriff's deputy and weakly smiled back. "Driver, move out."

As the Bradley pulled away, they stared at White in silence while he watched them drive off. Some of the infected passed by him, near enough to touch but did not even notice the huge man with a shotgun, waving to the others. One or two stopped to sniff at him but then kept on going, on the hunt for fresh meat. They didn't bother with him at all anymore.

He was one of them now.

***

"White Four, this is Two Three. Over."

"*Who am I speaking with? Where is Chamberlain? Over.*"

"This is Matthews. Chamberlain's dead. They got him. Saw it myself. Over."

There was a pause while Savage considered what he'd just been told. "*Send your traffic. Over.*"

"I've got a wounded man aboard my track, we need a medic. Over." The column jumped up onto I-69 westbound. The lieutenant put the slowest vehicle in the lead, which happened to be the M-88 recovery vehicle, with a squad of grunts sitting on top. Following close behind were the two tanks, and then the rest, looking like some sort of up-armored gypsy caravan.

"*Is he bit? If so, you need to pop his grape and roll him over the side before he turns. Over.*" The highway was littered with cars and trucks and they maneuvered their way through the mess, pushing some of them out of the way when they could. I-69 was the most direct route to the closest remaining bridge. They didn't have time to screw around with the side streets, hoping that this would be faster.

Every now and again, one of the dead would emerge and give chase, drawing a fusillade from the infantry. With ammunition less of a problem, they all got a lot more trigger-happy. Mostly it was out of frustration and anger rather than fear.

"White Four, this is Two Three. Negative, he's not bit. He's got a gunshot wound and it's bad. He won't make it if we don't get a medic. Over."

"*Bags is in the back of my track but we ain't stopping.*"

Mark saw an open stretch up ahead where the road was clear. "Roger, no need. Stand by." He toggled the intercom. "Burbey, punch it. Get us up beside White Four. And stay there. Get us as close as possible."

"You got it."

Burbey mashed the accelerator to the floor and the IFV lurched forward, passing several of the others in the convoy. The other crews and dismounts looked at them in surprise when they raced past, until they were even with the platoon sergeant's vehicle, only inches away. The name "Ball Busters Inc" was stenciled on the platoon sergeant's track in black spray paint.

Savage, as short as he was, had the commander's seat raised as high as it would go, so he could stand and still see over the edge of the turret. He looked right at Mark like he was crazy, keying the transmitter on his radio. *"What exactly do you think you're doing?"*

"No time to argue. Have the medic hop over. We'll hold steady next to you."

Savage looked and saw some scattered obstacles up ahead. *"Fine."* He said something into his intercom and within seconds, the medic popped her head up from the cargo hatch, slinging her combat lifesaver bag over her shoulder. The others helped her climb up to the top of the back deck, where she steadied herself, careful to keep her balance.

The vehicles moved along together smoothly on the surface of the road, trying to keep a steady direction and speed when Savage's track ran over some wreckage causing it to lurch. Bags swayed precipitously and nearly fell off, seeing the chasm between the vehicles briefly open up, then close again. Once the distance tightened, she took the leap.

She tripped and stumbled, falling face forward. Luckily for her the people on Mark's track had their arms outstretched and they caught her, gently lowering the medic into the troop compartment, unscathed.

Once there she found the deputy laying on the diamond-plate floor plates. His normally dark, African-American complexion glowed white as a ghost from blood loss. She ripped open her aid bag, pulling out a tourniquet and wrapped it around his upper thigh, on the wounded leg, cinching it down as tight as she could to stop the bleeding.

It was hard working in the back, there were legs all around her and it was crowded in there with almost no room to move. The soldiers stood on the bench seats where they could, standing up in the hatch and facing out in every direction with their weapons, while the civilians crouched in the corners and generally tried to stay out of the way. Bags looked up briefly to make eye contact with the big German Shepherd who sat calmly, watching her while Carnegie petted him.

"He going to make it, Doc?" Carnegie said, still stroking the dog's head.

"Too soon to tell but I'll do the best I can," Bags said, pulling an IV from the kit. Angel and Consuela huddled together in the darkened corner of the troop compartment, watching the medic work, while the other teenage girl named Bailey took orders and helped out.

As Bags worked to save the man's life, not another word was said to her as they continued to cruise down the road.

Chapter 12

North Side, US-69 Bridge
1115 Hours Local

It took them nearly an hour to negotiate their way through the detritus, burned out hulks and toppled trailers from wrecked big-rigs. The city behind them sounded like downtown Mogadishu coming unglued. There were bodies scattered everywhere, some in the ditches, some in the roads, others hanging out of scorched cars. The heat of the sun baked them without mercy and many of them were getting ripe, bloating in the heat. Clouds of flies hovered over them and the stink was unbearable. It was so bad that a few of the soldiers donned their gas masks to deal with the smell, while others improvised neckerchiefs, pulled tightly over noses and mouths.

Along the way civilian foot traffic picked up gradually at first, then grew to a crowd. Practically everyone was on foot, though a few bicycles and motorbikes made their way through the throng. Somehow, with all the cell towers down, and the radio and TV signals inundated with the Emergency Broadcast System, people managed to spread information through word of mouth. And the word was, they needed to get to the Kansas-side of the border where it was safe. People carried their most prized belongings with them, dragging them in wagons, strollers and backpacks. It was the largest concentration of refugees any of them had ever seen.

"Hey, El-Tee, is that it up there?" Yokey's voice was muffled from the rag he had tied around his face. He pointed up ahead beyond the M-88 which still held the lead position in their little convoy. The grunts sitting on it bobbed and swayed in unison with each bump in the road, seemingly in a daze.

"Yeah, that's it alright. We're finally there but it's covered with vehicles and foot traffic." Lieutenant Baker reached down inside and dug out a pair of binoculars. He focused them carefully to get a better look while steadying himself with his elbows. "It's also swarming with Jayhawks. Looks like Combat Engineers. And if I'm not mistaken, they are finishing up and pulling out."

The M-88's engine rumbled and the driver laid on the horn, which sounded rather pathetic in comparison to the vehicle's large size. They tried to get the civilians to clear out of the way. Some of the grunts hollered and swore at them but most didn't listen. Everyone was singularly focused on getting across that bridge and on to salvation. Still, they moved along, albeit at a snail's pace.

Yokey ripped off a loud fart, so loud in fact, that Baker even heard it through his CVC headphones.

"Ugh! Goddammit, Yokey! It smells bad enough already without you shitting your pants in here!" The loader, Specialist Volks, was down in the turret of the tank and his face entirely too close to Yokey's wretched ass. And in the confined space within, there was nowhere to run. "El-Tee, permission to turn on the overpressure system to clear out the smell of whatever crawled up Yokey's ass and died."

"Permission granted." Baker turned to his gunner. "Do you not have any respect for your fellow crew members?"

"Come on, sir. It's good training for them. Teaches 'em how to survive in a contaminated chemical and biological environment!"

"I wonder what I would do without you," Baker said, bringing the binoculars back up to his eyes.

"Probably get inferior gunnery scores for one thing," Yokey quipped, reaching down and scratching his balls. "What do you see up there?"

"One giant, fucking logjam."

The civilians massed on the north side of the bridge in a growing mob. The Combat Engineers from the National Guard set up trucks and APCs to physically block the bridge, while some of them worked on the ground in a crowd-control function. They allowed a slow trickle of refugee foot-traffic to pass onto the bridge while holding most of them back. This allowed military vehicles to still move freely from one side to the other, allowing the Engineers to work, setting their demolition charges.

The people grew panicked and more desperate with each passing minute and many of them were armed. It wasn't going to be long before things got out of control.

"Battle Axe Six, this is Battle Axe Seven. Over." Baker and Yokey looked at each other and groaned. First Sergeant Landreau had been a pain in everyone's ass the minute they linked up with him at the LRP.

"Seven, this is Six. Go ahead. Over." Baker rolled his eyes and shook his head. Yokey made a stroking motion in the air with his hand like he was masturbating.

"Six, this is Seven. We need to expedite getting across that bridge. I recommend we get the dismounts on the ground and clear the people out of the way so the vehicles can pass. We don't have much time, it looks like those Engineers are getting ready to light the fuse." Landreau had been calling him constantly, asking to see if there were updates from Battalion, if they were there yet, and generally badgering the living shit out of him. His gravelly voice was getting on Baker's last nerve.

"Seven, this is Six, stand by." Baker sighed and looked through his binoculars again. The people weren't interested in letting them pass, the "Thank you for your service" honeymoon now officially over. He pulled up the sleeve of his Nomex and checked his Casio G-Shock. They were running out of time. "Well, Yokey, what do you think?"

"You're asking my opinion?"

"Yup."

"I think you should let me go punch First Sergeant Landreau in the dick."

"That wasn't what I was asking."

"Oh, you meant about getting across the bridge." Yokey lowered his goggles. "I think we should go full 'crunchie' mode."

"I don't know why I bother to ask you anything, you fucking mongoloid."

"It's because his parents were brother and sister, sir," Volks chimed in from down below.

"Okay, fuck this. Time to get things sorted out." Baker disconnected the cable from his CVC and climbed out of the hatch, then lowered himself down off the tank. He went jogging off toward the front of the column, armed with nothing more than an unloaded semi-automatic.

Yokey watched him in stunned silence for a moment. "Stay here you guys."

"Wait, where are *you* going?" Volks said.

Yokey pulled off his helmet and then took off after his lieutenant. Along the way he came up alongside the M-88 to see the grunts looking down at him. "Hey, are you just going to sit there? We need to protect the El-Tee!" They looked at each other in puzzlement, then a couple shrugged their shoulders and climbed down, chasing after Yokey.

When they caught up with Baker, he was pushing and shoving his way through the crowd. Some big bruiser got angry and gave the young officer a shove before drawing back a fist to strike him with. Before he knew it, one of the dismounts stuck the muzzle of their M-4 in the ornery guy's face and he immediately backed down, then disappeared into the crowd.

Baker looked relieved to see Yokey and his two new friends. "Thanks, fellas. Now, let's go."

Before long they reached the checkpoint, suffering through a few sharp elbows and foul words along the way. When they arrived a surly Staff Sergeant gave them an annoyed look, then proceeded to try and ignore them. The crowd was getting louder and they were beginning to throw things at the soldiers manning the position.

"Sergeant, who's in charge here?" Baker lowered his bandana in order to be heard more clearly. Someone pushed him from behind and Yokey punched him in the throat, sending him reeling.

"I am." The Staff Sergeant turned his back to the officer while speaking into a handmike.

"Sergeant, we're with Bravo Company, 1-18 Infantry out of Fort Riley. We've got orders to get across that bridge." Baker hoped that he sounded more convincing than he felt right about then.

"Look, man. I've got orders myself. And that's to keep a lane open on the bridge so our people can move. If I let your convoy on the bridge, it'll block it up." The Staff Sergeant deliberately ignored the rank on Baker's uniform. "You can cross the minute me and my boys break down this checkpoint and leave. You can fall in right behind us."

Baker looked over his shoulder at the crowd just behind him. They were growing even more agitated, sensing that their window of opportunity was closing. Hundreds of them crushed in even tighter, yelling and screaming at the soldiers.

"The minute you leave, these people are going to rush this bridge and it's going to be impossible to cross with my vehicles and equipment."

"Not my problem, dude. But in a few minutes when they give the order, me and my boys are out of here, now if you don't mind, I got work to do." The NCO turned his back to the officer and began talking into the radio once again. Meanwhile, all around them the Engineers physically held the crowd back with their rifles. It was getting to be like one giant mosh pit without any music.

Baker turned to his gunner. "Come on, Yokey. Let's get back to the company."

***

On orders from the lieutenant, Savage ordered the platoon forward, passing the rest of the company, forcing their way through the angry mob. At first they beeped their horns and even tried shooting warning shots into the air but nothing seemed to get their attention. Eventually the frustrated platoon sergeant just ordered them to drive forward slowly but not to stop. They'd either get out of the way, or they wouldn't.

Reluctantly, they all got out of the way.

The crowd parted in the face of the advancing armored vehicles, many of the people slapping the sides of the Bradleys in frustration. The soldiers riding on them ended up on the receiving end of a hail of insults and a few tossed rocks. Still, they pressed on until they reached the Combat Engineers and their checkpoint. By the time they arrived the National Guardsmen were mounting their vehicles and preparing to leave.

Without fanfare the boys from Kansas rolled out with haste, picking up speed as they crossed the bridge heading southbound. They nearly ran over several refugees on the way, not bothering to swerve out of the way to miss them. It was obvious at this point they didn't give a shit.

As they pulled out, 2nd Platoon filled the gap, physically blocking the bridge with their IFVs. The infantry hopped down and dismounted, wading into the mass of humanity doing their best to push them back, while the rest of the company pressed forward toward them.

The M-88 was still in the lead and had its digging blade lowered practically all the way to the ground. It acted as a cow-catcher like an old steam-powered locomotive, only this was a "human-catcher" pushing folks out of the way. After getting a gentle nudge from the huge behemoth, most got the hint and got the hell out of the way. The rest of the company followed close behind, bumper to bumper.

Arriving at 2nd Platoon's makeshift checkpoint, Savage ordered the Bradleys to open a lane and the rest of the company passed through, one at a time. First the M-88, then the tanks, then the company command element, with the stragglers and then 3rd Platoon pulling up the rear. For the first time in a long time, they noticed First Sergeant Landreau standing up and exposed, anxiously supervising the operation from the back of his M-113.

Mark dismounted the track and joined the rest of the

squad on the ground, doing their best to keep the bridge clear so the company could cross. The pushing and shoving increased in intensity as each armored vehicle drove by. A few of the civilians made a mad dash through the opening and got onto the bridge but they kept most of them back. They didn't need to keep them all off the bridge, just enough of them so they could drive through the cleared center lane.

When the M-113 drove up Mark couldn't help but to look up and see Landreau staring back down at him, giving an evil look. He continued to stare with those hateful eyes as he passed through the checkpoint and onto the bridge, before losing sight of him.

When Mark turned back around, some big bruiser took a swing and punched him square in the face, knocking him off his feet and landing on his ass. In a daze, he tried to get up only to get kicked in the ribs by someone else. Raising his hand up to protect his face a woman spat on him. The rest of the squad had their hands full and before he knew it, the crowd closed in on him with kicks and punches. He wanted to grab his rifle but he couldn't and before he knew it, he was in the fetal position on the ground getting the shit pounded out of him.

Then, the staccato-sound of a machine gun tore through the air, followed by the barking and snarling of a dog. When Mark forced his eyes back open he saw Gray standing over him, firing bursts into the air, forcing the crowd back, while Carnegie unleashed Saxon, who went straight at the big bruiser who had punched him. The dog lunged and latched onto the poor bastard's balls and the tattoo-covered guy screamed like a six-year-old girl.

The sound of the SAW and the sight of the dog had the desired effect and most of the mob backed off. If only a few feet but enough to give the platoon some breathing room. Johnson offered a hand and helped Mark back to his feet.

"You okay, sarn't?" Johnson rested a hand on Mark's shoulder, waiting to make sure he didn't fall over.

"Yeah, I'm good. Thanks."

A three-round burst crackled behind them. It was Savage up in the turret of his Bradley, firing into the air, trying to get their attention. "Alright, mount 'em up. *Time to go!*"

Mark and the rest of the squad climbed back up onto their vehicles in record speed. The moment they got back aboard the civilians started streaming around them onto the bridge, making a break for the far side. He checked his watch, dismayed to see that it read "11:36."

"We good on time, sarn't?" Donahue said, checking his own watch from the gunner's hatch.

"Yeah, we're good," Mark lied. "We've got plenty of time."

***

Baker put the handset down after ordering their rear-guard platoon to displace and catch up with the rest of the company. He wanted to go faster but the M-88 was in the lead and the big beast wasn't known for speed. It was probably a good thing though, since he didn't want to leave anybody behind. Still, it moved along at a good clip.

He peered through his binoculars and saw that the last of the Combat Engineers had cleared the bridge and all of them were on the south side of the river now. The trickle of civilians on the bridge ahead of them must have sensed that things were getting down to the wire and they were no longer walking, they were running as fast as their feet could carry them.

He turned around to see 2nd Platoon was far behind the rest of them and just starting to move. The moment they moved their Bradleys, it opened up the floodgates and the mob began pouring through. He picked up the handmike once again. "White Four, this is Battle Axe Six. You need to move out as fast as you can. Put the pedal to the metal. Over."

"*Axe Six, White Four. Acknowledged. We'll kick it in the ass. Over.*"

The lead elements of the company were nearly across now and Yokey got even more animated than before. He was smiling from ear to ear.

Here it comes, you better start running
Here it comes, you better start running...

***

Lieutenant Bethel's track took the lead while Sergeant Savage and his crew followed close behind. Third in the order of movement was "B-22" with Staff Sergeant Frakes in the hatch. Once the other three moved out, Mark ordered Burbey to fall in behind the others.

People streamed in from both sides and didn't care if they ran in front of the Infantry Fighting Vehicles. Not wanting to kill innocent civilians, they had to slow down so they didn't run anybody over. They watched helplessly as the rest of the company crossed unimpeded, moving out at impressive speed, nearly reaching the far side.

Still, they pressed on.

Once they reached about a third of the way the world seemed to come apart with a thunderclap from the gods. The charges set underneath the bridge detonated in unison, sending chunks of debris flying in every direction. The explosion rocked their Bradley hard on its suspension and Burbey slammed on the brakes.

The shock wave hit Mark in the face like a sledgehammer, knocking him painfully into the back of the commander's hatch. If he'd not just happened to have his mouth open, the concussion would have burst his eardrums. A cloud of dust washed over them and they were instantly blinded, sitting there in the haze with ears ringing.

When he regained his wits he toggled the intercom. "You guys alright?"

Burbey was the first to respond. "I'm up, sarn't."

"I am too but I got my bell rung good." Donahaue stood

in the hatch next to him, wiping blood from his nose.

"That's what Candi said," Burbey quipped.

"Stop talking about my wife, cocksucker!"

Mark leaned over the back and looked over the bustle rack to check on the squad. Some of them were sprawled out on top of one another in the troop compartment, while others were getting back up on their feet. "Is everyone okay?"

He got nods in the affirmative and a couple of shaky "thumbs up" from them before turning back around. When the dust cloud settled, coating everything in its path, he saw hundreds of refugees picking themselves up from the road. Nearly all of them had been knocked down from the blast and most of them looked like they were in a daze.

Up ahead the center of the bridge was completely gone. He saw that the lead elements of the company had made it safely across but 2nd Platoon had not. Lieutenant Bethel's track was nowhere to be seen, and Sergeant Savage's vehicle was missing as well. Bravo 22 was just ahead of them, hanging precariously on shattered chunks of asphalt, concrete and twisted strings of rebar.

"Dear god," Mark said to himself. "Half the platoon is gone."

Sergeant Frakes, up in the Bradley Commander's position in the turret, began barking orders. The troop door on the back ramp creaked open and the soldiers on board came tumbling out. They stumbled over the rubble and one of them nearly fell through a hole to his death but a buddy caught him in the nick of time. They all started putting distance between themselves and the IFV that barely hung on, near the edge of the abyss.

Mark waved them forward. "Come on you guys, this way!"

When he looked up, he saw Frakes speaking into the boom mike on his helmet, giving orders to his crew. Then he watched a plume of exhaust belch from the manifold.

"He's not doing what I think he's doing is he?" Donahue turned to Mark, a concerned look etched on his face.

"I sure as hell hope not." Mark picked up the transmitter. "White Two Two, this is White Two Three. Come in. Over." There was no response. The vehicle's transmission went into reverse and the sprockets grabbed onto the steel track, applying torque and taking out the slack. They were trying to back up, away from the edge of the shattered bridge.

"Two two, don't try it! Abandon the vehicle. Get out of there now!" Mark yelled into the handset, only to see that the antennas on Frake's vehicle were sheared away in the blast. They couldn't hear any radio transmissions at all.

The Bradley started to back up a few inches at a time, and it rocked unevenly. It didn't make it more than a foot or so when the rubber track pads lost purchase and the tracks began to slip. Then, a creaking and groaning rang out, and then a loud crack.

The wreckage beneath them gave way and the Bradley Fighting Vehicle leaned forward and fell. It tumbled ass over teakettle into the roiling brown waters of the Missouri, hitting the surface with an audible splash.

"Jesus Christ." Donahue's mouth hung agape, his eyes wide.

Mark simply sighed, shaking his head. The dismount squad from Frakes' Bradley ran toward them, not looking back. "Okay, fellas. Let's get those guys loaded up and get the hell out of here. It looks like we've got a long day ahead of us."

***

The nine members of 3rd Squad piled onto *BOHICA*, sitting and hanging on wherever they could find room. With no room in the troop compartment, they covered every unoccupied surface, grasping onto the Bushmaster autocannon, the bustle rack, or even the antenna mounts. Legs dangled off the sides while everyone faced out.

The crowd of civilians that survived the blast and lucky enough not to get dropped into the river milled around without direction. Some stared off at the far banks on the southern side, while others stripped off their clothes and jumped in, trying to swim across. Some families with small children began fashioning floatation devices for their kids in an attempt to make it over to safety. A few asked the soldiers with tears streaming down cheeks, begging for help and protection. They couldn't bear to look and ignored them, with looks of stone on their faces.

Staff Sergeant Bates, the leader of 3rd Squad, leaned in next to Mark. "Where's Chamberlain?"

"He didn't make it." Mark jabbed a thumb in the direction they had come from earlier. "He bought it in the LRP."

"That really sucks." Bates scratched his chin and stood up, trying to get a better look at the landscape behind them. The sweat ran freely down his cheeks and neck, streaking the concrete dust that covered his skin. "What'll we do now? Any ideas?"

Mark pulled out his map and showed it to the other Squad Leader, pointing to their position and the major road networks. "I figure there's no sense in heading south looking for a bridgehead to cross. The Kansas Guard has probably blown every bridge in the city."

"So what'll we do then? Hang out here?"

"We could. Maybe find another building to hole up in until somebody gets to us. There isn't enough room in the track to button-up inside of and wait. Not for all of us anyway."

"That didn't work out so hot at the school, remember?"

Mark nodded. He took off his CVC and ran fingers through his wet hair. He just realized how thirsty he was getting. "Yeah, things kind of went sideways." He pointed down at the map again. "Our other option is making a run for the border to the northwest." A lump grew in his throat which he forced down with a hard swallow. "Maybe head toward Leavenworth." The thought of going back there sat like a chunk of ice in his gut.

"That works for me, better than sitting here waiting to be torn to pieces by those… things."

"Right. Well, we're wasting time then. Let's move." He pulled the CVC back on and toggled the intercom key. "Okay, Burbey. Get us out of here."

"Where to, sarn't?"

"Turn us around. Then we'll head to the northwest."

"Roger."

Burbey put the vehicle in gear and gently applied the accelerator, revving the engine. The tracks on either side of the vehicle worked in opposite directions, and the IFV did a "pivot steer," turning around 180 degrees, without moving from the spot. Then, he popped it into "Drive" and creeped forward.

Once again, the soldiers had to yell at the civilians to get out of the way with similar results as before. They simply didn't care, focused on self-preservation with utter disregard for government authority. While not overtly hostile at the moment, they weren't cooperative either.

They were forced to move along the shoulder of the road, with people begrudgingly moving out of the way. It was extremely slow-going and the soldiers ground their teeth in frustration.

"Burbey, take this exit up here." Mark looked up ahead, searching for a cleared lane with very little luck. There was a mangled wreck in front of them but few people hanging around, so it appeared to have some potential. "Dog-leg around to the right."

"Roger, sarn't."

There were five cars piled up together on the exit ramp. It appeared that a Dodge Durango had come racing up from the wrong direction and made a head-on collision into a Hyundai. Three other cars had crashed into the mess as well, making it one hell of a pile-up. There was a cloud of flies hovering around the charred wrecks, suggesting that there were plenty of bodies still inside.

Burbey eased the IFV over onto the shoulder to the right-hand side of the mess. There was a patch of grassy slope that was open, and offered clear passage. It was fairly steep however but nothing they hadn't traversed a hundred times before.

The vehicle came around leaning precariously off to the right, and all the passengers piled on top hung on a little tighter. The grade was steeper than they had anticipated but still okay. They crawled along right up until they heard the loud popping sound of the track. The teeth on the drive sprocket were losing their grip and began making a terrible noise.

"Driver, stop!" Mark said into the boom mike but it was too late. The heavy steel track came off the sprocket and the road wheels, folding underneath the vehicle. They immediately ground to a halt.

"Fuck!" Bates exclaimed, slapping his hand down on the turret.

Mark climbed out and pushed past the soldiers sitting on the front deck of the Bradley. They made no move to get off, perfectly content to stay where they were. When he got down and took a look, it didn't take long to see the problem. The weight of the vehicle with the grade of the slope they were on, forced the track off its road wheels. Throwing track wasn't an uncommon occurrence in the mechanized world but it always seemed to happen at the most inopportune time. Like now.

Bates jumped down and crouched down next to Mark. "You gotta be shitting me."

Mark put his hands on his hips, looking at the problem. "Let's get a perimeter established, then we'll get to work. We should be able to break track and get this fixed in no time."

Screams echoed from the crowd on the road above them. Down on the exit ramp on the far side of the wreck they couldn't see much but what had been a relatively calm assembly of dazed survivors quickly devolved into a stampede with people scattering in every direction. The sounds of desperation punctuated by the crack of firearms and the ungodly howls of the dead.

Suddenly scores of them came barreling down the grassy embankment, completely ignoring the soldiers. They ran for their lives, some of them pushing others over or out of the way, with no concern for their fellow man, singularly focused on survival.

Bates turned to Mark while unslinging his rifle. "I don't think we've got time to break track."

"Yeah, I think you're probably right." Mark cupped his hands around his mouth and hollered. "Everybody un-ass the track. We need to beat feet *and we need to do it now!*" He watched with a bit of sadness as the group jumped off and dismounted the vehicle with *BOHICA* stenciled on the TOW missile launcher housing.

Death before dismount, he thought to himself, checking his rifle to ensure there was a round in the chamber. "Donahue, Burbey, don't forget to grab the VS-17 panels on your way out!"

***

They managed to keep themselves more or less in a tactical formation. Bates had 3rd Squad broken up by fire team, with Alpha Team in the lead and Bravo taking up the rear. Jefferson lay on a litter in the center of the formation, carried by four of the men, bouncing up and down with each agonizing step. Bags jogged alongside, holding an IV in the air, still stuck in the man's arm. He moaned in pain but did his best not to cry out.

Bates kept pace alongside Mark looking all around as a massacre unfolded behind them. They did their best to put distance between themselves and flesh-eaters but with a wounded man and the equipment they carried, they'd not likely outrun them for long. For the time being they were distracted by all the fresh meat still scattering near the road.

"Got any ideas, Matthews?" The magazine pouches attached to Bates' plate carrier bobbed up and down with each stride. They weren't running fast at all but with all the gear they wore, and the heat of mid-day running across a sun-baked parking lot, their pores opened up like they were in a sauna.

"I figure we get in there and hunker down. Then we figure out our next move." Mark pointed to the casino straight ahead. It was the only building around, except for a hotel off to the northeast but that was over a half mile away. They needed to get somewhere with walls to protect them. And they needed to get there fast.

"That place is huge. We ain't got enough people to secure it."

"We don't need to secure the whole thing. Just a few rooms will do. Anything is better than being stuck out here in the open."

"Hard to argue with that."

Up ahead dozens of fleeing civilians raced toward the casino's front entrance, having the same idea. The lights were on, dancing and flashing in preset rhythms. The power grid may have been down but the backup generators here were working perfectly.

Reaching the main entrance, they found everyone pounding on the doors trying to get in. Much earlier, someone had made it inside and barricaded the entranceway, sealing it off. Civilians bashed at the reinforced panes of glass with fists and rifle butts, trying to get inside.

"It looks like every man for himself," Bates said, wiping drops of perspiration from his nose. "These fuckers might stand half a chance if they bothered to work together."

The Alpha Team Leader, Specialist Rodriguez, brutally kicked the doors. "Open up and let us in, damn you!"

"Maybe we can work our way around back. Maybe we can get in through a loading dock or something." Bates removed his helmet and then took off his ballistic glasses. He used the tail of his shirt to clean the sweat off the lenses so he could see.

Mark watched the civvies hammer away at the reinforced

windows to no avail. "I guess it's worth a try."

The two NCOs were interrupted when Saxon began barking like crazy. Coming across the parking lot they'd just crossed were more people fleeing, only these were being chased by the infected.

The Bravo Team Leader, Sergeant Medicine Bear, crouched behind his weapon, peering down his sights at the approaching deluge of the dead. "We don't have any more time. Whatever we're gonna do, we need to do it fast!"

Mark looked down at Jefferson, laying on the litter. "Okay, you guys pick him up. Let's get a fire team wedge to take the lead, then we'll work our way around to the northeast…"

"Fuck this." Medicine Bear stood, snatching up the twenty-seven-pound M-240 Bravo medium machine gun he'd acquired from the back of Bravo-22. "Get out of the way you assholes!" As he swung the belt-fed weapon around, the soldiers scattered, getting the hell out of the way. The NCO barely waited until they were clear before firing the heavy weapon from the hip, spraying 7.62mm full metal jacket into the reinforced glass doors. Under the hail of bullets, the doors exploded into a million pieces, covering them all in tiny shards.

"You dumb-ass, with the doors gone, those things can get in too!" Bates berated his subordinate, stabbing a finger in his face.

"No time for this, let's get inside. We'll figure it out later!" Mark started pushing his people through the breach, with an eye on the parking lot and the approaching wave of death.

***

Baker looked through his binoculars and cringed. As the dust settled the enormity of the disaster gradually settled in. The center spans of the bridge were completely gone, while the northern and southern sections sagged and drooped toward the river below, with jagged pieces of concrete hanging by threads of rebar. Two of the tracks were completely gone while the two trail vehicles remained, though one hung on precipitously.

He snatched up the handset. "Any White element, any White element. This is Battle Axe Six. Come in. Over!

Nobody answered his call and he watched as the infantry escaped the lead vehicle which barely hung on by bits of shattered rubble. He saw the crew trying to self-recover the track and the pitch in his voice raised.

"Any White element, this is Battle Axe Six. Do not try and back up. Over!" He turned to Yokey, his eyes wild. *"Why the fuck don't they answer?"*

"You're calling them on the company frequency. They're probably tuned in on their platoon internal freq." He ducked down inside the tank, not needing to be told what to do. He hunched down next to the radios and desperately tried to find the platoon radio frequency for Bravo Company, 2nd Platoon. "It'll take me a minute, El-Tee!"

They didn't have a minute, and Baker watched helplessly as the Bradley Fighting Vehicle struggled to back up, then slipped and fell. He squeezed his eyes together, unable to watch.

"I found it! Punching up the freq now!" Yokey exclaimed.

"Don't bother, dude. It's too late." His hands clenched into fists and he gritted his teeth together so hard he thought he might crack a molar. All around his tank, Combat Engineers were packing up their gear and making ready to move out. The surviving members of Bravo Company on the other hand, slowly gathered along the road, looking toward the northern bank from where they'd just come from. "Go find me First Sergeant Landreau. I want a status report on the company right away."

Yokey popped his head back up through the hatch. "Roger that. What're you gonna do?

"I'm going to let Battalion know that we've still got

people trapped over there, and we need a rescue mission organized ASAP."

***

Rodriguez was the first one through the shattered doors, running right smack into a barricade of furniture piled up nearly to the ceiling on the far side. He climbed up and toppled the chairs and tables stacked hastily at the entrance. The other members of his fire team joined him, along with a number of civilians who wanted to get inside too.

"Here they come!" Medicine Bear opened up with the 240 Bravo from the prone position, the weapon resting on its bipod. The sharp, rapid, report of the weapon signaled the others and the rest of Bravo Team joined in.

PFC Weber off to his right poured it on thick with his SAW, using the optic mounted on the feed-tray cover to take careful aim, going for headshots. The smaller machine gun sounded like a toy in comparison to its bigger brother. But that hardly mattered, when employed properly, it was effective enough.

To the left Devons and Espinoza let fly with their carbines. Devons had a grenade launcher mounted to the underside of the barrel but with no rounds for it, the thing was nothing more than an elaborate paper weight.

While Bravo Team engaged from the prone, lying on the hot pavement, Mark's people fired over top of them while kneeling or standing. They looked almost like a Revolutionary War painting, with one rank firing over the other. Except that these people were armed with automatic weapons.

The infected only picked up the pace, drawn to the noise, oblivious to the buzzsaw they were running into. Dozens of them fell, crumpling to the ground, only to be trampled by the hundreds coming up from behind. And as fast as the soldiers could dispatch them, it did little to slow down their rapid advance, moving at the speed of Olympic sprinters.

"What's taking so long?" Bates pulled an empty mag and stuffed it into a cargo pocket before reloading his weapon. He shouldered the M-4 and put the Aimpoint red dot at head level of the charging mass of flesh-eaters. He let fly with three-round bursts, scoring hit after hit. The closer they got, the harder it was to miss.

Private Hong and Swanson shoved a massive potted plant out of the way, while Rodriguez and McDermott tossed aside some bar stools. Finally, they made a hole large enough to get through.

"We're in!" Shouted Rodriguez who ducked inside, followed closely behind by his men.

"Burbey, Donahue, Dubois and Johnson, grab the litter and take Jefferson!" Mark popped off another two rounds, then his bolt locked to the rear. He looked over his shoulder briefly to see the four of them struggling with the litter, each man carrying a corner, climbing up the hastily erected obstacle, trying to get the wounded deputy inside.

Saxon went nuts, a white froth running from his sharp canines, straining at his leash. Carnegie stood firmly on it with the heel of her boot to hold him back, while she used both hands to fire a rifle, pouring it on as fast as she could.

The parking lot filled full of animated bodies, faces contorted in madness, rushing toward the sound of the guns. As far as the eye could see they kept coming in an unending stream, as if the whole city were descending upon them at once.

A hand landed on Mark's shoulder, grabbing his attention. It was Roberts, the civilian with the Mini-14 with his wife and daughter standing right next to him. "They got the wounded deputy inside!" Even shouting, he could scarcely be heard over all the noise.

"Alright, you people next!" He pointed at the Roberts family and then to Angel and Consuela. The two teenage lovers nodded in understanding, though they couldn't comprehend a single word spoken.

While soldiers and civilians pushed and shoved their way

through the gap, the rear guard continued to pour on the fire, scything through the stampeding mass of undead, doing their best to hold back the inevitable.

***

"First Sergeant, the lieutenant wants you to organize a team to head over to the other side of the river to evacuate our survivors." Beltran emerged from the M-113 after getting a call from the company commander. He stood there uneasily, looking around like a cornered animal looking for escape. "He said Battalion has arranged for some helicopters to conduct an extraction."

"What the fuck are you talking about? Is he out of his mind? There's no way we'll get them back from over there. Those people are finished. You call him back and tell him we can't do it!" Landreau shook his fist at the driver, taking some pleasure in yelling at him. It was bad enough that they put a lieutenant in charge of the company but now some of the soldiers were starting to take Baker seriously and listen to him. *This stupid kid will get us all killed. Lieutenants don't know shit*, he thought to himself.

Between the thoughts of the flesh-eaters attacking and killing everyone in the city, Landreau's mind would shift gears and he would see that bastard Foley's face. The same guy who he thought he'd put in prison forever. And yet, there he was, standing there in an MP's uniform, reaching for his gun. It was a nightmare.

How the hell did he get out of prison anyway? More importantly, how did he end up here, now, in my company?

Most of the platoon died over there when the engineers touched off the demo charges but some of them survived. They all watched what happened from the southern bank of the river. And Landreau could see the MP brassard through his binoculars, even at this distance. Somehow Foley made it and he was over there right now.

If Lieutenant Baker got some sort of rescue operation

going, they might actually get them back and with Foley too. If that happened, that sonofabitch might come after him.

He couldn't convince the men in the company that "Matthews" was an imposter, and by the time he did, Foley might put a bullet in his head. That was a chance Landreau was not willing to take.

No matter what, there could be no rescue mission. It's just too bad that a whole platoon had to be sacrificed in order to make sure that Foley ended up dead. But there simply was no other way. He couldn't afford to take any chances.

He decided right then and there that he'd lead the lieutenant's idiotic mission, and then he'd sabotage it. He'd make sure that whatever happened, Foley, and any other witnesses ended up dead. Then, once and for all, he'd be rid of him. There was no other way.

Landreau's expression softened. "Okay, Beltran. Forget it. It's alright. I'll go over and talk to the lieutenant. We'll start organizing a team and we'll get our people out. Everything's going to be fine. Everything is going to be *just* fine."

***

Some woman sat there bawling uncontrollably, sitting there helpless by herself as desperate people dashed through the breach in the barricade, completely oblivious of her. Mark nearly did the same, almost not noticing but stopped and shook her. She looked at him briefly, longingly, and he placed his hands on her shoulders while staring into her tear-filled eyes. "You're going to be okay. You understand me?"

She nodded, wiping the snot from her nose.

"Okay then, in you go." He pushed her through the hole and hands on the other side pulled her in. He turned to Medicine Bear and his fire team, suddenly channeling the movie *Aliens* for some reason. "Mariiiines, we are *leaving!*"

Medicine Bear got up on a knee and shouldered the M-240 Bravo machine gun like a rifle, holding the heavy piece of iron as if it were made of paper. He fired a steady stream of NATO full metal jacket in a wide arc, dropping a dozen or more of the dead. *"Everybody fall back!"*

Mark laid down cover fire for Weber and Devons while they peeled off the line, practically leaping through the breach in the make-shift wall of scavenged furniture. Once they were in, he followed with Medicine Bear and Espinoza covering their retreat.

The infected descended on the two of them with singular focus, coming on at unbelievable speed. The Team Leader scooped up the last of the linked ammo and made a break for it with Espinoza right behind him.

Medicine Bear tripped on the leg of a stool and came crashing through the other side, rolling onto the floor. He was up on his feet in an instant reaching out for his subordinate. Espinoza nearly cleared the breach but the things on the other side were too quick and a dozen pairs of hands latched on to him, pulling him thrashing and kicking back outside. His blood curdling screams made them all wince.

The dead wasted no time and were clawing their way through the breach, greeted by a hail of gunfire. Undeterred, they fell on top of each other, eventually blocking the hole with their motionless bodies and providing temporary relief. It didn't take long before the platoon heard them on the other side, tearing the obstacle down.

The group stood in the foyer, catching their breath and looking around. It was brightly lit and the floor tiles glistened. A few of them shook, suddenly aware that the air conditioning was on and working overtime. They hadn't been this cool in days.

Bates felt the ammo pouches on the front of his plate carrier, suddenly realizing that he was getting low on ammunition.

Some of the civvies that managed to get inside with the platoon struck out on their own without waiting to see what the soldiers intended to do. Small groups broke off in different directions, some headed onto the main casino floor, while others went toward the restaurants or the hotel. The five civivies from the strip mall elected to stay close to the grunts for protection, feeling a connection and safer with the platoon.

They set up a hasty perimeter in the foyer while the NCOs huddled together to come up with a plan. The others scanned their sectors nervously, listening to the infected outside tearing at the improvised wall. They worked in a frenzy since the obstacle surely wouldn't last for long.

Johnson and Dubois knelt next to Jefferson on his litter from the center, surrounded by the rest of their buddies. Carnegie and Saxon lingered close to the nervous civilians who clung to one another.

"Dubois, this reminds me of the Shadowfell Campaign when we got chased into that church by waves of zombies. You remember that?" Johnson adjusted his knee pad so he could kneel on the hard-tiled floor. His face was covered in a fine sheen and his chest worked overtime to catch his wind.

"Holy shit, you're right. That's the one where we stacked up pews to keep the zombies out, then we taunted them mercilessly between attacks." Dubois' smile grew from ear to ear. "I started off with the Monty Python taunts of farting in their general direction."

"Yeah, then you said 'Verily doth ingest a satchel of Richards.' That shit was dope!" Johnson raised his hand and the two of them gave each other a "high five," which then devolved into their own secret handshake that only the two of them knew.

"Seriously, will you two dorks knock it off?" Gray looked over her shoulder, giving the two of them the stink-eye. She unfolded the bipod on her SAW and set the weapon down, peering through the scope in the direction of the main casino floor.

"You know, Gray. We might not be long for this world. There still might be a chance for us." Dubois winked at Johnson, his smile growing toothy.

"I'd rather attend a Tijuana donkey show. As a

performer." Gray removed her patrol cap and wiped the perspiration from her brow.

"Will you guys knock it off with all the sexy talk? I'm getting aroused over here," Harris said, unable to resist jumping in with the shit-talk.

Nearby, Mark, Bates and Medicine Bear huddled together having a conference. Donahue and Burbey lingered near them, both carrying radios in rucksacks. The two of them looked miserable, clearly not accustomed to being dismounted and preferring to be on the track.

A shot rang out from inside the main casino floor, followed up soon thereafter by another. Then it erupted into a massive firefight. The soldiers in the foyer all instinctively dropped from a knee to their bellies, scanning their fire lanes.

"What's that all about?" Bates said, checking to see if he had a round chambered.

"Sounds like we've got different armed bands cooped up in here and they don't ascribe to the 'caring is sharing' philosophy." Mark looked back to check and see if his people were switched on and watching their lanes. They were and he turned back to the two other NCOs.

"What now, boss?" Medicine Bear busied himself by linking together two belts of 7.62 link, then neatly arranging them next to the gun.

Bates looked over at the furniture piled high at the entrance, listening to the grunts and howls on the other side while the dead systematically deconstructed it. They might have been ravenous, flesh-eating monsters but they still retained a certain level of intelligence and they were leveraging it at the moment to work as a team to get at the people barricaded inside. "Well, we can't stay here. They'll be through that in a matter of minutes."

"Agreed. What do you have in mind then?" Mark reached for a canteen attached to his web gear. He intended to only take a sip but quickly drained it. He didn't realize how thirsty he was.

Bates produced a pack of "cowboy killers" and offered

one to Mark and Medicine Bear. They both accepted and Bates lit their cigarettes with his lighter. "Anywhere but here. Maybe we can find some hotel rooms or offices and barricade ourselves in. Then once we buy ourselves some time and breathing room, we figure something out."

Mark took a deep drag and blew out the smoke. It'd been a long time since he smoked and it didn't feel right. Not that he cared at the moment, any distraction was a welcome one. "Sounds good to me, I'll get my people ready to move."

Another shot thundered inside the enclosed space and Rodriguez went limp.

Chapter 13

"*Contact!*" Private Jimmy Hong cut loose with his SAW, peppering the hallway next to the elevators located thirty meters away. Chunks of tile and concrete exploded under withering fire. The deafening sound made it impossible for anyone to hear as he let fly with burst after burst.

Weber and Devons hopped to their feet and assaulted forward, moving as a buddy team, leapfrogging toward the elevators. Weber sprinted a few feet crying out, "I'm up, they see me, I'm down!" before dropping onto his belly and laying down his own covering fire.

Hong watched his two buddies get dangerously close to his beaten zone and let up on the trigger. Devons slammed his back up against the nearest set of elevators, taking a deep breath before rounding the corner, blazing away with his carbine.

Then all of a sudden, he stopped.

"*Clear!*" Devons called out.

Bags went over to check on Rodriguez, running her hands across his torso, looking for blood. Unresponsive, she rolled him over to find a neat little hole at the bridge of his nose. Her shoulders slumped and she looked over to Sergeant Bates, shaking her head.

Before the Squad Leader could say anything the top of the obstacle near the entrance came crashing down. Furniture came tumbling inside and the dead clawed their way over the top.

Harris opened up with his SAW, dumping spent brass and steel links onto the floor. Wooden furniture splintered and shattered, and several infected went flying back outside. But more of them flooded the opening, while others continued to tear down what remained.

"Let's move!" Mark ordered, picking up one of the handles of Jefferson's litter. Gray dropped down next to Harris and the two light machine gunners sent streams of hot lead into the attacking mob coming over the top.

"Where are we going?" Bates said, firing wildly into the creatures summiting the obstacle. They were so close, he didn't bother aiming.

"Anywhere but here!"

Donahue took the handle of the litter from Mark. "I got this, sarn't!"

Mark pushed past all the others, until he was up with Devons and Weber. On the floor were two dead men, one armed with a Remington 700 deer rifle, and the other with a Winchester pump shotgun. Devons had shot them both on the run, then gave them a double-tap before taking a knee on the far side of their bodies. He oriented his M-4 carbine down the hallway at the door.

"They came from there," Devons said, pointing at the doorway. Above it was a sign that read "stairs."

Mark looked back to see the furniture collapsing in a small avalanche. Tables, chairs, and the reanimated dead came crashing down in a heap. The platoon fired wildly into them but a mass charged from outside, trampling each other to get in.

"This way!" Mark went to the stairwell and kicked open the door, ducking inside. He was received by a hail of gunfire that smacked the concrete walls and floors all around him. It was even louder inside the enclosed space and each report thundered with such force it rattled the teeth in his skull. He fired upwards, blindly, not bothering to search for a target.

Devons came in right behind, blazing away up the staircases, attempting to lay down suppressing fire. Weber nearly crashed into the both of them when he came in next, adding to the noise and confusion. Bits of concrete spalling filled the air, cutting the skin, while bullets zipped by in both directions, splattering and ricocheting in the confined space.

It went on for what seemed like forever but in reality was only a few seconds. Then, without warning, the shooting from up above stopped. Doors slammed and echoed while ears rang.

"Give me an up!" Mark shouted, barely able to hear

himself.

"I'm good," Weber called out.

"I'm hit," Devons groaned.

Mark looked over to see the grenadier laying on the floor, both hands pressed onto a wound on his upper leg. Blood seeped through his fingers in a steady flow. He opened the door and shouted to the others, "*Come on!*"

The platoon came barging in while Weber tried to help Devons up the first flight of stairs. Practically deaf from the shooting, Mark could still hear the dead howling and screeching, nearly on top of them.

The litter team came in with Jefferson looking confused but Mark pulled them inside, urging them up the stairs. The rest came in after them in ones and twos, pounding up the stairs, the able-bodied stomping up past the wounded, taking the lead. They continued coming through the door while Medicine Bear held the rear, his M-240 Bravo hammering away, chewing up their pursuers.

Finally, Swanson came through the door, holding it open. Medicine Bear came crashing in, then kicked the door shut. He leaned up against it with all his might, resting the machine gun on his hip. There were no rounds loaded into the feed tray, the barrel smoking and shimmering.

Weber bounded up the stairs three at a time and nearly made it to the landing on the second floor when more rifle fire boomed from up above, sending him sprawling to the cold concrete. He fired back wildly at the opening in the center of the stairwell, not actually seeing any targets, while bullets panged off the thick steel handrails. He continued firing until something slammed into his shoulder with the force of a ball-peen hammer. His face contorted in pain and he pulled himself into the corner and out of the line of fire.

A stray round hit Swanson in the neck and he clasped his neck, arterial spray painting the walls of the stairwell until he collapsed. By the time Bags got to him he was nearly unconscious and going into shock.

Bates cracked off a few shots and his bolt locked to the

rear on an empty magazine. "Matthews, we're getting murdered in here! What's your status?"

The door behind Medicine Bear thumped relentlessly as the dead tried to get in. He braced his legs and pushed back with all of his might trying to keep them out. He glanced down at Swanson who lay on the cold ground bleeding out but dared not move to help him or else he'd let the floodgates loose, and they'd get inundated in a deluge of the dead.

Hong and McDermott took the lead, laying down a punishing amount of fire, leap-frogging up the stairs. They nearly made it to the 3rd Floor landing but the volume of fire coming from above stopped them cold, forcing them to the ground.

The platoon crowded the stairwell, most nearly standing on top of one another. The landing on the 2nd Floor was worst of all, serving as a hasty Casualty Collection Point. Bags used her own body to cover Jefferson and Devons, protecting them from the random ricochets and bullet fragments bouncing off the walls.

Carnegie held the civilians back, out of the line of fire as best she could manage, while covering Saxon's ears with both hands. The noise was brutal for the men and women but unbearable for the dog.

Mark tried to catch his breath, the sweat running down his temples oblivious to the cool air. He could barely hear Bates down on the stairs below him but he heard enough. The dead were trying to get at them from below, and armed civilians up above had them bottled up, clearly disinterested in letting anyone else join them. They were stuck, and probably goners if he didn't come up with something quick.

Nearly two floors above them rifles, pistols and shotguns crossed over railings, popping off a few rounds, then retreated back to cover. Most of the time the shooters just did a "pray and spray," never actually aiming at anything. Only rarely did one of the belligerents cowboy up and pop their head over to take a look. They didn't need to aim, the platoon was caught in one giant "fatal funnel" and it was only a matter of time before they were all hit and bleeding out. Or worse.

Bates pushed his way through on the 2ⁿᵈ Floor landing, taking a look at the door there. He wanted to get them out of there as quickly as possible so he tried the handle. It did not budge and it was then that he noticed the card reader next to the latch. Without a key card they could not gain access, though anybody on the other side could open it up and get at them. It presented yet another unpleasant tactical dilemma he had to deal with, while his number of combat effectives continued to drop.

He looked up and saw Matthews crouched near a railing, peering upwards through the center of the stairwell. Bates shoved his way through the group and joined the other NCO. "Doors are locked on the 2ⁿᵈ Floor, we can't get out that way," he shouted into Mark's ear. He eased his face out a few inches to get a look upward but flinched and snapped back when a bullet smacked the railing next to his face. "It's getting sporty in here!"

Mark looked over at Bates and saw him still wearing full kit and body armor but what caught his attention was the mount on the front of his helmet. He also still had a large pouch affixed to his FLC with a piece of parachute cord snaking out of it, tied to the rest of his rig. It was known as a "dummy cord," and it was there for securing sensitive items so they couldn't easily be lost. "Do you and all your people still have your night vision goggles?"

Bates looked down at his pouch, "Yeah, I guess so. Why?"

"Put 'em on." Mark leaned backward down the flight of stairs and yelled as loud as he could. *"Everyone get your nods on, right now!"* He then turned back to Bates. "Time to shoot out the lights in here."

Bates' face grew a feral grin. "Roger that." He pulled the goggles from his pouch and deftly mounted them to the front of his helmet, checking them to ensure they functioned properly. "Time to get hot!" Be stomped up the stairs until he was even with McDermott and Hong and gave them the instructions.

Nearly at once, Mark and the other three leaned out and started knocking out the lights. The others in the platoon saw what they were up to and immediately joined in. It wasn't easy and they all exposed themselves to a ton of incoming fire but from their various angles distributed throughout the lower levels of the staircase, they were able to get most of them.

Night vision goggles flipped down over faces from helmet mounted "rhino mounts." Those that had tossed their helmets and plate carriers away earlier, still had their goggles but had to hold them to their faces with a free hand. All of them had Infrared laser designators mounted to their weapons and they switched them on, allowing the firers to aim their weapons in the dark.

Bates didn't wait for a signal, choosing to go full berserker instead. Stunned, it took a moment for it to register but Hong and McDermott picked up and tried to catch up.

They drove upwards, sweeping the front with their IR lasers, popping any remaining lights along the way, turning things inky black. With their illuminators on, everything appeared a bright green hue, if just a bit grainy.

Climbing to the 4th Floor they saw the first of their armed opponents, still slinging lead down toward their buddies. Totally in the dark they fired blind, desperation evident on their faces even through the night vision optics.

Bates brought the IR laser up, invisible to the naked eye unassisted. It moved as if in slow-motion, rising from the man's legs to his chest. Out of freshly borne habit he waited until the dot rested on the man's face before pulling the trigger, watching him drop to the ground as if someone had turned off a switch.

The young man's companions, hearing the thunder of rifle shots so close, turned and panic-fired into the inky blackness, lighting up the enclosed space with fireballs belched from the muzzles of their weapons. Bates shot the next one, sending him slamming into the wall before Hong and McDermott came from behind, silencing the other two.

The door was propped wide open, held in place by a wedge. Bates rushed it but two more came rushing out, guns blazing. He caught two to the chest, center mass of his body armor, slamming harmlessly into his E-SAPI plates. The third caught him just below the chin. The .270 Winchester soft-tip entered his throat, cutting through and smashing into his spine, severing the cord. Bates stumbled backward and fell into Hong and McDermott, sending all three crashing backward down the stairs.

Mark grabbed Gray by the combat harness. "We're up, it's go time!" Both stepped over the tangled mess of arms and legs trying to get out from underneath the dead Squad Leader. They held their night vision goggles in place with their left hands, holding their weapons with the right. Gray had her machine gun slung over her shoulder, making it manageable to manipulate single-handedly. Using the IR lasers to aim, they did not need to shoulder their weapons, fully able to aim and shoot accurately from the hip.

Climbing up to the landing Mark caught sight of the two survivors and had no time to react, looking down the barrel of a deer rifle. The weapon boomed in the enclosed space and his nods whited out with the flash. He felt something hit him in the face and he too went flying backward.

Gray, off to his right and nearest the railing, opened up with a long burst from her belt-fed gun. The muzzle flash was barely visible with the military-grade flash suppressor but the tracer rounds definitely were. Every fifth round zipped out, bright red, moving at supersonic speed, with four invisible companions in between. She stitched the first one across the chest and arced the stream of 5.56 NATO over, sending his companion stumbling back through the open doorway.

She readied herself to bound forward when someone on the other side opened up with a shotgun, sending her to the deck, diving for cover. The weapon was a semi auto and the shooter blasted away, filling the air with 00 Buck. After seven shots, the gun went dry.

Gray tried to get back up while the other man reloaded but she'd dropped her night vision goggles and gotten the tie-down cord tangled up in the rest of her rig. Fully aware she only had a few seconds, she struggled with her kit, internally raging in frustration. So focused on trying to get sorted, she almost didn't notice something bolt past her from behind, climbing the stairs like they weren't even there and launching through the open doorway.

From the light emanating from the open door, she caught a glimpse of something brown and hairy, chugging forward like a mini-locomotive. It charged inside and instantly triggered a wail from the shooter on the far side of the doorframe.

She finally unsnarled the mess of her gear and charged forward over the threshold. To her right, Saxon was latched onto the shooter's groin and he was desperately trying to get the animal off. He'd dropped his shotgun and was using both hands to get the dog's jaws unlocked from his balls. Gray wasted no time and dumped a burst into the man's chest, watching him execute the Spandau Ballet before crumpling to the floor.

It was well lit in the hallway outside the stairwell, and three more heavily armed people came rushing out from around a corner, stopping only inches away, nearly bumbling into her. Eyes went wide as saucers and weapons started to come up but Gray mashed the trigger of her SAW and tore the three of them to shreds, killing them where they stood. She only stopped shooting when the bolt of the weapon went "kerchunk" on an empty chamber.

She stood there, chest heaving, with the sting of burnt powder hanging in her nose. It took her a moment before she shook herself out of it, then quickly checked to see if there was anyone else there. To her relief, there wasn't. She leaned back into the darkened stairwell. "*Clear!*"

Carnegie whistled loudly and Saxon's ears perked up,

then he darted back into the stairwell.

Mark managed to get back on his feet, feeling a burning sensation on his cheek with a wetness running down to his collar. The bullet had grazed him but done no significant damage. He saw the illuminated doorway with Gray just inside of it, on a knee, snapping a fresh drum of ammunition into place. The door was propped open by a body slumped up against it. "Come on, get the lead out!" The others came pounding up the stairs, their footfalls barely audible over the ringing in his ears.

Hong and McDermott rolled Bates' body off and helped the rest carry the wounded, man-handling them as best they could. Down below Medicine Bear dug his heels into the concrete and leaned into the door, barely able to keep it shut. He gritted his teeth, feeling the pounding from the other side against his back, listening to the awful sounds the infected made on the other side. With great effort he retrieved a belt of ammo from a cargo pocket and reloaded his M-240, straightening out the links so they would not bind up.

Gray slapped the feedtray cover closed on the SAW when the world exploded around her. Bullets and lead shot slammed into the wall inches away and she spun around to catch a glimpse of several people coming at her. She got to her feet and sprayed down the hallway from the hip, backing out the doorway to get out of the line of fire. She backed into the body slouching against the door and tripped, dropping flat on her ass out on the darkened landing. She knocked the dead man over and the door came free, slamming shut with a thud.

Mark came up and pulled on the handle but it did not budge, locked securely in place. "Shit!"

From the next level up another door opened, barely illuminating the area. It was enough for them to catch sight of a metal cylinder tumbling down, sailing past the soldiers. Then, it too slammed back shut.

The metal cylinder kept going all the way down until it bounced off the concrete floor at Medicine Bear's feet with a clack. The NCO looked down and saw a burning fuse on one end that was nearly at the steel end cap.

It was a pipe bomb.

He pushed himself away and made for the first flight of stairs but didn't make it ten feet before the improvised device detonated in a deafening blast. It sent him face-first into the stairs with such force it nearly knocked him unconscious. He quickly pushed himself up and shook the fog from his head, rising to his feet when the door he'd been holding closed with his body came flying open, nearly torn from its steel hinges.

The dead poured in, filling the empty void in an instant with a crush of their violated bodies.

Medicine Bear brought the heavy weapon around and hammered the first few, the heavy jacketed-slugs tearing off huge chunks of flesh and shattering bone. He did his best to stem the tide but didn't even slow them down. A dozen of the things were on him in the span of a heartbeat and set to work rendering him into nothing more than bits of shredded meat. Mercifully, he was dead in seconds as hundreds of them trampled over him, smashing his body into the concrete stairs.

***

The choppers came roaring in from the east, setting down in a clearing next to the river. They were UH-60 Blackhawks from the Missouri Army National Guard, brought in on request from Battalion. The Brigade commander had somehow convinced the local boys to allow them to land and not shoot them out of the sky, and the two birds landed without incident, taking instructions by radio from a Pathfinder.

Across the river lay the casino, and to the rear was a large industrial area. The brigade had a hasty cordon set, establishing a perimeter around the area. Civilian refugees gathered in a large marshaling area in a nearby parking lot, where Army trucks lined up, preparing to move them to an established safe zone. Members of the Brigade Support Battalion handed out bottles of water and MREs while taking down names for manifests. Many of the people gathered there a mere fifty meters away looked on, fascinated by the sight of the whirly-birds.

Landreau watched the helicopters gently settle to earth, the grass blowing wildly under the rush of their powerful blades. Once down, the crew chiefs exited through the side doors, their large helmets still attached to long "spaghetti cables" so they could talk to the pilots inside. They motioned the First Sergeant and his men to approach, making it clear they wanted them to board from the side and to stay clear of the rearward-mounted rotor.

He looked at Beltran, Medina and a handful of others he'd scraped together from the headquarters element. These men made up the "Quick Reaction Force" he'd managed to cobble together for this rescue mission. He jerked his chin toward the waiting Blackhawks. "Let's go."

They got up and followed Landreau as he calmly approached the aircraft. All the while he ran the plan through his mind.

Everyone had last spotted the survivors from 2nd Platoon enter the casino across the way, with an army of the dead in hot pursuit. The company commander and even battalion tried multiple times to raise them on the radio without any luck. Nobody was certain the platoon had a radio with them and even if they had, it would be difficult if not impossible to get a transmission through the thick concrete walls of the structure, so they made the assumption that they were still alive.

The plan was to insert Landreau and his team on the roof, then they would go inside and look for the remaining members of the platoon. What nobody knew was that Landreau had no intention of actually looking for the platoon. He'd take his boys inside, out of line of sight, make a good show of it, then call for extraction after an unsuccessful search. Then he'd be rid of that bastard Foley once and for all.

A ruckus broke out behind them. The gawkers who'd been standing there calmly watching the helicopters land and getting manifested onto trucks, suddenly scattered in terror. Soldiers dropped their clipboards and water bottles, snatching up their weapons and firing into the crowd. Confusion set in and people ran everywhere while troops shot in every direction.

Landreau froze in his tracks, seeing three infected women leap on top of an officer firing his pistol, clawing and biting him while he tried to fight them off. Civilians and soldiers alike went down as dozens of the dead came sprinting from around the corner of a nearby warehouse, having no time to react.

Beltran shouldered his weapon, looking through the Aimpoint. He aimed the carbine at people but could not bring himself to fire. "First Sarn't, what do we do?"

Refugees ran toward the helicopters, trying to get aboard and get away to safety. The crew chiefs of the two UH-60s leapt back into their choppers and the pilots powered up. They hastily strapped in behind their door guns as the two aircraft lifted off and nosed forward, flying away just before the first of the civilians could reach them.

Landreau and his men stood there dumbfounded with people running in every direction all around them. The shooting rapidly increased in intensity, with automatic weapons adding to the din. He looked at his men and then at the madness consuming the entire Brigade Support Area. All he knew at that point was that he needed to get the hell out of there. He looked over to his company training NCO. "Medina, you're in charge."

The young sergeant gave him a confused look. "Roger, First Sarn't. What do you want me to do?"

"Stay here!" Landreau didn't wait for a response, instead turning on his heel and taking flight. Through the manic crowd he saw an unoccupied Humvee parked next to a couple of heavy trucks.

He pushed past a family huddled together, knocking one of the kids out of the way. When he got to the Humvee he tossed his rifle inside and slammed the door shut. To his delight, the cable lock for the steering wheel was disengaged. He fired up the engine easily, put it into drive and took off. He didn't even spare a glance into his rearview mirrors as he sped away, leaving the madness behind.

***

Coming up to the landing, the door opened a crack and a hand tossed another pipe bomb out, hurtling straight at them. In the darkened enclosure the lit wick sizzled and popped in slow motion as the improvised device sailed over Mark's head, falling down in and among his companions on the staircase below. "*Incoming!*"

Another eardrum-shattering blast detonated, followed up by wails of agony.

"Harris and Donahue are hit!" called out a disembodied voice, barely piercing through the noise and ringing.

The mad bomber pulled the door shut after lobbing the device. Mark dumped the rest of his magazine, riddling the door with holes, hoping he hit their attacker on the other side. *What I wouldn't give for just one hand grenade, or even a claymore right about now*, he thought to himself, frustrated by how helpless he felt.

Hong and McDermott stood shoulder-to-shoulder, pulling rearguard and blasting away at the dead who kept clawing their way toward them. The infected pushed and crammed into the stairwell, boxed in tight between the walls and the railings, effectively channeling themselves. It made them easy targets and the two young soldiers took careful aim, conserving their dwindling ammunition supply, while holding back the tide.

The Roberts family worked with Angel and Consuela to assist Bags with the wounded. It took two of the girls to help Swanson, while the rest struggled with Devons and Weber.

Johnson and Dubois, manhandled the injured sheriff's deputy, while Burbey and Gray helped Harris and Donahue. That left Mark and Carnegie with Saxon, working in intervals to clear the rest of the way, pushing forward. Nearly out of ammo, they were quickly running out of able-bodied trigger-pullers as well.

"I'm out!" Hong bellowed. "Anybody got any mags?"

"Here, it's my last one!" McDermott said, handing the last of his spare ammunition over.

The dead continued pushing forward, reaching up toward the living, arms outstretched. Through the green glow of the night vision devices, their eyes seemed even more evil, lit with Infrared illuminators. They couldn't see the soldiers but they could hear and smell them, and that was good enough. They crawled and clawed their way over their fallen, steadily pressing forward, inch by inch, stair by stair.

"Take the lead," Mark said to Carnegie. She held one of the wounded soldier's goggles with one hand over her eye, and held her pistol in the other. Saxon's barks were drowned out by the rest of the noise but he stayed by her side. She did not respond to the NCO but picked up her pace, passing the landing and continuing to climb.

Mark stood next to the bullet-riddled door and kept the muzzle of his weapon trained on it in case it opened again. He stood off to the side and out of the way to allow the others to pass. They all staggered past, the wounded doing the best they could. He stayed there until Hong and McDermott were even with him and he handed them the last two of his magazines. "Make 'em count, I ain't got no more!" He then turned and threw one of Harris's arms over his shoulder, supporting him under the armpit and helping him along.

When they made it up another flight of stairs, the first of the dead made it to the landing just as the door opened again. Another pipe bomb was tossed out but this time it landed among the flesh-eaters. The moment the door cracked open the light from inside shone brightly, and the infected on the landing ran to it like moths to a flame.

The explosive went off and hobbled several of the creatures, who got immediately trampled by the others coming from below. The rest went at the door, flinging it open and rushing inside by the dozens. Mark and the others could clearly hear the sound of panicked gunfire coming from inside, the dead drawn in from the light and the cracks of the shots. Whoever it was holed up inside who had been shooting the hell out of the survivors of 2nd Platoon, now had a real problem on their hands.

This was the breathing room they needed but they knew it was only temporary. The men and women continued trudging upwards, legs and lungs burning from the strain. Carnegie and Saxon led the way while everyone else did their best to keep up.

Finally, Carnegie got to the top of the stairs. The lights hadn't been knocked out up here, and the bar across the door was marked with "Exit." They had finally reached the roof.

The group came stumbling outside onto the casino's rooftop, immediately hit in the face by the heat and humidity. The sun had been baking it and the temperature seemed almost unbearable, especially in their state of exhaustion.

The brief respite from their pursuers was short-lived when many of the infected caught wind of the smell of fresh blood spilled on the stairs. Hong and McDermott started shooting again when scores of the creatures came chasing up after them. Once outside in the sunlight, they slammed the door shut behind them and leaned against it with their full weight. It started drumming and thumping from the other side almost immediately, shaking and vibrating with each strike. They pushed as hard as they could to keep it closed but they were only just barely able to do it.

Seeing them struggle, Clay Roberts quickly set Donahue down and helped the two soldiers, pressing his shoulder into the door. Bags set to work with her aid kit, patching up the wounded to the best of her ability, with what little supplies she had left while the others patched up their buddies with individual aid kits.

"Quick, go find something to wedge against the door," Mark said to Johnson and Dubois, dropping the magazine from his weapon to count the remaining rounds.

"Like what?" Dubois asked, shrugging his shoulders and looking around.

"Like anything, now hurry up!" The two of them took off to see if a maintenance crew had left any tools or equipment lying around on the roof that they could use. Mark jogged over to the ledge to get a good look at the surroundings, and hopefully, some way to get down and out of there.

Small arms fire cracked and popped inside the casino and the dead continued coming in from all directions, unable to resist the siren song of man-made noise. There was a fire ladder in back leading to the loading docks in the rear of the facility but it was no good. The infected wandered around down there near the base of the ladder, looking for a way inside the building. There was no obvious way out.

Machine guns rattled in the distance and he jerked his head up to see all hell breaking loose on the other side of the river. There were Army vehicles and even helicopters on the far side but civilians scattered in all directions over there and some of the soldiers fired into the dispersing crowd. It didn't take a rocket scientist to figure out what was going on.

Some of the people made a break for the helicopters, ignoring the soldiers trying to stop them. The Blackhawks did not sit idle, electing to take off and get the hell out of there.

He looked back over and saw Donahue wincing and gnashing his teeth while Burbey applied a field dressing to a nasty leg wound. Next to him sat a rucksack with a radio in it, the short-whip antenna sticking out the top.

"Burbey, bring the radio over there. And move with a purpose!"

Burbey looked up and nodded, patting his buddy on the shoulder before picking up the backpack and jogging over. Instinctively, he offered the hand-mike to the NCO who stood transfixed on the two helos on the far bank, lifting off from their earthly bonds.

"This on the company command freq?"

"Roger, sarn't."

He keyed the mike. "Battle Axe Six, this is White Two Three. Over."

There was silence for a moment, then came the response. "*White Two Three, this is Six. What's your location? Over!*"

"Roger, Six. We're on the roof of the casino directly north of the two Blackhawks taking off. We need extraction immediately. Our situation is extremely tenuous. Over!"

"*Okay, got it. Stand by.*"

Burbey watched him in anticipation. "It's going to be alright, dude. The El-Tee has got this." He hoped he sounded more convincing than he felt. His bowels were starting to do backflips while he looked at the helicopters. "Shit, I almost forgot. Grab the VS-17 panels!"

Burbey looked confused and then the lightbulb flicked on. He dropped the rucksack and dug out two pieces of cloth, one side colored olive drab, the other a blaze orange. These were marker panels used for all sorts of purposes, one of them for marking landing zones.

They unfurled the markers and waved them like mad, doing their best to get the attention of the pilots who were easing away from the anarchy breaking out on the other side of the river. They called out as well, knowing full well they couldn't be heard but they did it anyway. Their already hoarse voices croaked, trying to get the air crews to notice them.

They grew ever more desperate as the giant birds eased off and began lifting away, flying overhead and heading off toward the center of the city. Their blades churned a roiling pillar of black smoke rising to heavens, mocking them as the aircraft gracefully flew away, seemingly careless of their looming fate worse than death.

Then, mercifully, they eased over to the left and lazily came back around, headed straight toward them. It was the most beautiful sight Mark had seen in years. His heart leapt and tears welled up in his eyes.

"*Two Three, this is Six. Battalion was able to contact the Blackhawks, they should be enroute to you now. Over.*"

"Roger, Six. They're on the way." He turned back to Burbey. "I could kiss the El-Tee on the mouth right about now!" He slapped the other man on the shoulder and handed the handset back, running over to the rest of the platoon.

He continued waving the VS-17 panel even as the first UH-60 flared in, settling down on the gravel- covered the rooftop, while the other hovered patiently.

"Gather up the wounded and get them on board!" Mark directed those nearest the injured to pick them up while the crew chief dismounted and waved them forward. He assisted with Jefferson, the wounded sheriff's deputy first, then helped with the rest.

They loaded up those hurt the worst and then Angel, Consuela, along with Bailey Roberts and her mom Cynthia. On Mark's signal, the crew chief climbed back on board and the aircraft lifted away, making room for the second one.

When it touched down Mark motioned for the crew chief to stay in place while shoving Dubois and Johnson through the gaping side door. On his order, Bags and Carnegie followed with Saxon, leaping up on board.

He turned to Gray. "How much ammo you got left for the Piglet?" He pointed his chin at the light machine gun she held.

"Half a belt, sarn't." She shifted her weight but held his gaze. She wasn't going anywhere without his say-so.

"Okay, when I give the signal, you lay down some fire until you're out. Then haul ass. Got it?"

"Roger, sarn't."

"Awesome." He turned to Burbey, "Load up, buddy."

Burbey nodded and smiled, then darted off for the bird.

Mark looked over his shoulder toward the crew chief on the Blackhawk. He sat behind his pintle-mounted M-240 Bravo medium machine gun. He wore a flight helmet with the visor pulled down but nodded at the NCO and leaned his shoulder into the gun. He turned back to the three holding the door shut, their heels dug into the gravel digging furrows into it, the door creeping open with each intense pounding. Awful-looking fingers and hands reached out from the other side, raking at the air. "You guys ready?"

Their pale faces covered in sweat and grime, they acknowledged while straining against the door.

"*Go!*" Mark nudged Gray and then shouldered his own weapon.

The three men broke away and dashed toward the helicopter as the door behind them flung open, spilling out dozens of the dead, who came sprinting into the sunshine, eagerly pursuing their prey.

As soon as the two soldiers and the civilian banker were clear, Mark opened fire, with Gray joining in. They cut down the first several, careful to keep their aim high while their friends raced past, leaping into the arms of their comrades aboard the chopper. They kept it up until Mark's bolt locked to the rear and Gray's slammed forward on an empty chamber. He grabbed her by the combat harness and shoved her toward the aircraft. "*Let's get the fuck out of here!*"

He pushed her forward, barely noticing when the crew chief opened up with his M-240 Bravo, scything down the flesh-eaters behind them, knocking them down like bowling pins.

Hands reached out for them and pulled them in as the bird lifted off, their legs still dangling out the open door as they gained altitude. Mark and Gray were too busy struggling to get on the chopper to notice the scores of snapping jaws and wretched claws reaching upward toward the sky as they lifted off.

When he finally got situated, he looked up and the first thing he saw was the civilian banker, husband and father Clay Roberts mouthing the words "Thank you" to him with tears in his eyes.

Mark just put a hand on the man's shoulder, too damned exhausted to respond in any other way.

Chapter 14

Tactical Assembly Area "Hammer"
1045 Hours Local
Day 3 of the Outbreak

Mark awoke, laying on a bare army cot in a dimly-lit tent. The air conditioner was barely working and it was warm but not oppressive. The canvas of the cot squeaked when he sat up, swinging his legs over the side. He'd rolled up his GI-issued jacket and used it as a pillow but shook it out and shrugged it back on before going for his boots. He'd been wearing and sweating in the same clothes for the last few days and they were starting to get ripe.

There were other cots in there with the rest of the platoon plus a few additions. Bags lie in the corner, snoring louder than a freight train while Johnson and Dubois sat on another, playing a game of *Magic: The Gathering*. Gray sat near the entrance underneath one of the field lights with her SAW disassembled, meticulously cleaning it. Hong and McDermott traded different components of their MREs after warming up the main meal packets, digging in with plastic spoons.

Consuela and Angel sat next to Bailey Roberts while she quietly gave them English lessons. Clay and Cynthia Roberts watched them contentedly, Cynthia slowly stroking Clay's graying hair.

Burbey came in through the tent flap with a cup of java in each hand and came straight over to Mark while he put on his boots, tightening the laces. He handed one of the paper cups over. "Here you go, sarn't. I thought you could use this."

"Thanks, dude." Mark accepted the cup and blew on it before taking a sip. He grimaced after tasting the thick, black, witch's brew. "God, where'd you get this? It's terrible. It tastes like varnish remover."

"The mess tent. It ain't good but it's got caffeine and

there's plenty of it."

Mark smiled. "Well, I've definitely had worse." He raised the paper cup in a salute, then took another drink, forcing the bitter stuff down.

"Anyway, Sergeant Medina sent me over. He says El-Tee Baker needs to speak with you."

"Okay, thanks." Mark set the cup down before buckling up his MP gun belt and grabbing his AR-15 before heading outside. Emerging from the temporary shelter, he squinted in the bright sunlight, raising a hand to shield his eyes. The area was a beehive of activity, growing busier with each passing hour.

A tent city grew up in the industrial area south of the river while military traffic continued to flow in. Throughout the night reinforcements arrived, bolstering the numbers of combat forces available to the area commanders. Along with that, the first supplies carried overland all the way from Fort Riley arrived by truck, though at great effort and cost.

The stories the truck drivers told did not inspire any confidence in the weary troops who had been hanging on by a thread in the suburbs of Kansas City, if they were to be believed. They spoke of a general breakdown of law and order, along with a frightening description of the spread of a plague that no one seemed able to contain. They made it sound as if it were the beginning of the end of the world.

Under normal circumstances it would have taken a few hours for the convoys to arrive from Fort Riley via I-70 but it had taken over a day for the first trucks to make it there loaded with mission-essential supplies. They'd heard of a pitched battle fought in the streets of Topeka but none of them were sure of how much of that was real or exaggerated. All they knew was that things were definitely not business as usual.

Pulling the patrol cap on his head, he slung his rifle and walked over to the company command post located roughly a hundred meters away. Military personnel drove Humvees and trucks everywhere, while forklifts moved pallets of equipment around. Over near Levee Road, fuel blivets were arranged in neat rows while a support unit set a fueling and rearming site for an aviation unit.

Nearing the CP he had to walk around an M-1 tank parked there with the name "Camel Toe" stenciled on the barrel of the main gun. Sergeant Yokey had a breaker-bar, attempting to dislodge a particularly stubborn nut on one of the track pins frozen in place by rust. He used profanity that would make a sailor blush, before yelling at the rest of his crew to go find a sledge hammer.

Mark walked into the company CP and found Lieutenant Baker sitting and talking to Sergeant Medina and Specialist Beltran. There were radio remotes sitting on the small folding table next to them, with reports crackling in from the company and battalion frequencies. The three men leaned over a laptop computer screen, likely going over the daily personnel status report before sending it up to Battalion. They all looked up from the report when he walked inside.

"You wanted to see me, sir?"

"Ah, Sergeant Matthews, come on in. Have a seat." Baker pointed to the folding chair located on the opposite side of the field table from him. It was covered in paperwork of all kinds, with improvised "In" and "Outboxes" fashioned from MRE cases and green duct tape. "Do you want a cup of coffee? It's not great but it's better than the stuff the cooks are making in the field kitchens. It's sweet nectar compared to that paint thinner they're serving over there."

"Sure. Thanks, sir." Mark unslung his rifle and had a seat. Beltran got up and poured a fresh cup from the "silver bullet" in the corner and set it in front of him before getting back to work, knocking out administrative duties. He picked up the cup, enjoying the warmth in his hand and the coolness in the tent. The air conditioner in the CP worked like a champ, and the generator outside thrummed happily.

"So, how's the platoon doing?" Baker took a sip from his own paper coffee cup, leaning back in his chair and scratching an armpit. He still wore the same Nomex suit he'd had on for days, and there were distinct salt rings formed on it.

With only eight effectives left, he'd hardly considered them a "platoon," but technically that's what they were. At least until somebody reorganized the unit and folded them in with someone else. "Everybody's doing well, now that they've had a chance to get some rest."

"I really appreciate what you've done while you've been here with us. Frankly, a lot of people are still alive because of what you did out there and we owe you a debt of gratitude at the very least." He set the cup down and leaned forward, propping his elbows on the table, before pointing at the MP brassard on Mark's shoulder. "We made some calls to try and get you back with your unit, since I'm sure you're anxious to get back. I'm guessing you have a family up in Leavenworth that you're worried sick about. Yes?"

The idea of going back to Leavenworth sent electric shocks through him and he started feeling sick to his stomach. As cool as it was in there with the air conditioning going full blast, beads of sweat formed on his forehead and upper lip. "Uh... no, sir. I don't have any family back at Fort Leavenworth. It's just me." He'd been too tired over the last day since they'd been whisked away from the roof of the casino to give much thought of an escape plan. But right about now he really wished he'd snuck off in the middle of the night to start making his way toward Ohio. If they sent him back to Leavenworth... well... he'd be fucked.

"Actually, I'm relieved to hear that." He paused before leaning back again. "The word we're getting is that Fort Leavenworth is a total nightmare. The Kansas Guard sent some patrols in there and reported back that the place was totally overrun with infected. It's pretty ugly." He took a deep breath and sighed. "There're probably survivors but with everything else that's going on, looking for some there is pretty low on the list of priorities."

"I see." Mark felt the tension ease a bit but he hoped the expression on his face didn't betray the sense of utter terror that gripped him at that very moment. If they found anyone up there that knew the real Sergeant Matthews, his cover would be blown, and God only knew what would happen to him after that. He could claim that Matthews had been infected and he had no choice but who would believe him? They didn't believe him when they sent him to prison the first time. They sure as hell wouldn't believe him this time either. He'd be lucky if he didn't get a summary execution in a ditch somewhere. No, he didn't think for one second he'd get a fair hearing or a decent shake if they found out who he really was. It was more important than ever that he get out of there. Fast.

"Listen, I called you here to talk about what's next." He took another sip and ran fingers through his short-cropped hair. "According to Division, things are going sideways just about everywhere. This... infection... whatever you want to call it, is spreading everywhere like a flash fire. What's worse is that law and order have utterly disintegrated. The government intends to reassert control but in order to do that we need every swinging dick in the field."

"I'm not sure what this has to do with me." Mark's mind raced as he thought of a way out of there. He tried to buy some time.

"The bottom line is I'm critically short of NCOs right now. The brigade took a shitload of casualties in the first forty-eight hours. This company is no exception. Hell, even the First Sergeant stole a Humvee and deserted. Nobody knows where he went. Anyway, I need you to stay here with us. We need your help. When the dust settles in the coming weeks, I'll do what I can to get you back to your unit at Leavenworth—if anyone there is still left alive—but for now, I need you here." Baker locked his gaze with a grave seriousness.

Mark considered what he'd been told. They were in no hurry to get him back to Leavenworth, or even make a serious attempt to locate his chain of command. He'd heard rumors that Landreau had gone AWOL, and now it was confirmed to be true. So the only person who could reveal his true identity was gone, and even if he returned, his credibility would be non-existent. It seemed that at least for the time being, he was reasonably safe. He could feel the pounding in his chest begin to slow and he didn't need to fight quite so hard to keep his breathing under control. He looked down at his boots and then back up at the officer. "Understood, sir. I guess I'll do what I can to keep helping out here in Bravo Company."

"Awesome." A smile cracked on Baker's face and he extended a hand across the table. "That makes you the new platoon sergeant of 2nd Platoon."

Mark leaned forward and shook the lieutenant's hand. He didn't really have a good response prepared and the words came spilling out. "Thanks, sir. I appreciate your confidence."

"No need to thank me. I'm not sure I'm doing you any favors. Anyway, I need you back here in two hours with the rest of the platoon leadership for a briefing. Battalion gave us orders to head back into the city tomorrow and we need to get everyone ready."

"Roger that." Mark stood and saluted the lieutenant before picking up his rifle and heading out. His head was spinning and he tried to make sense of everything that had been discussed. He wasn't sure of anything right now but as long as the world was falling apart being here in Bravo Company was as good a place to be as any.

And with that, he headed back to his platoon to get them ready for their next mission.

***

Ellis Heights Housing Area
Fort Riley, Kansas
1423 Hours Local
Day Four of the Outbreak

It took a couple of days for Landreau to make it back to Fort Riley after escaping the death trap back in Kansas City. There were military and police checkpoints all over the place, along with armed patrols roaming everywhere. Things were devolving quickly and he needed to get out of there. It was the end of the world and the further he got from people the better.

He tried to stay off the main roads but was entirely too conspicuous in a military Humvee. It brought him no joy when he hijacked a family's minivan somewhere between Basehor and Tonganoxie but he didn't have any choice. It would have been better if the father hadn't tried to resist on the side of the road, or else Landreau wouldn't have had to shoot him in front of his wife and kids. It was a shitty thing but a man had to do what a man had to do.

Landreau couldn't think straight for a long while but when he got his wits about him, he realized that he needed a plan. There was no point wandering the Midwest aimlessly in a stolen minivan. He couldn't keep that up forever and he needed a place to go and sit this thing out. Whatever this was. He remembered finally that his wife Cindy had family in Utah with land and lots of food. Those people out there were preppers and if he could make it out there then he could fall in with them. If anyone was going to make it through this, it'd be people like that. So he decided to go get his wife, and she'd take them to her relatives where they would be safe.

Changing into civilian clothes, Landreau struck north, paralleling I-70 but giving it a wide berth. He tried to stay on the small side roads, avoiding anyone he came across, sleeping inside of the car when necessary. He stole some food and water along the way, which turned out badly for some other people but he put those thoughts out of his mind. If they'd have just shared some of it with him, he'd have let them go. So, in a way, it was really their own fault.

After taking his time he finally arrived at Fort Riley, rolling through an abandoned gate. He was shocked to find the place nearly a ghost town, with nearly no activity anywhere to be seen. He caught sight of a military convoy moving out on the far side of the installation but he ducked into a parking lot and laid low, doing his best not to draw attention to himself. When he picked up and moved again, he did so deliberately, driving slowly and moving with particular care.

It didn't take long after that before he arrived at his home in one of the designated housing areas. Some of the neighbors had cars in their driveways and some did not. Things were eerily quiet and it was more than a little disconcerting to see some of the homes with their front doors hanging wide open. Still, when he got to his house the place appeared secure and Cindy's car was on the curb right where she always parked it.

He pulled into the drive and turned off the ignition, stuffing the keys into a jacket pocket. He looked around to see if anybody was around but didn't see a soul. He thought about grabbing the M-4 carbine from the back seat but elected not to. If someone came by, that might draw the wrong kind of attention. He elected to stuff his issued 9mm automatic in his waistband instead.

Unlocking the front door, he entered the house and carefully closed it behind him, finding things dark inside. "Cindy, are you home?" She had to be in there somewhere, she never went anywhere without her car. The woman was too damned lazy to walk anywhere.

Not wanting to wait he grabbed a couple of suitcases and then went to the bedroom and began to pack. Even though it was July, Utah got cold in the winter so he dug up some hats, coats and gloves. He didn't figure that this was going to blow over anytime soon and they were in it for the long haul. He also opened his small safe and grabbed all the jewelry and cash he had in there, along with his grandmother's silver coin collection. That stuff would be worth something and he could use it for trade later.

He rifled through drawers, tossing clothes and other items into the suitcases laying open on the bed. Some things were practical, some had sentimental value but he did his best to pack light. He didn't want to have to lug too much around. When he finished in there, he'd go to the safe in the other room and grab some more guns and ammo. You couldn't have too many of those these days, that was for sure.

Zipping up the suitcase he heard a hiss that sent a chill down his spine. He immediately froze in place, staring straight ahead to the other side of the room. He swallowed hard and slowly turned around to see his wife Cindy standing in the bedroom doorway, carefully studying him.

She was dressed in her street clothes as if she'd been out shopping but they were covered in clotted, brown gore. Her head turned to the side when she made eye contact with him, red and almost luminescent. This contrasted with the pronounced veins on her face and the darkness of her lips. A thick, oily-black drool ran down her chin from a snarling mouth, dripping to the carpet.

"*Keeeevvviiiiinnnn,*" she growled, "*I loooooovvvvee yoooooo.*"

"Oh my god," he said, reaching for the pistol stuck in his belt.

She pounced on him before he could get the weapon clear, clawing and biting like a wildcat. The pistol went flying across the room.

They fell to the ground, writhing and struggling, knocking over a nightstand, sending a lamp crashing. The creature that had once been his wife raked his neck with her nails, then sunk her teeth into his left forearm he'd raised high to defend his face.

The struggle went on for a long while until Landreau was covered in deep bites and scratches. Then, as suddenly as the attack had begun, she stopped and stood up, quietly watching him again as he lay there bleeding and weeping on the bedroom floor. She made no more aggressive move on him, only standing there, seemingly curious.

When he got up and stumbled toward the master bathroom she simply watched, doing nothing to stop him. He clumsily closed the door behind and locked it, then went for the first aid kit located in the cupboard. He dressed his wounds carefully and eventually got the bleeding to stop. Landreau sat on the toilet with tears rolling down his face. He sat there for a long time, considering what he should do next but his thoughts came more slowly as time passed. His mind grew foggier and ever more sluggish until he could think no longer.

Then, after a long while he fell over. He lay motionless for hours as the sun sank beneath the horizon.

The next morning, when the sunlight creeped in from the window near the shower, Landreau's eyes peeled open. Shakily, he stood and when he was upright he saw himself in the mirror over the sink. It took awhile for things to come into focus but when they did he found his reflection staring back at him, with a pair of awful, blood-red eyes.

About Shane Gries

I'm a career soldier, student of history and writer. I've spent over sixteen years serving overseas in Europe, Asia and Oceania, and can order beer in several languages. I started off as a young enlisted man and then commissioned later on as an Infantry officer. I'm a graduate of Airborne School, Ranger School, earned my Expert Infantryman Badge, and did some time in combat. I've even got a family around here someplace that constantly puts up with my nonsense.

If you enjoyed this book, please check out Irregular Scout Team One by J.F. Holmes. A parallel series to The Thin Dead Line, IST-1 follows the adventures of a mixed Team of military and civilian scouts as they advance back across a devastated America. Contains the Dragon Award Finalist novel, "Falling".

For even more great Military Science Fiction check out:

www.cannonpublishing.us

Fallen Empire

What's a soldier to do when the war is over? When he's only known conflict his whole life? Since time immemorial the solution has been to find another war, this time for pay. Whoever has the credits and wins the high bid gets the experienced fighter. Sometimes, though, the credits aren't enough to over the price.

Empires rise, but Empires also fall. The Terran Union has spent five centuries under the control of the alien Grausians, like a barbarian tribe under the thumb of Rome. Now, after almost two decades of civil war and succession struggles, the formerly subject races have settled back in their ancient territories to lick their wounds and rearm, leaving hundreds of settled planets to exist in a political vacuum. Into that space steps the free companies, mercenary units that fight for gold, honor, power and glory. Veterans who can't get the wars out of their souls, new recruits looking for adventure, corporations with their own agenda.

An ancient enemy invades Earth, returning to claim their home world. The men and women of the U.S. Military find themselves matching technology against magic as cities burn and armies clash.

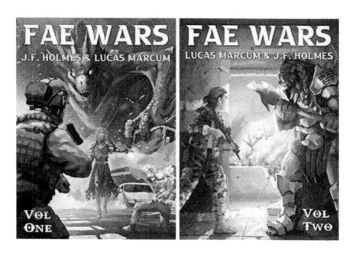

Printed in Great Britain
by Amazon

15661410R00180